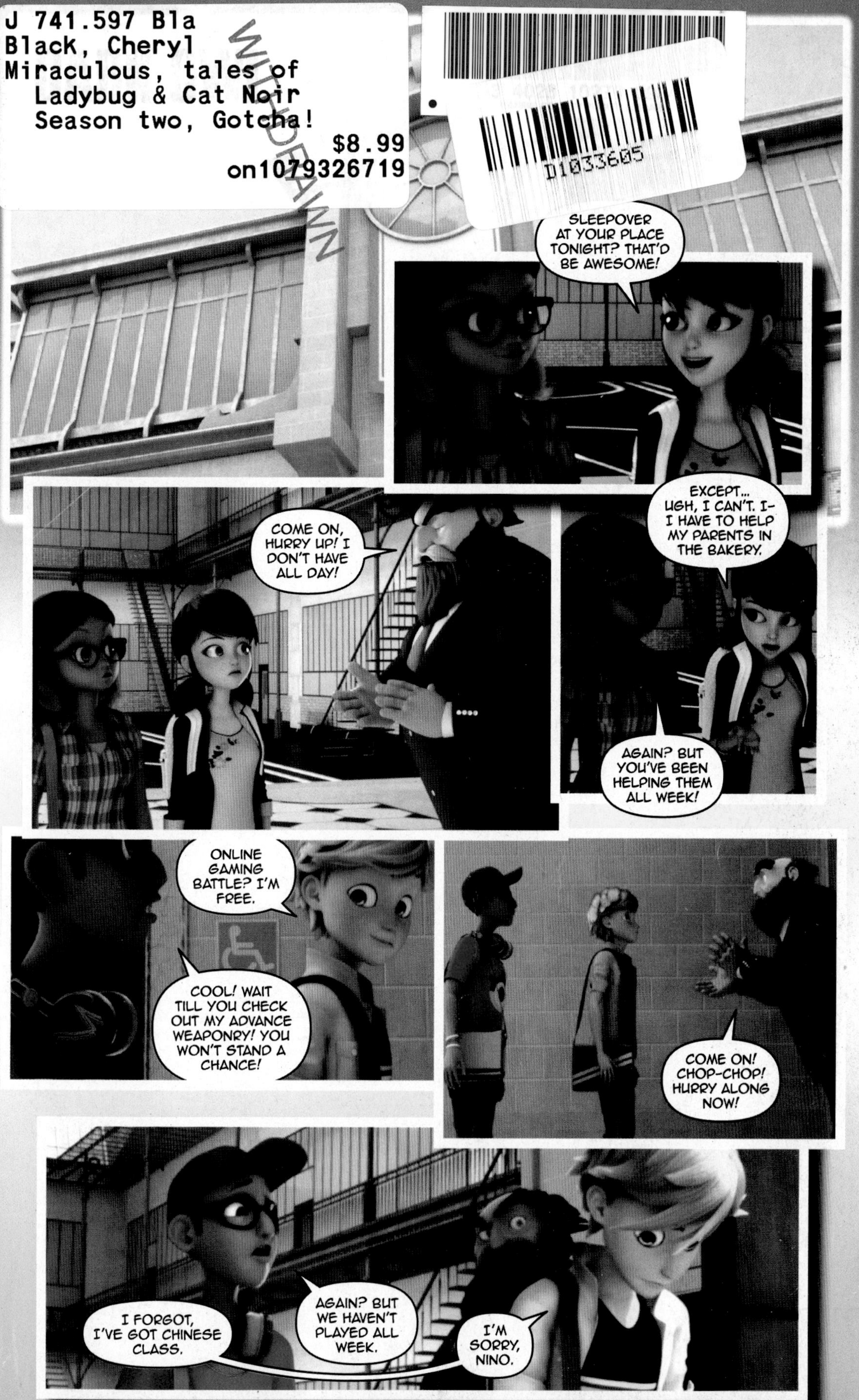
SLEEPOVER AT YOUR PLACE TONIGHT? THAT'D BE AWESOME!
COME ON, HURRY UP! I DON'T HAVE ALL DAY!
EXCEPT... UGH, I CAN'T. I- I HAVE TO HELP MY PARENTS IN THE BAKERY.
AGAIN? BUT YOU'VE BEEN HELPING THEM ALL WEEK!
ONLINE GAMING BATTLE? I'M FREE.
COOL! WAIT TILL YOU CHECK OUT MY ADVANCE WEAPONRY! YOU WON'T STAND A CHANCE!
COME ON! CHOP-CHOP! HURRY ALONG NOW!
I FORGOT, I'VE GOT CHINESE CLASS.
AGAIN? BUT WE HAVEN'T PLAYED ALL WEEK.
I'M SORRY, NINO.

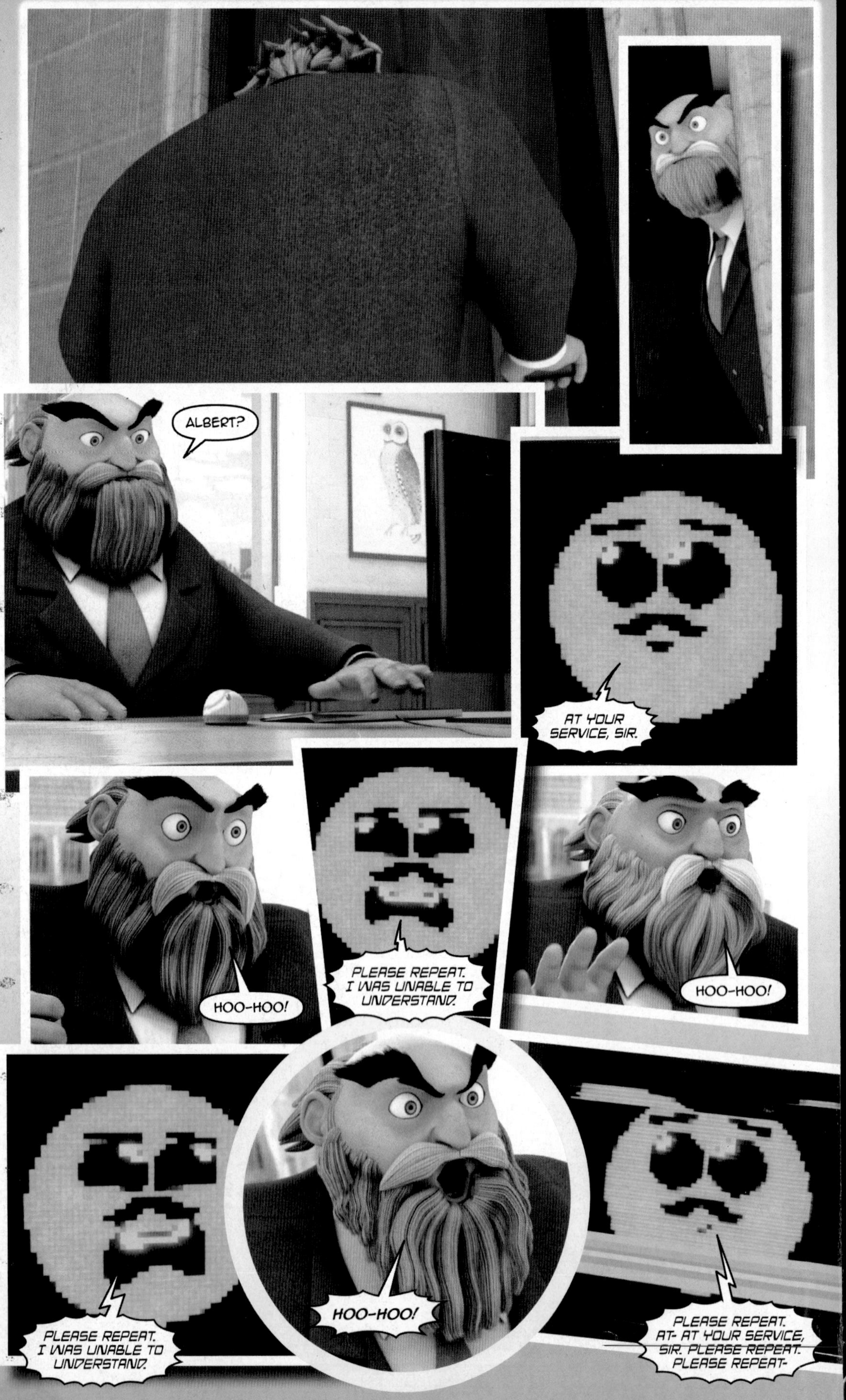
ALBERT?
AT YOUR SERVICE, SIR.
HOO-HOO!
PLEASE REPEAT. I WAS UNABLE TO UNDERSTAND.
HOO-HOO!
PLEASE REPEAT. I WAS UNABLE TO UNDERSTAND.
HOO-HOO!
PLEASE REPEAT. AT- AT YOUR SERVICE, SIR. PLEASE REPEAT. PLEASE REPEAT-

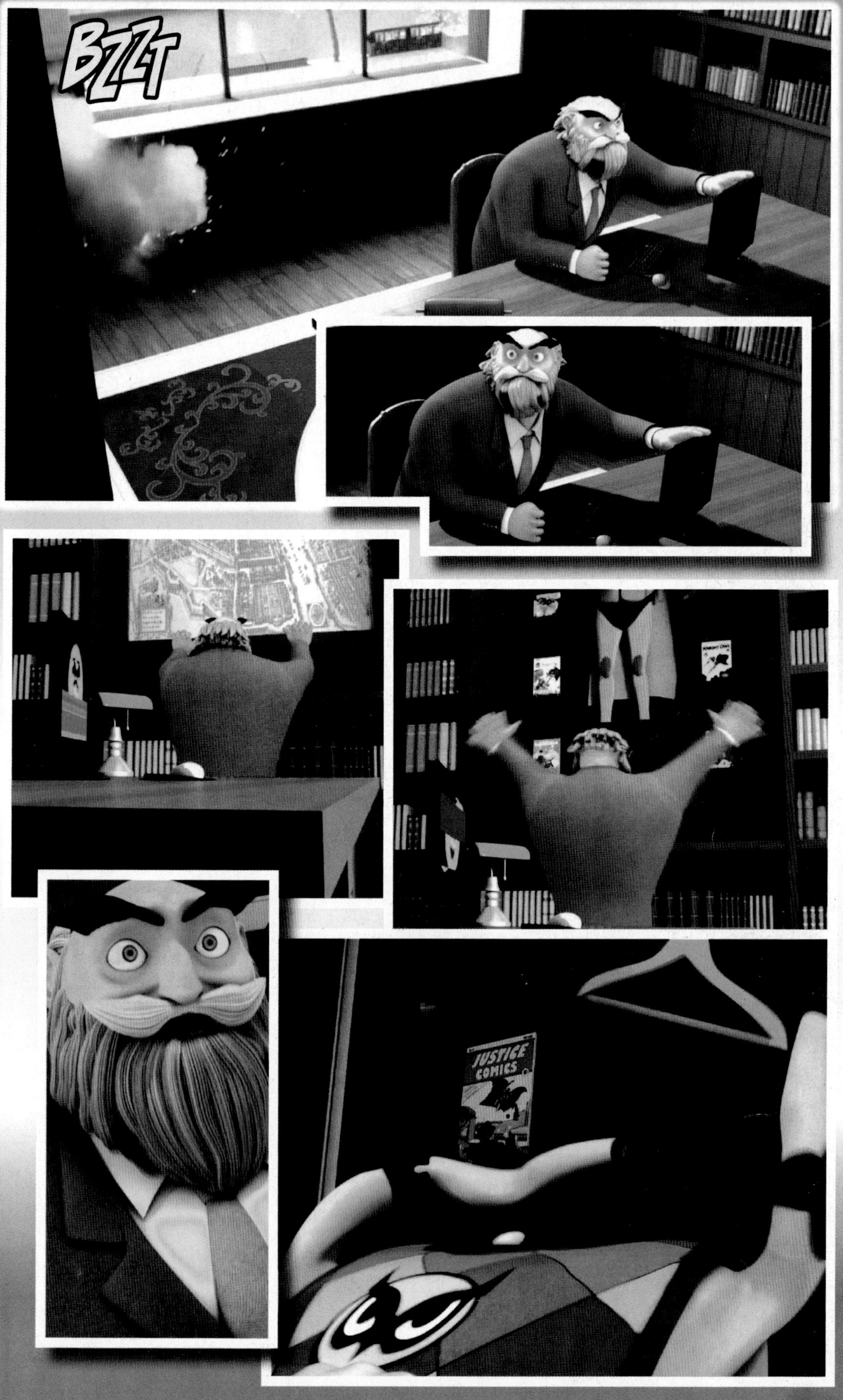
BZZT
JUSTICE COMICS

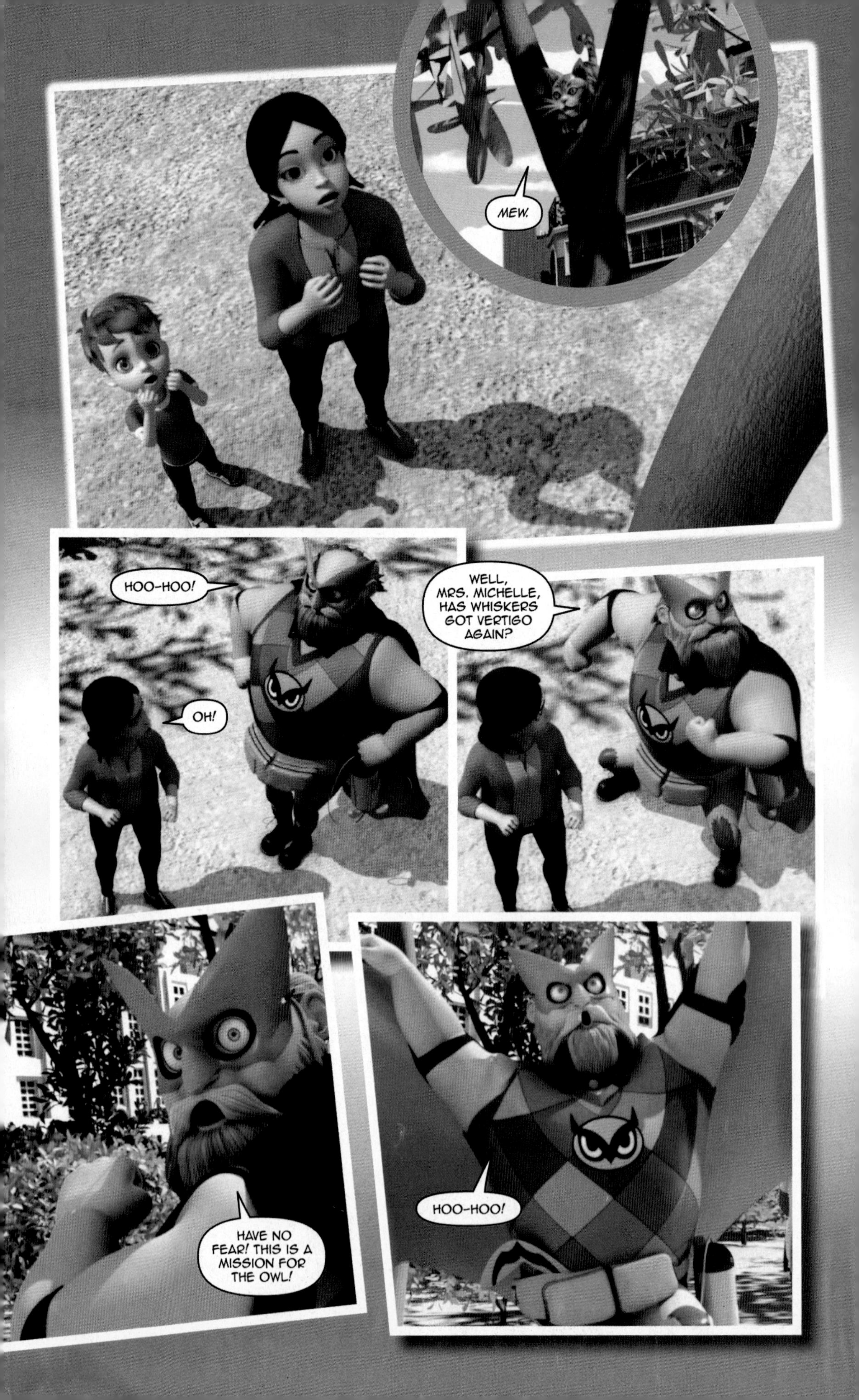
MEW.
HOO-HOO!
OH!
WELL, MRS. MICHELLE, HAS WHISKERS GOT VERTIGO AGAIN?
HAVE NO FEAR! THIS IS A MISSION FOR THE OWL!
HOO-HOO!

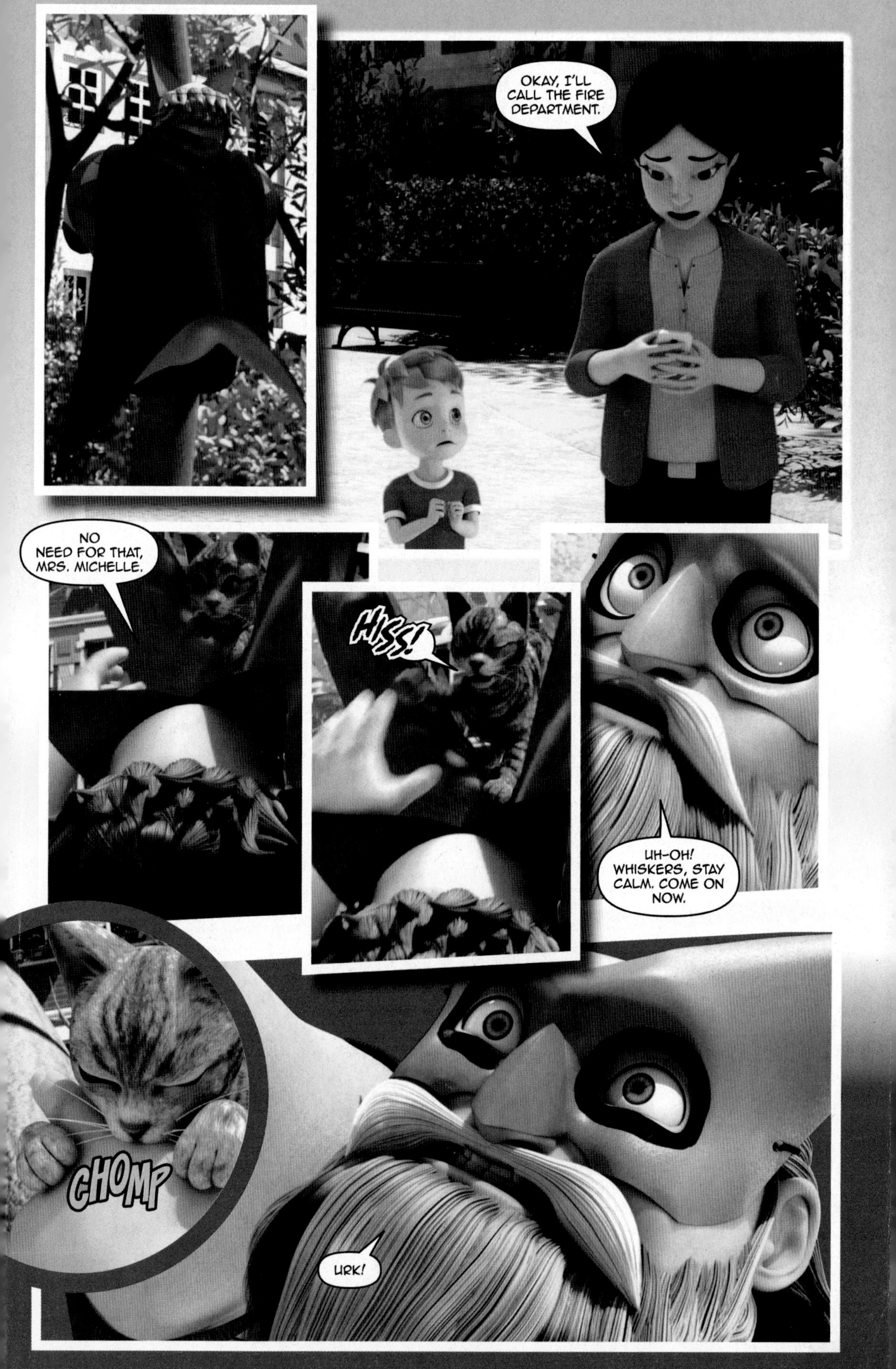
OKAY, I'LL CALL THE FIRE DEPARTMENT.
NO NEED FOR THAT, MRS. MICHELLE.
HISS!
UH-OH! WHISKERS, STAY CALM. COME ON NOW.
CHOMP
URK!

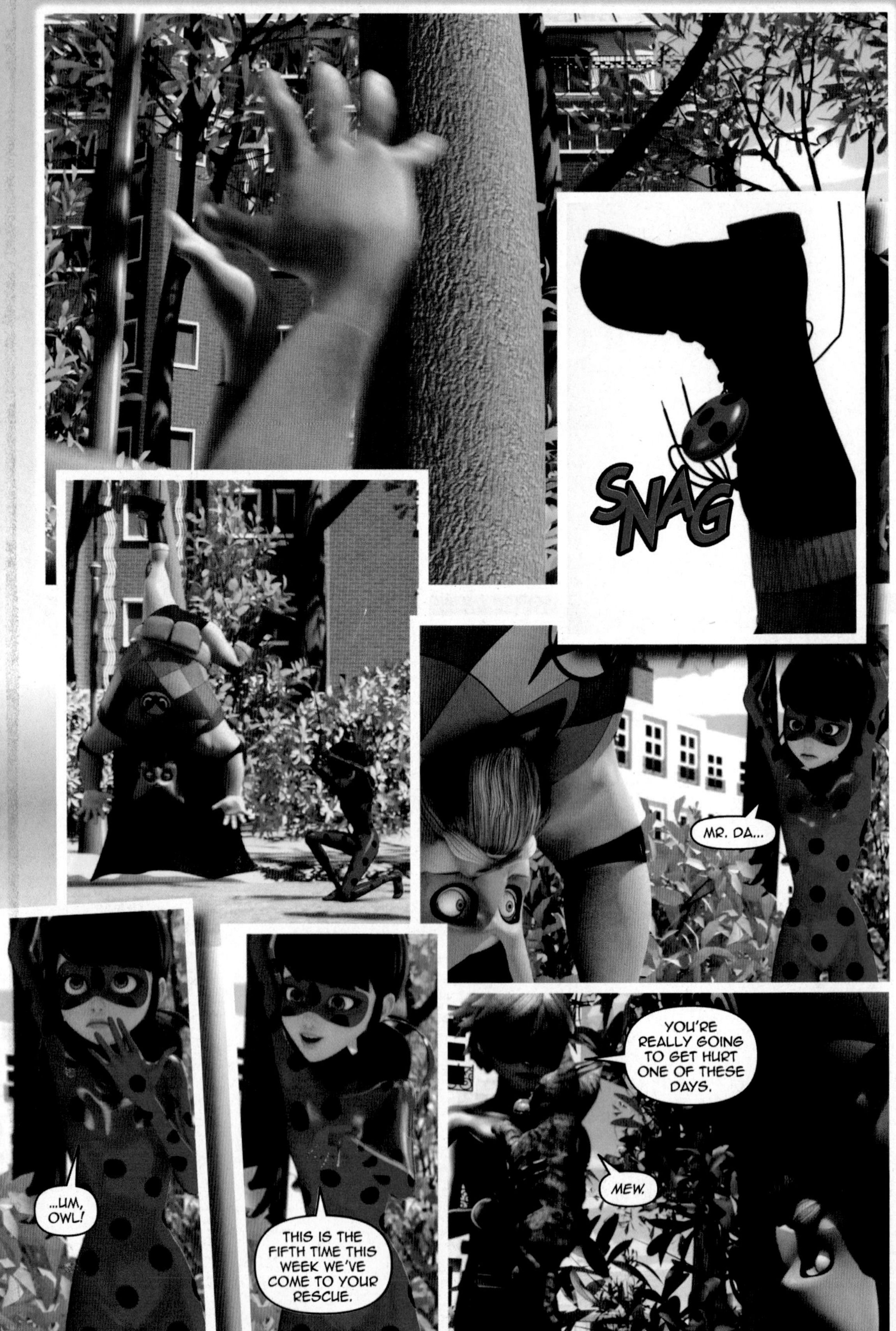
SNAG
MR. DA...
...UM, OWL!
THIS IS THE FIFTH TIME THIS WEEK WE'VE COME TO YOUR RESCUE.
YOU'RE REALLY GOING TO GET HURT ONE OF THESE DAYS.
MEW.

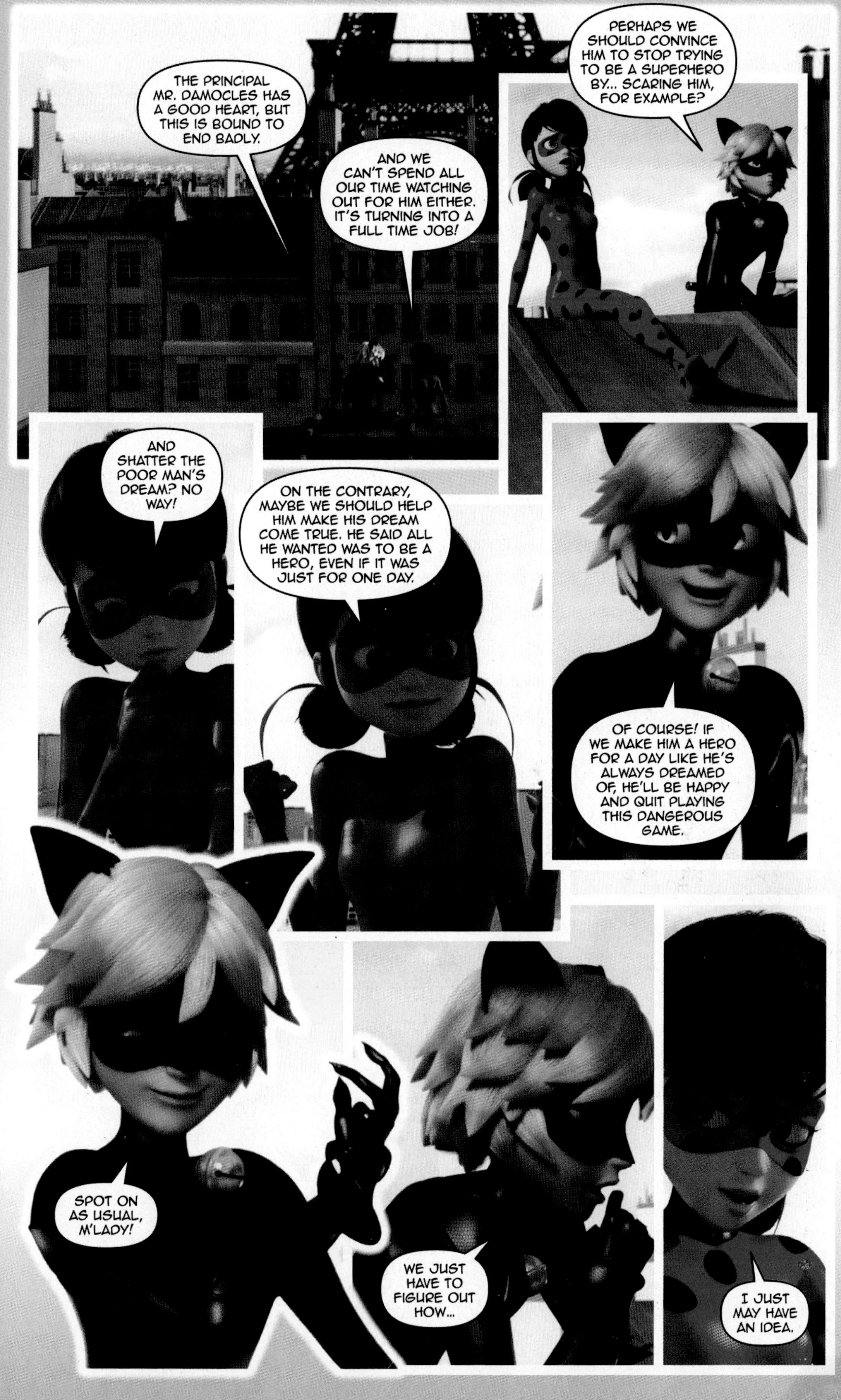
THE PRINCIPAL MR. DAMOCLES HAS A GOOD HEART, BUT THIS IS BOUND TO END BADLY.
AND WE CAN'T SPEND ALL OUR TIME WATCHING OUT FOR HIM EITHER. IT'S TURNING INTO A FULL TIME JOB!
PERHAPS WE SHOULD CONVINCE HIM TO STOP TRYING TO BE A SUPERHERO BY... SCARING HIM, FOR EXAMPLE?
AND SHATTER THE POOR MAN'S DREAM? NO WAY!
ON THE CONTRARY, MAYBE WE SHOULD HELP HIM MAKE HIS DREAM COME TRUE. HE SAID ALL HE WANTED WAS TO BE A HERO, EVEN IF IT WAS JUST FOR ONE DAY.
OF COURSE! IF WE MAKE HIM A HERO FOR A DAY LIKE HE'S ALWAYS DREAMED OF, HE'LL BE HAPPY AND QUIT PLAYING THIS DANGEROUS GAME.
SPOT ON AS USUAL, M'LADY!
WE JUST HAVE TO FIGURE OUT HOW...
I JUST MAY HAVE AN IDEA.

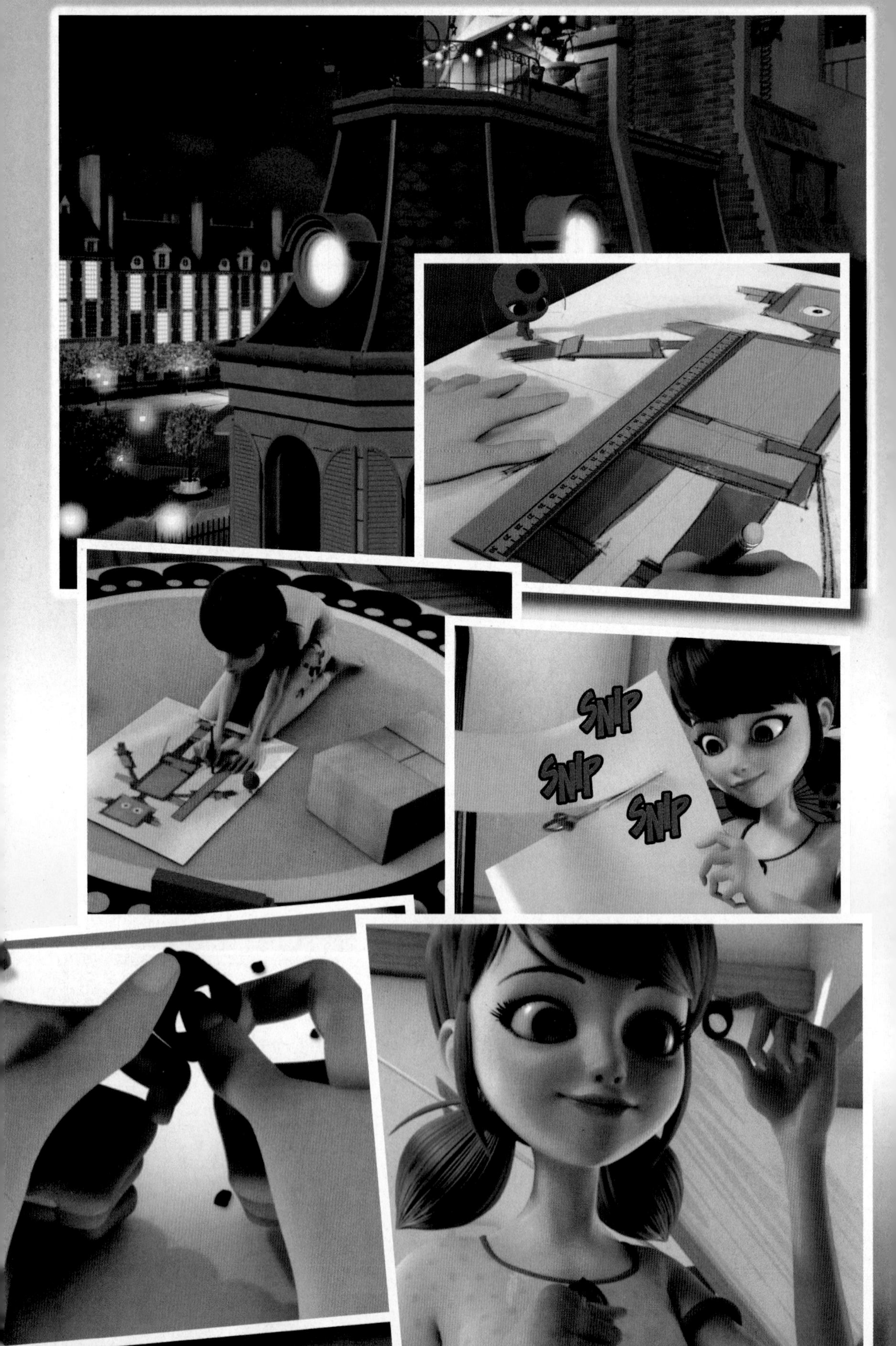
SNIP
SNIP
SNIP

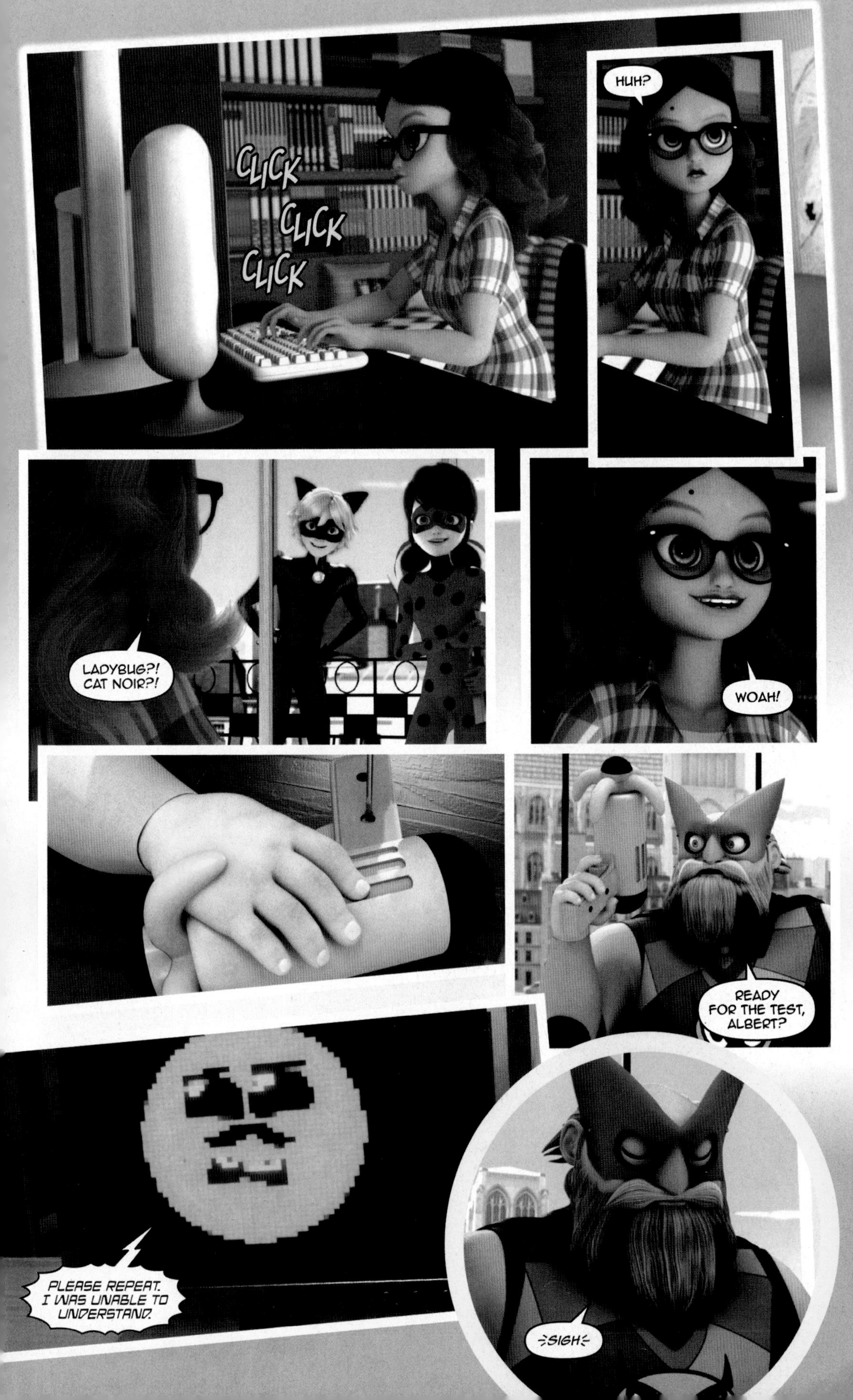
CLICK
CLICK
CLICK
HUH?
LADYBUG?! CAT NOIR?!
WOAH!
READY FOR THE TEST, ALBERT?
PLEASE REPEAT. I WAS UNABLE TO UNDERSTAND.
SIGH

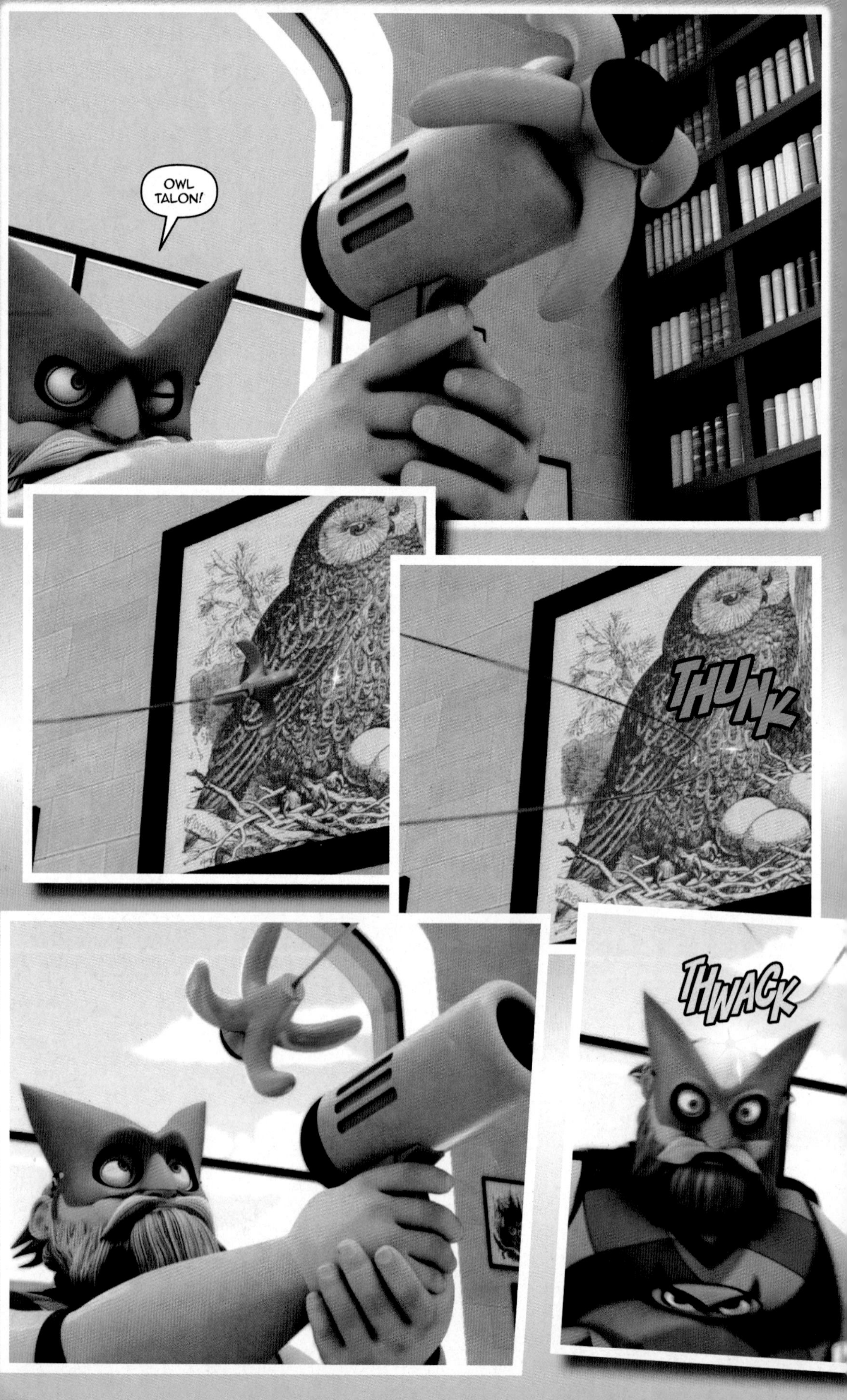
OWL TALON!
THUNK
THWACK

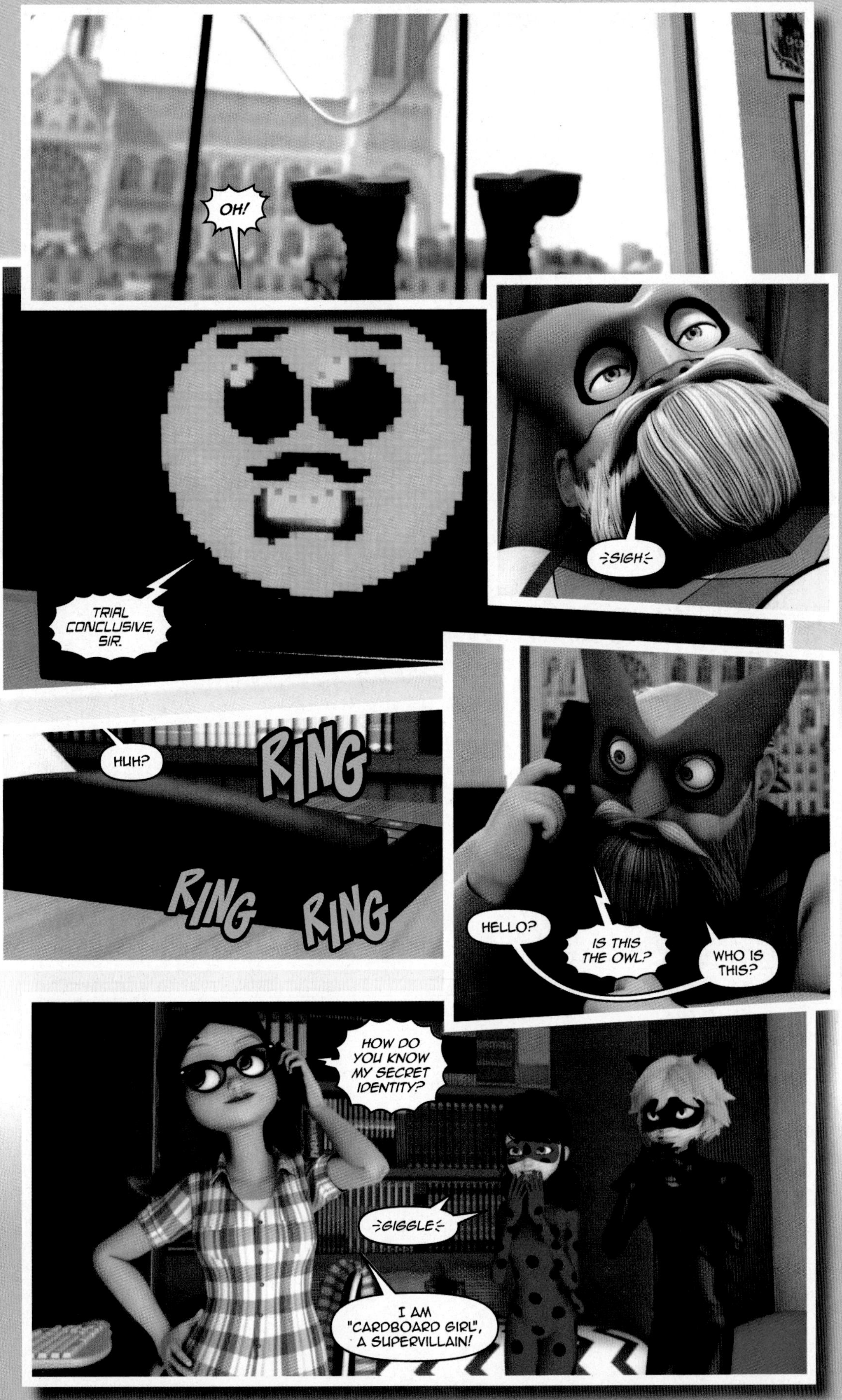
OH!
TRIAL CONCLUSIVE, SIR.
SIGH
HUH?
RING
RING
RING
HELLO?
IS THIS THE OWL?
WHO IS THIS?
HOW DO YOU KNOW MY SECRET IDENTITY?
GIGGLE
I AM "CARDBOARD GIRL", A SUPERVILLAIN!

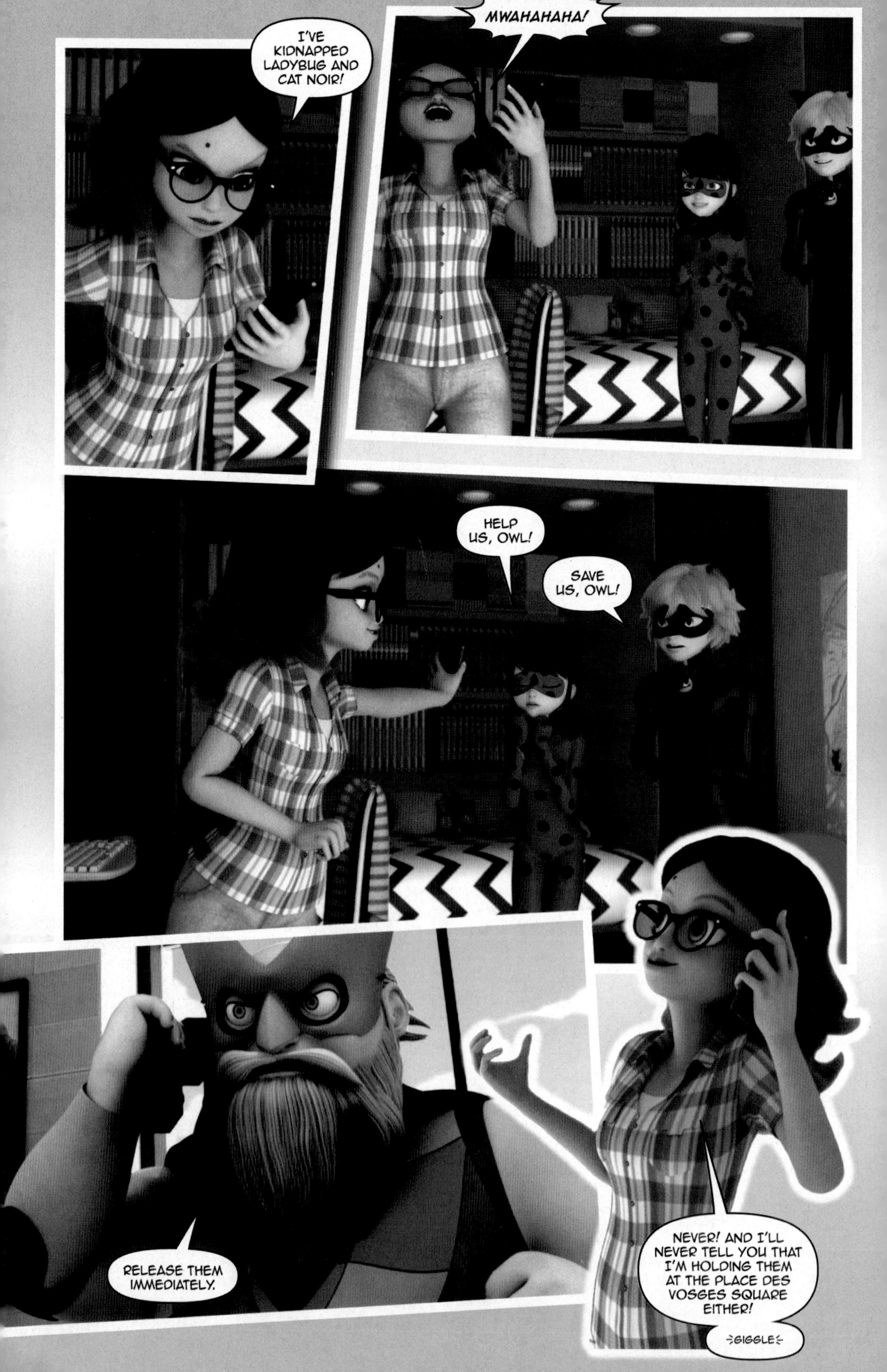
I'VE KIDNAPPED LADYBUG AND CAT NOIR!
MWAHAHAHA!
HELP US, OWL!
SAVE US, OWL!
RELEASE THEM IMMEDIATELY.
NEVER! AND I'LL NEVER TELL YOU THAT I'M HOLDING THEM AT THE PLACE DES VOSGES SQUARE EITHER!
GIGGLE

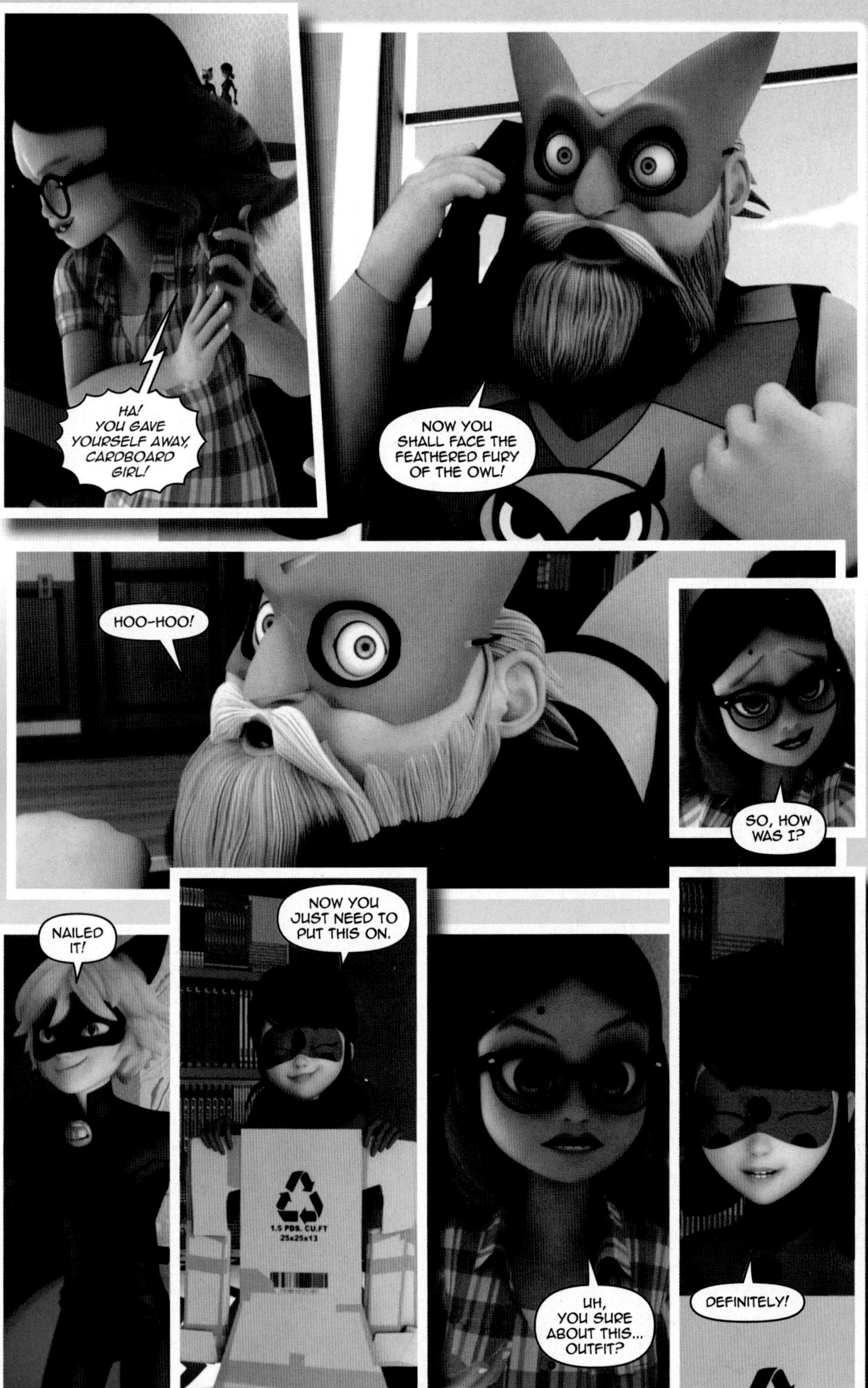
HA! YOU GAVE YOURSELF AWAY, CARDBOARD GIRL!
NOW YOU SHALL FACE THE FEATHERED FURY OF THE OWL!
HOO-HOO!
SO, HOW WAS I?
NAILED IT!
NOW YOU JUST NEED TO PUT THIS ON.
1.5 PDS. CU.FT
25x25x13
UH, YOU SURE ABOUT THIS... OUTFIT?
DEFINITELY!

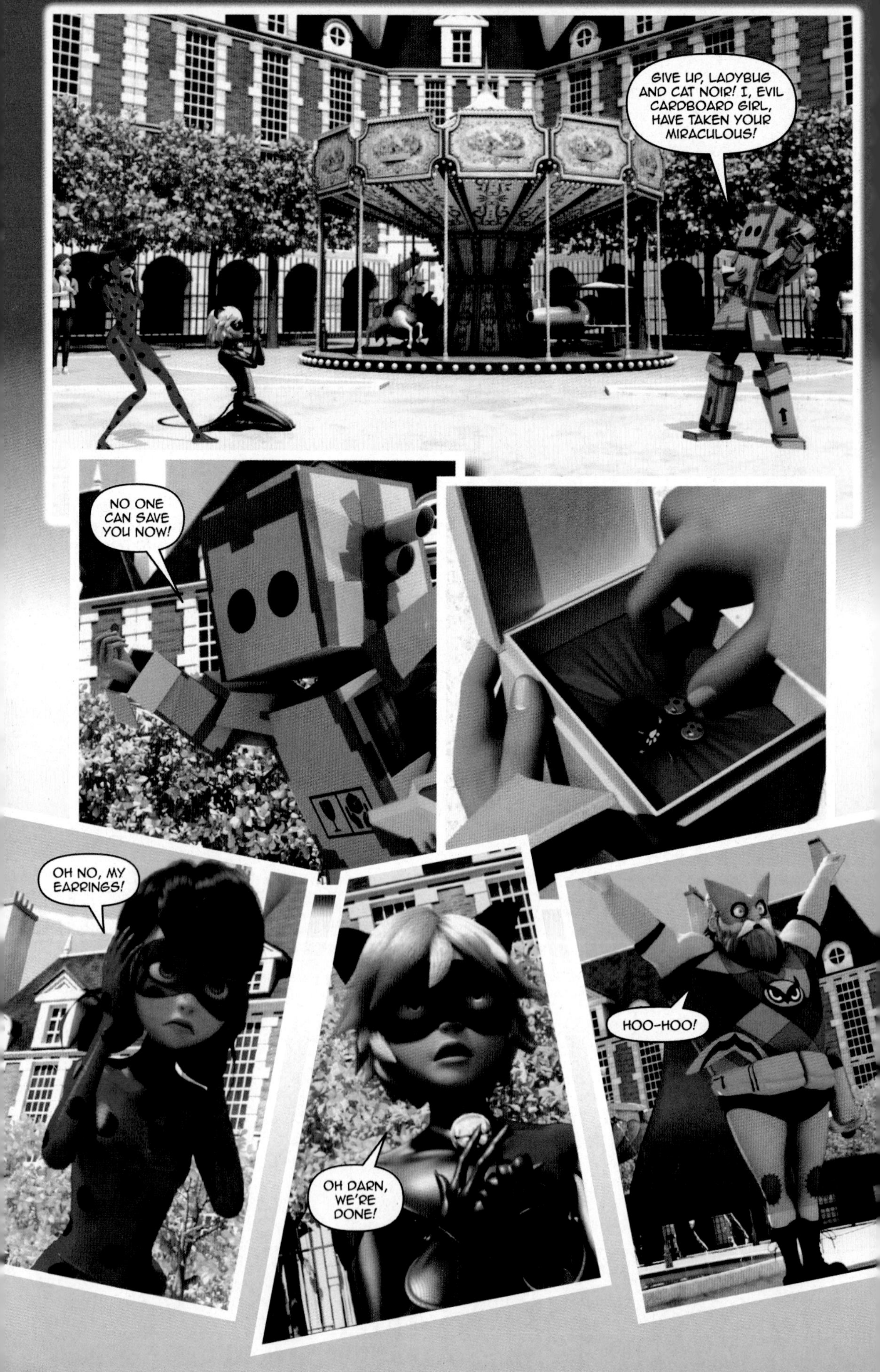

GIVE UP, LADYBUG AND CAT NOIR! I, EVIL CARDBOARD GIRL, HAVE TAKEN YOUR MIRACULOUS!
NO ONE CAN SAVE YOU NOW!
OH NO, MY EARRINGS!
OH DARN, WE'RE DONE!
HOO-HOO!

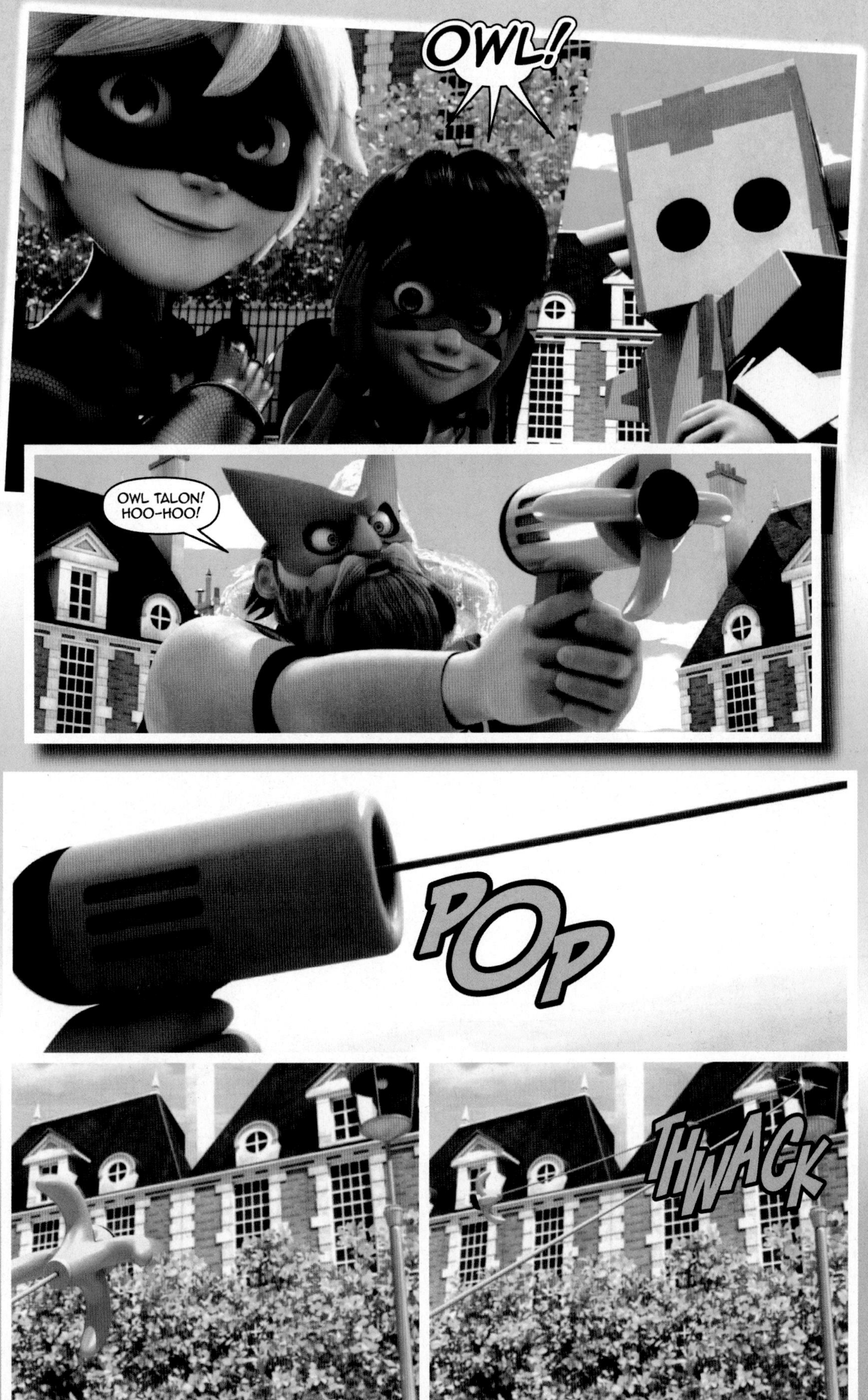
OWL!
OWL TALON! HOO-HOO!
POP
THWACK

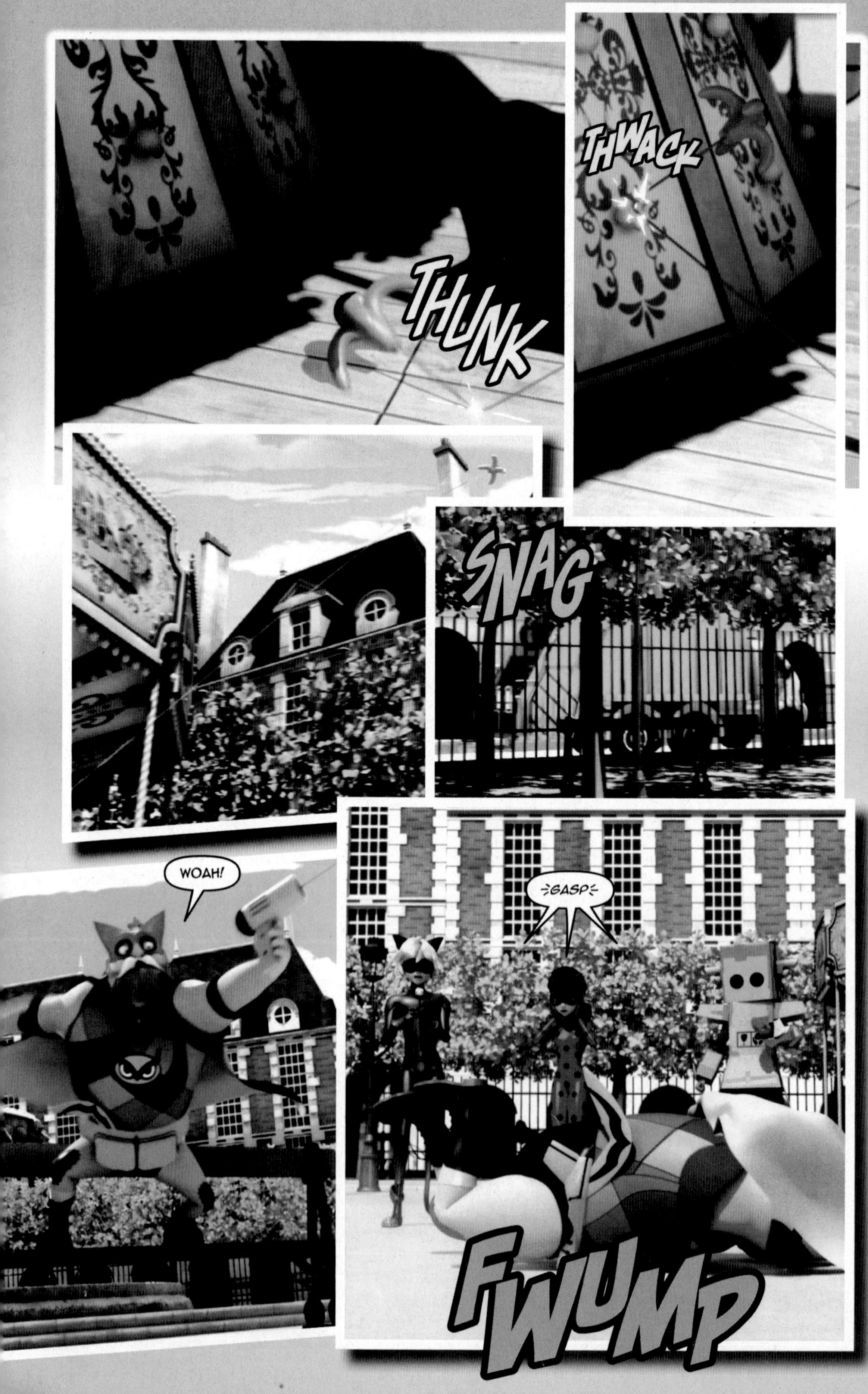
THUNK
THWACK
SNAG
WOAH!
GASP
FWUMP

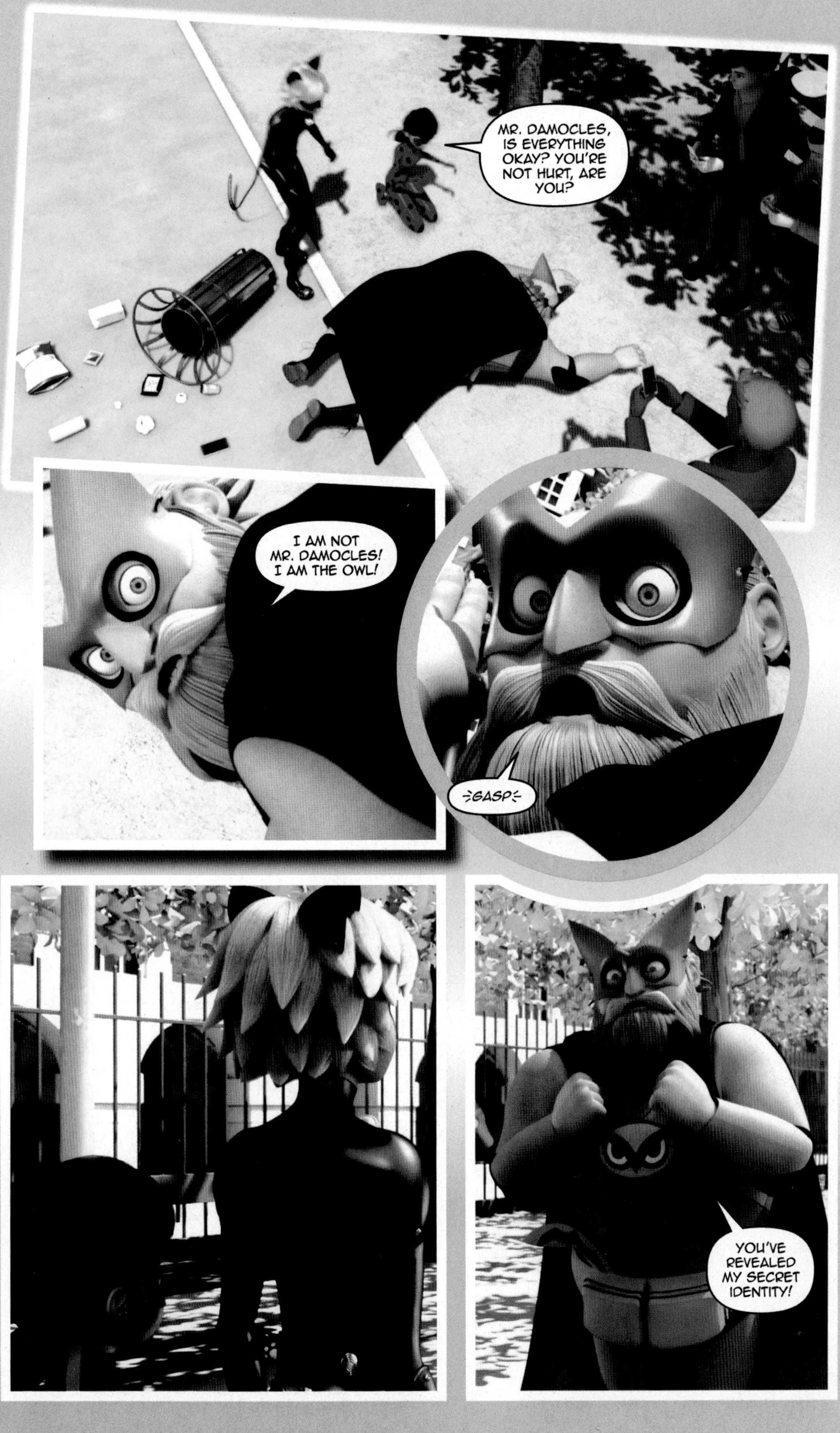
MR. DAMOCLES, IS EVERYTHING OKAY? YOU'RE NOT HURT, ARE YOU?
I AM NOT MR. DAMOCLES! I AM THE OWL!
GASP
YOU'VE REVEALED MY SECRET IDENTITY!

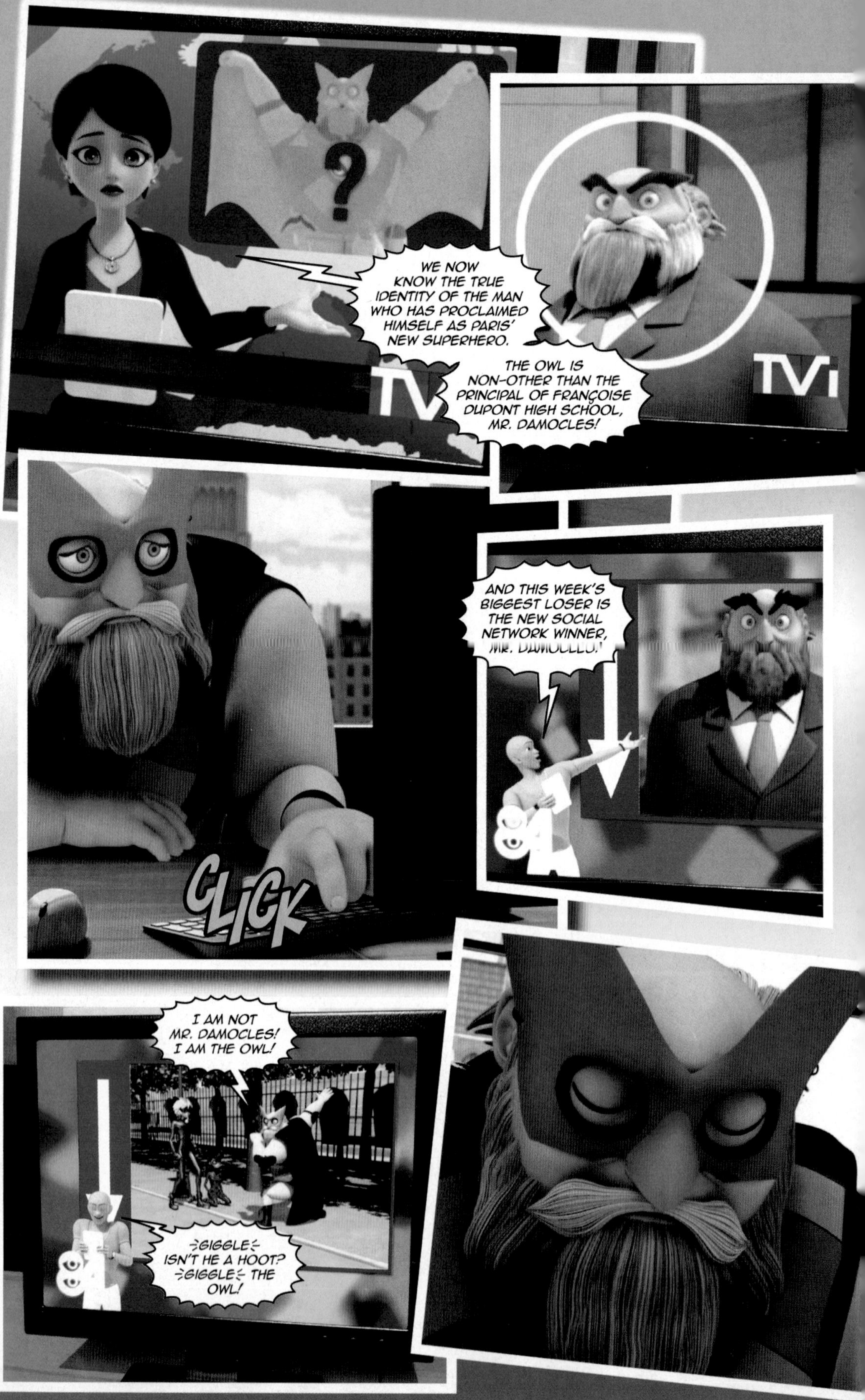

WE NOW KNOW THE TRUE IDENTITY OF THE MAN WHO HAS PROCLAIMED HIMSELF AS PARIS' NEW SUPERHERO.
THE OWL IS NON-OTHER THAN THE PRINCIPAL OF FRANÇOISE DUPONT HIGH SCHOOL, MR. DAMOCLES!
TV
TVi
CLICK
AND THIS WEEK'S BIGGEST LOSER IS THE NEW SOCIAL NETWORK WINNER, MR. DAMOCLES!
I AM NOT MR. DAMOCLES! I AM THE OWL!
GIGGLE ISN'T HE A HOOT? GIGGLE THE OWL!

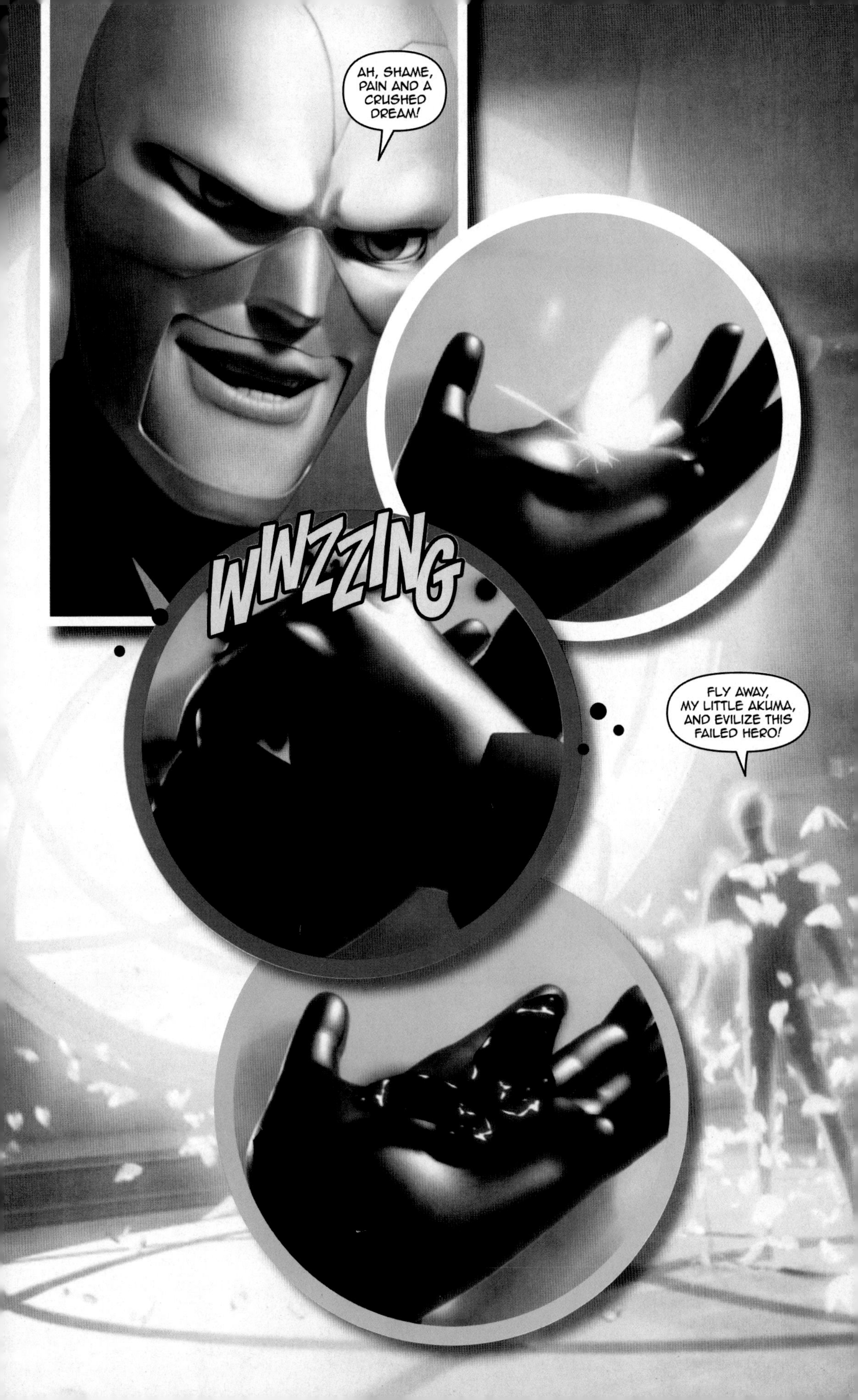
AH, SHAME, PAIN AND A CRUSHED DREAM!
WWZZING
FLY AWAY, MY LITTLE AKUMA, AND EVILIZE THIS FAILED HERO!

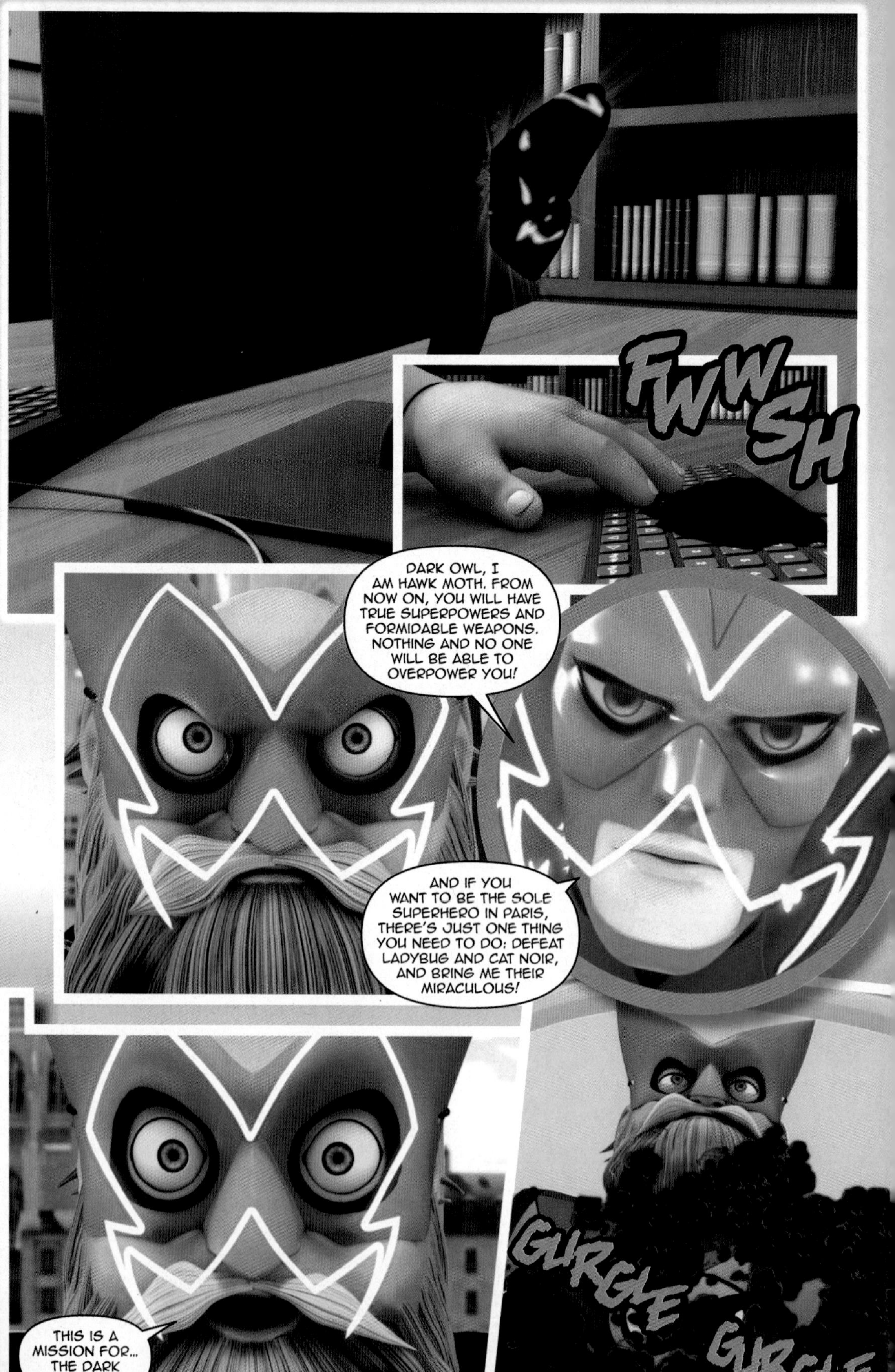
FWWSH
DARK OWL, I AM HAWK MOTH. FROM NOW ON, YOU WILL HAVE TRUE SUPERPOWERS AND FORMIDABLE WEAPONS. NOTHING AND NO ONE WILL BE ABLE TO OVERPOWER YOU!
AND IF YOU WANT TO BE THE SOLE SUPERHERO IN PARIS, THERE'S JUST ONE THING YOU NEED TO DO: DEFEAT LADYBUG AND CAT NOIR, AND BRING ME THEIR MIRACULOUS!
THIS IS A MISSION FOR... THE DARK OWL!
GURGLE
GURGLE

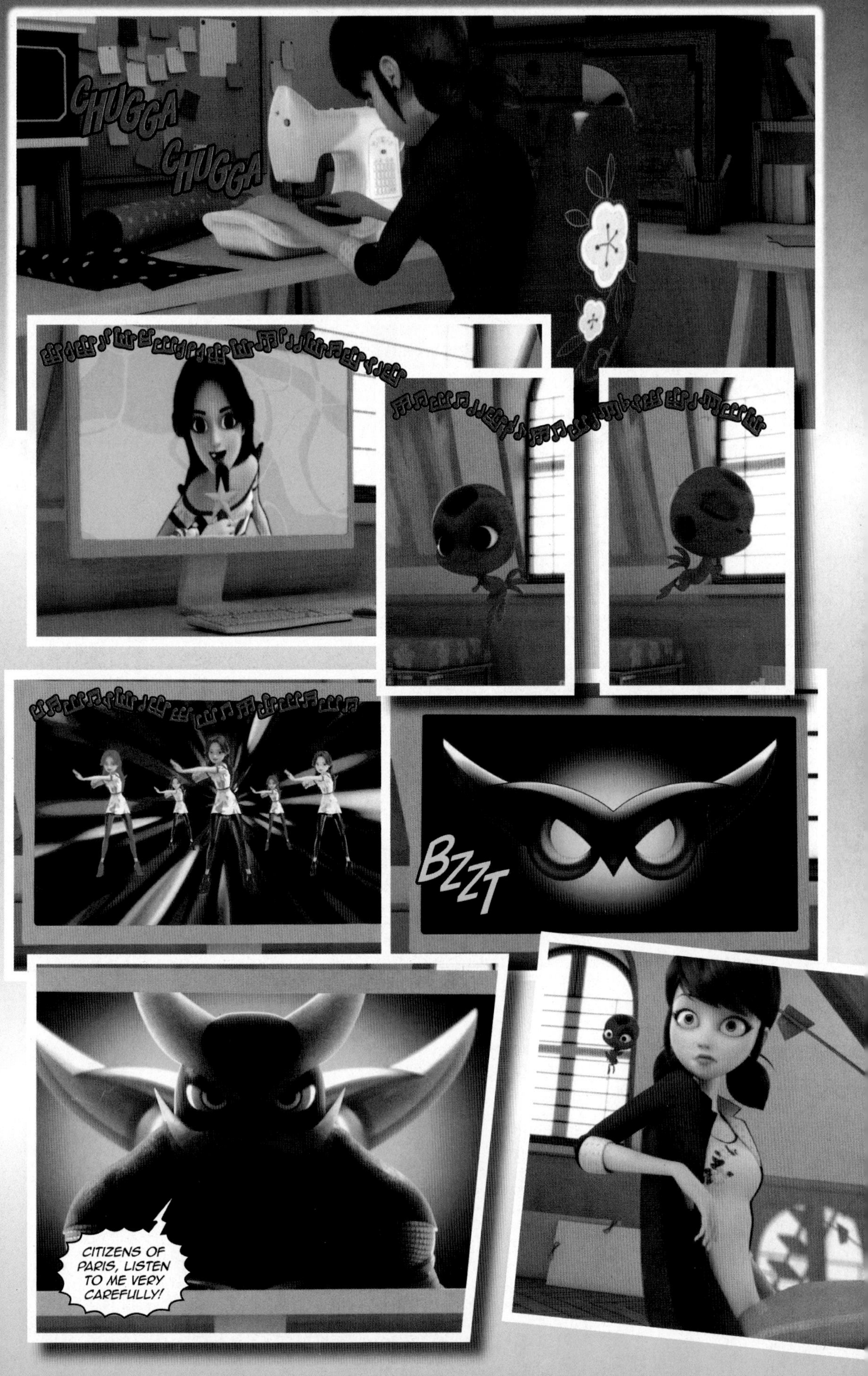
CHUGGA
CHUGGA
BZZT
CITIZENS OF PARIS, LISTEN TO ME VERY CAREFULLY!

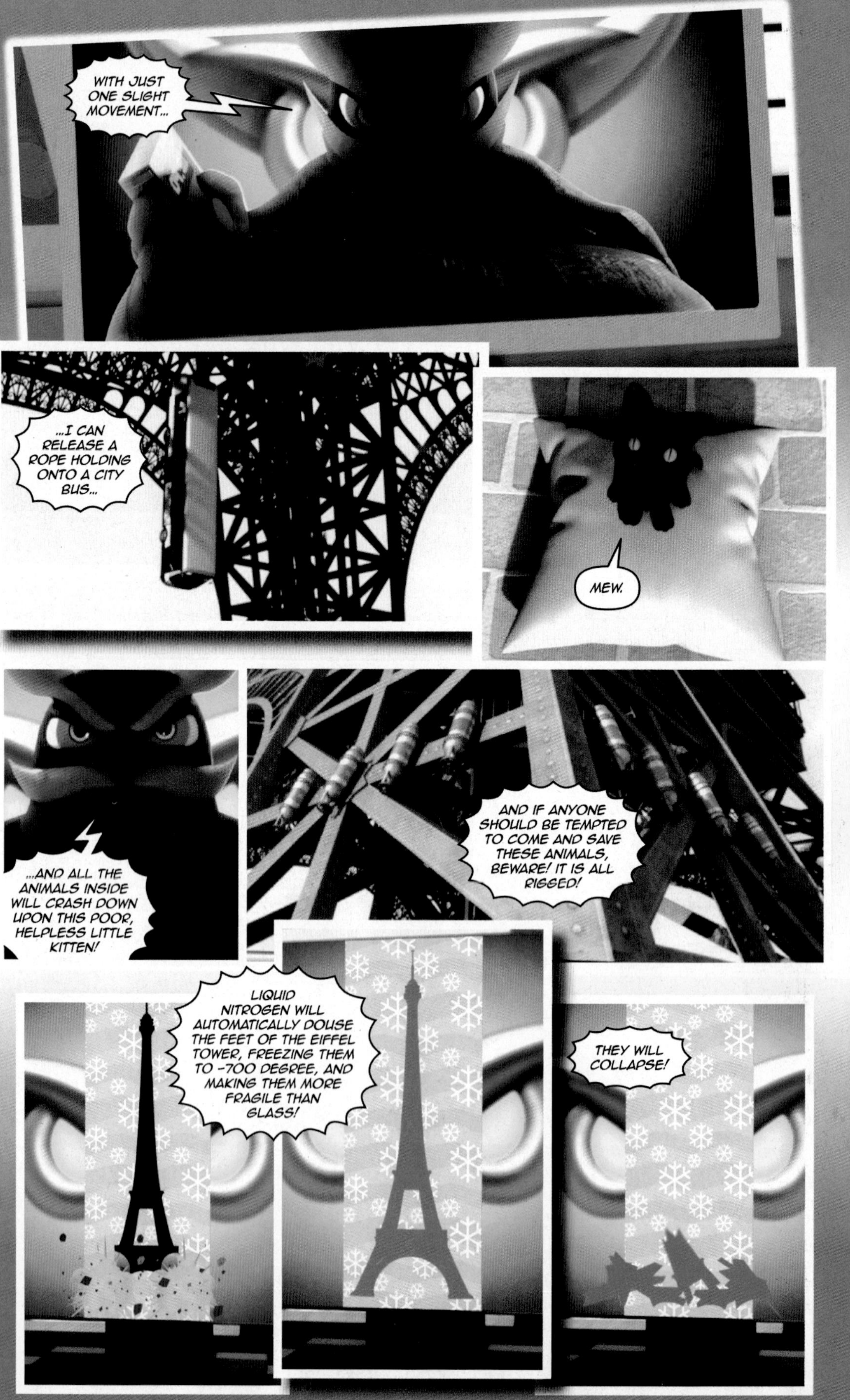
WITH JUST ONE SLIGHT MOVEMENT...
...I CAN RELEASE A ROPE HOLDING ONTO A CITY BUS...
MEW.
...AND ALL THE ANIMALS INSIDE WILL CRASH DOWN UPON THIS POOR, HELPLESS LITTLE KITTEN!
AND IF ANYONE SHOULD BE TEMPTED TO COME AND SAVE THESE ANIMALS, BEWARE! IT IS ALL RIGGED!
LIQUID NITROGEN WILL AUTOMATICALLY DOUSE THE FEET OF THE EIFFEL TOWER, FREEZING THEM TO -700 DEGREE, AND MAKING THEM MORE FRAGILE THAN GLASS!
THEY WILL COLLAPSE!

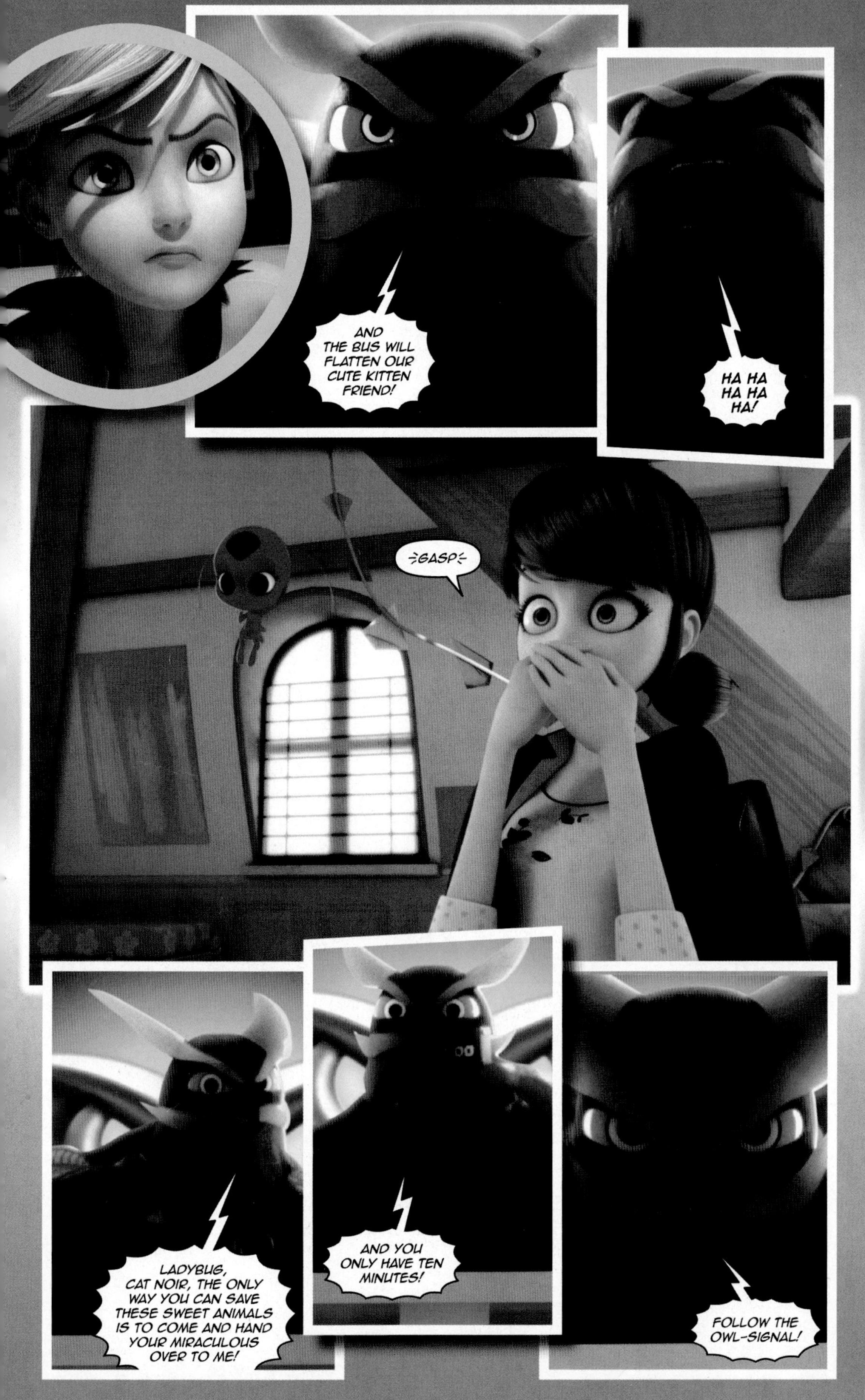
AND THE BUS WILL FLATTEN OUR CUTE KITTEN FRIEND!
HA HA HA HA HA!
GASP
LADYBUG, CAT NOIR, THE ONLY WAY YOU CAN SAVE THESE SWEET ANIMALS IS TO COME AND HAND YOUR MIRACULOUS OVER TO ME!
AND YOU ONLY HAVE TEN MINUTES!
FOLLOW THE OWL-SIGNAL!

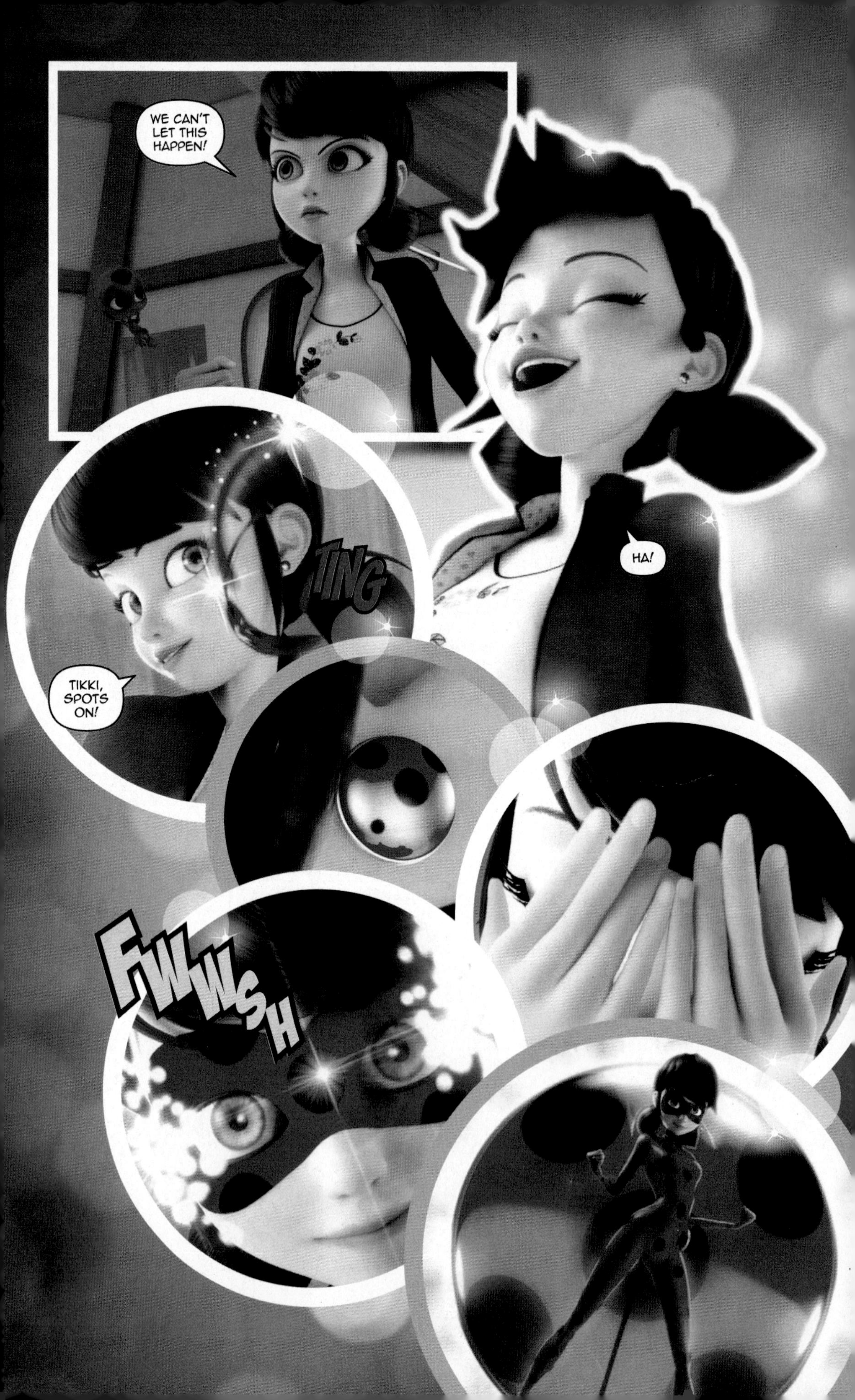
WE CAN'T LET THIS HAPPEN!
HA!
TING
TIKKI, SPOTS ON!
FWWSH

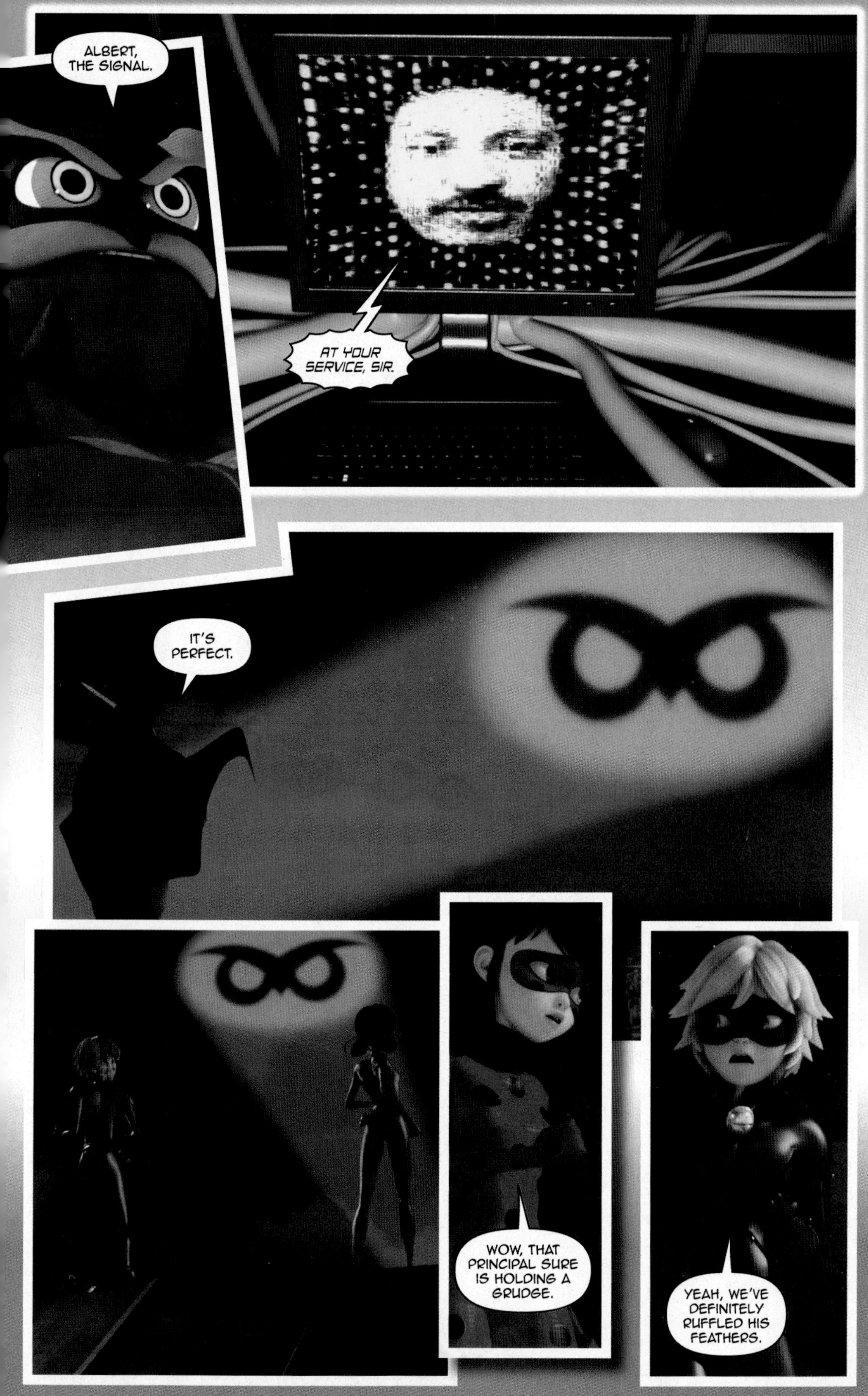
ALBERT, THE SIGNAL.
AT YOUR SERVICE, SIR.
IT'S PERFECT.
WOW, THAT PRINCIPAL SURE IS HOLDING A GRUDGE.
YEAH, WE'VE DEFINITELY RUFFLED HIS FEATHERS.

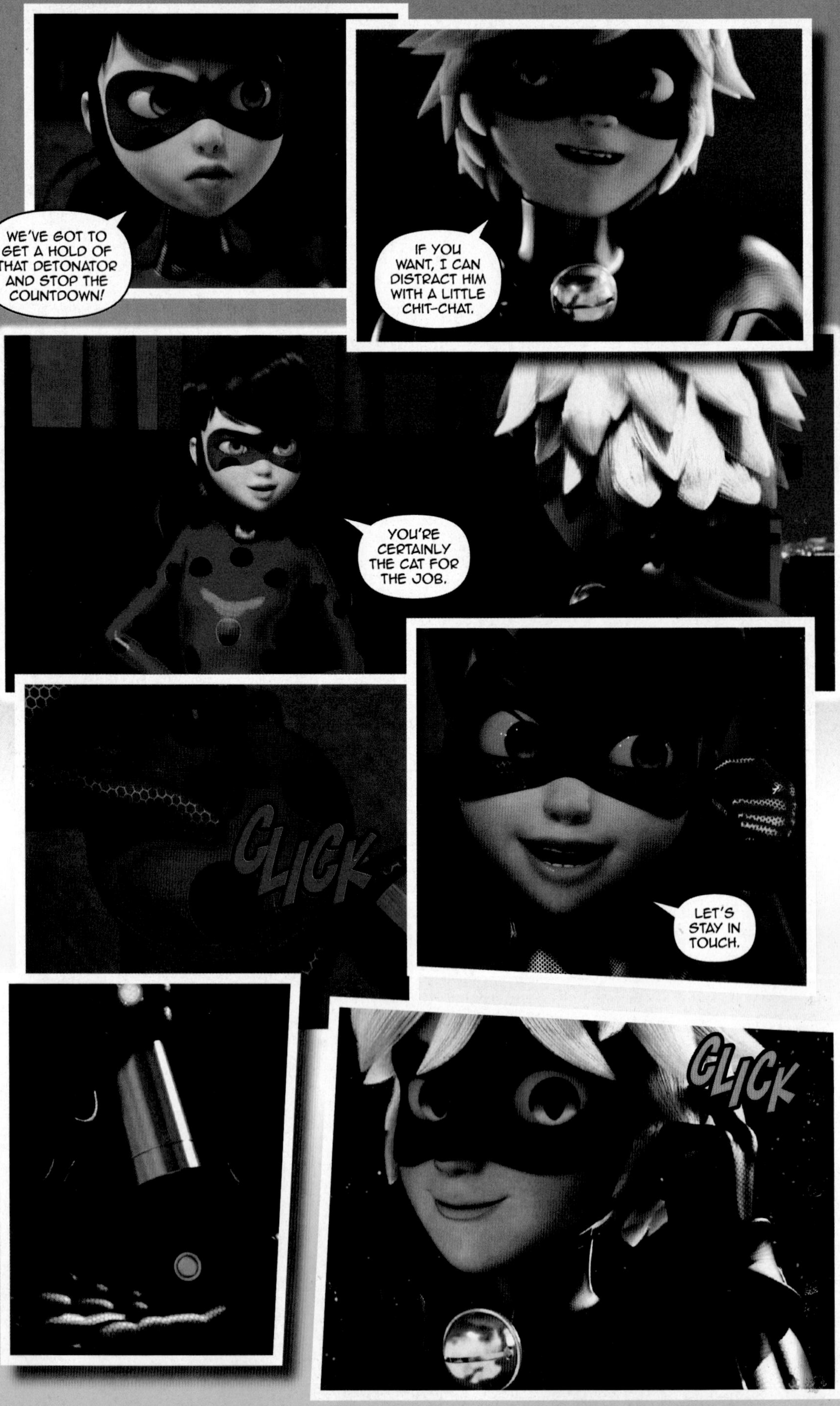

WE'VE GOT TO GET A HOLD OF THAT DETONATOR AND STOP THE COUNTDOWN!
IF YOU WANT, I CAN DISTRACT HIM WITH A LITTLE CHIT-CHAT.
YOU'RE CERTAINLY THE CAT FOR THE JOB.
CLICK
LET'S STAY IN TOUCH.
CLICK

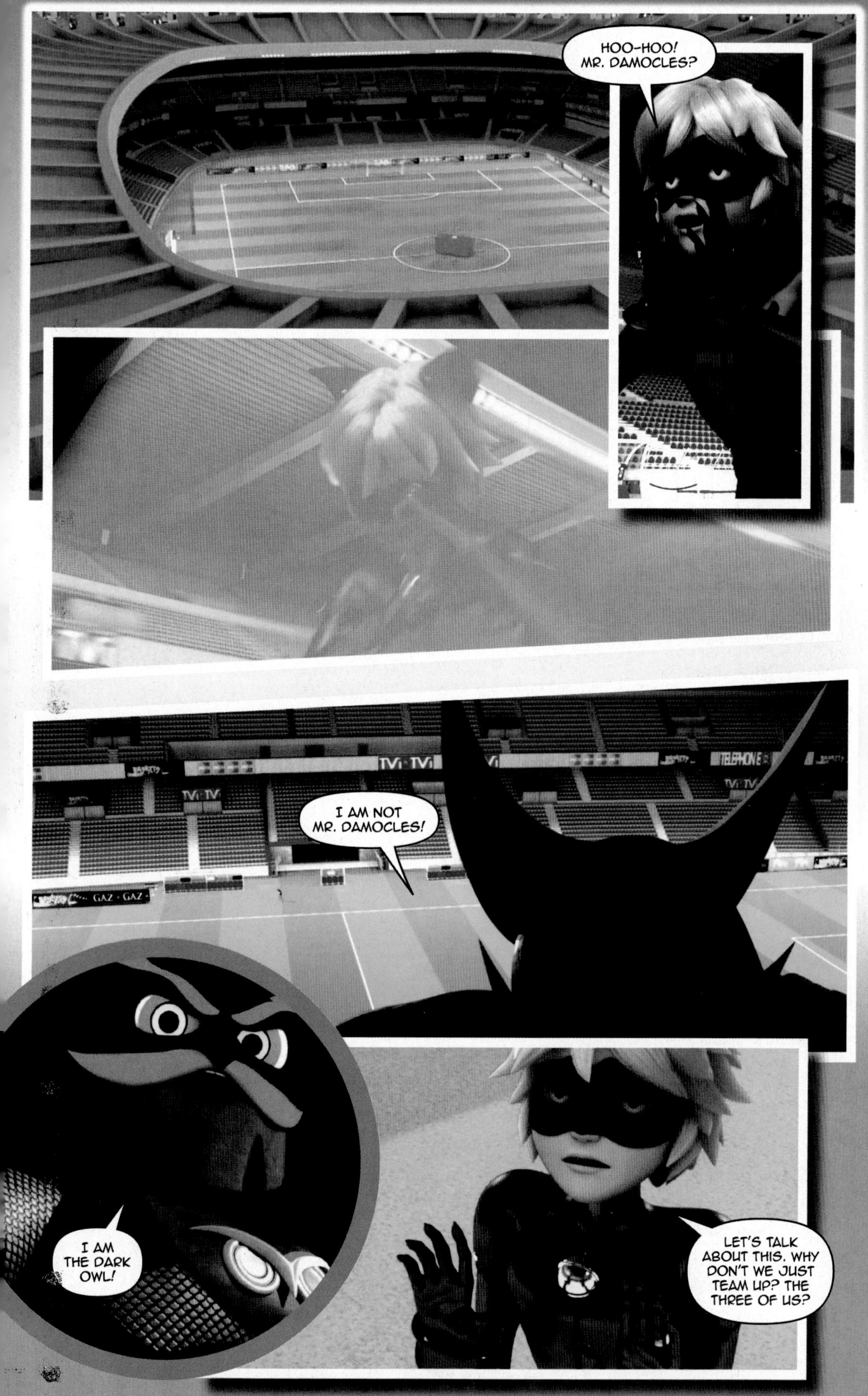
HOO-HOO!
MR. DAMOCLES?
TVi TVi
TELEPHONE
GAZ - GAZ
I AM NOT
MR. DAMOCLES!
I AM
THE DARK
OWL!
LET'S TALK
ABOUT THIS. WHY
DON'T WE JUST
TEAM UP? THE
THREE OF US?

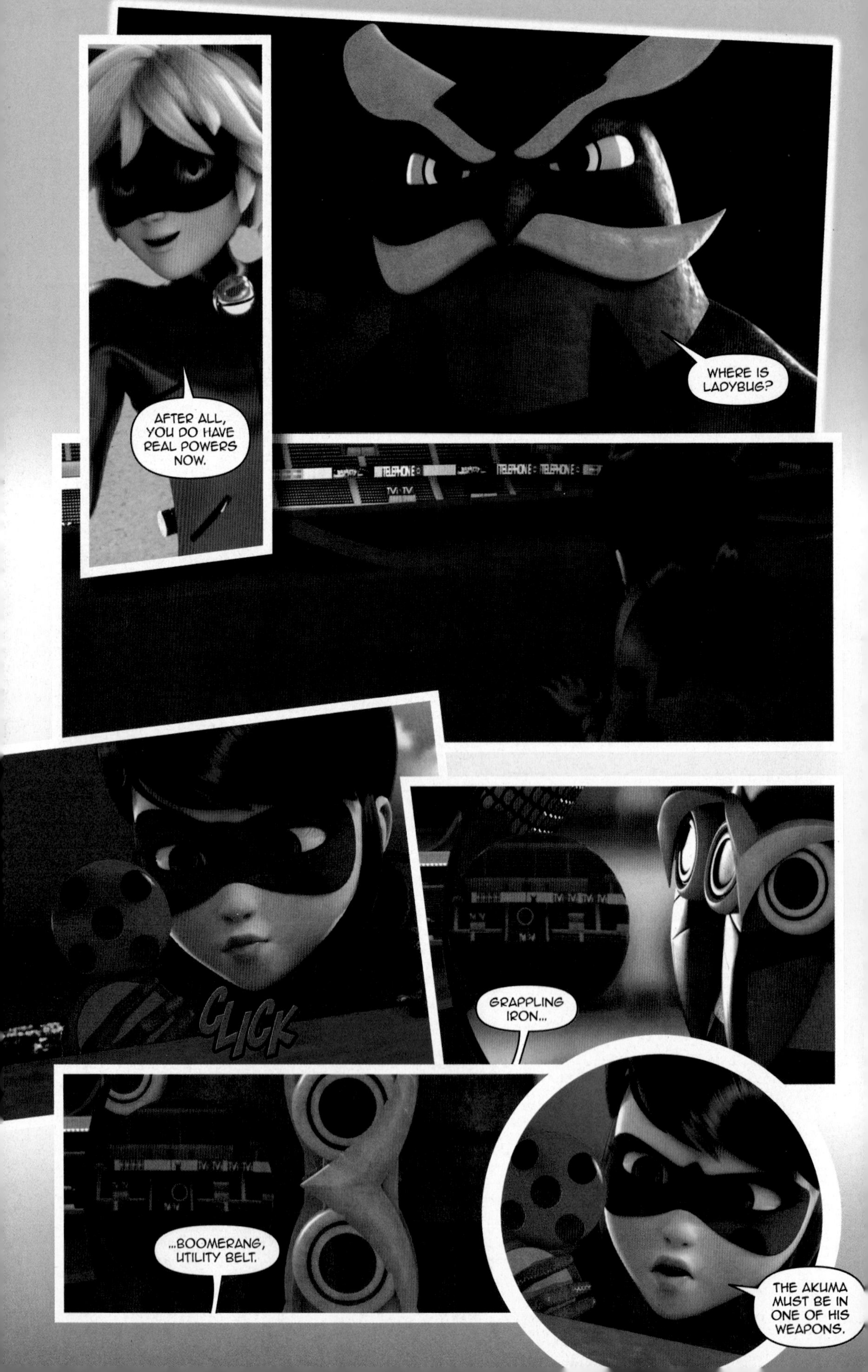
AFTER ALL, YOU DO HAVE REAL POWERS NOW.
WHERE IS LADYBUG?
CLICK
GRAPPLING IRON...
...BOOMERANG, UTILITY BELT.
THE AKUMA MUST BE IN ONE OF HIS WEAPONS.

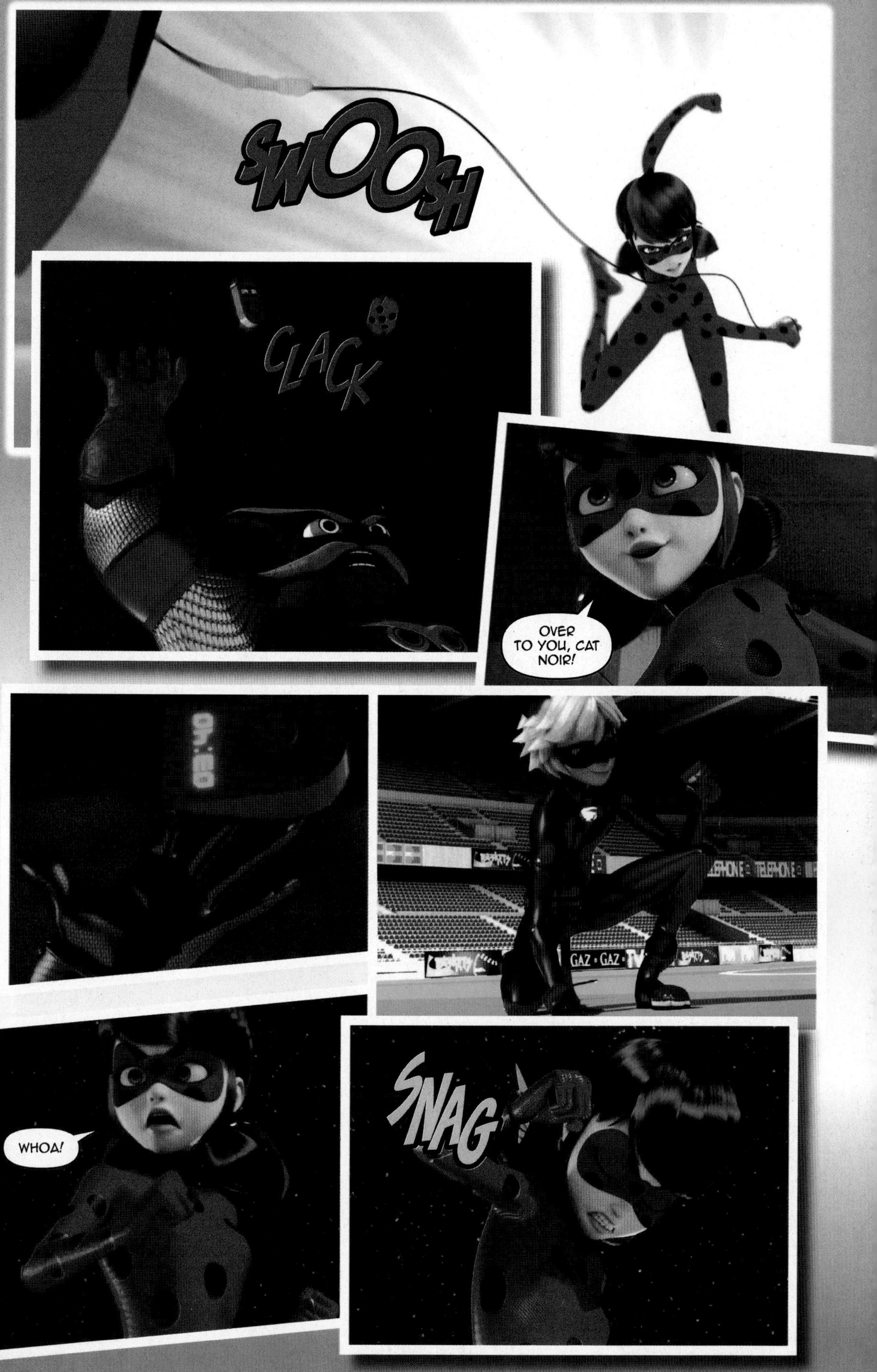
SWOOSH
CLACK
OVER TO YOU, CAT NOIR!
WHOA!
SNAG

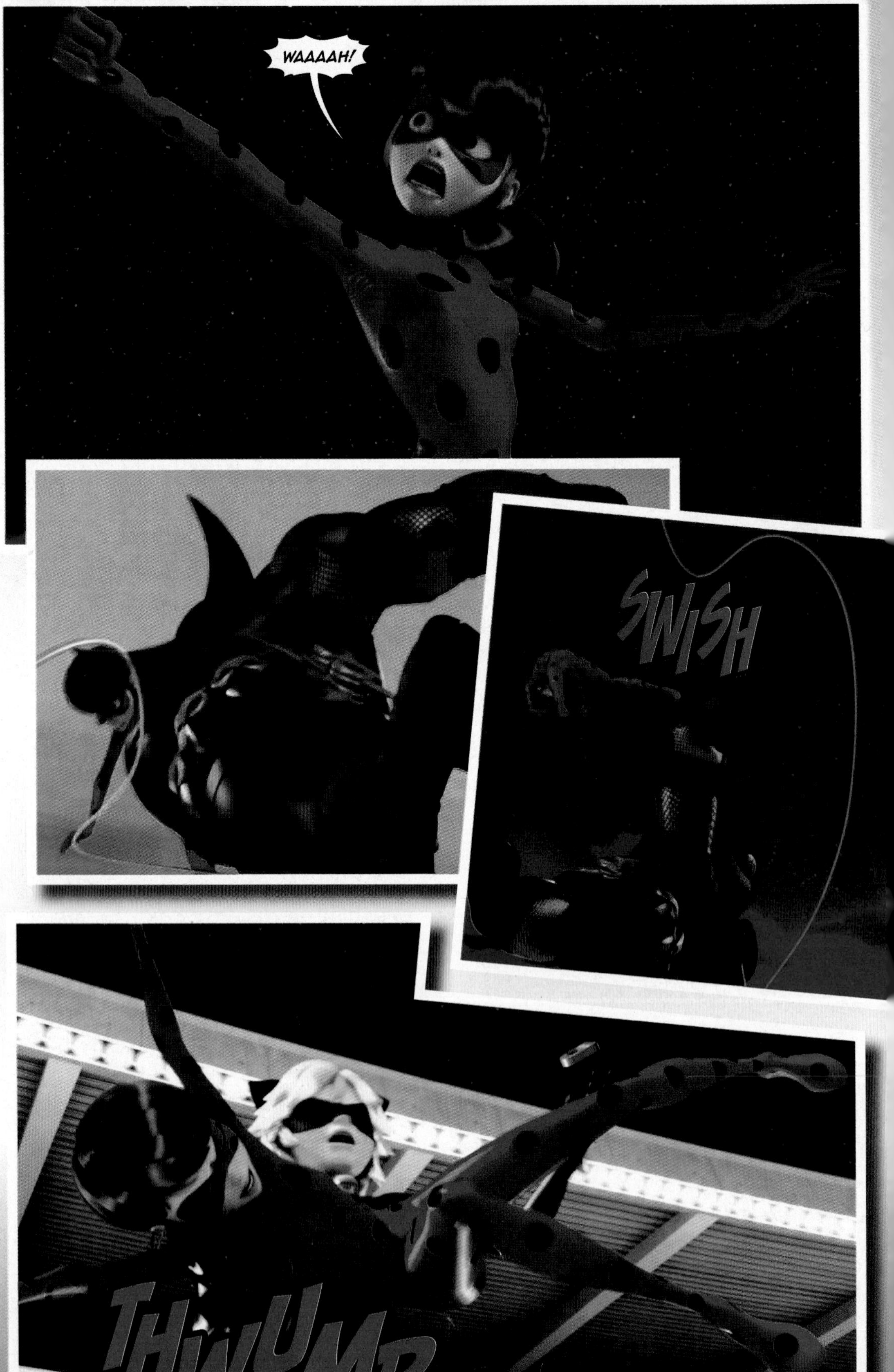
WAAAAH!
SWISH
THWUMP

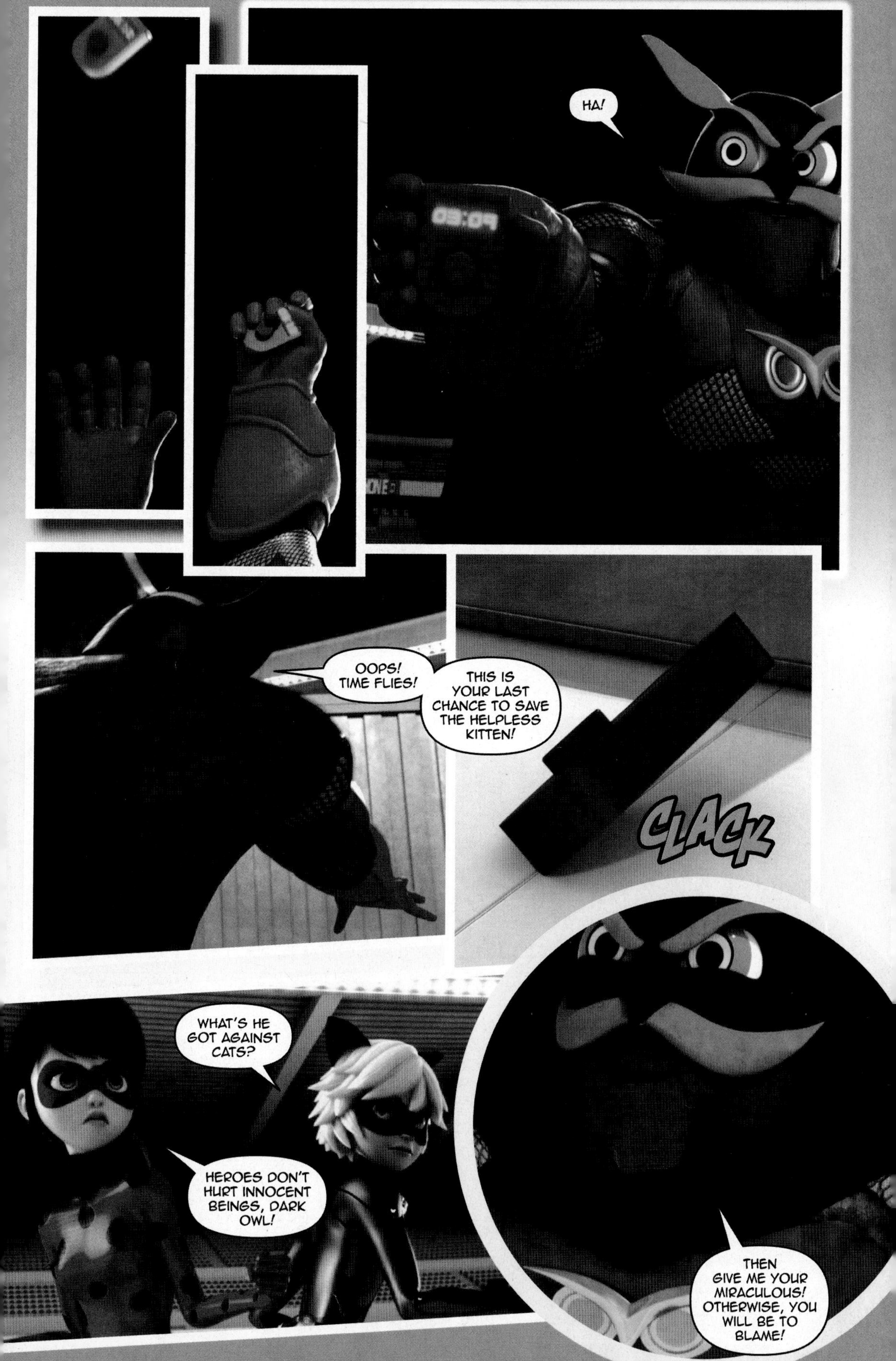
HA!
OOPS! TIME FLIES!
THIS IS YOUR LAST CHANCE TO SAVE THE HELPLESS KITTEN!
CLACK
WHAT'S HE GOT AGAINST CATS?
HEROES DON'T HURT INNOCENT BEINGS, DARK OWL!
THEN GIVE ME YOUR MIRACULOUS! OTHERWISE, YOU WILL BE TO BLAME!

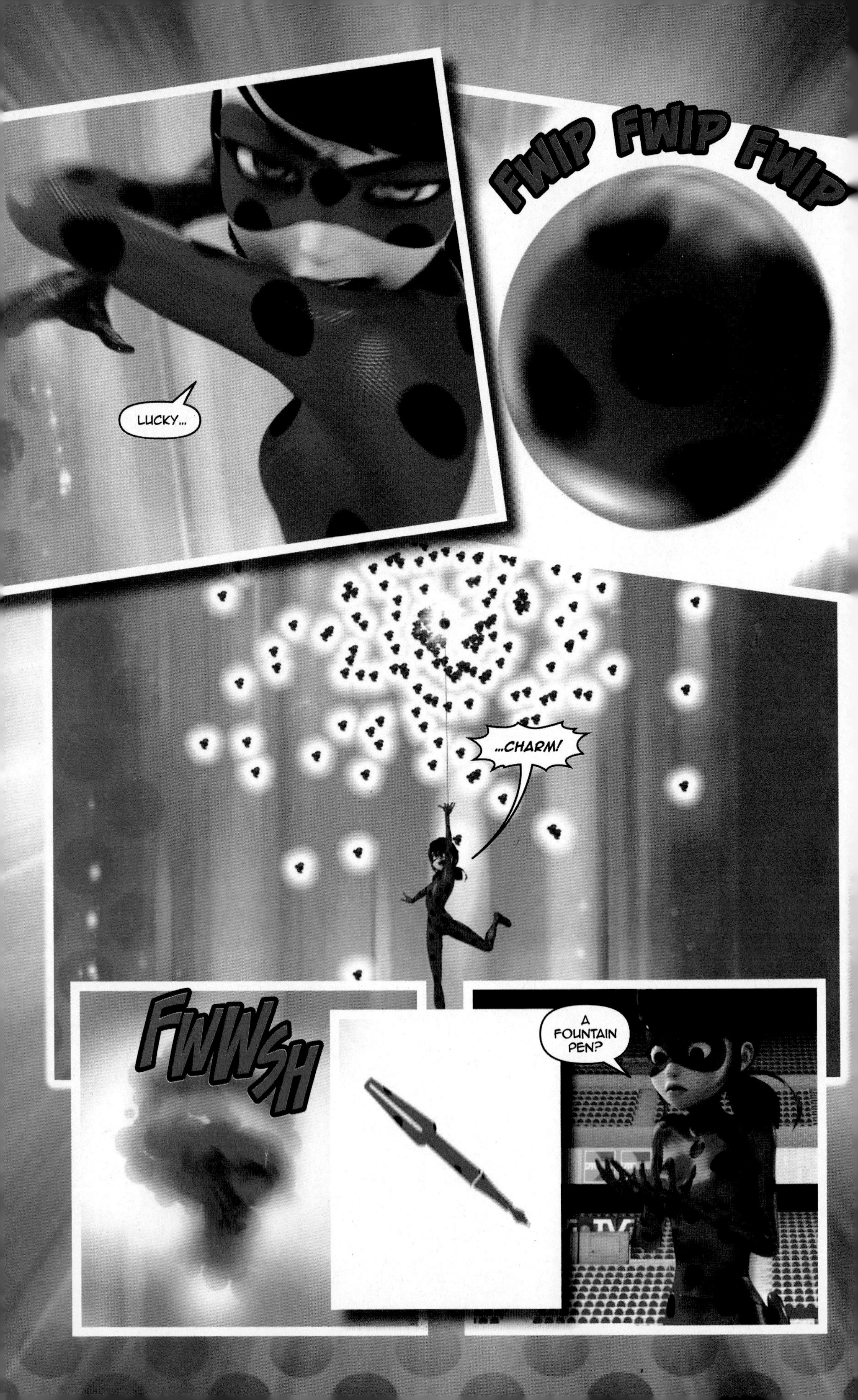
LUCKY...
FWIP FWIP FWIP
...CHARM!
FWWSH
A FOUNTAIN PEN?

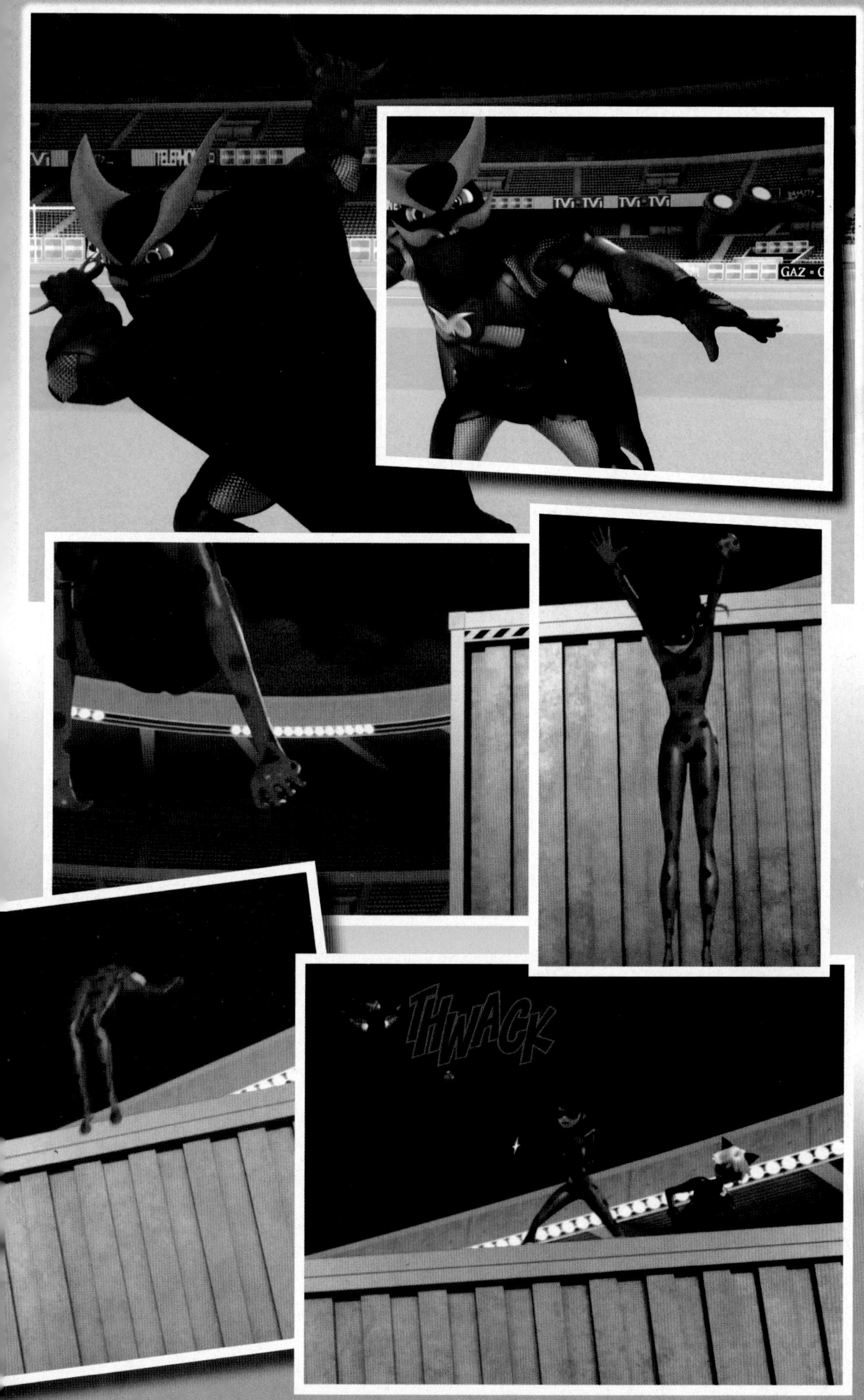
THWACK

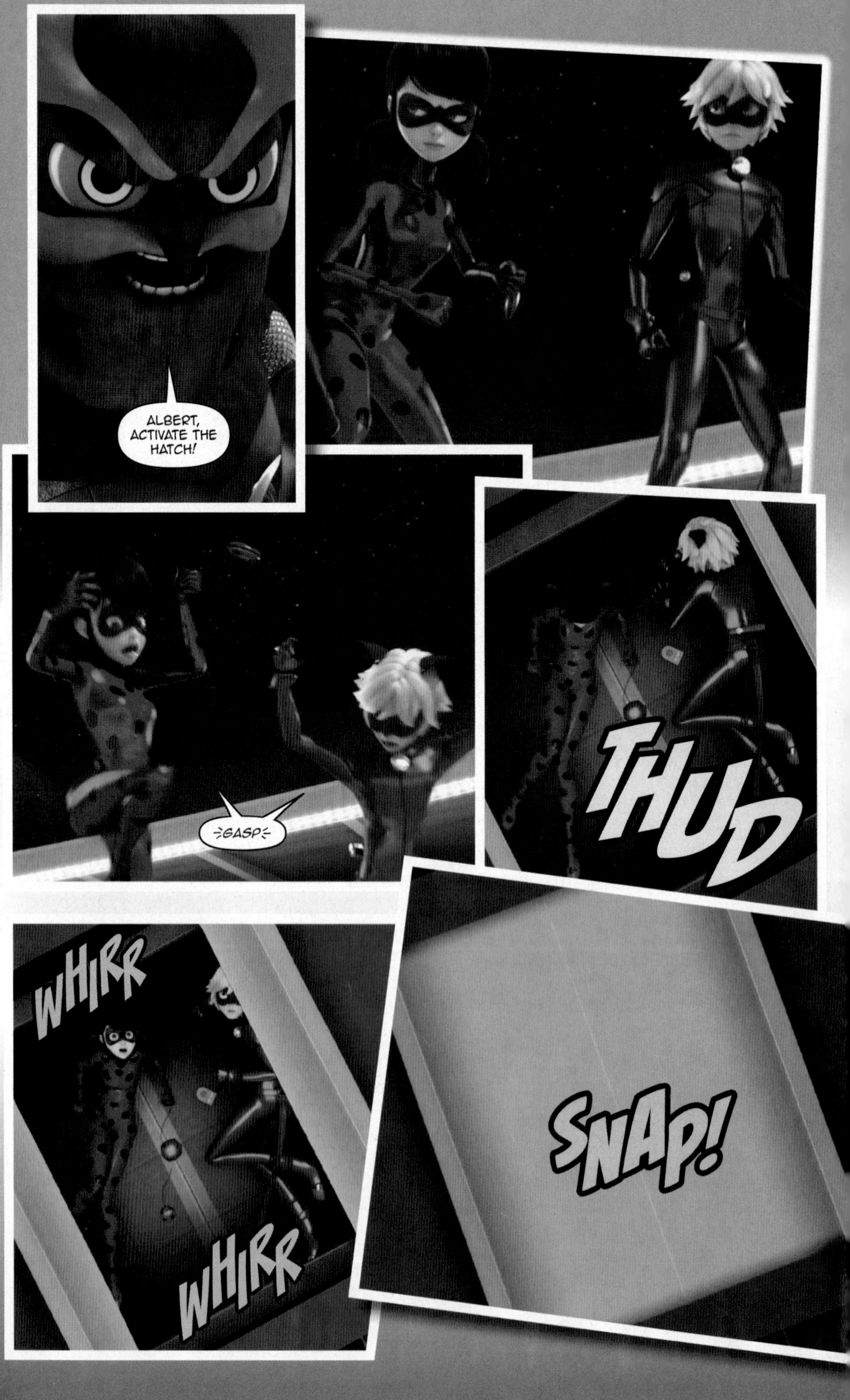
ALBERT, ACTIVATE THE HATCH!
GASP
THUD
WHIRR
WHIRR
SNAP!

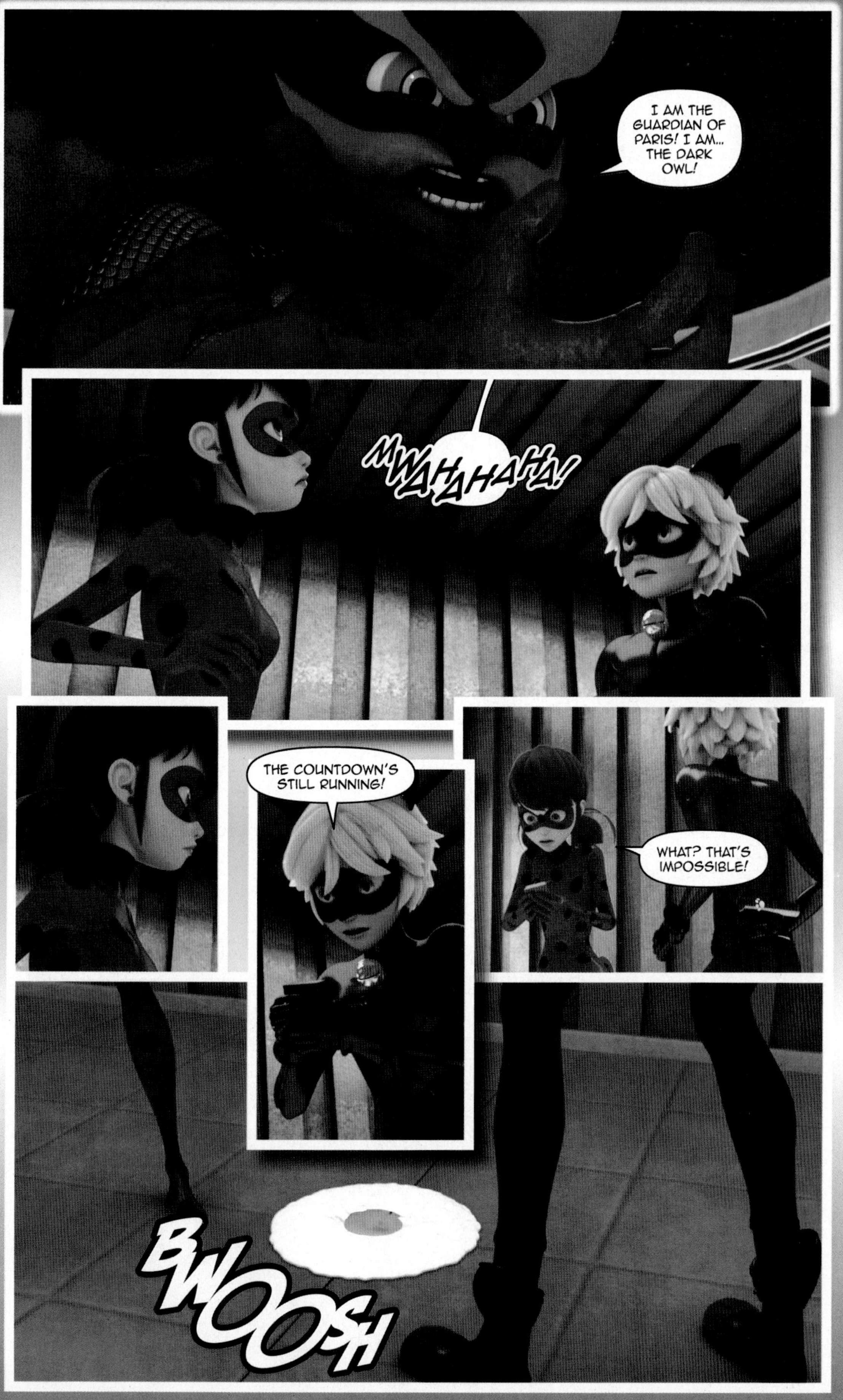
I AM THE GUARDIAN OF PARIS! I AM... THE DARK OWL!
MWAHAHAHAHA!
THE COUNTDOWN'S STILL RUNNING!
WHAT? THAT'S IMPOSSIBLE!
BWOOSH

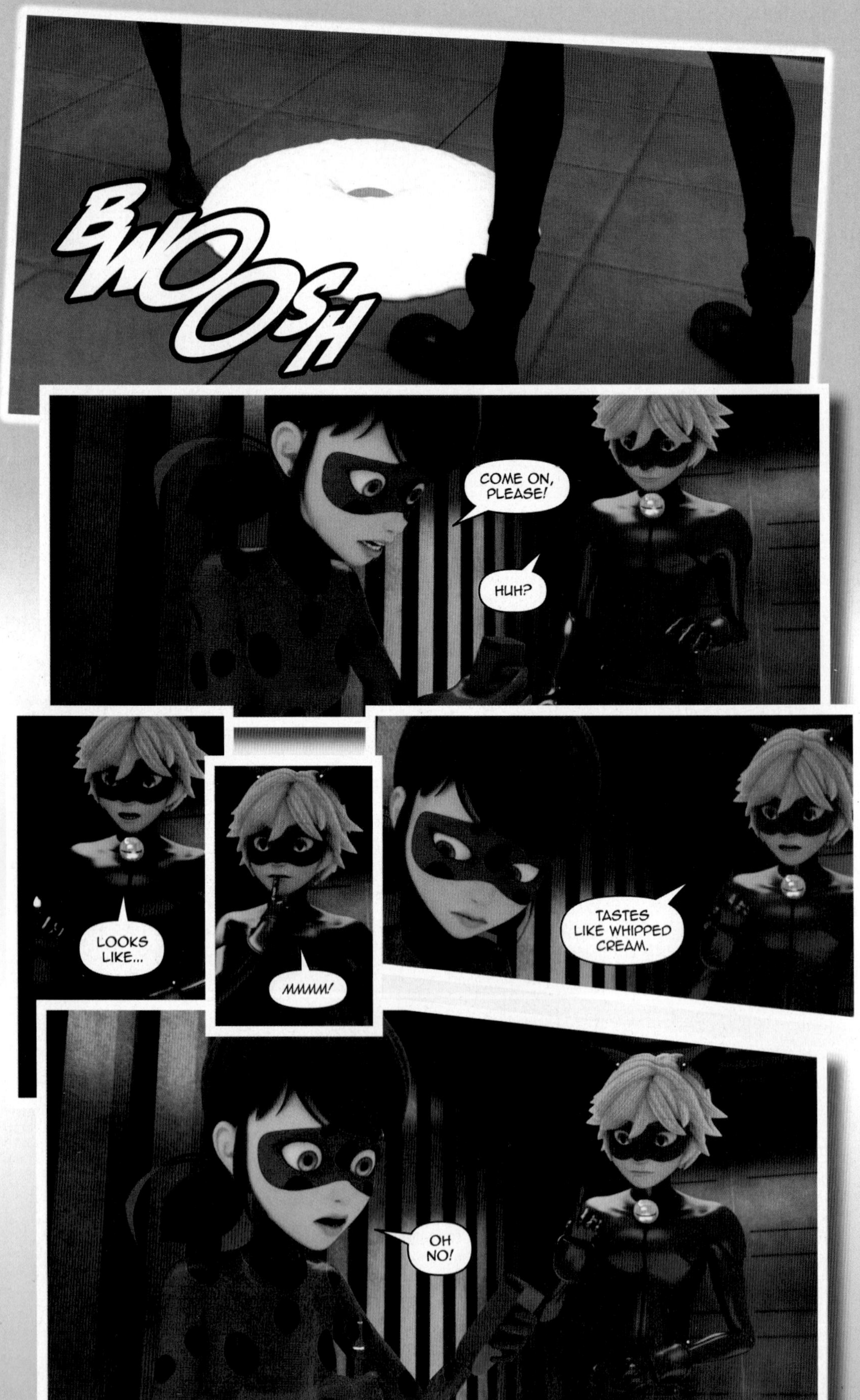
BWOOSH
COME ON, PLEASE!
HUH?
LOOKS LIKE...
MMMM!
TASTES LIKE WHIPPED CREAM.
OH NO!

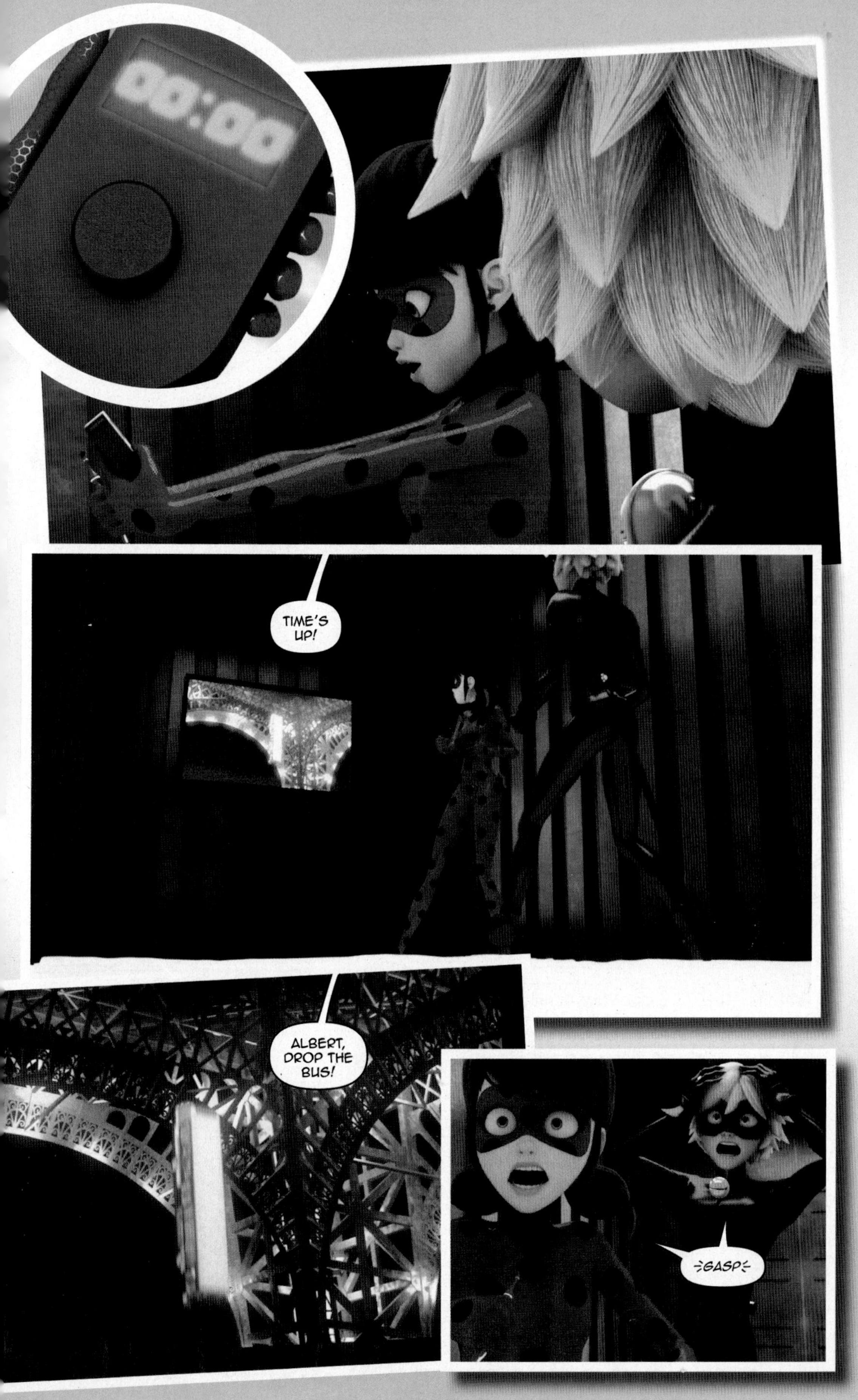
00:00
TIME'S UP!
ALBERT, DROP THE BUS!
GASP

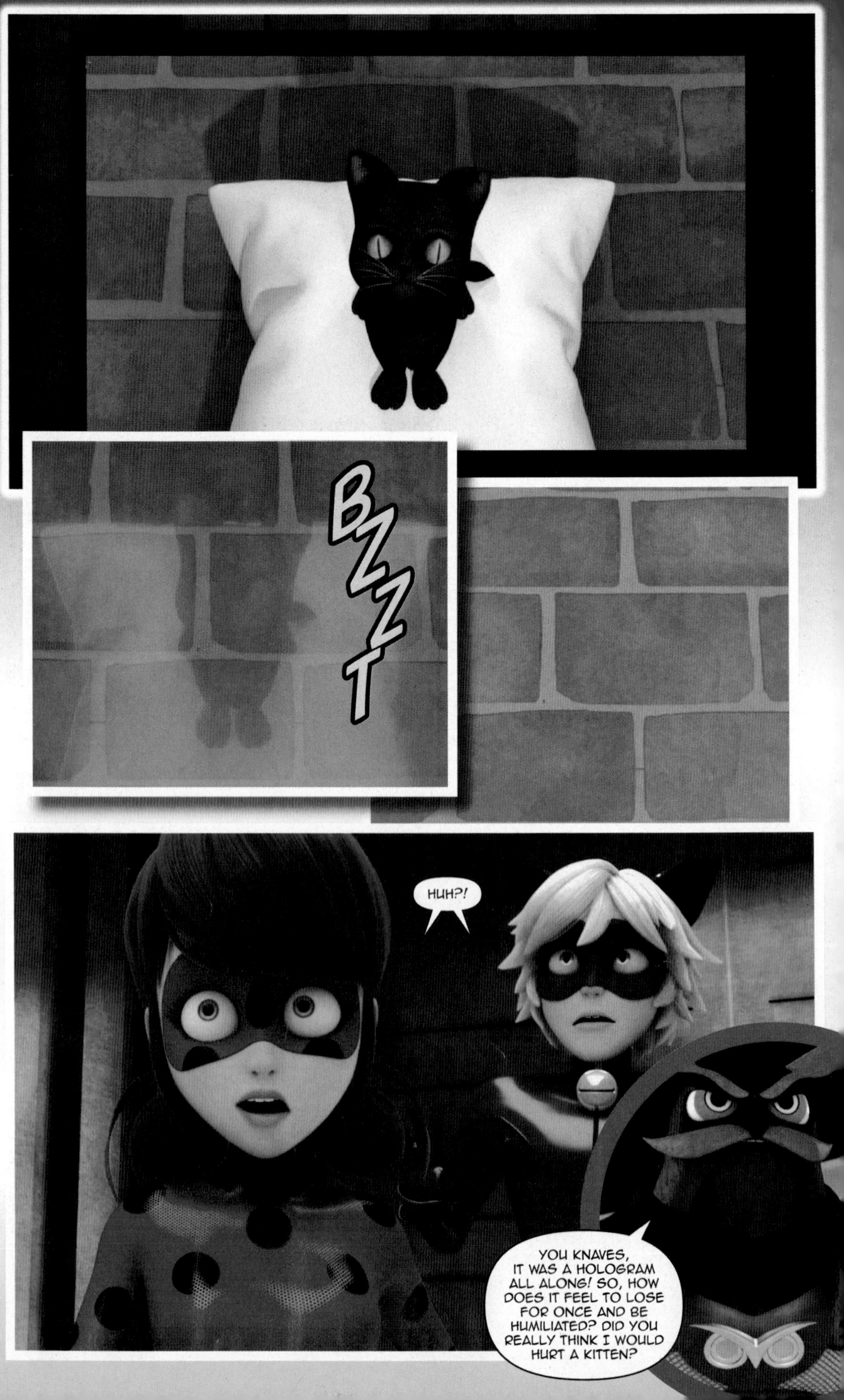
BZZZT
HUH?!
YOU KNAVES, IT WAS A HOLOGRAM ALL ALONG! SO, HOW DOES IT FEEL TO LOSE FOR ONCE AND BE HUMILIATED? DID YOU REALLY THINK I WOULD HURT A KITTEN?

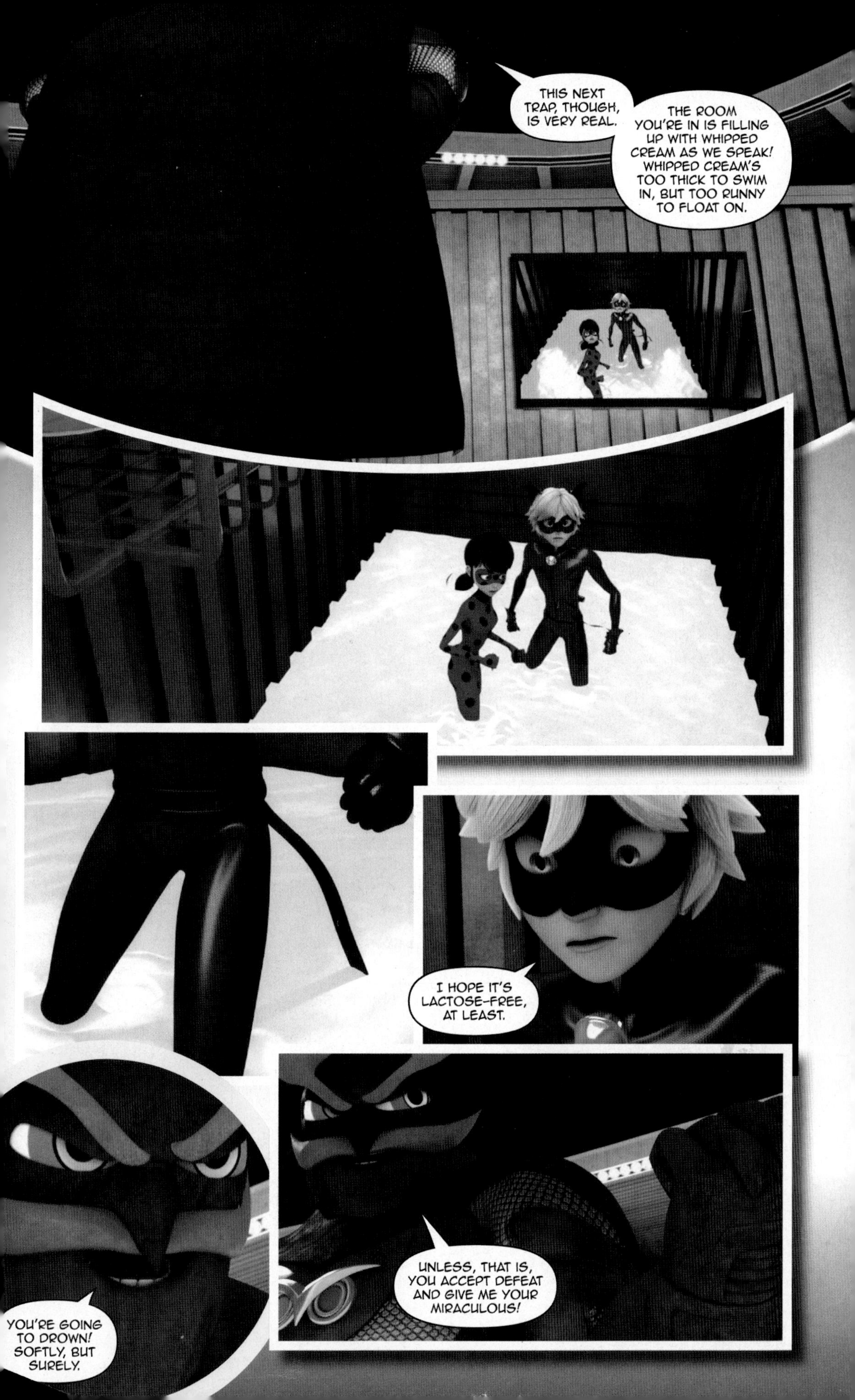

THIS NEXT TRAP, THOUGH, IS VERY REAL.
THE ROOM YOU'RE IN IS FILLING UP WITH WHIPPED CREAM AS WE SPEAK! WHIPPED CREAM'S TOO THICK TO SWIM IN, BUT TOO RUNNY TO FLOAT ON.
I HOPE IT'S LACTOSE-FREE, AT LEAST.
YOU'RE GOING TO DROWN! SOFTLY, BUT SURELY.
UNLESS, THAT IS, YOU ACCEPT DEFEAT AND GIVE ME YOUR MIRACULOUS!

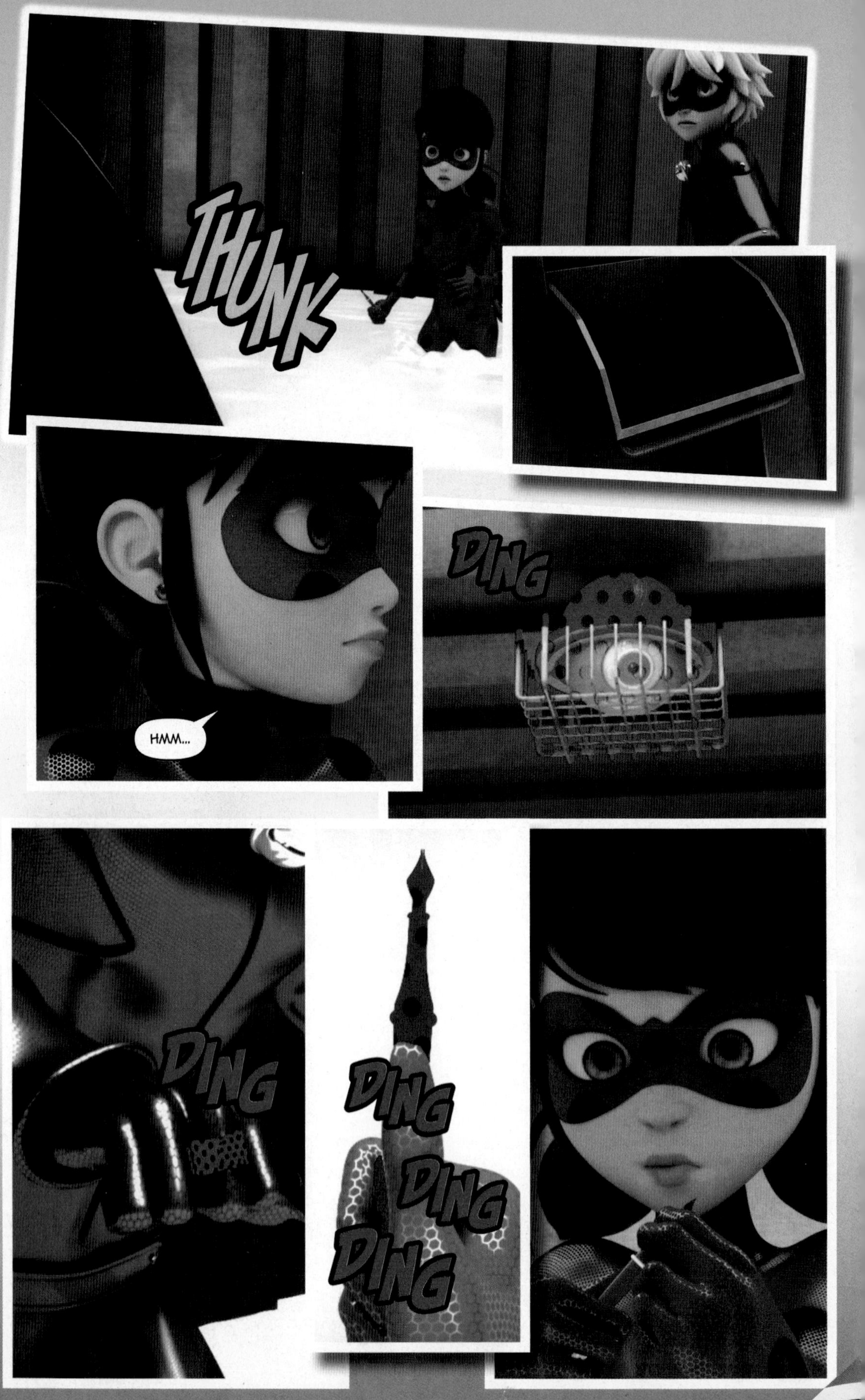
THUNK
HMM...
DING
DING
DING
DING
DING

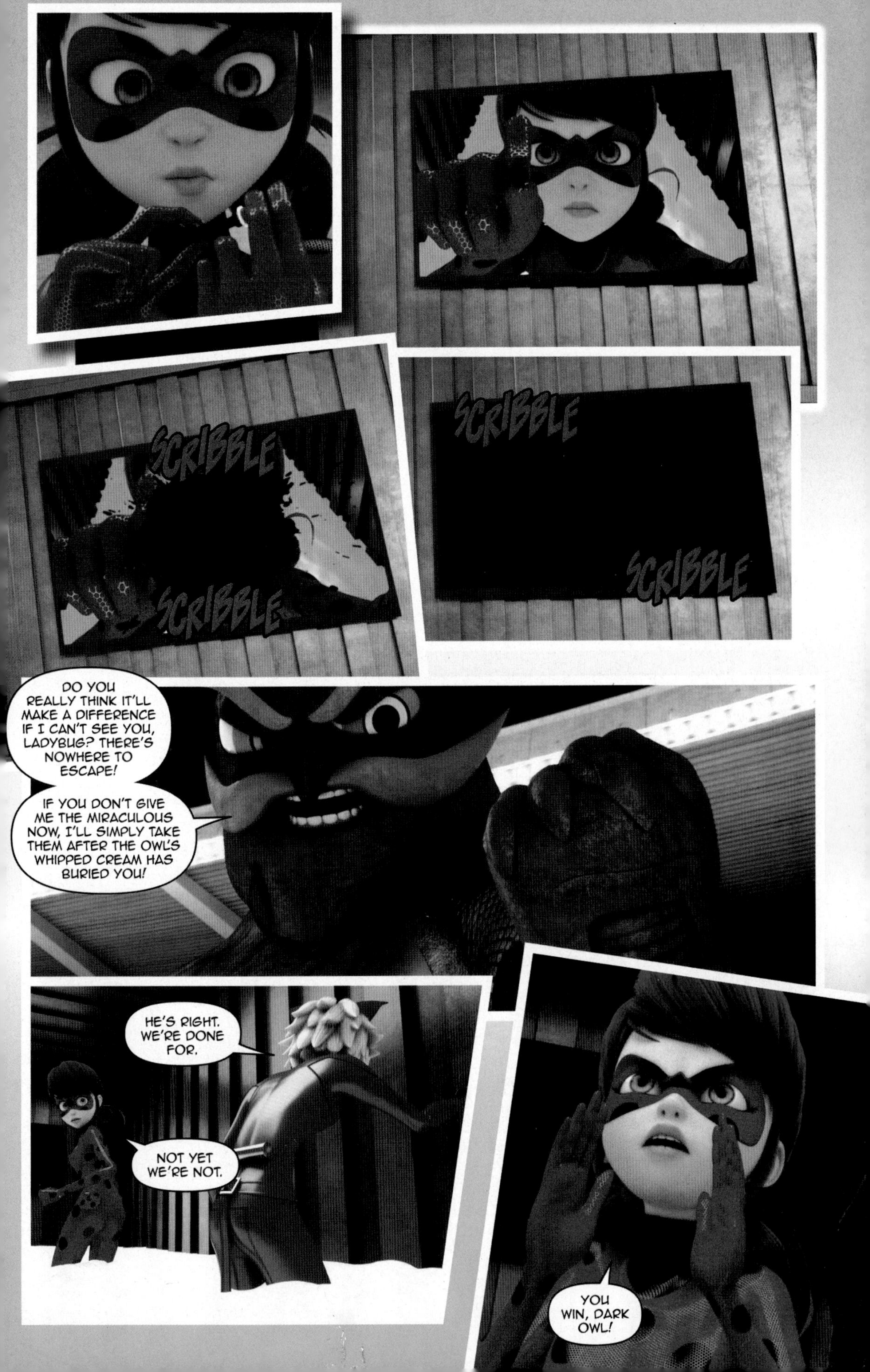
SCRIBBLE
SCRIBBLE
SCRIBBLE
SCRIBBLE
DO YOU REALLY THINK IT'LL MAKE A DIFFERENCE IF I CAN'T SEE YOU, LADYBUG? THERE'S NOWHERE TO ESCAPE!
IF YOU DON'T GIVE ME THE MIRACULOUS NOW, I'LL SIMPLY TAKE THEM AFTER THE OWL'S WHIPPED CREAM HAS BURIED YOU!
HE'S RIGHT. WE'RE DONE FOR.
NOT YET WE'RE NOT.
YOU WIN, DARK OWL!

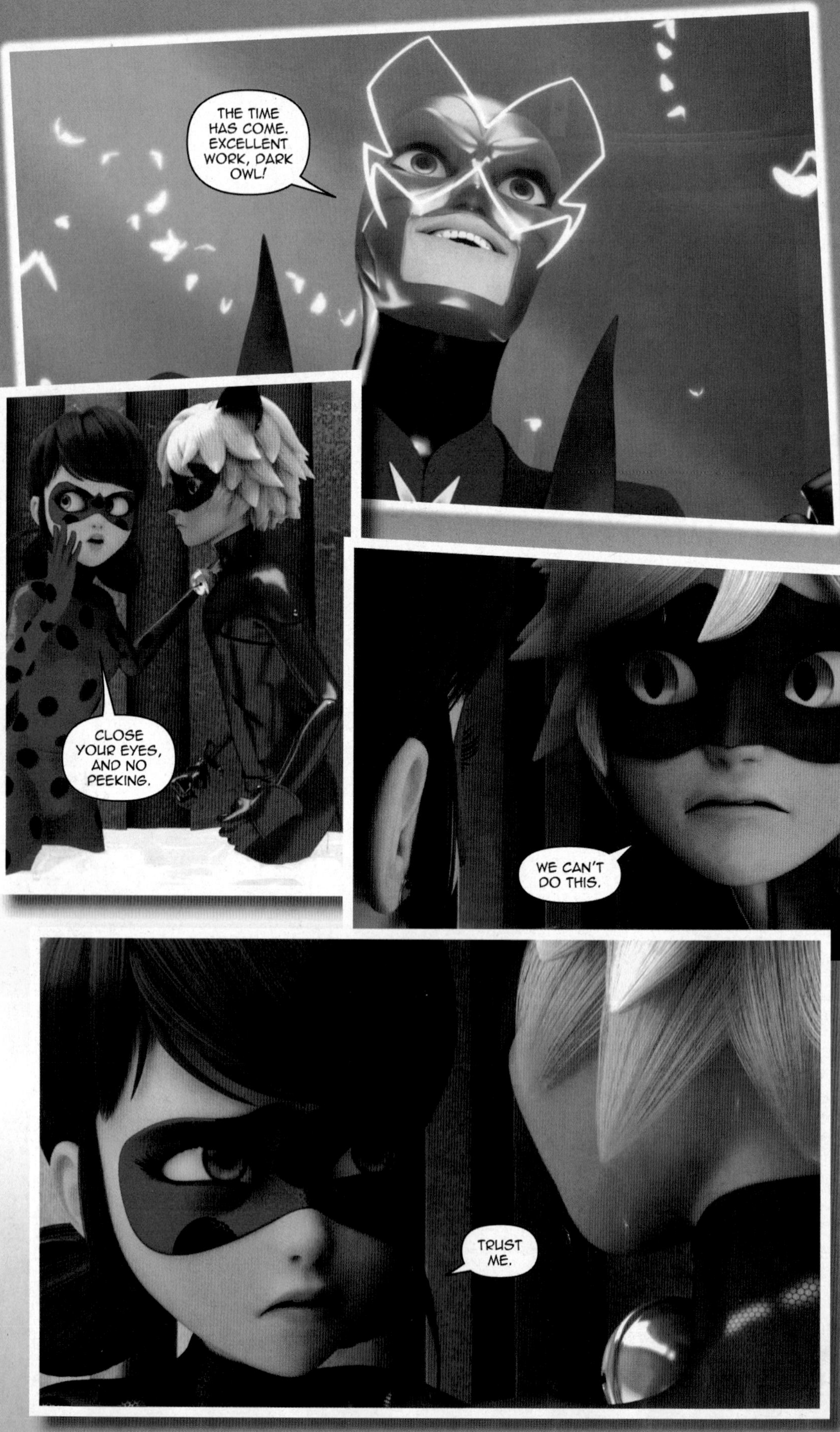
THE TIME HAS COME. EXCELLENT WORK, DARK OWL!
CLOSE YOUR EYES, AND NO PEEKING.
WE CAN'T DO THIS.
TRUST ME.

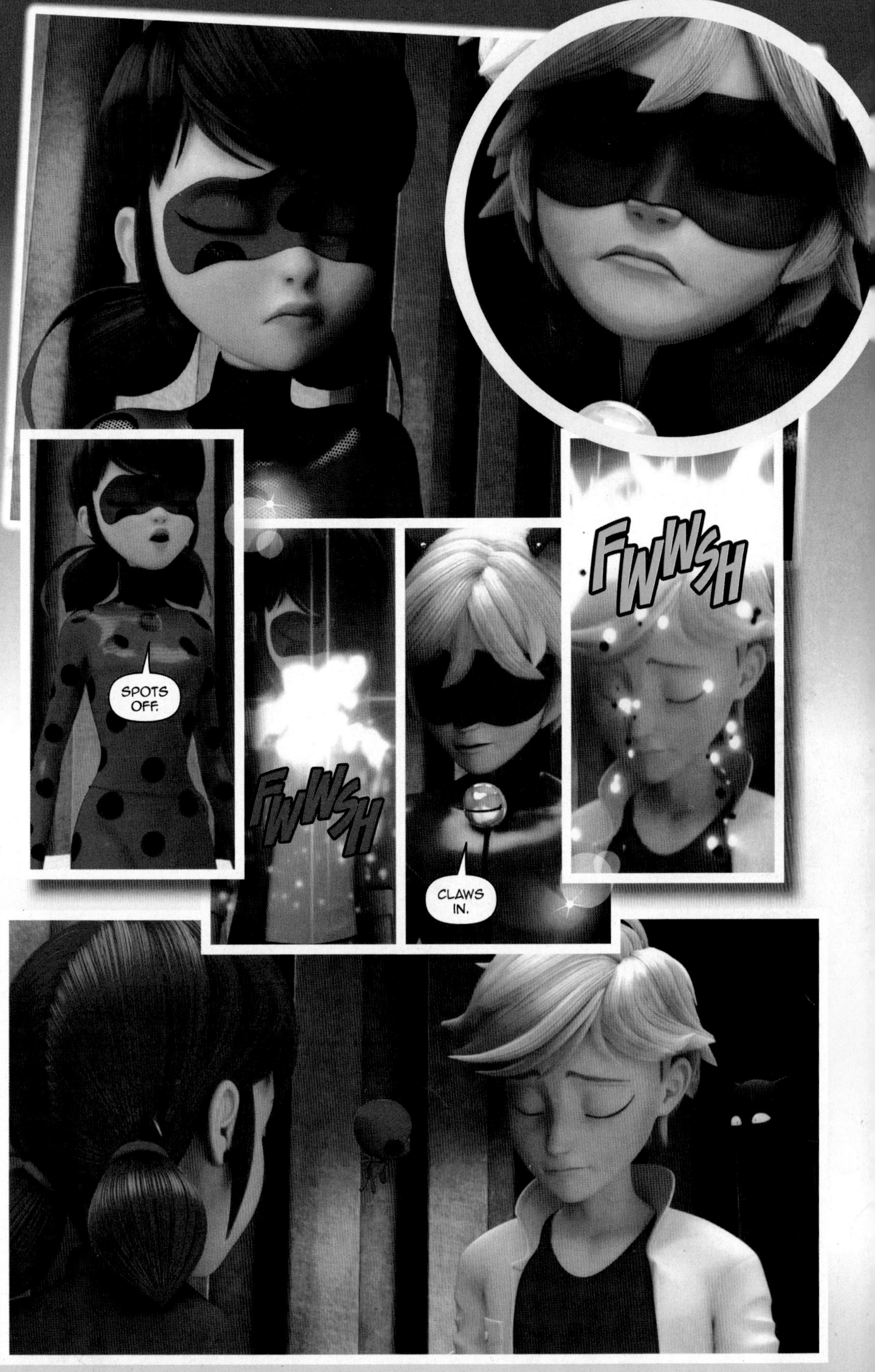
SPOTS OFF.
FWWSH
CLAWS IN.
FWWSH

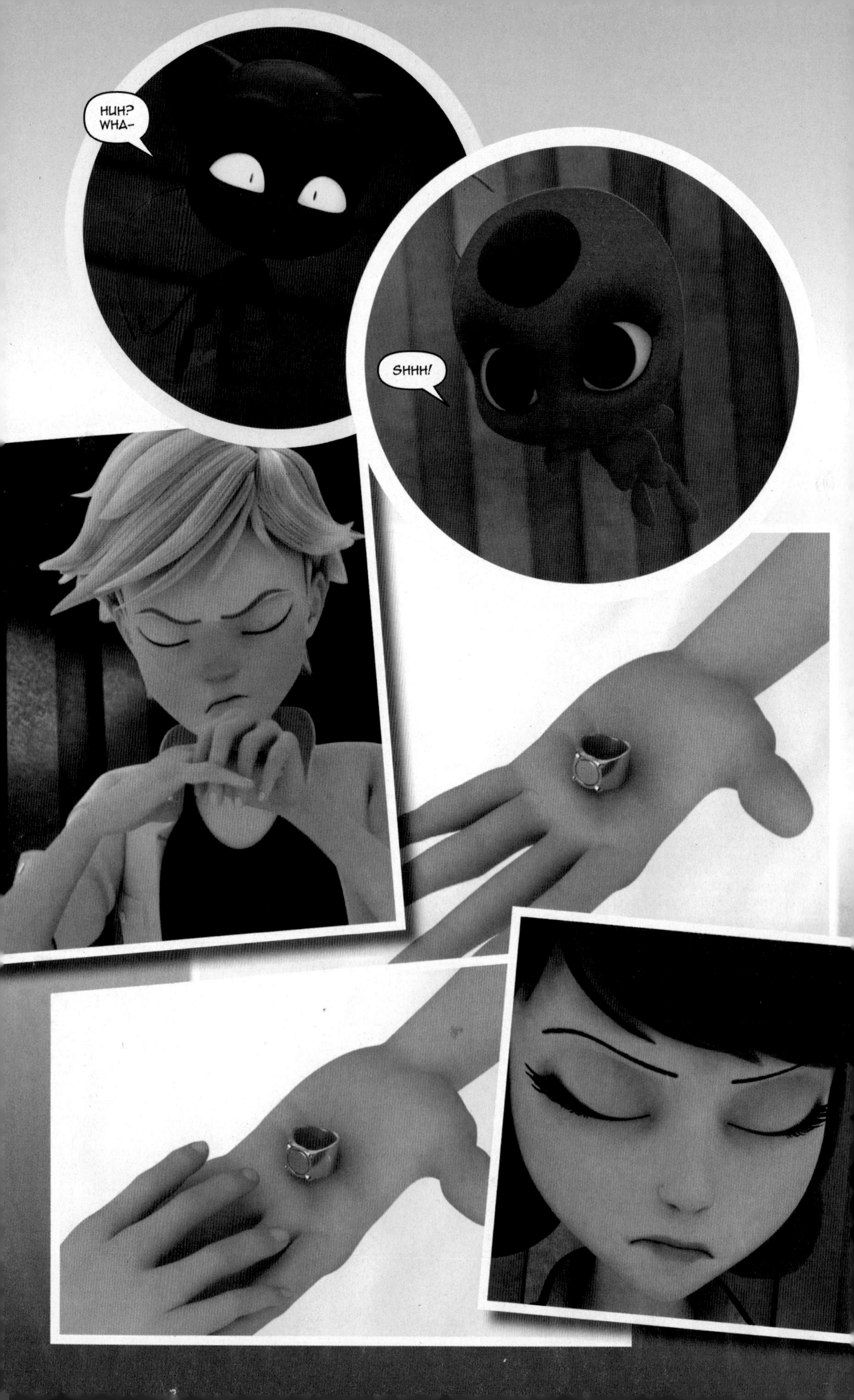
HUH? WHA-
SHHH!

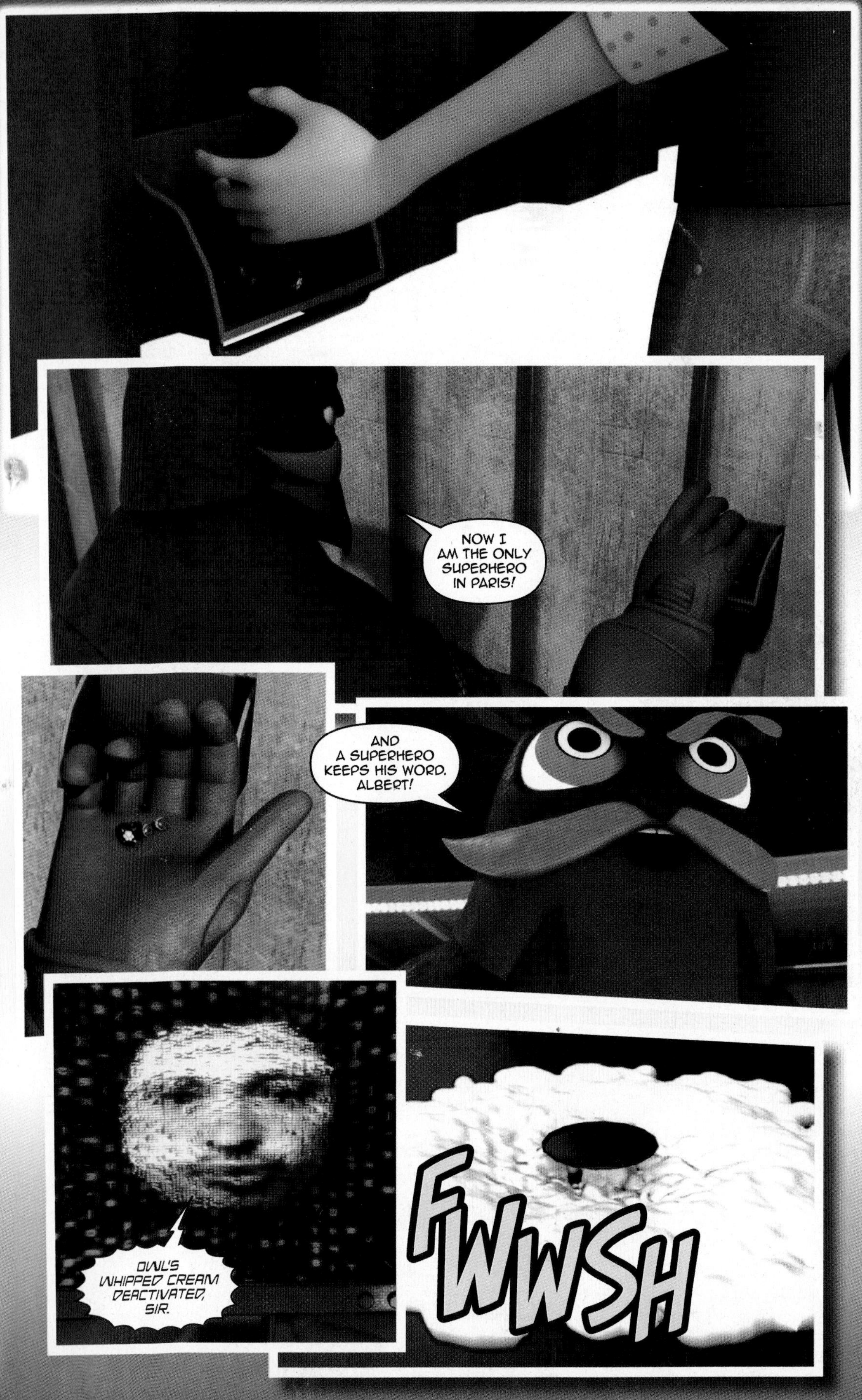
NOW I AM THE ONLY SUPERHERO IN PARIS!
AND A SUPERHERO KEEPS HIS WORD, ALBERT!
OWL'S WHIPPED CREAM DEACTIVATED, SIR.
FWWSH

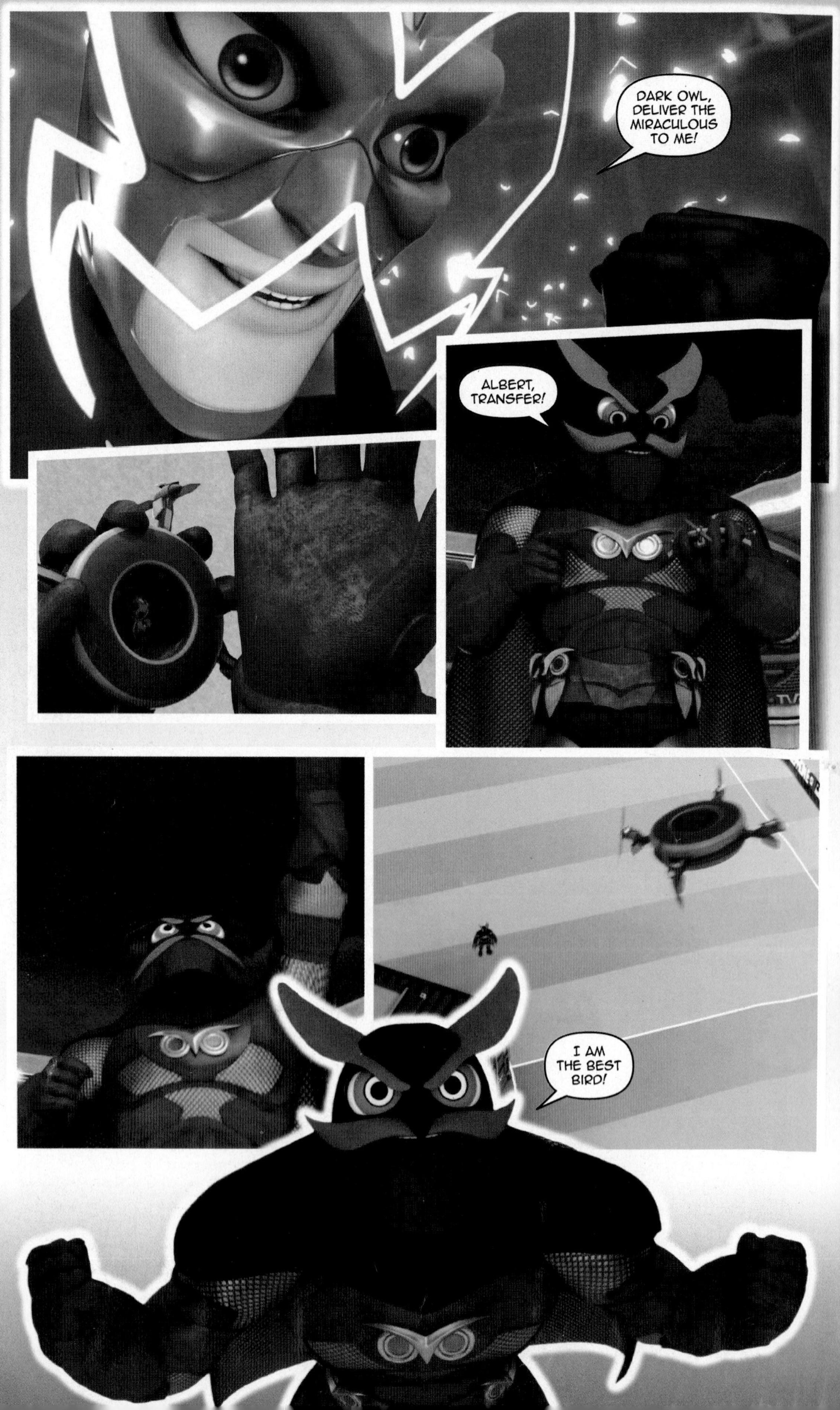
DARK OWL, DELIVER THE MIRACULOUS TO ME!
ALBERT, TRANSFER!
I AM THE BEST BIRD!

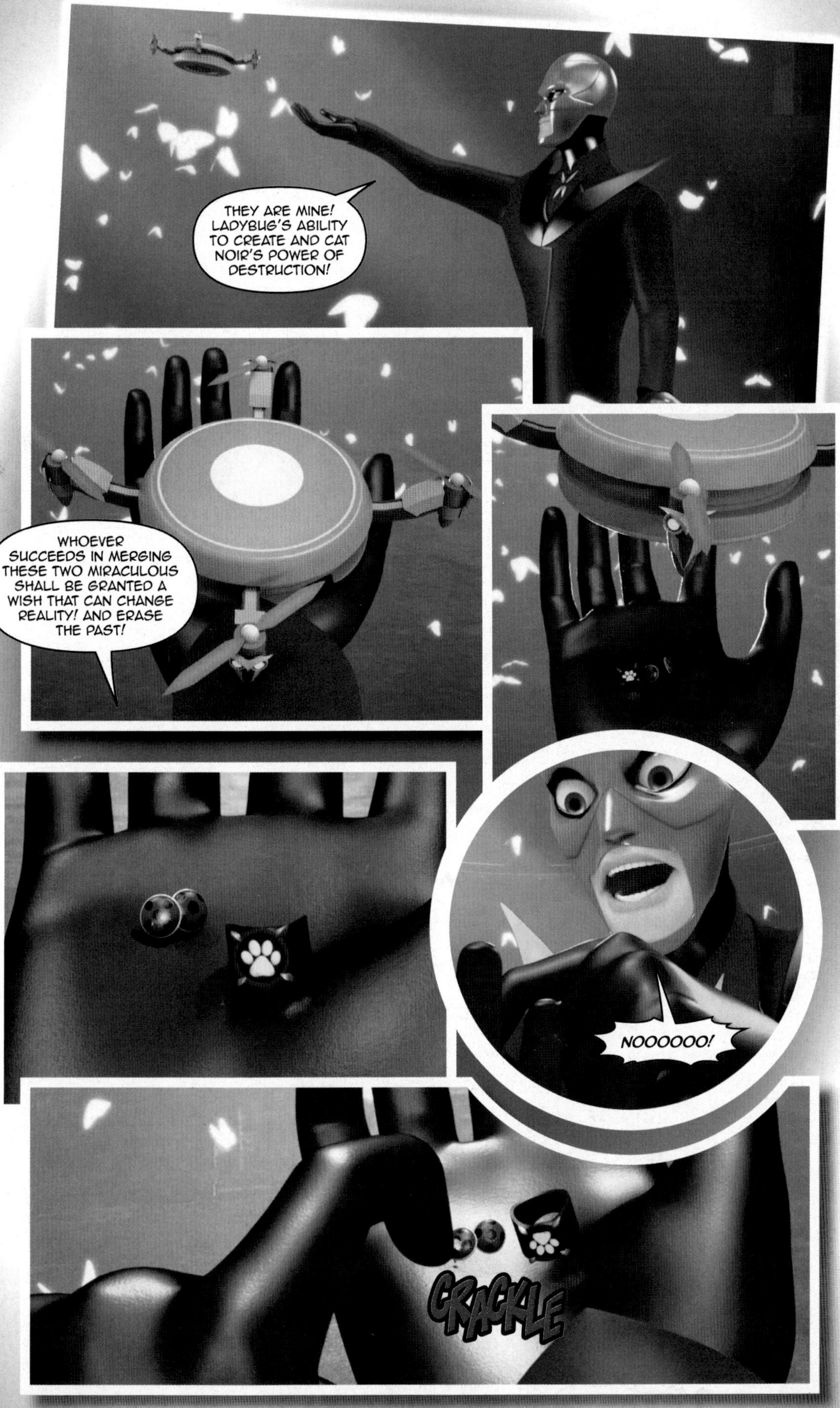
THEY ARE MINE! LADYBUG'S ABILITY TO CREATE AND CAT NOIR'S POWER OF DESTRUCTION!
WHOEVER SUCCEEDS IN MERGING THESE TWO MIRACULOUS SHALL BE GRANTED A WISH THAT CAN CHANGE REALITY! AND ERASE THE PAST!
NOOOOOO!
CRACKLE

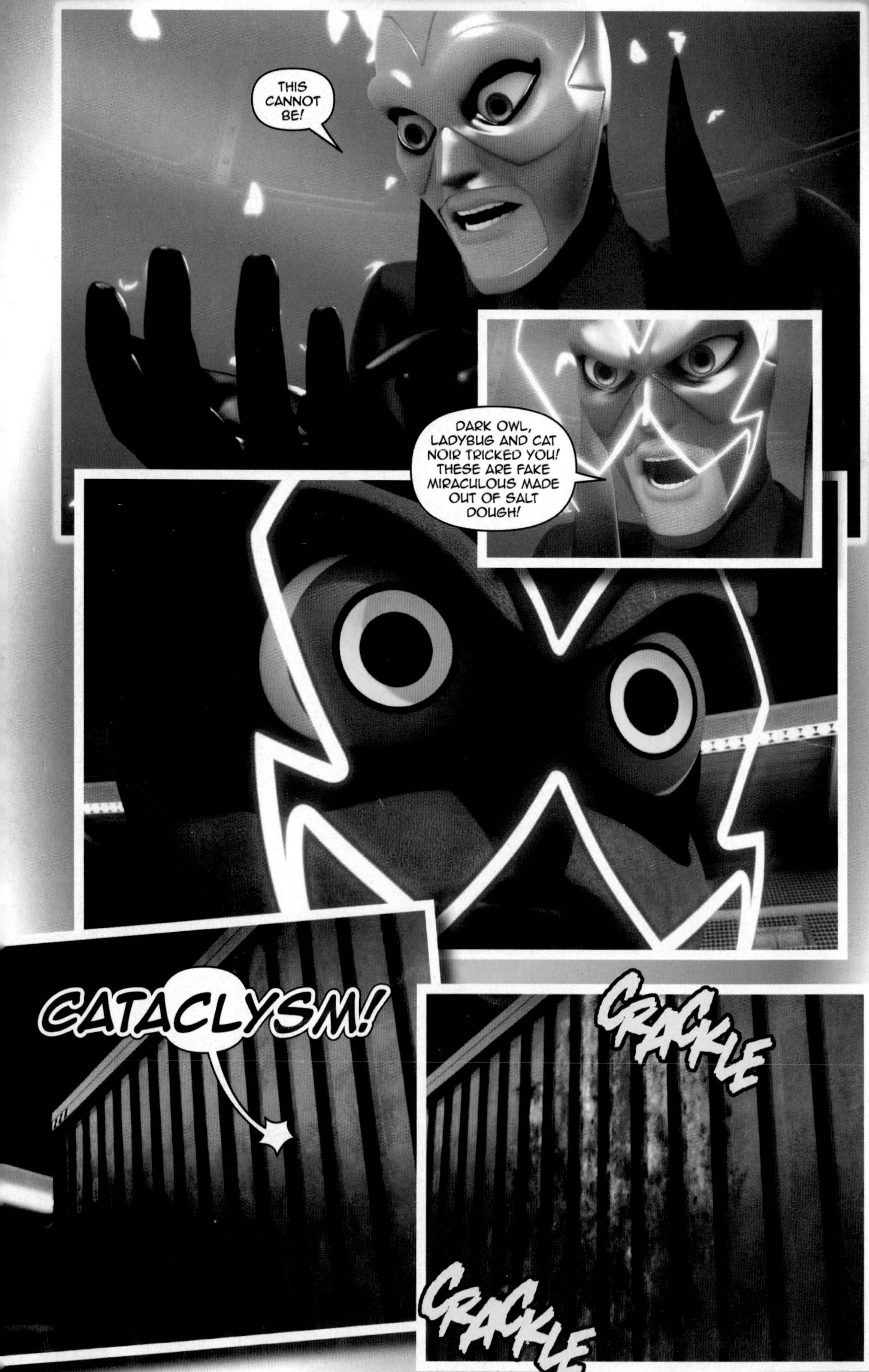
THIS CANNOT BE!
DARK OWL, LADYBUG AND CAT NOIR TRICKED YOU! THESE ARE FAKE MIRACULOUS MADE OUT OF SALT DOUGH!
CATACLYSM!
CRACKLE
CRACKLE

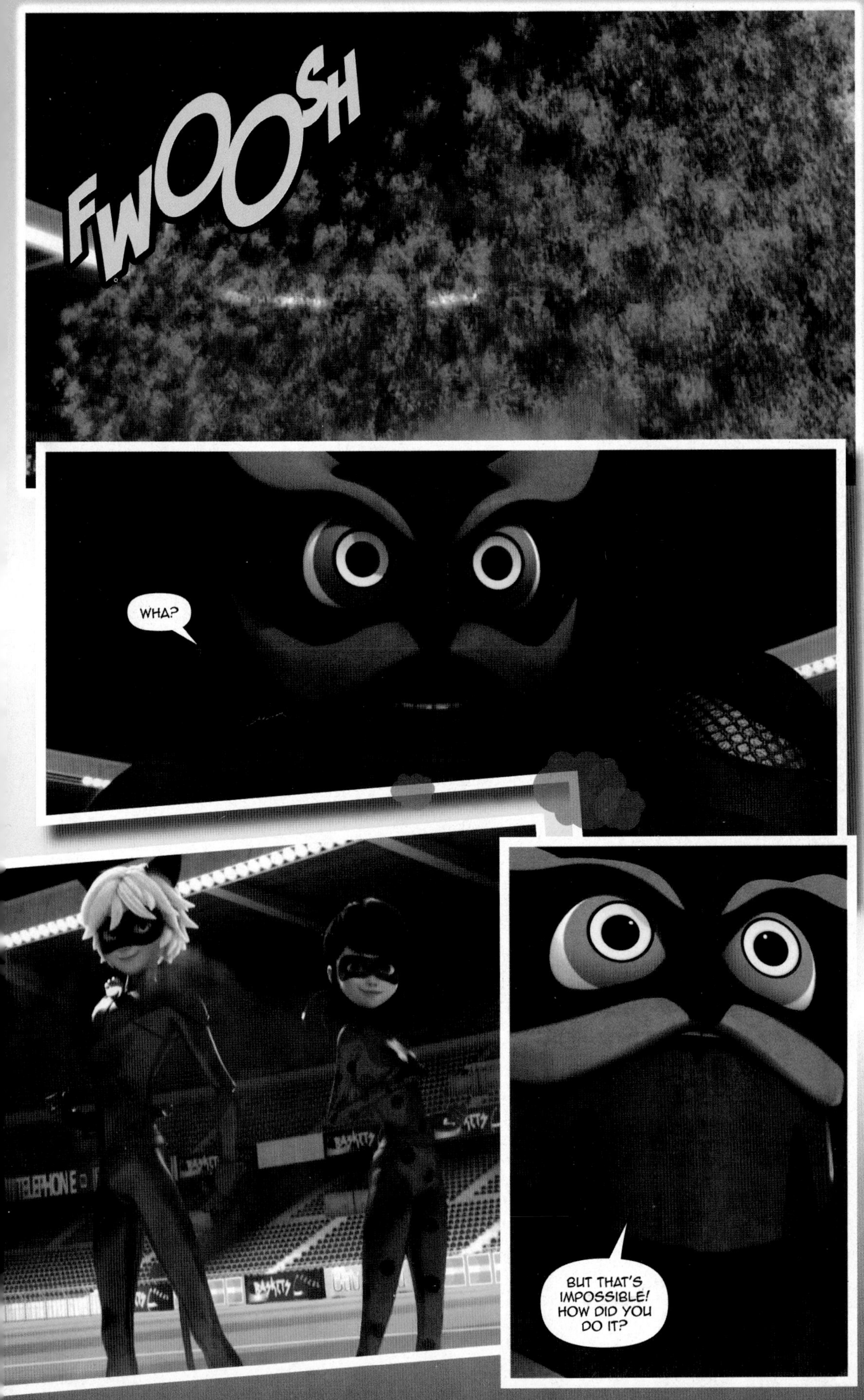
FWOOSH
WHA?
BUT THAT'S IMPOSSIBLE! HOW DID YOU DO IT?

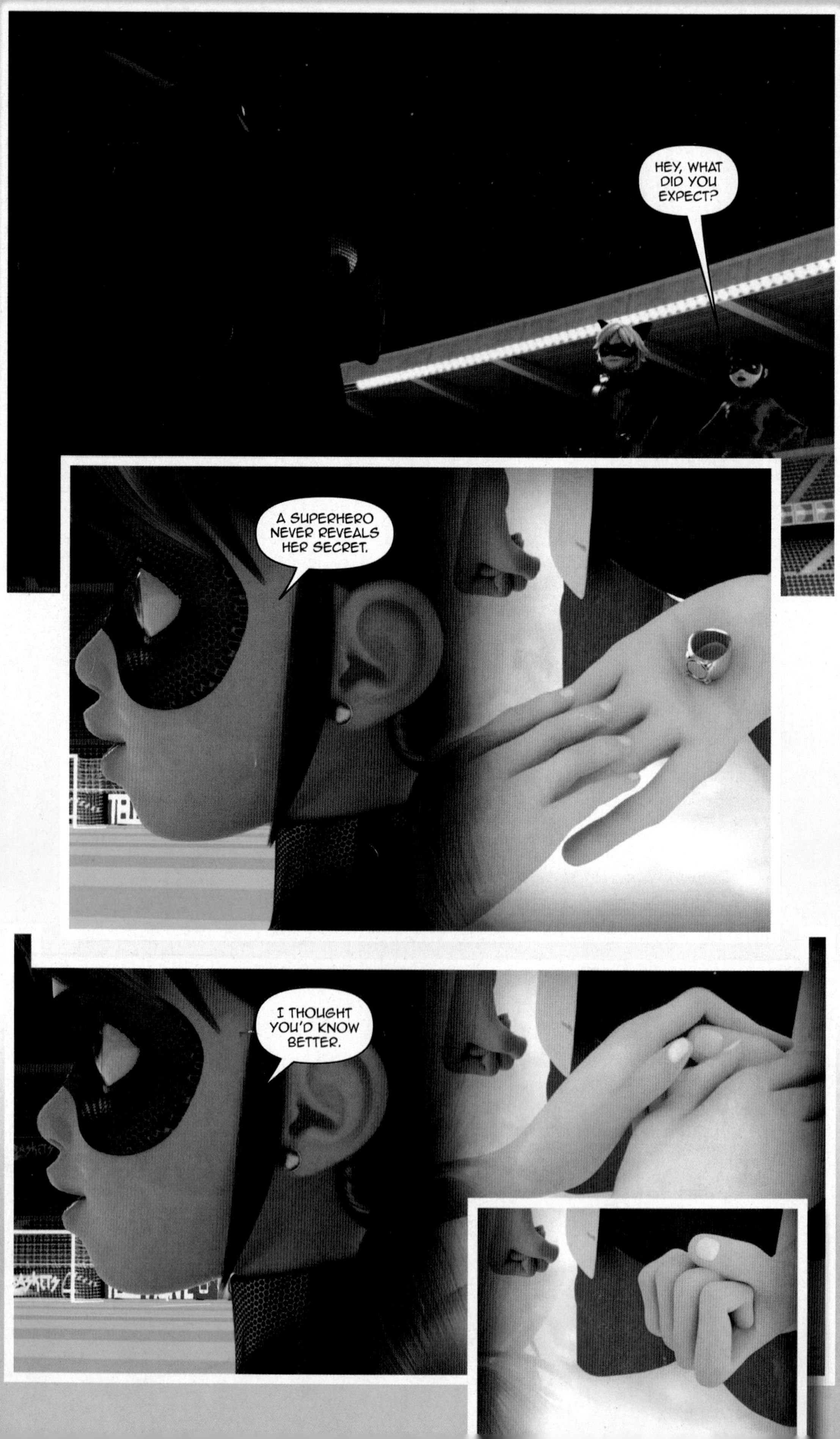
HEY, WHAT DID YOU EXPECT?
A SUPERHERO NEVER REVEALS HER SECRET.
I THOUGHT YOU'D KNOW BETTER.

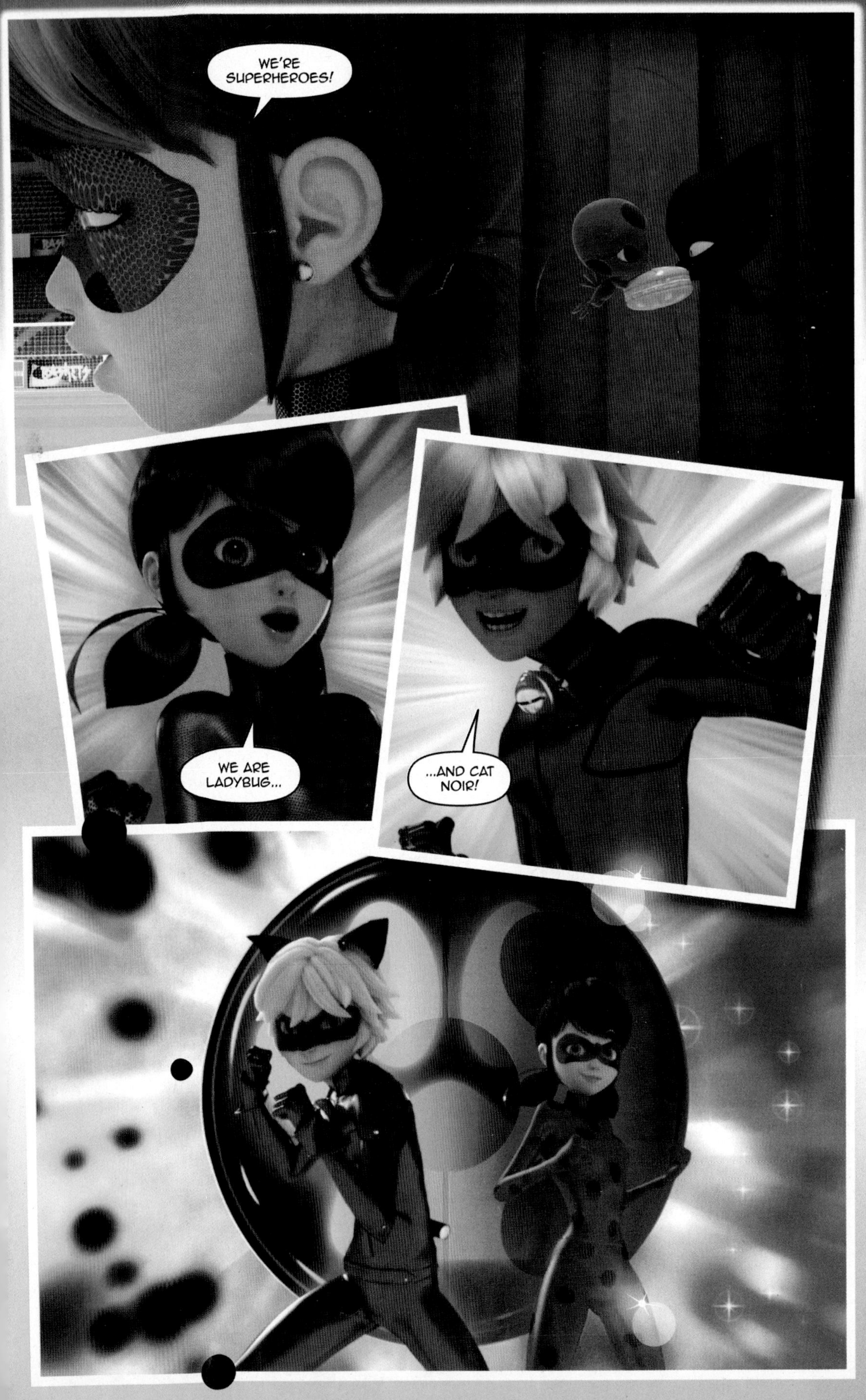
WE'RE SUPERHEROES!
WE ARE LADYBUG...
...AND CAT NOIR!

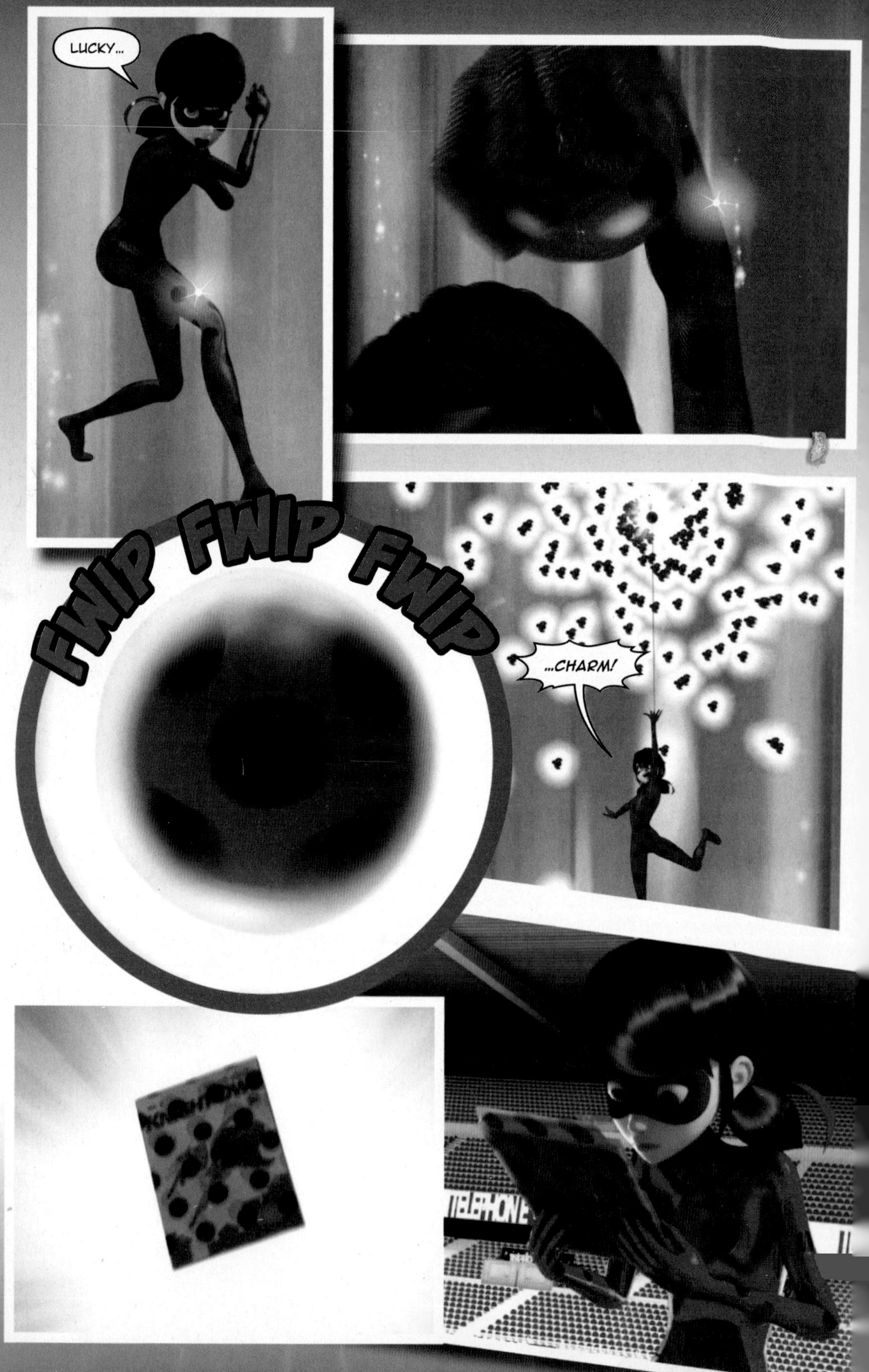
LUCKY...
FWIP FWIP FWIP
...CHARM!
TELEPHONE

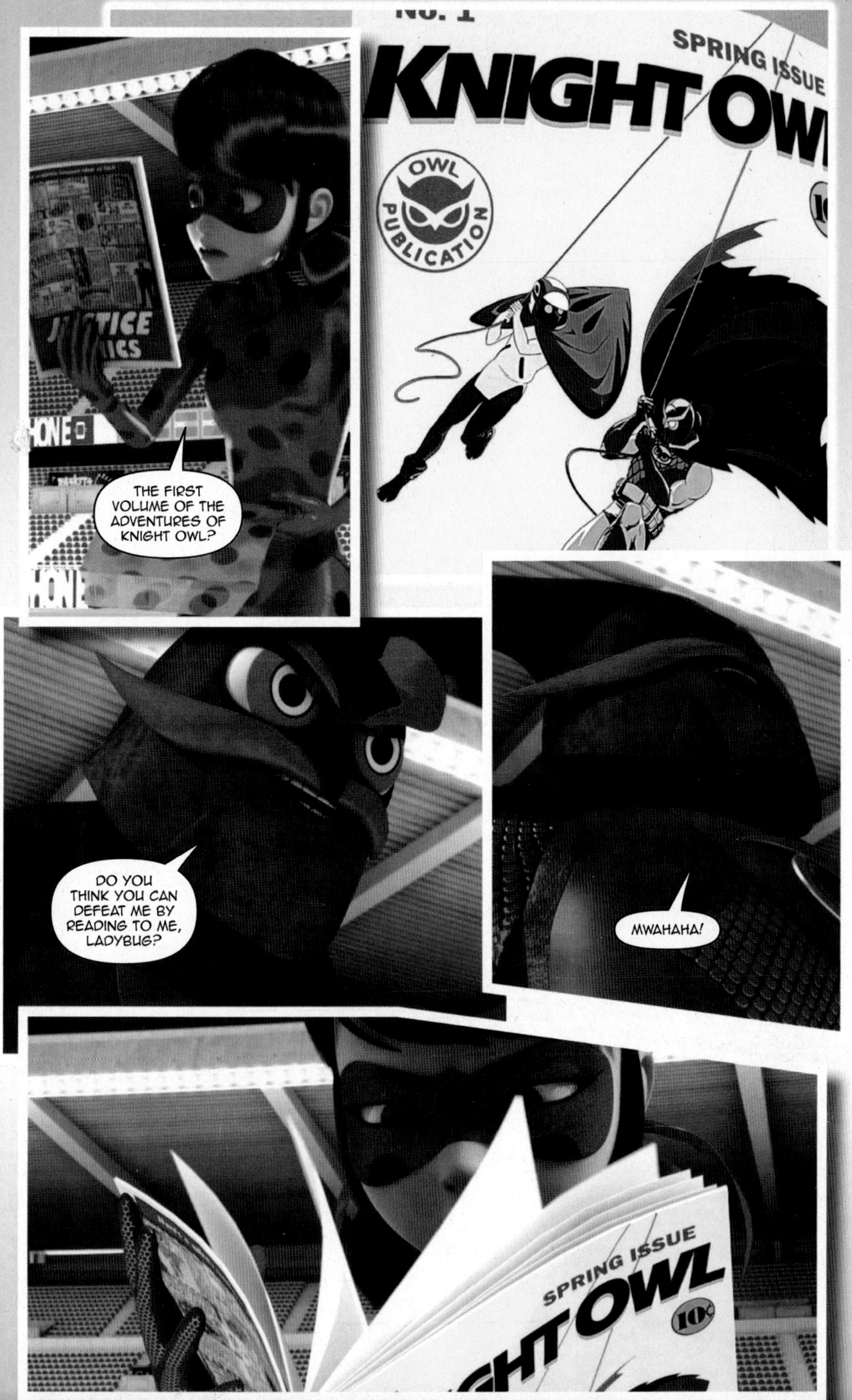
NO. 1
SPRING ISSUE
KNIGHT OWL
OWL PUBLICATION
JUSTICE COMICS
THE FIRST VOLUME OF THE ADVENTURES OF KNIGHT OWL?
DO YOU THINK YOU CAN DEFEAT ME BY READING TO ME, LADYBUG?
MWAHAHA!
SPRING ISSUE
GHT OWL

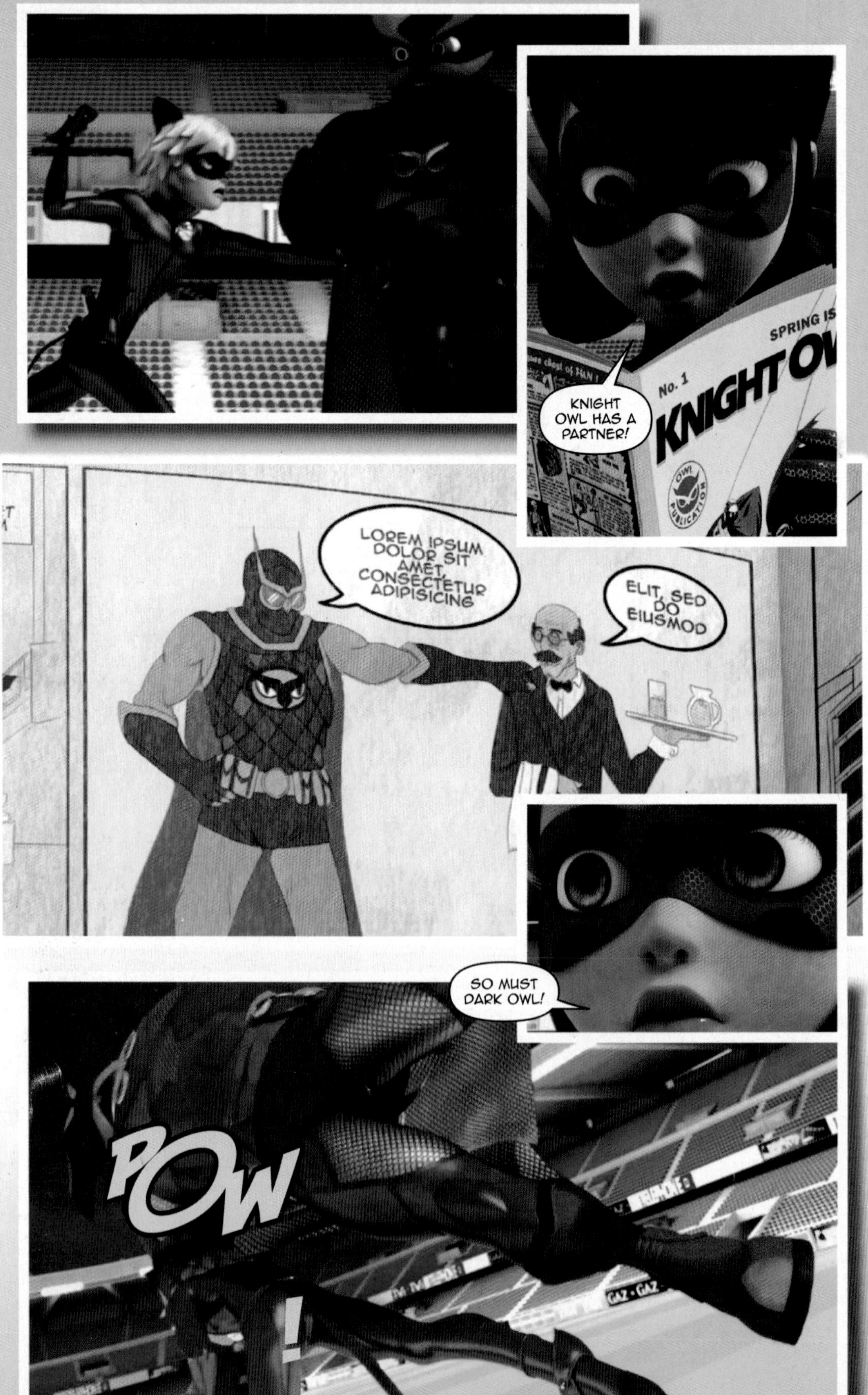

No. 1
OWL PUBLICATION
KNIGHT OWL HAS A PARTNER!
LOREM IPSUM DOLOR SIT AMET, CONSECTETUR ADIPISICING
ELIT, SED DO EIUSMOD
SO MUST DARK OWL!
POW!

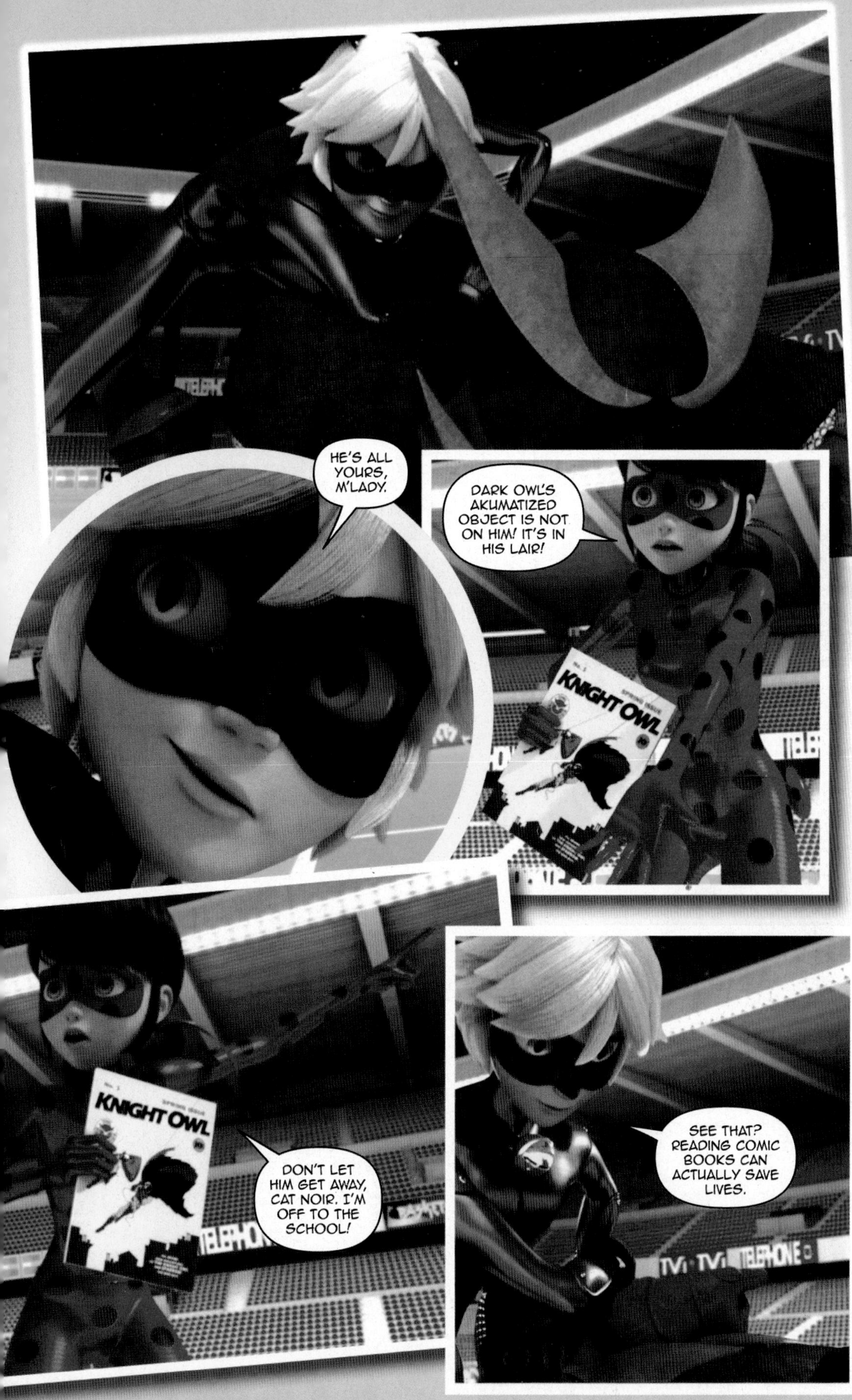
HE'S ALL YOURS, M'LADY.
DARK OWL'S AKUMATIZED OBJECT IS NOT ON HIM! IT'S IN HIS LAIR!
KNIGHT OWL
KNIGHT OWL
DON'T LET HIM GET AWAY, CAT NOIR. I'M OFF TO THE SCHOOL!
SEE THAT? READING COMIC BOOKS CAN ACTUALLY SAVE LIVES.
TELEPHONE
TVi TVi TELEPHONE

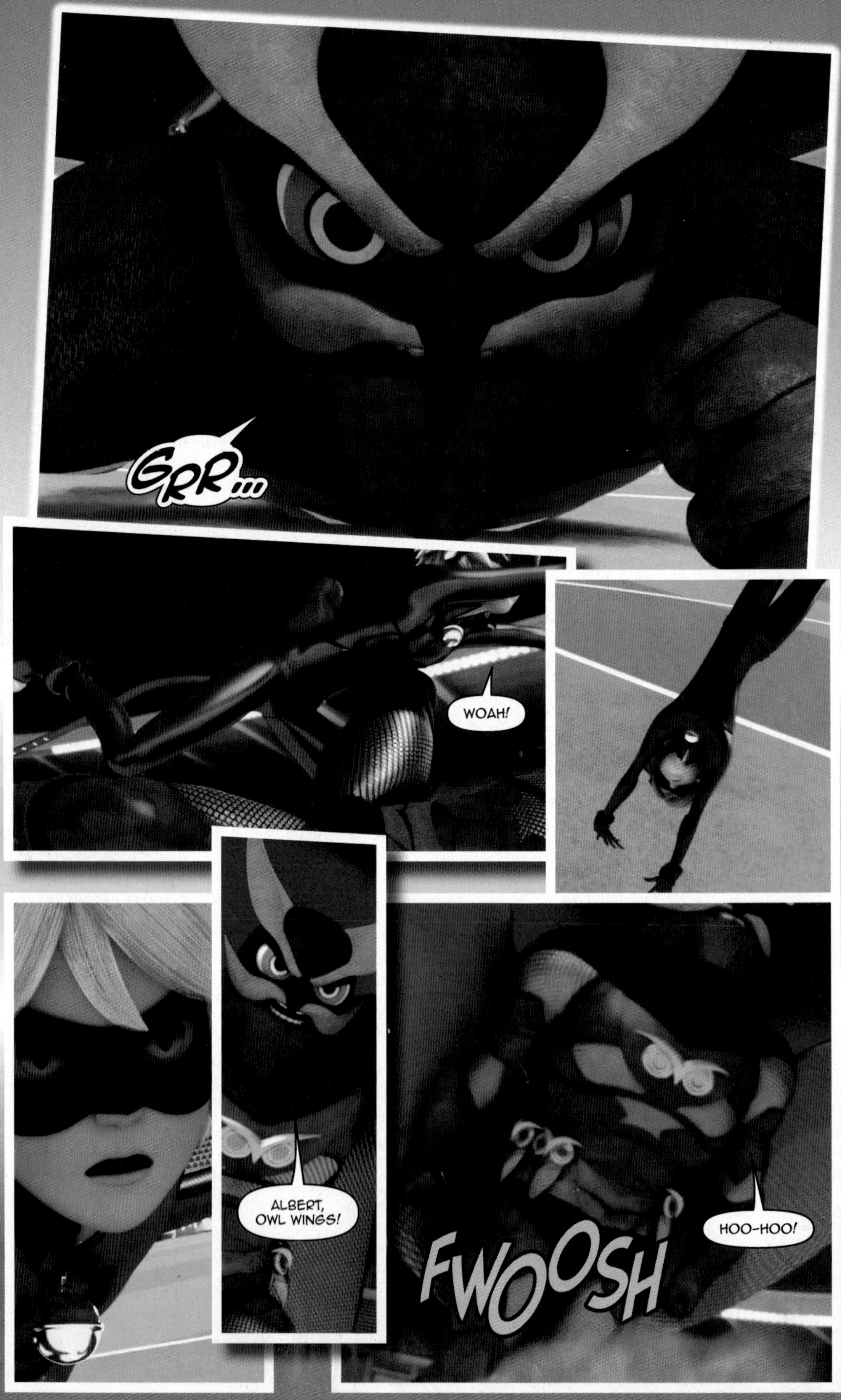
GRR...
WOAH!
ALBERT, OWL WINGS!
HOO-HOO!
FWOOSH

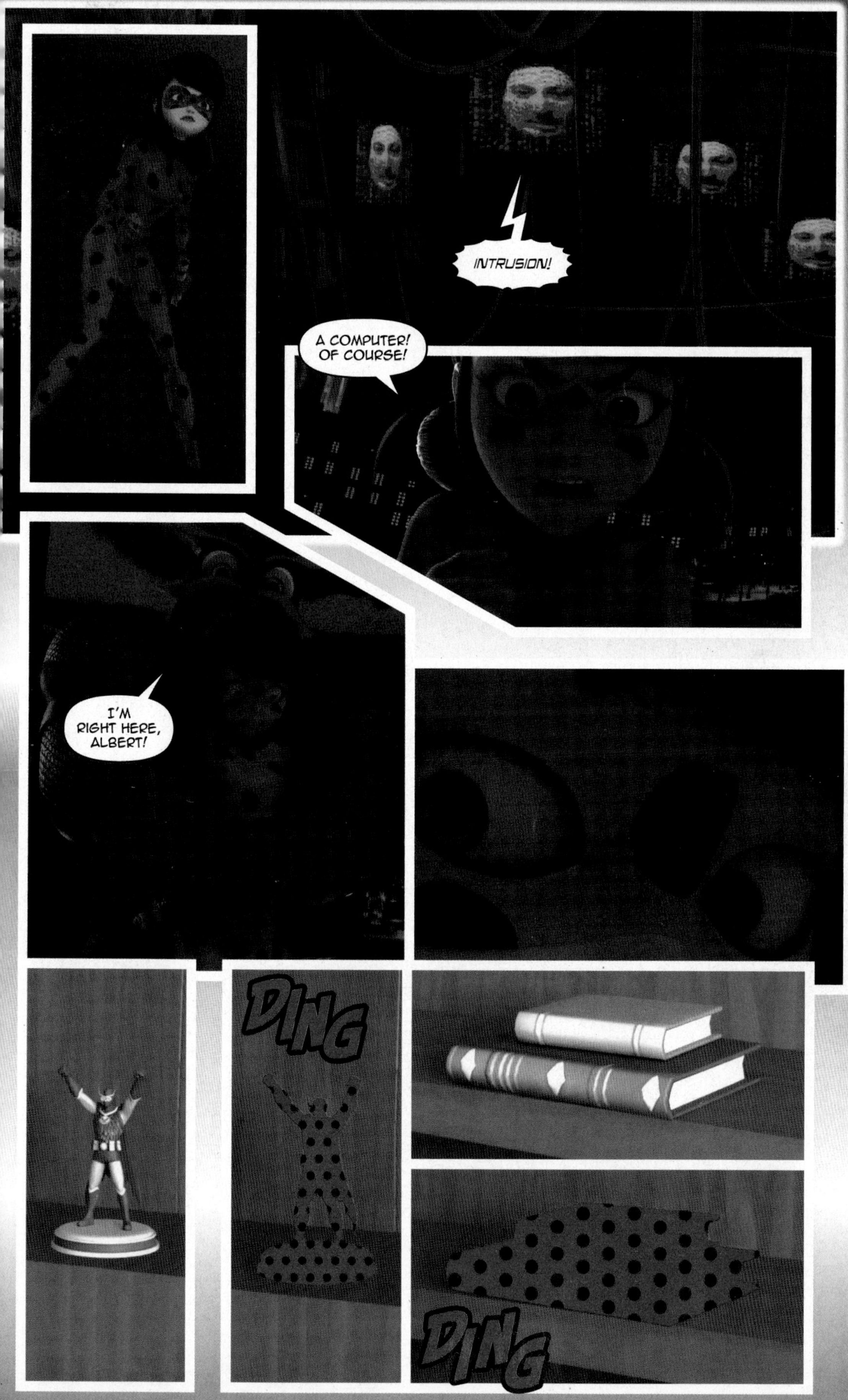
INTRUSION!
A COMPUTER! OF COURSE!
I'M RIGHT HERE, ALBERT!
DING
DING

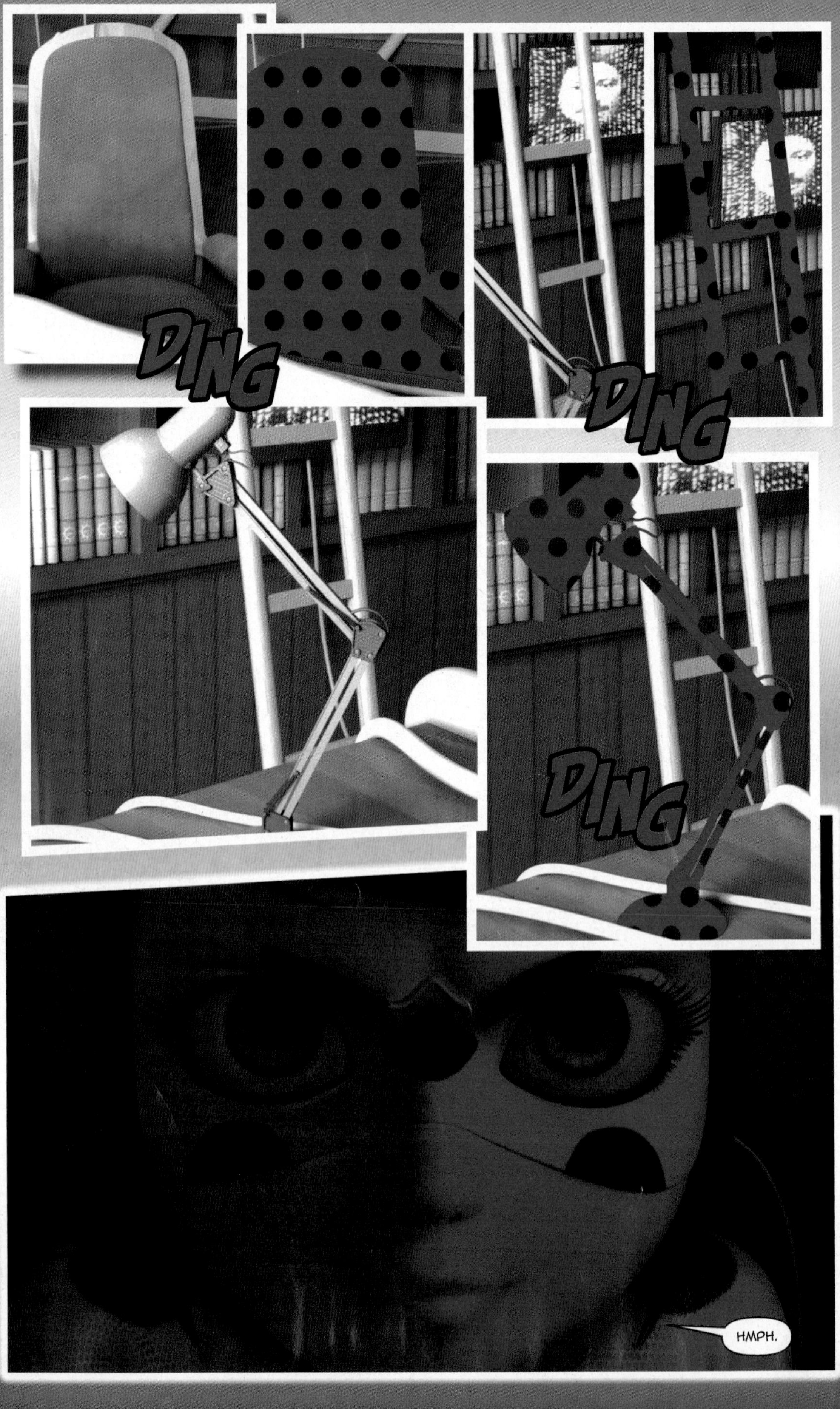
DING
DING
DING
HMPH.

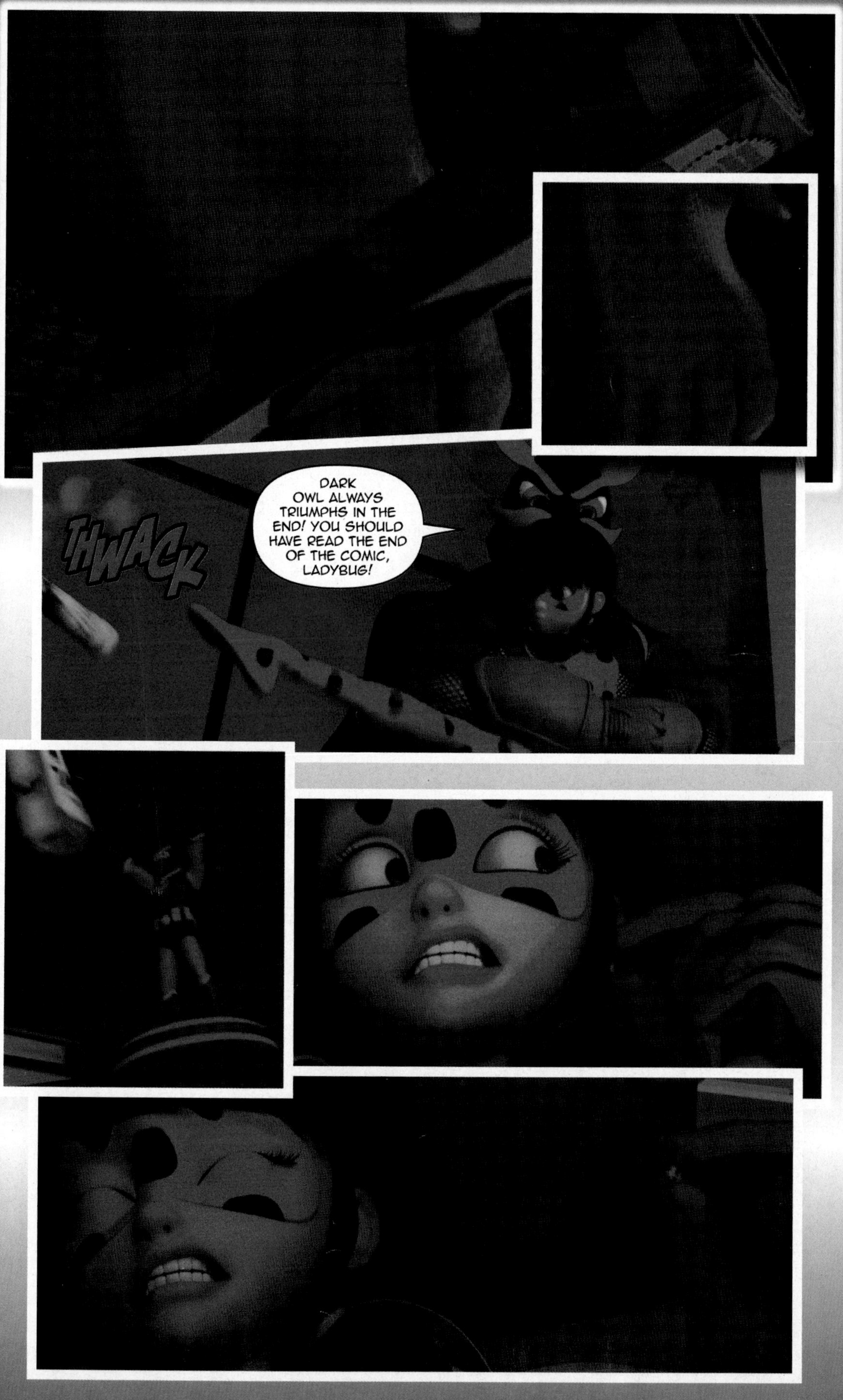
THWACK
DARK OWL ALWAYS TRIUMPHS IN THE END! YOU SHOULD HAVE READ THE END OF THE COMIC, LADYBUG!

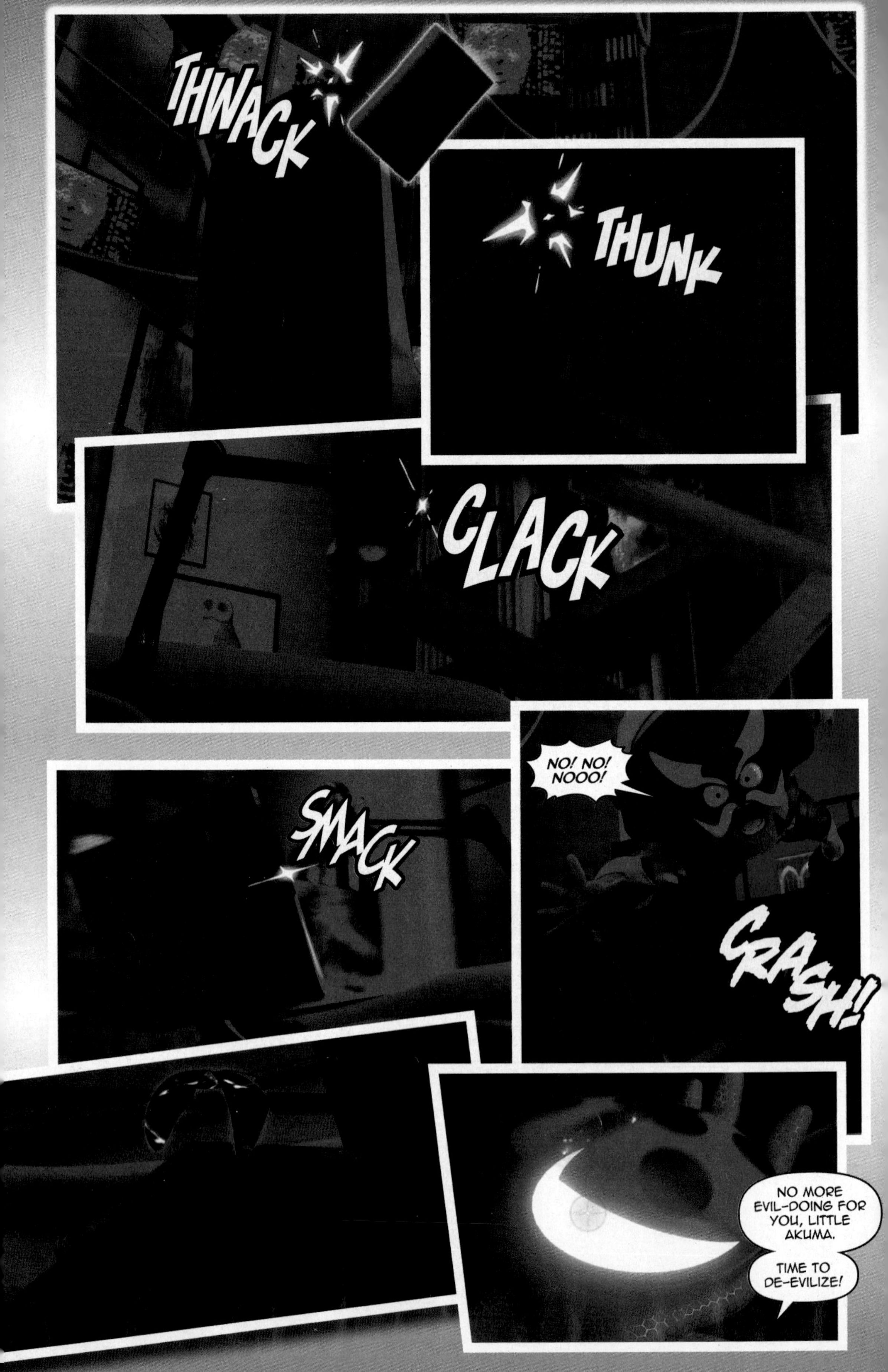
THWACK
THUNK
CLACK
SMACK
NO! NO! NOOO!
CRASH!!
NO MORE EVIL-DOING FOR YOU, LITTLE AKUMA.
TIME TO DE-EVILIZE!

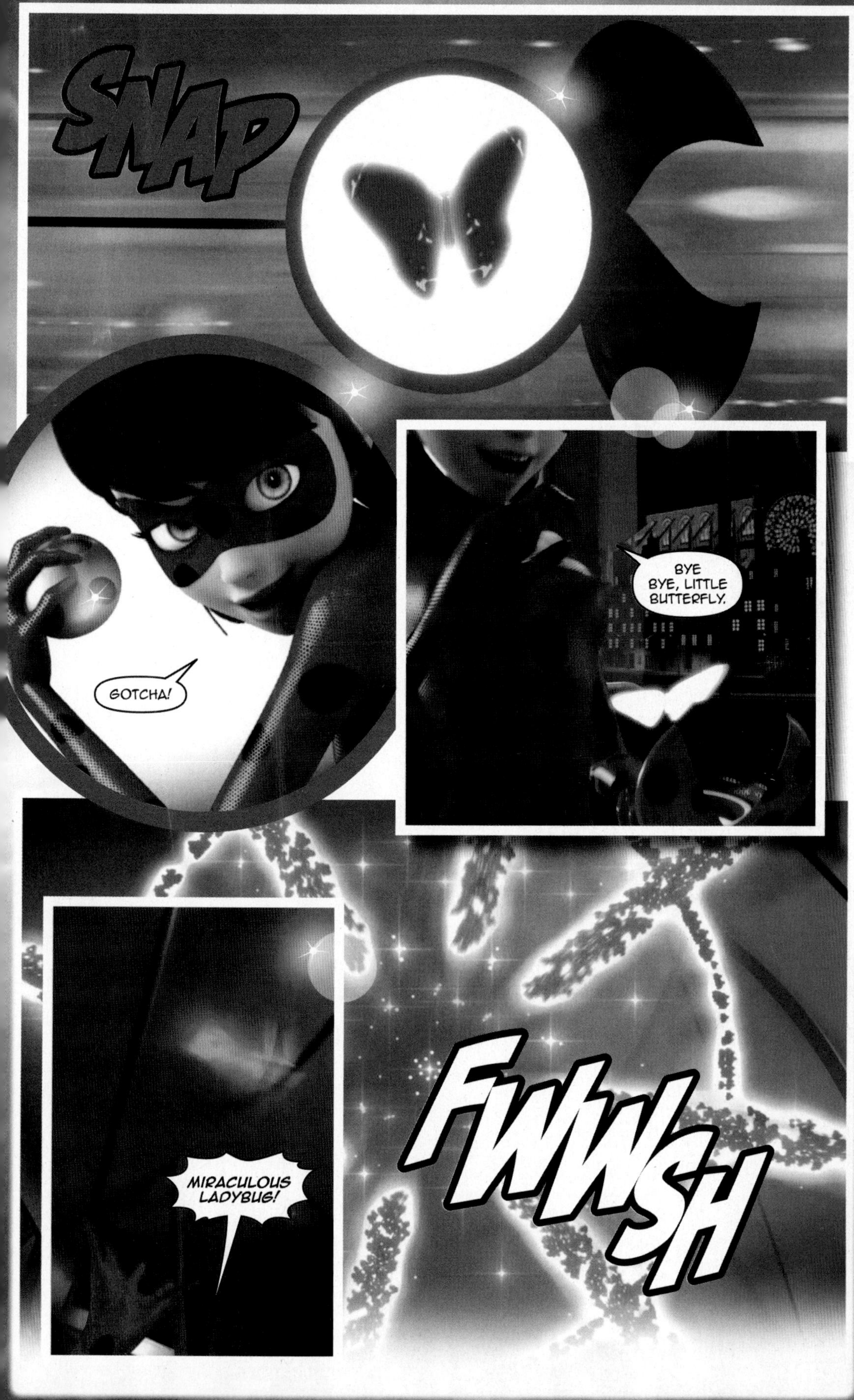
SNAP
GOTCHA!
BYE BYE, LITTLE BUTTERFLY.
MIRACULOUS LADYBUG!
FWWSH

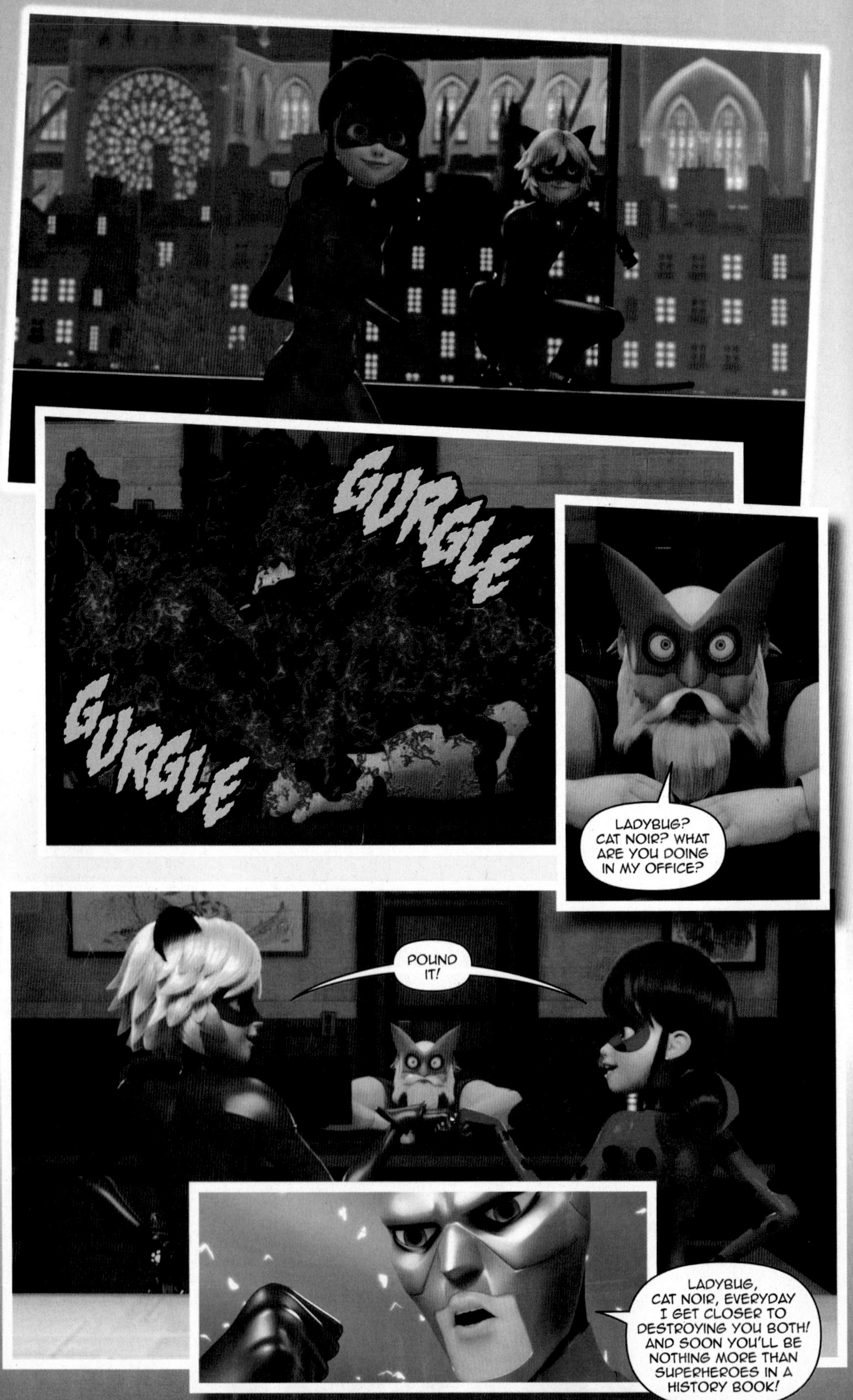
GURGLE
GURGLE
LADYBUG? CAT NOIR? WHAT ARE YOU DOING IN MY OFFICE?
POUND IT!
LADYBUG, CAT NOIR, EVERYDAY I GET CLOSER TO DESTROYING YOU BOTH! AND SOON YOU'LL BE NOTHING MORE THAN SUPERHEROES IN A HISTORY BOOK!

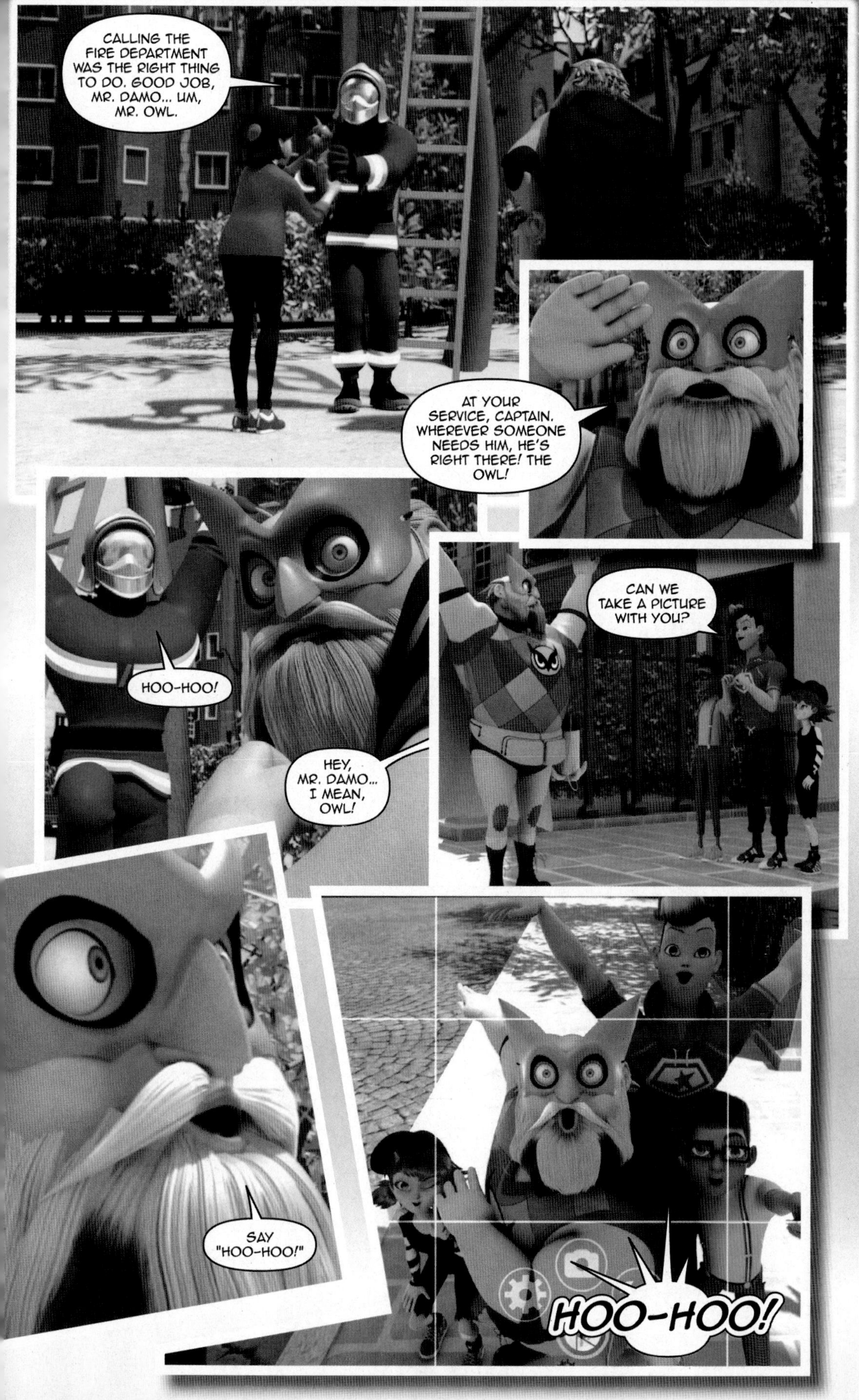
CALLING THE FIRE DEPARTMENT WAS THE RIGHT THING TO DO. GOOD JOB, MR. DAMO... UM, MR. OWL.
AT YOUR SERVICE, CAPTAIN. WHEREVER SOMEONE NEEDS HIM, HE'S RIGHT THERE! THE OWL!
HOO-HOO!
HEY, MR. DAMO... I MEAN, OWL!
CAN WE TAKE A PICTURE WITH YOU?
SAY "HOO-HOO!"
HOO-HOO!

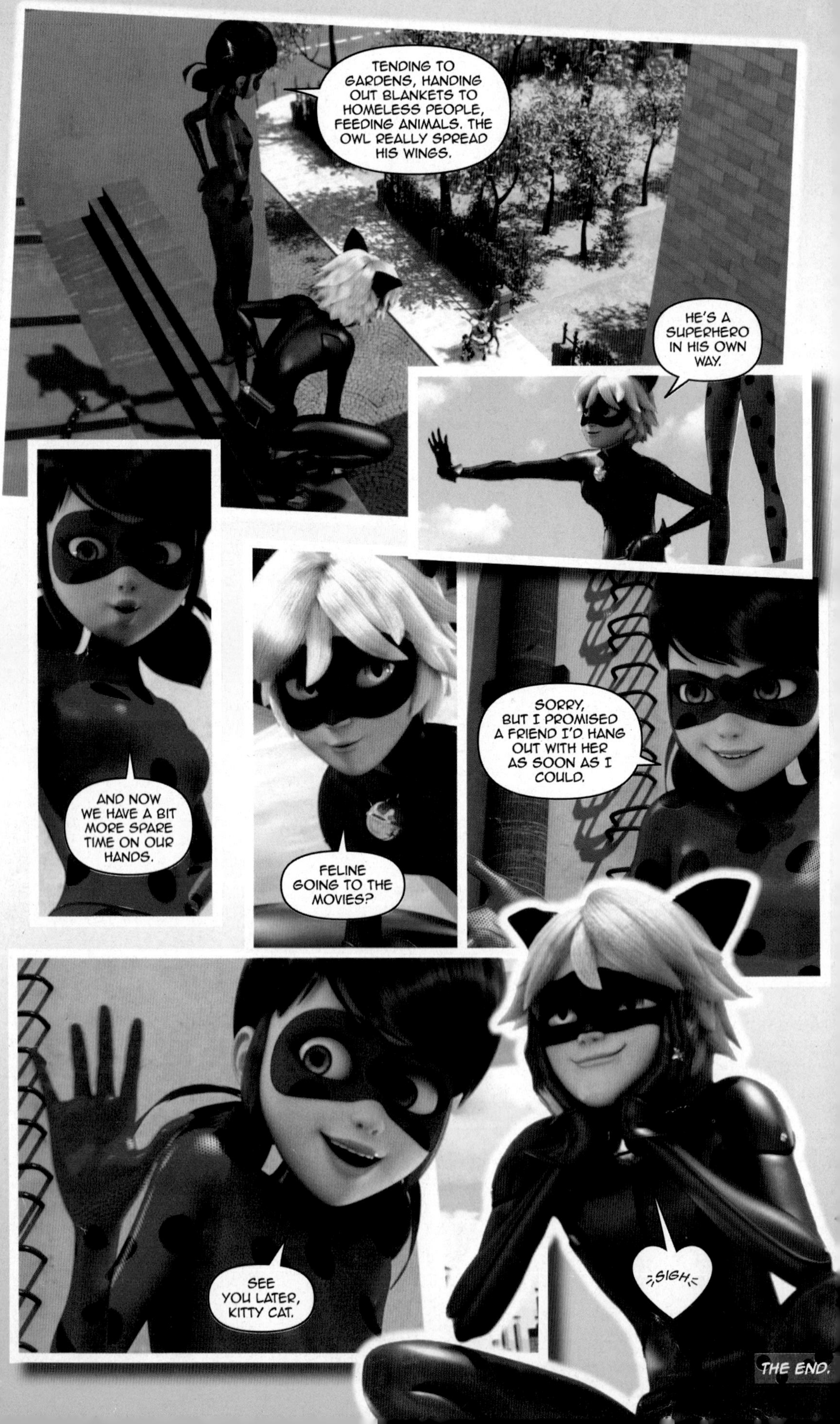
TENDING TO GARDENS, HANDING OUT BLANKETS TO HOMELESS PEOPLE, FEEDING ANIMALS. THE OWL REALLY SPREAD HIS WINGS.
HE'S A SUPERHERO IN HIS OWN WAY.
AND NOW WE HAVE A BIT MORE SPARE TIME ON OUR HANDS.
FELINE GOING TO THE MOVIES?
SORRY, BUT I PROMISED A FRIEND I'D HANG OUT WITH HER AS SOON AS I COULD.
SEE YOU LATER, KITTY CAT.
SIGH
THE END.

Gigantitan

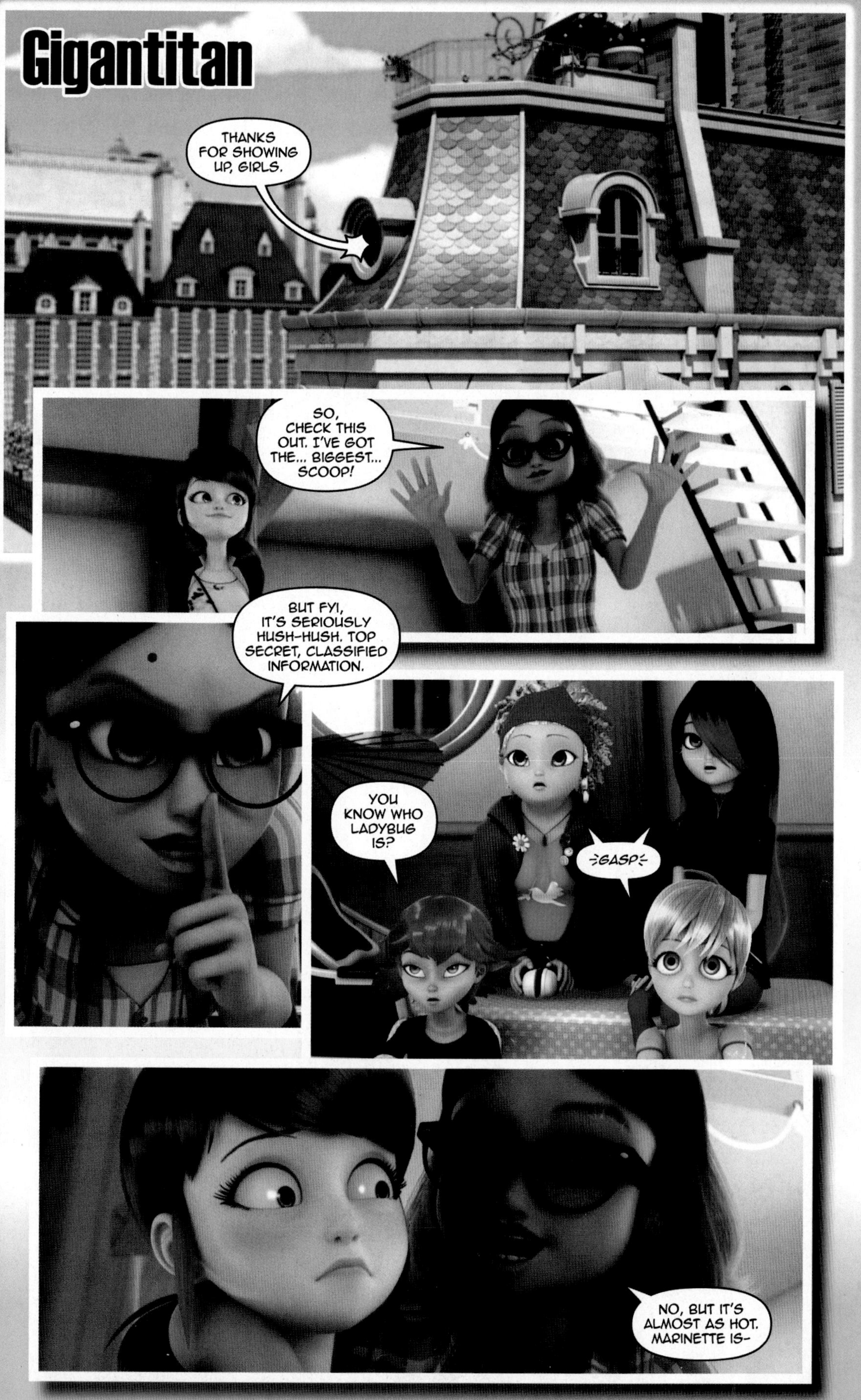
THANKS FOR SHOWING UP, GIRLS.
SO, CHECK THIS OUT. I'VE GOT THE... BIGGEST... SCOOP!
BUT FYI, IT'S SERIOUSLY HUSH-HUSH. TOP SECRET, CLASSIFIED INFORMATION.
YOU KNOW WHO LADYBUG IS?
GASP
NO, BUT IT'S ALMOST AS HOT. MARINETTE IS-

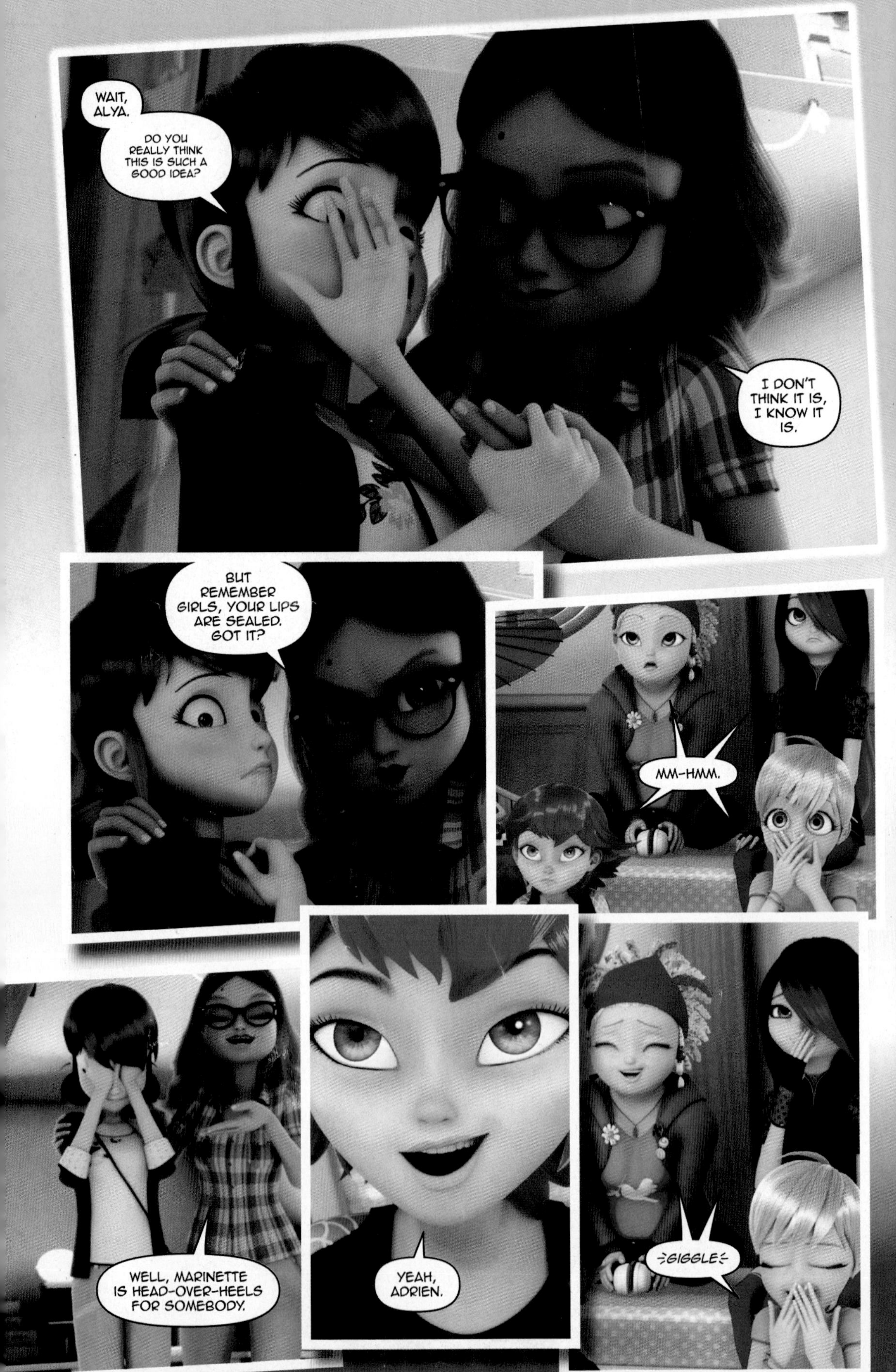
WAIT, ALYA.
DO YOU REALLY THINK THIS IS SUCH A GOOD IDEA?
I DON'T THINK IT IS, I KNOW IT IS.
BUT REMEMBER GIRLS, YOUR LIPS ARE SEALED. GOT IT?
MM-HMM.
WELL, MARINETTE IS HEAD-OVER-HEELS FOR SOMEBODY.
YEAH, ADRIEN.
GIGGLE

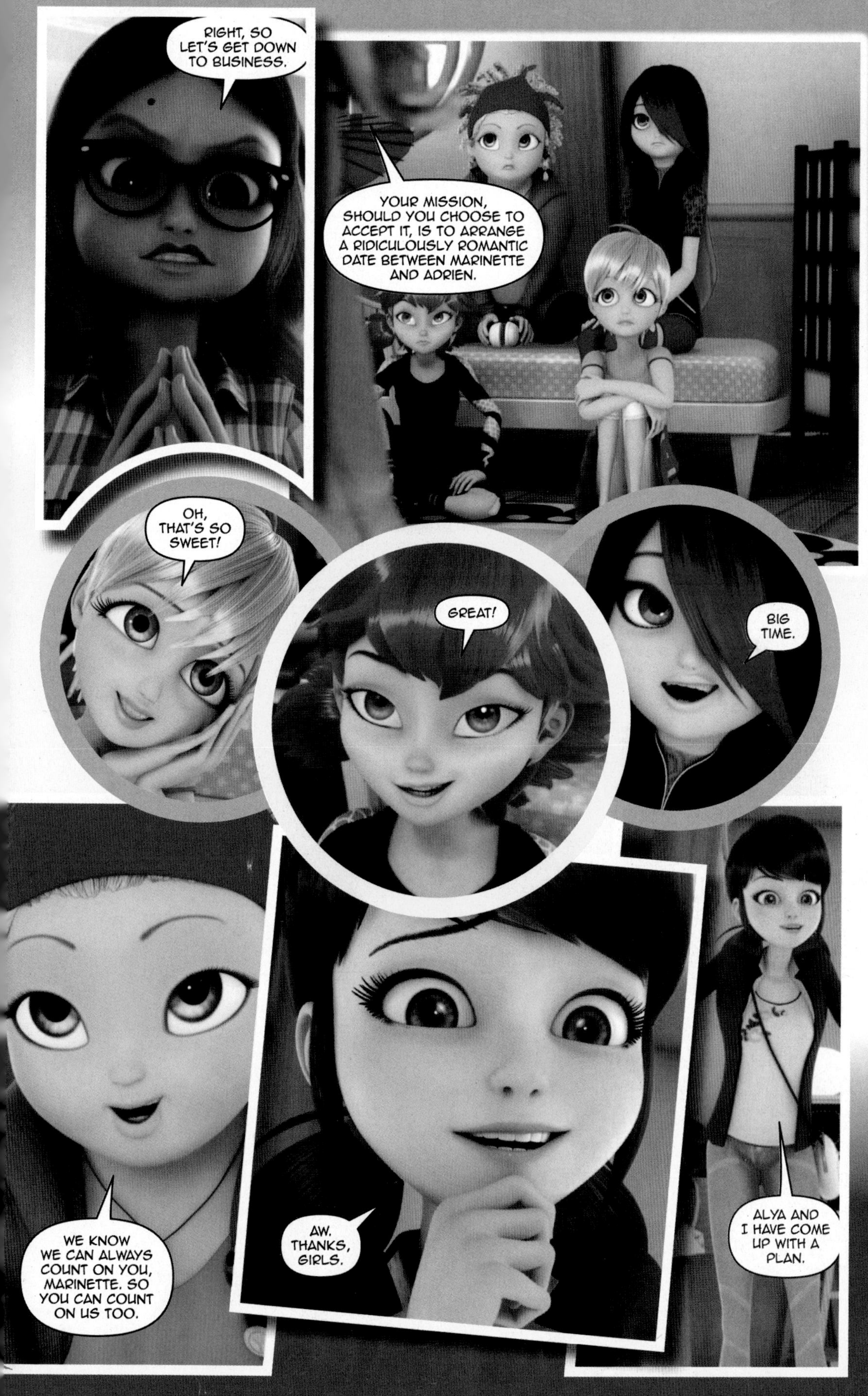
RIGHT, SO LET'S GET DOWN TO BUSINESS.
YOUR MISSION, SHOULD YOU CHOOSE TO ACCEPT IT, IS TO ARRANGE A RIDICULOUSLY ROMANTIC DATE BETWEEN MARINETTE AND ADRIEN.
OH, THAT'S SO SWEET!
GREAT!
BIG TIME.
WE KNOW WE CAN ALWAYS COUNT ON YOU, MARINETTE. SO YOU CAN COUNT ON US TOO.
AW. THANKS, GIRLS.
ALYA AND I HAVE COME UP WITH A PLAN.

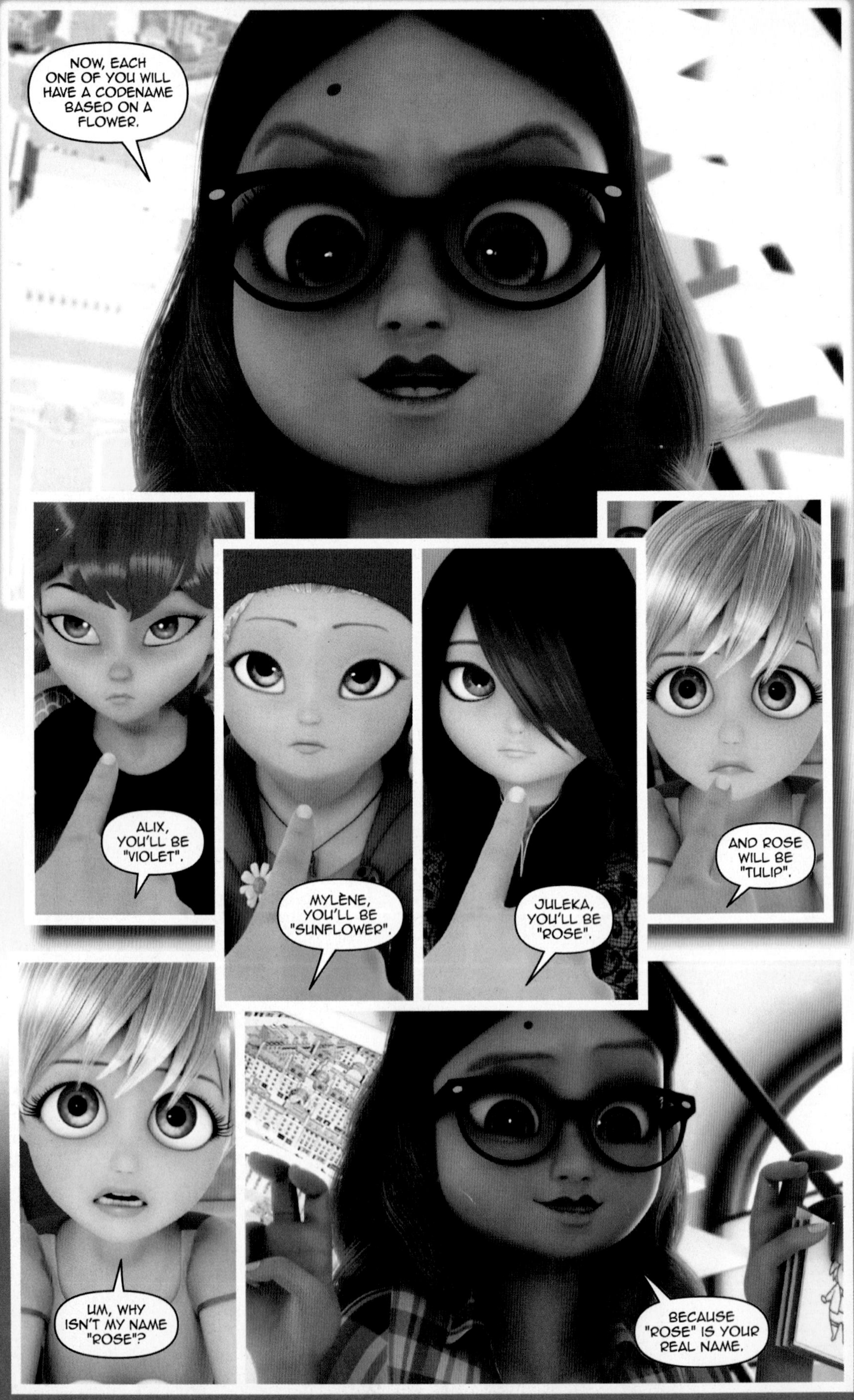
NOW, EACH ONE OF YOU WILL HAVE A CODENAME BASED ON A FLOWER.
ALIX, YOU'LL BE "VIOLET".
MYLÈNE, YOU'LL BE "SUNFLOWER".
JULEKA, YOU'LL BE "ROSE".
AND ROSE WILL BE "TULIP".
UM, WHY ISN'T MY NAME "ROSE"?
BECAUSE "ROSE" IS YOUR REAL NAME.

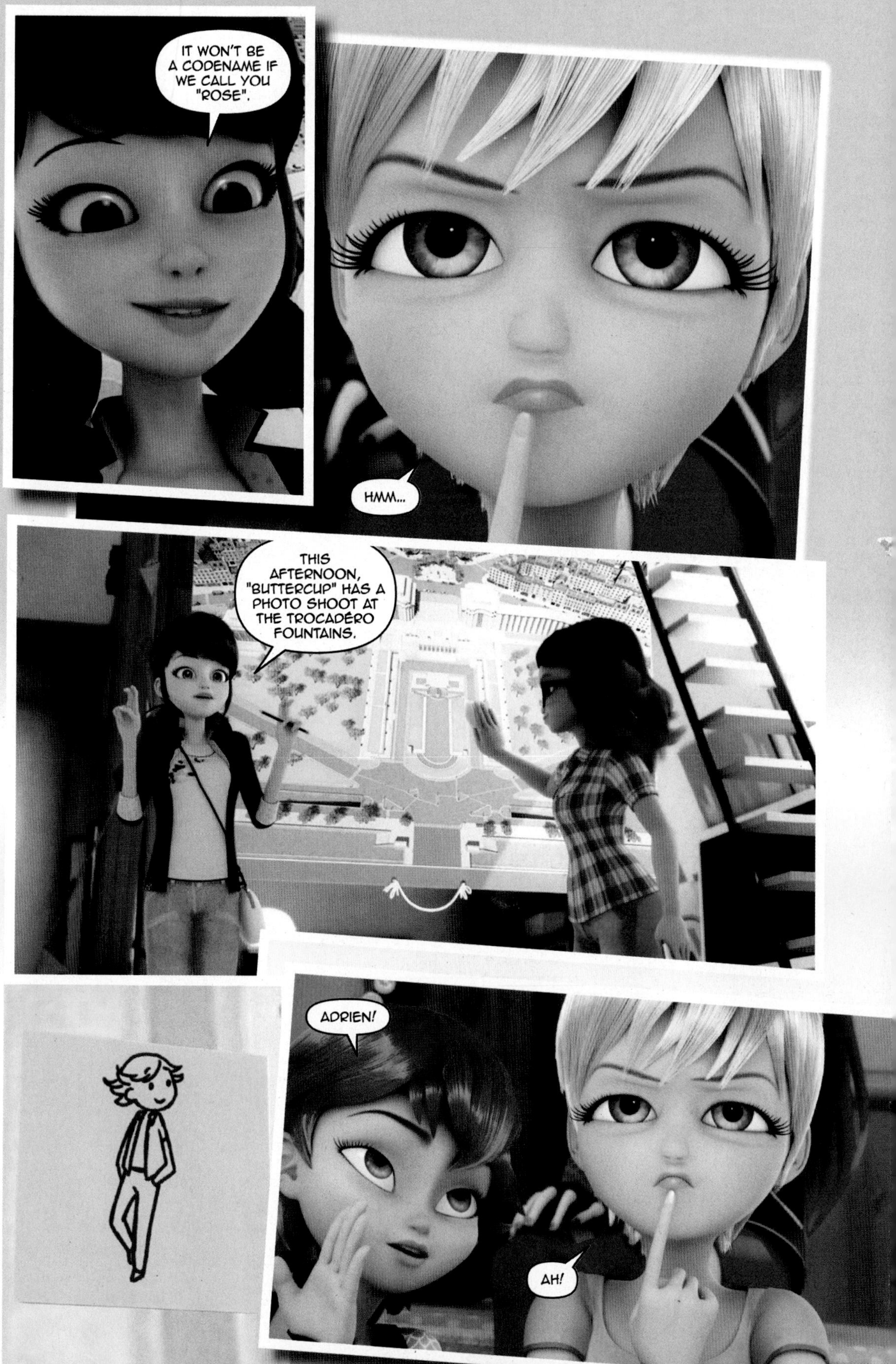
IT WON'T BE A CODENAME IF WE CALL YOU "ROSE".
HMM...
THIS AFTERNOON, "BUTTERCUP" HAS A PHOTO SHOOT AT THE TROCADÉRO FOUNTAINS.
ADRIEN!
AH!

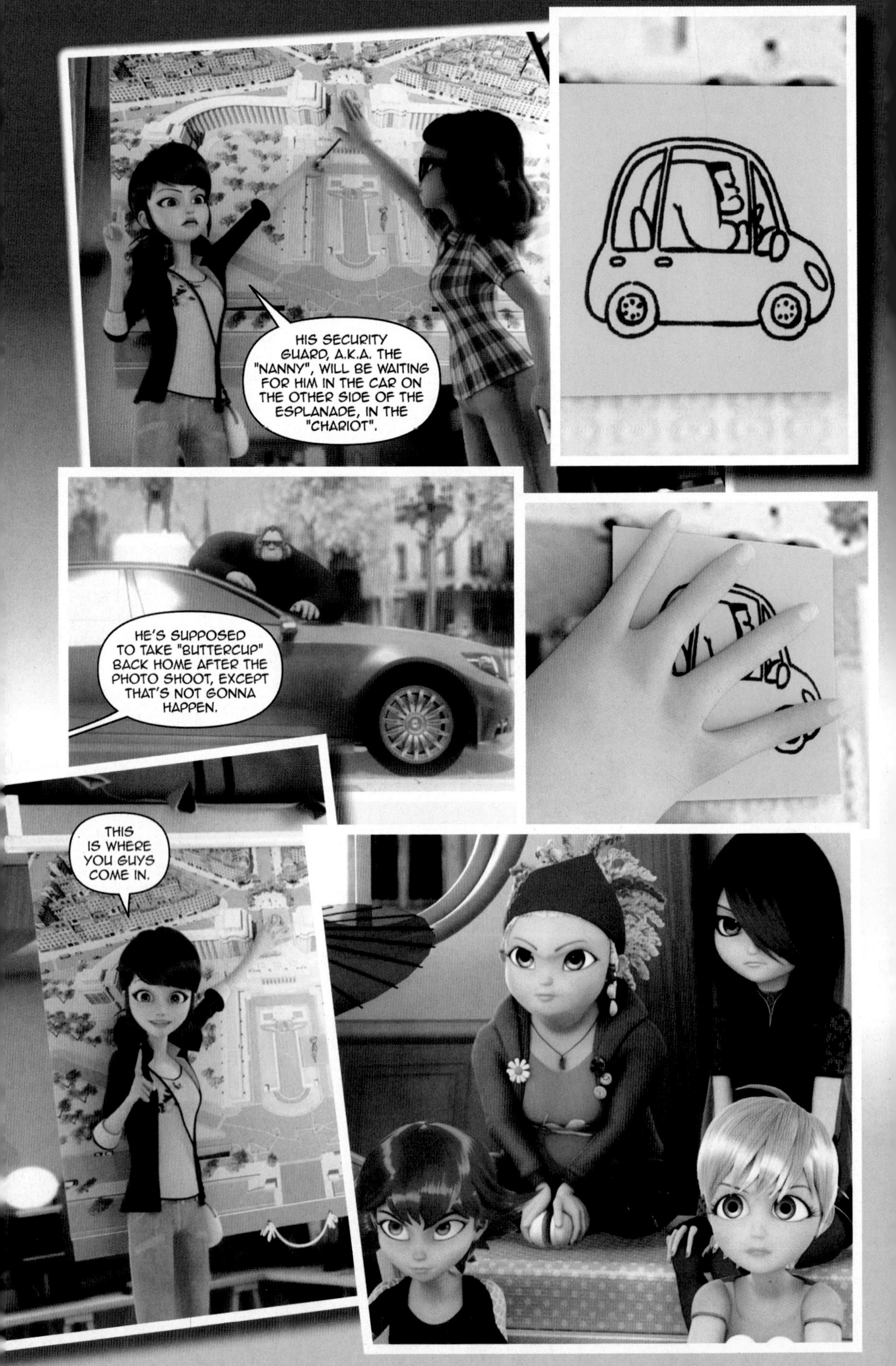
HIS SECURITY GUARD, A.K.A. THE "NANNY", WILL BE WAITING FOR HIM IN THE CAR ON THE OTHER SIDE OF THE ESPLANADE, IN THE "CHARIOT".
HE'S SUPPOSED TO TAKE "BUTTERCUP" BACK HOME AFTER THE PHOTO SHOOT, EXCEPT THAT'S NOT GONNA HAPPEN.
THIS IS WHERE YOU GUYS COME IN.

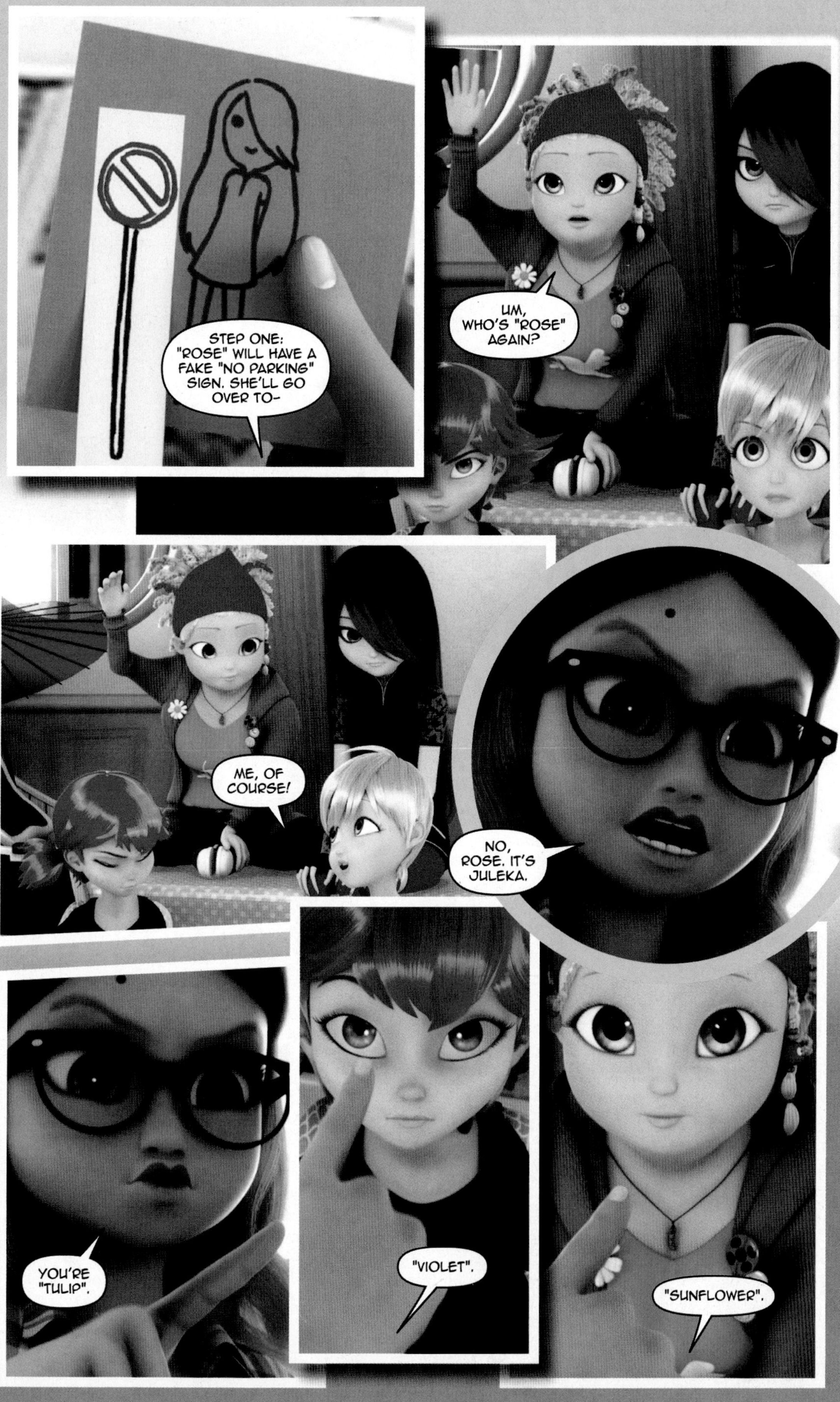
STEP ONE: "ROSE" WILL HAVE A FAKE "NO PARKING" SIGN. SHE'LL GO OVER TO-
UM, WHO'S "ROSE" AGAIN?
ME, OF COURSE!
NO, ROSE. IT'S JULEKA.
YOU'RE "TULIP".
"VIOLET".
"SUNFLOWER".

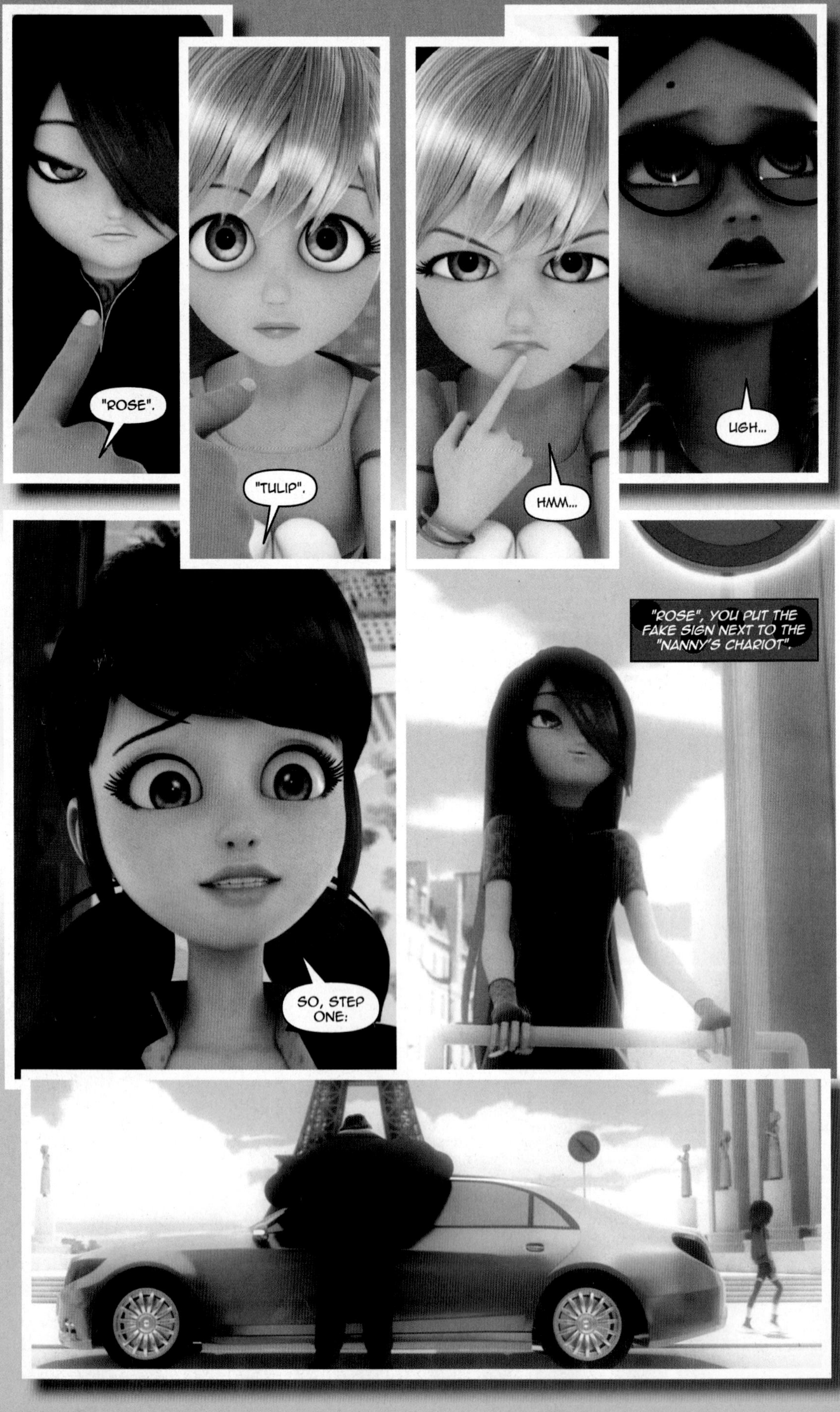
"ROSE".
"TULIP".
HMM...
UGH...
SO, STEP ONE:
"ROSE", YOU PUT THE FAKE SIGN NEXT TO THE "NANNY'S CHARIOT".

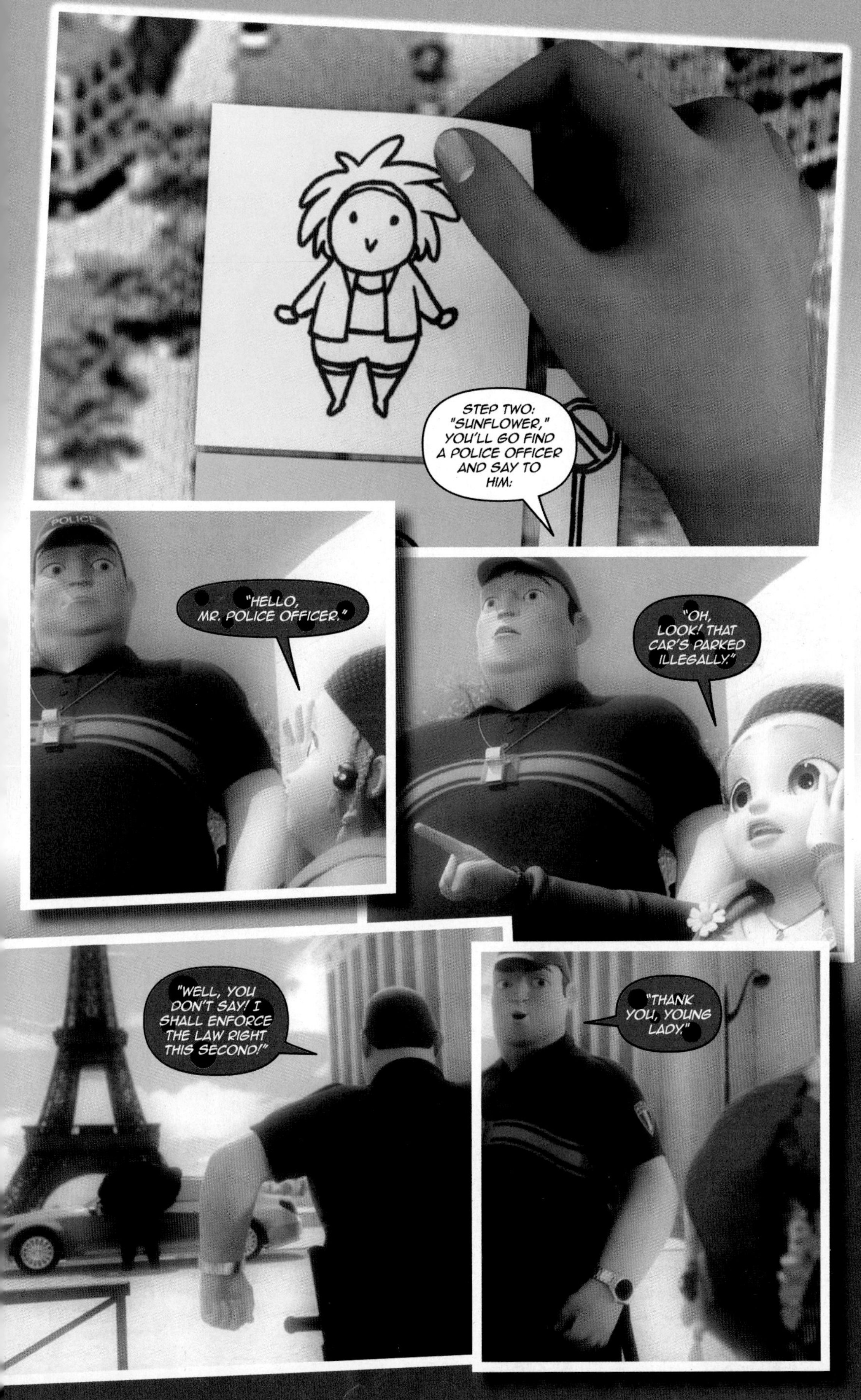
STEP TWO: "SUNFLOWER," YOU'LL GO FIND A POLICE OFFICER AND SAY TO HIM:
POLICE
"HELLO, MR. POLICE OFFICER."
"OH, LOOK! THAT CAR'S PARKED ILLEGALLY."
"WELL, YOU DON'T SAY! I SHALL ENFORCE THE LAW RIGHT THIS SECOND!"
"THANK YOU, YOUNG LADY."

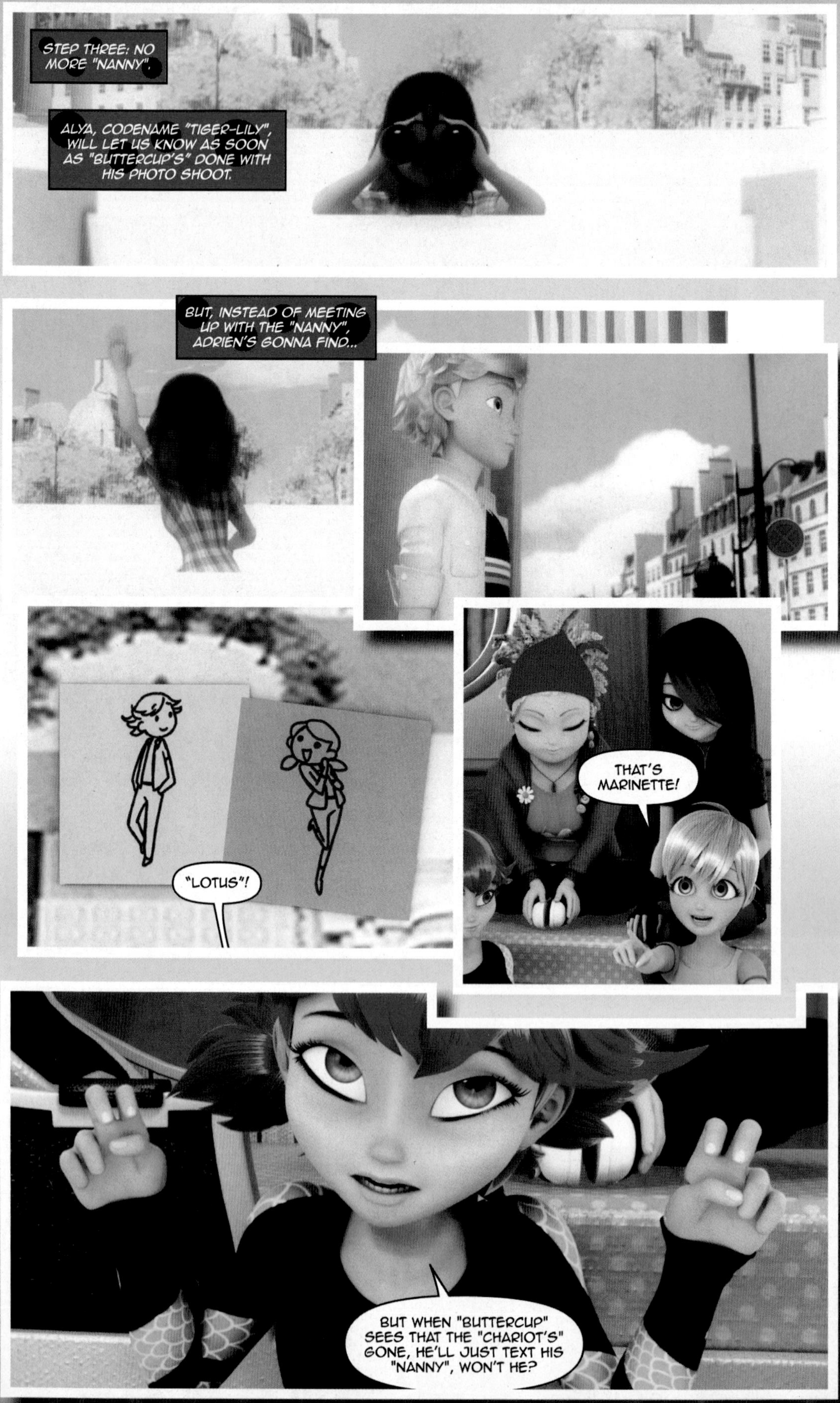
STEP THREE: NO MORE "NANNY".
ALYA, CODENAME "TIGER-LILY", WILL LET US KNOW AS SOON AS "BUTTERCUP'S" DONE WITH HIS PHOTO SHOOT.
BUT, INSTEAD OF MEETING UP WITH THE "NANNY", ADRIEN'S GONNA FIND...
"LOTUS"!
THAT'S MARINETTE!
BUT WHEN "BUTTERCUP" SEES THAT THE "CHARIOT'S" GONE, HE'LL JUST TEXT HIS "NANNY", WON'T HE?

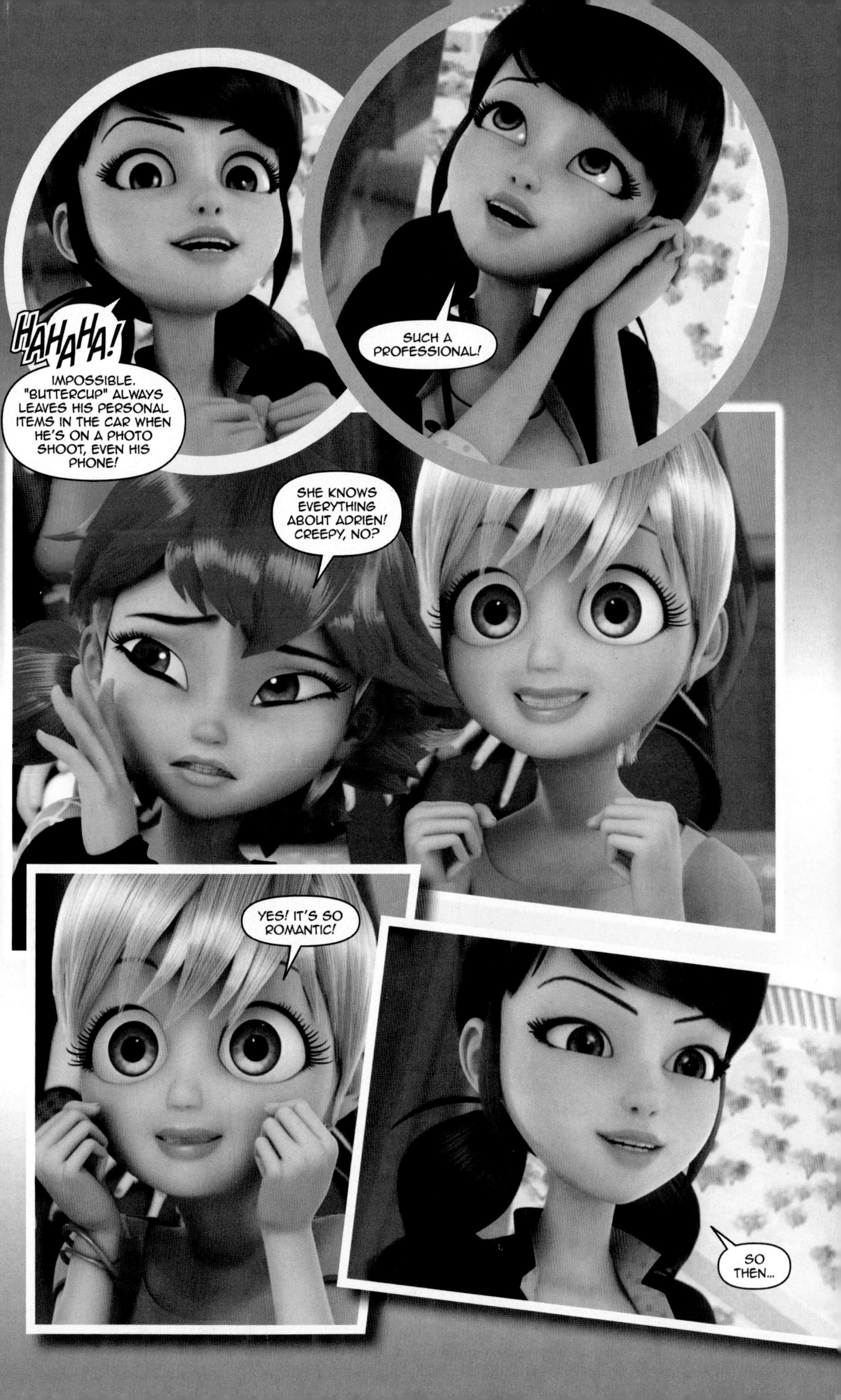
HAHAHA!
IMPOSSIBLE. "BUTTERCUP" ALWAYS LEAVES HIS PERSONAL ITEMS IN THE CAR WHEN HE'S ON A PHOTO SHOOT, EVEN HIS PHONE!
SUCH A PROFESSIONAL!
SHE KNOWS EVERYTHING ABOUT ADRIEN! CREEPY, NO?
YES! IT'S SO ROMANTIC!
SO THEN...

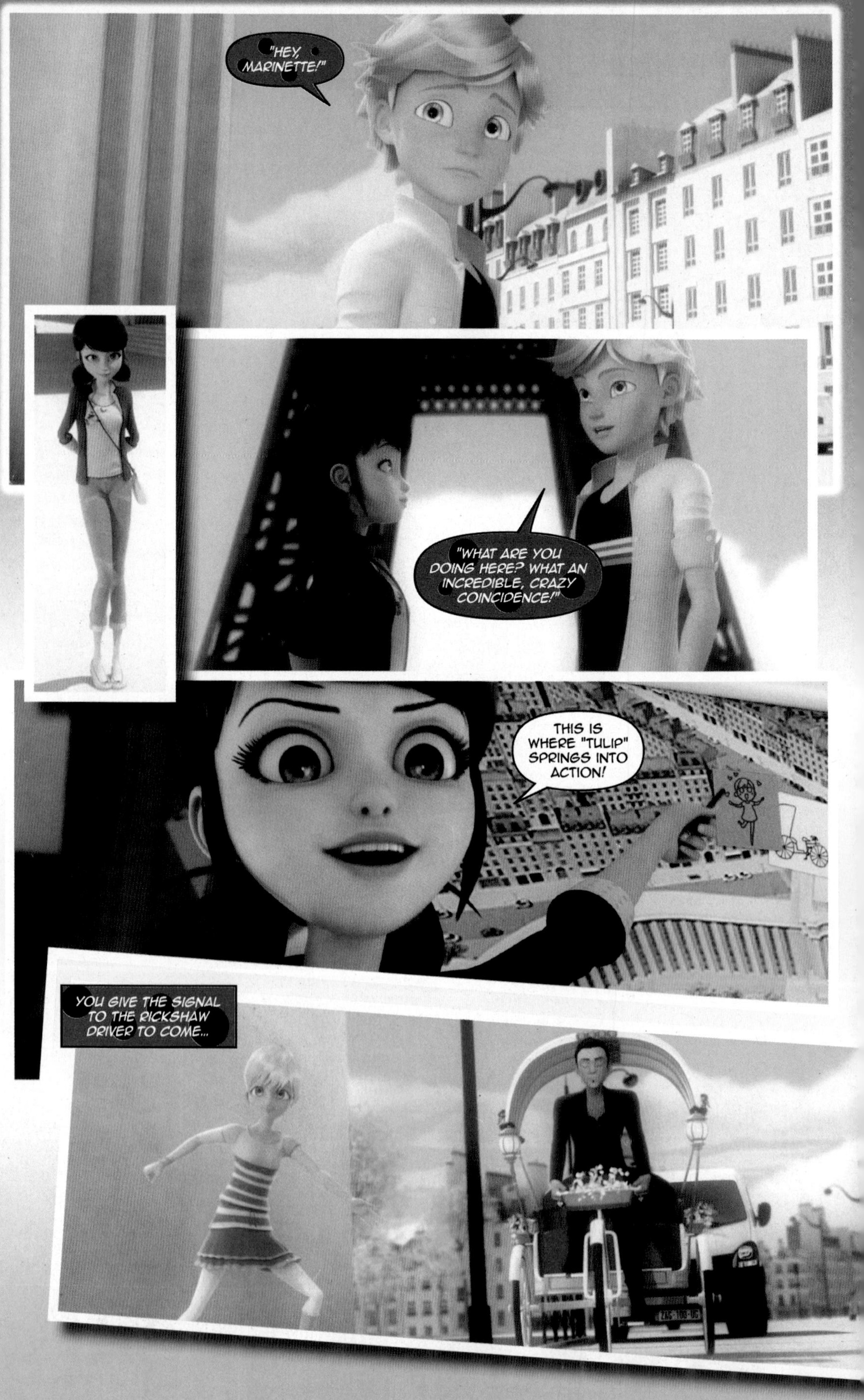
"HEY, MARINETTE!"
"WHAT ARE YOU DOING HERE? WHAT AN INCREDIBLE, CRAZY COINCIDENCE!"
THIS IS WHERE "TULIP" SPRINGS INTO ACTION!
YOU GIVE THE SIGNAL TO THE RICKSHAW DRIVER TO COME...

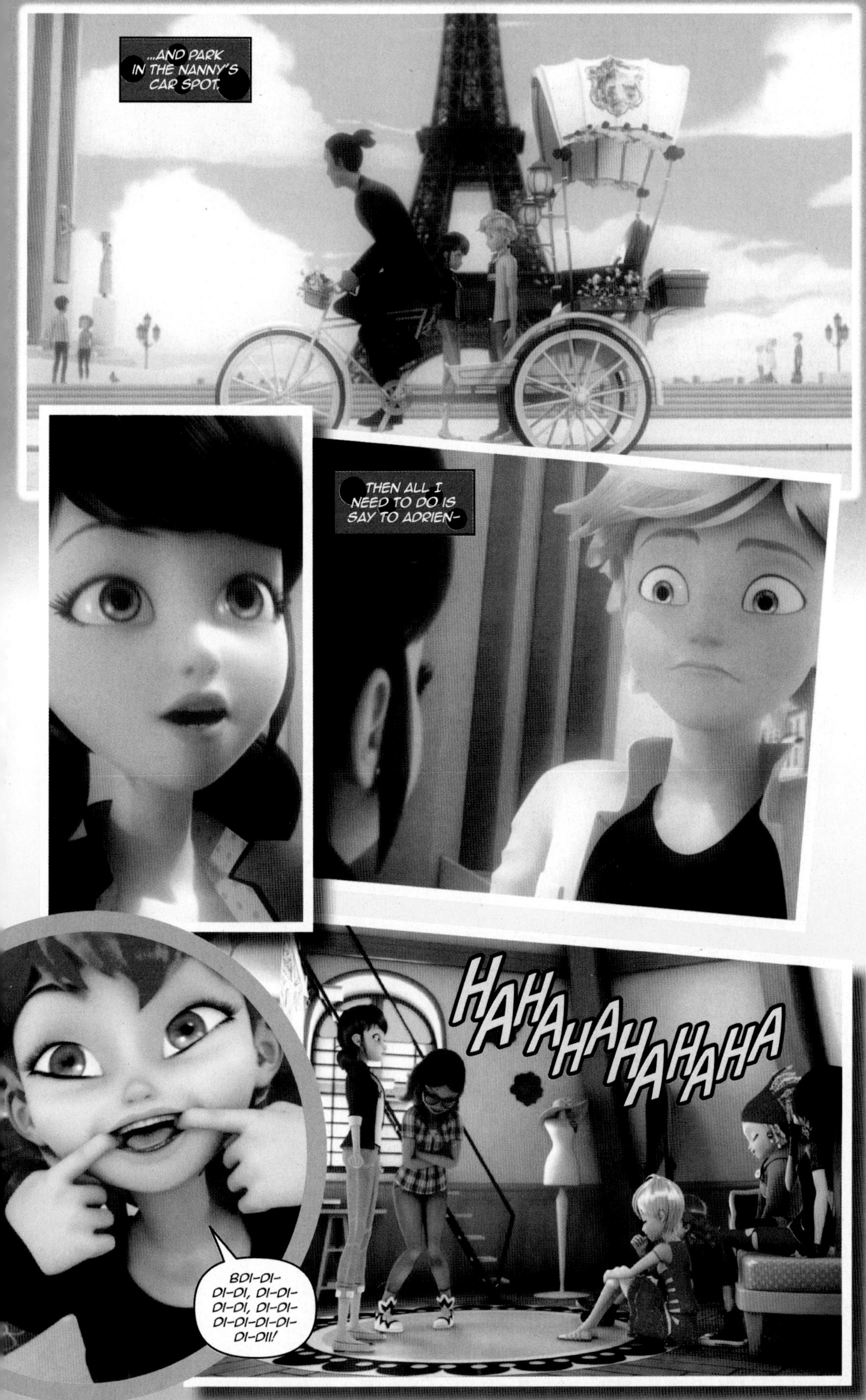

...AND PARK IN THE NANNY'S CAR SPOT.
THEN ALL I NEED TO DO IS SAY TO ADRIEN–
BDI-DI-DI-DI, DI-DI-DI-DI, DI-DI-DI-DI-DI-DI-DI-DII!
HAHAHAHAHAHAHA

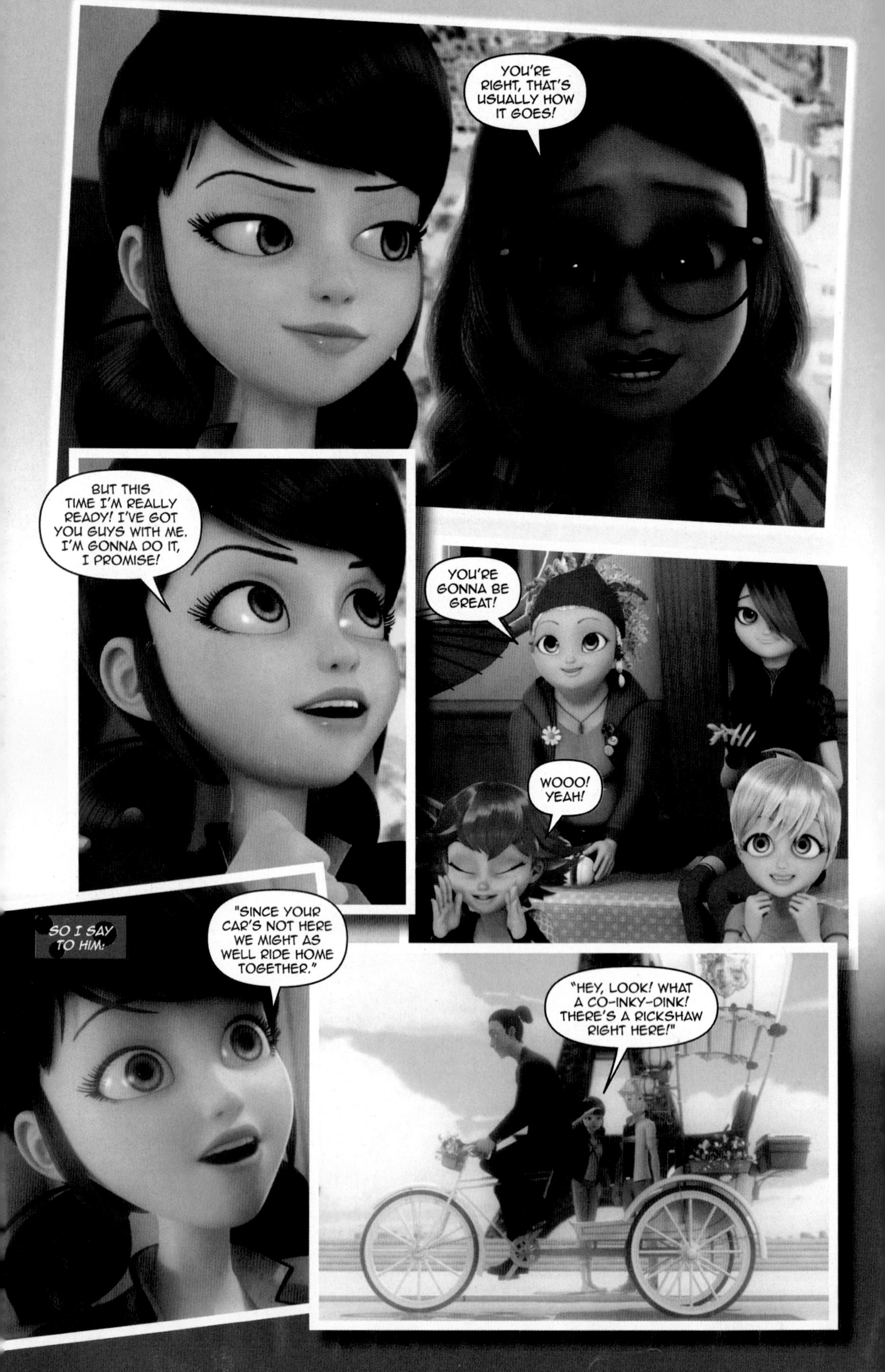
YOU'RE RIGHT, THAT'S USUALLY HOW IT GOES!
BUT THIS TIME I'M REALLY READY! I'VE GOT YOU GUYS WITH ME. I'M GONNA DO IT, I PROMISE!
YOU'RE GONNA BE GREAT!
WOOO! YEAH!
SO I SAY TO HIM:
"SINCE YOUR CAR'S NOT HERE WE MIGHT AS WELL RIDE HOME TOGETHER."
"HEY, LOOK! WHAT A CO-INKY-DINK! THERE'S A RICKSHAW RIGHT HERE!"

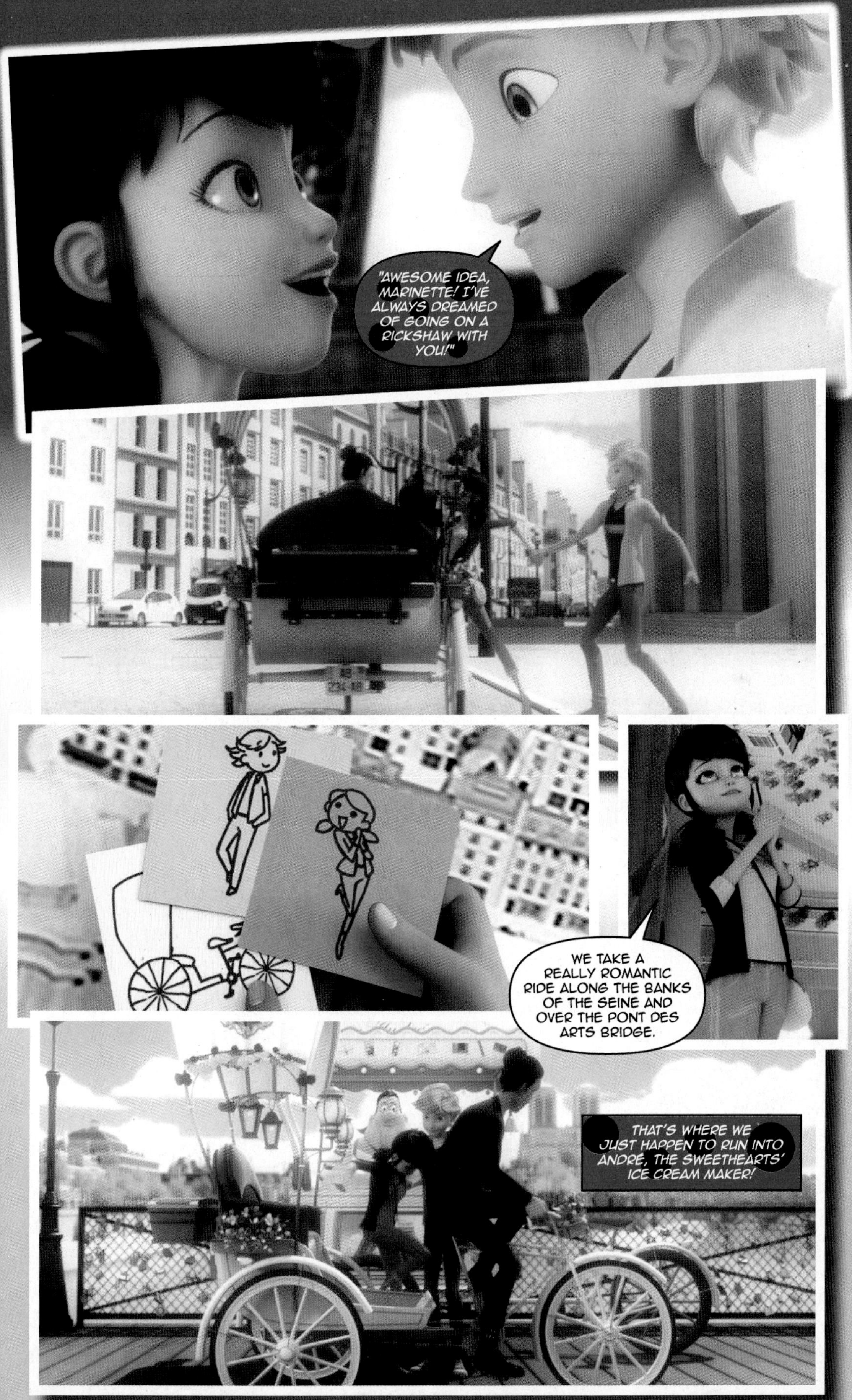
"AWESOME IDEA, MARINETTE! I'VE ALWAYS DREAMED OF GOING ON A RICKSHAW WITH YOU!"
WE TAKE A REALLY ROMANTIC RIDE ALONG THE BANKS OF THE SEINE AND OVER THE PONT DES ARTS BRIDGE.
THAT'S WHERE WE JUST HAPPEN TO RUN INTO ANDRÉ, THE SWEETHEARTS' ICE CREAM MAKER!

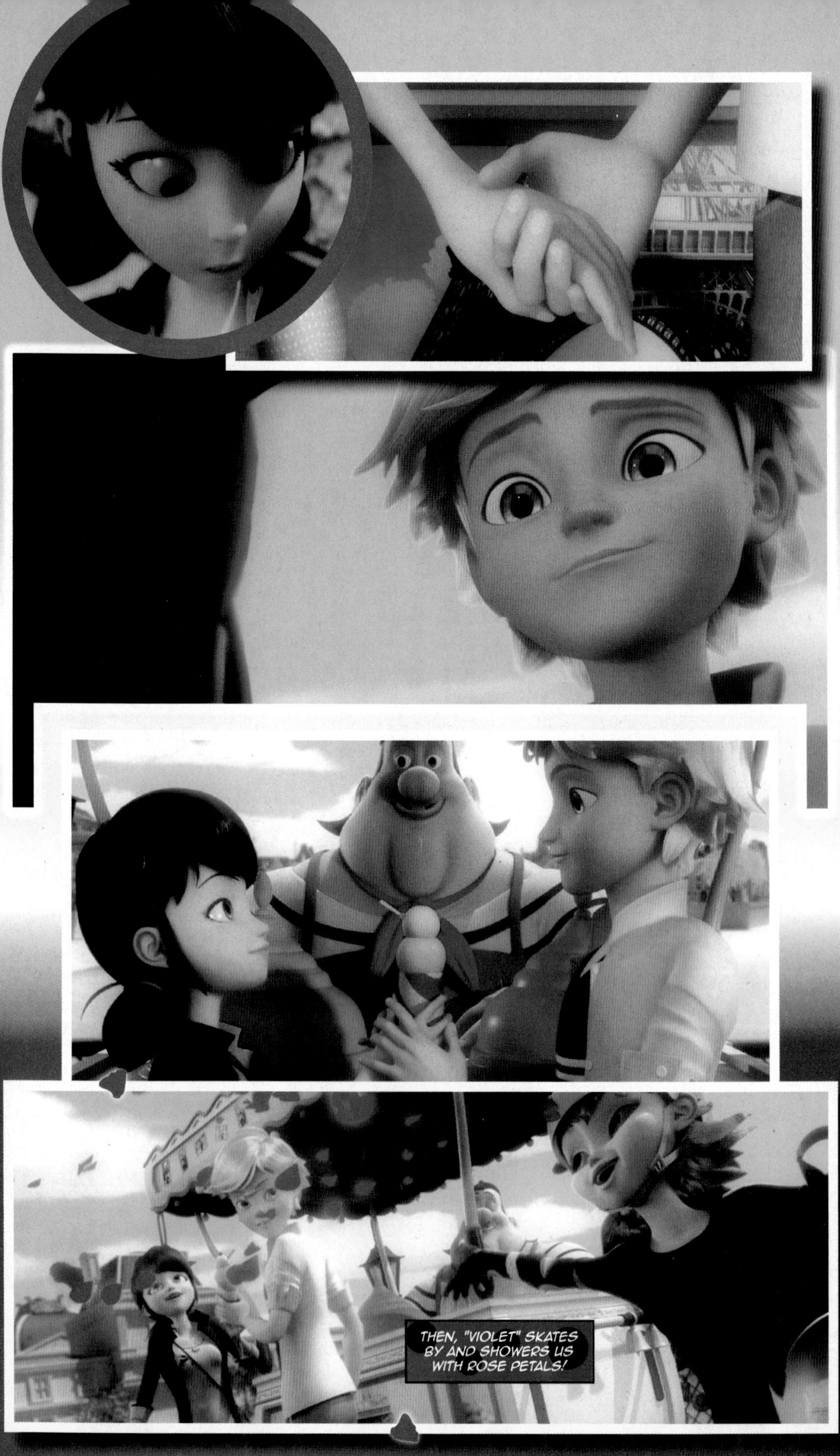
THEN, "VIOLET" SKATES BY AND SHOWERS US WITH ROSE PETALS!

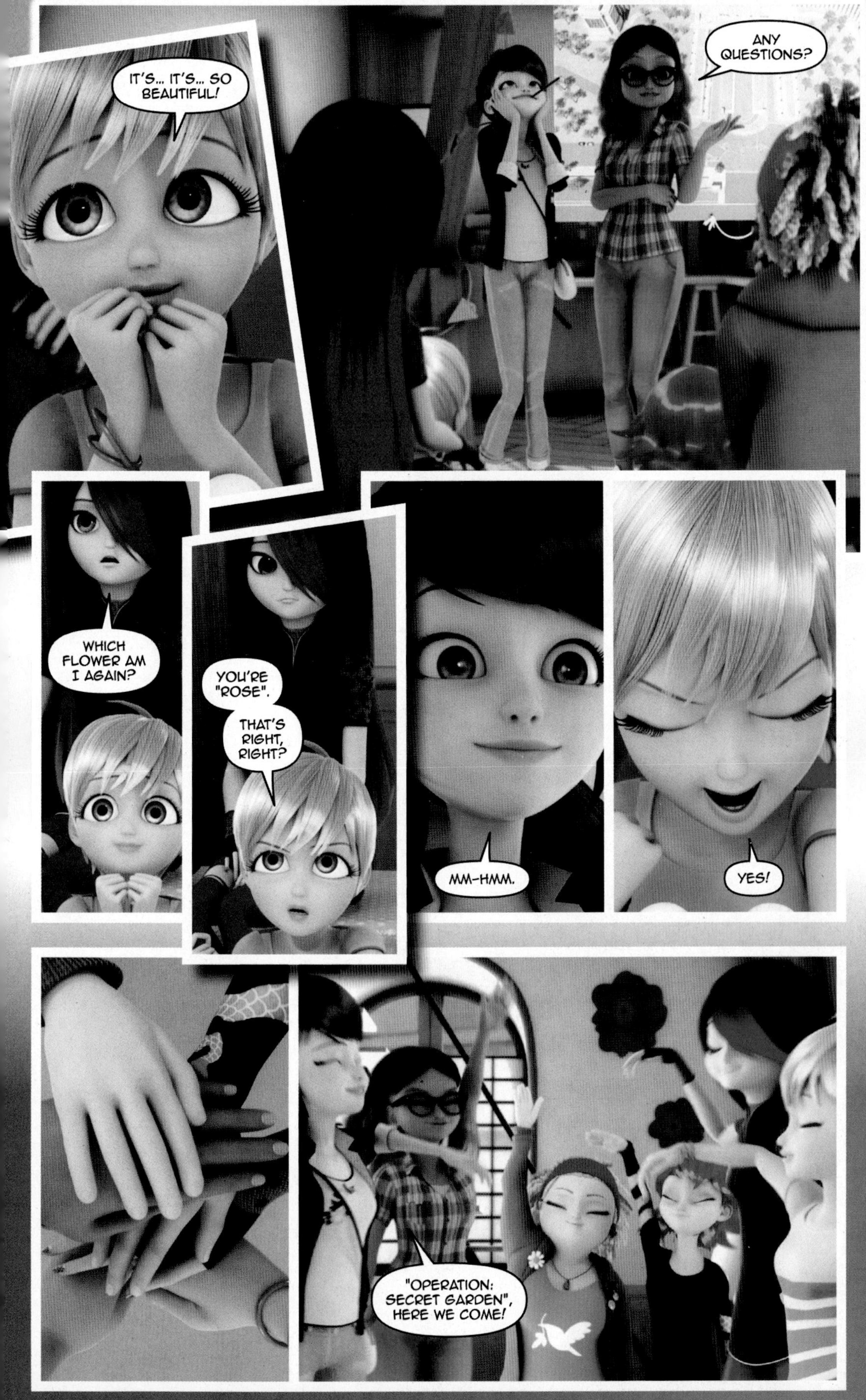
IT'S... IT'S... SO BEAUTIFUL!
ANY QUESTIONS?
WHICH FLOWER AM I AGAIN?
YOU'RE "ROSE".
THAT'S RIGHT, RIGHT?
MM-HMM.
YES!
"OPERATION: SECRET GARDEN", HERE WE COME!

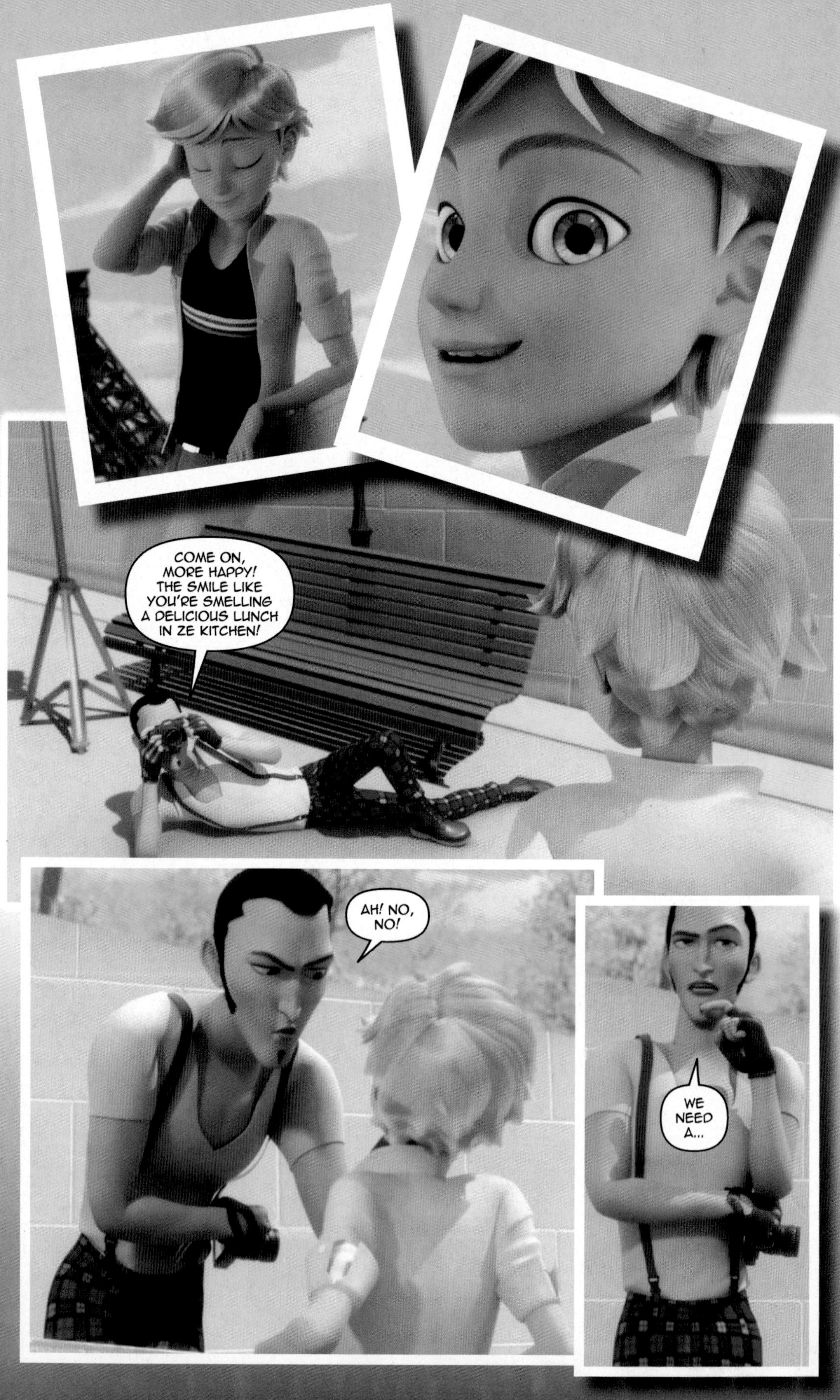
COME ON, MORE HAPPY! THE SMILE LIKE YOU'RE SMELLING A DELICIOUS LUNCH IN ZE KITCHEN!
AH! NO, NO!
WE NEED A...

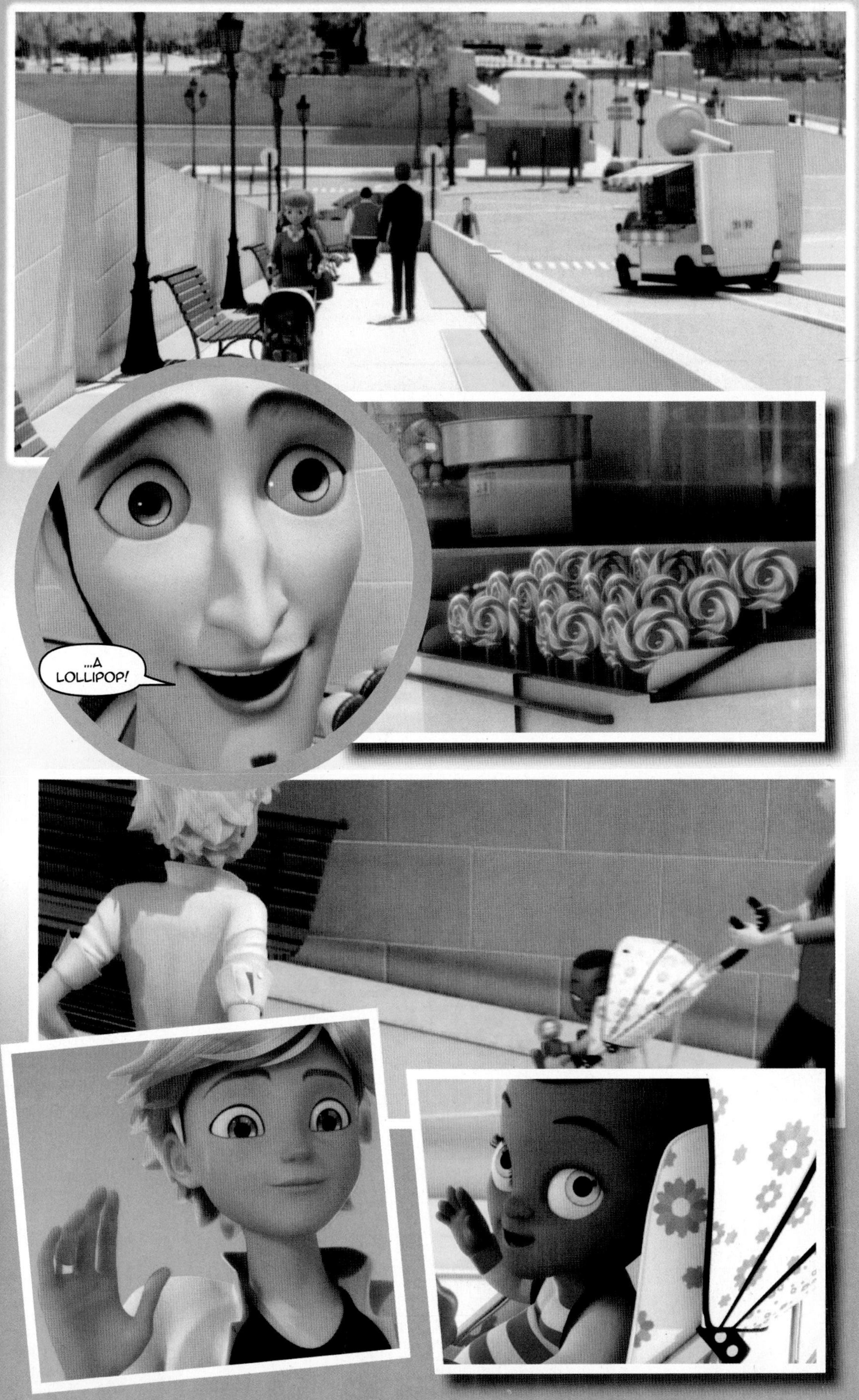
...A LOLLIPOP!

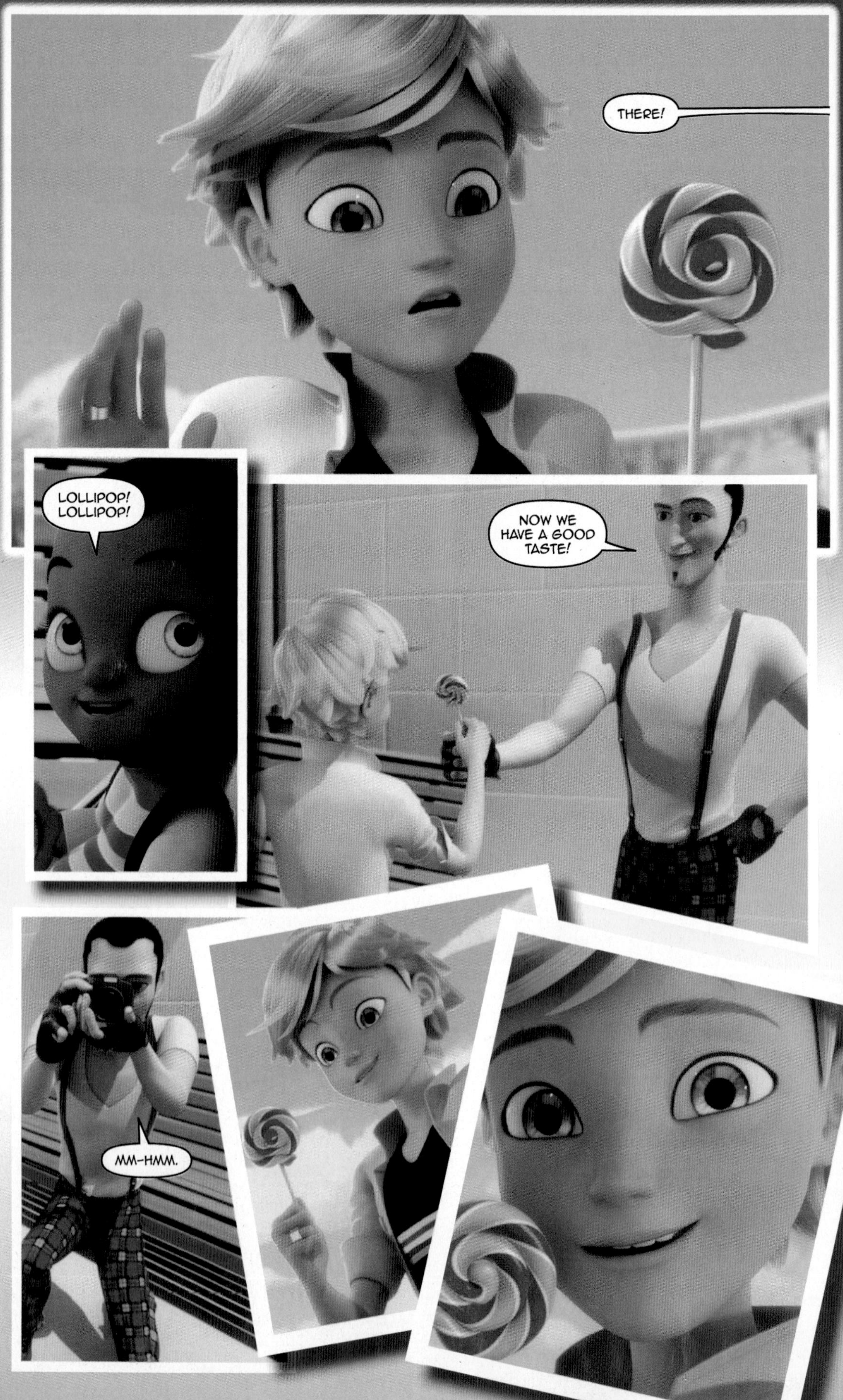
THERE!
LOLLIPOP! LOLLIPOP!
NOW WE HAVE A GOOD TASTE!
MM-HMM.

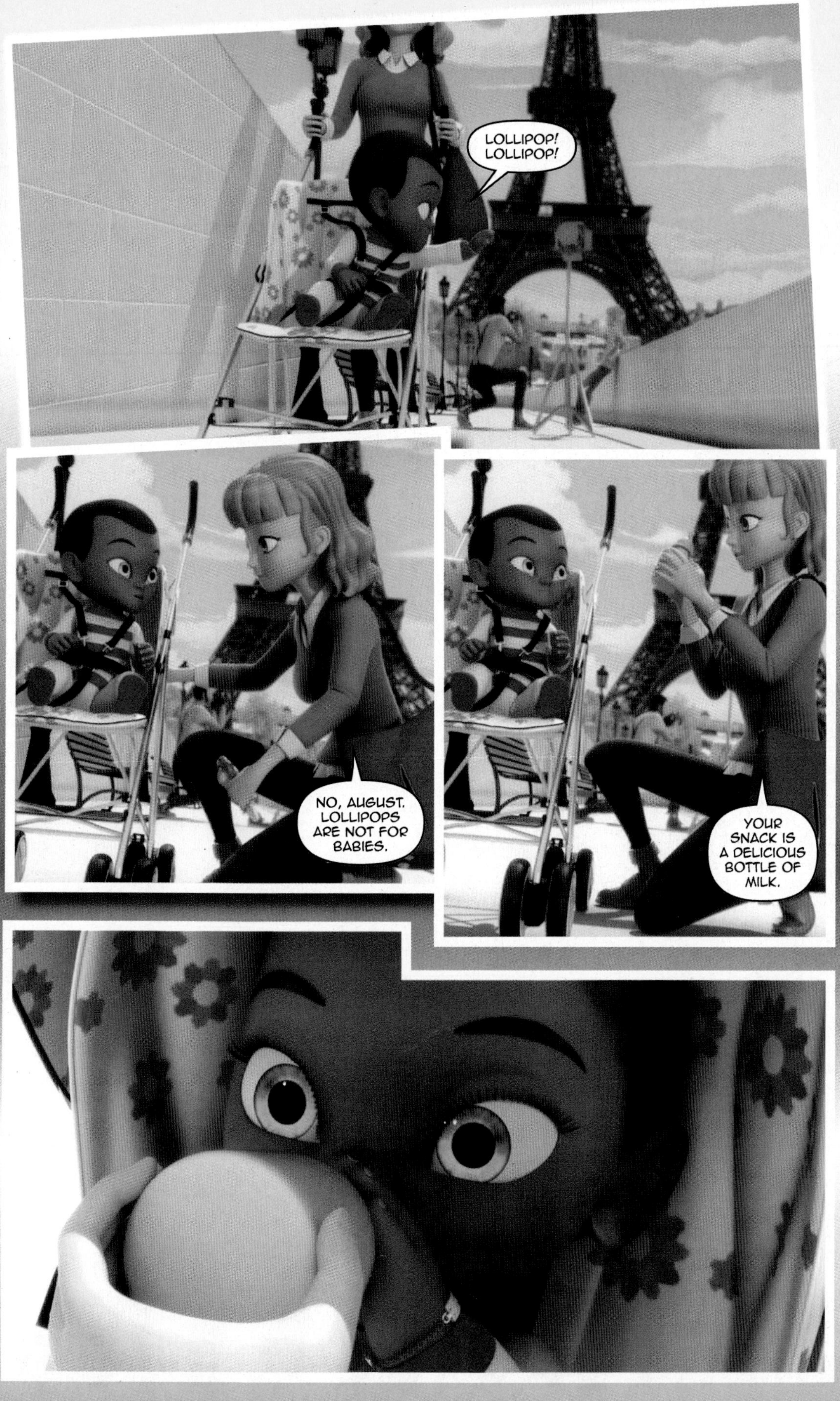

LOLLIPOP! LOLLIPOP!
NO, AUGUST. LOLLIPOPS ARE NOT FOR BABIES.
YOUR SNACK IS A DELICIOUS BOTTLE OF MILK.

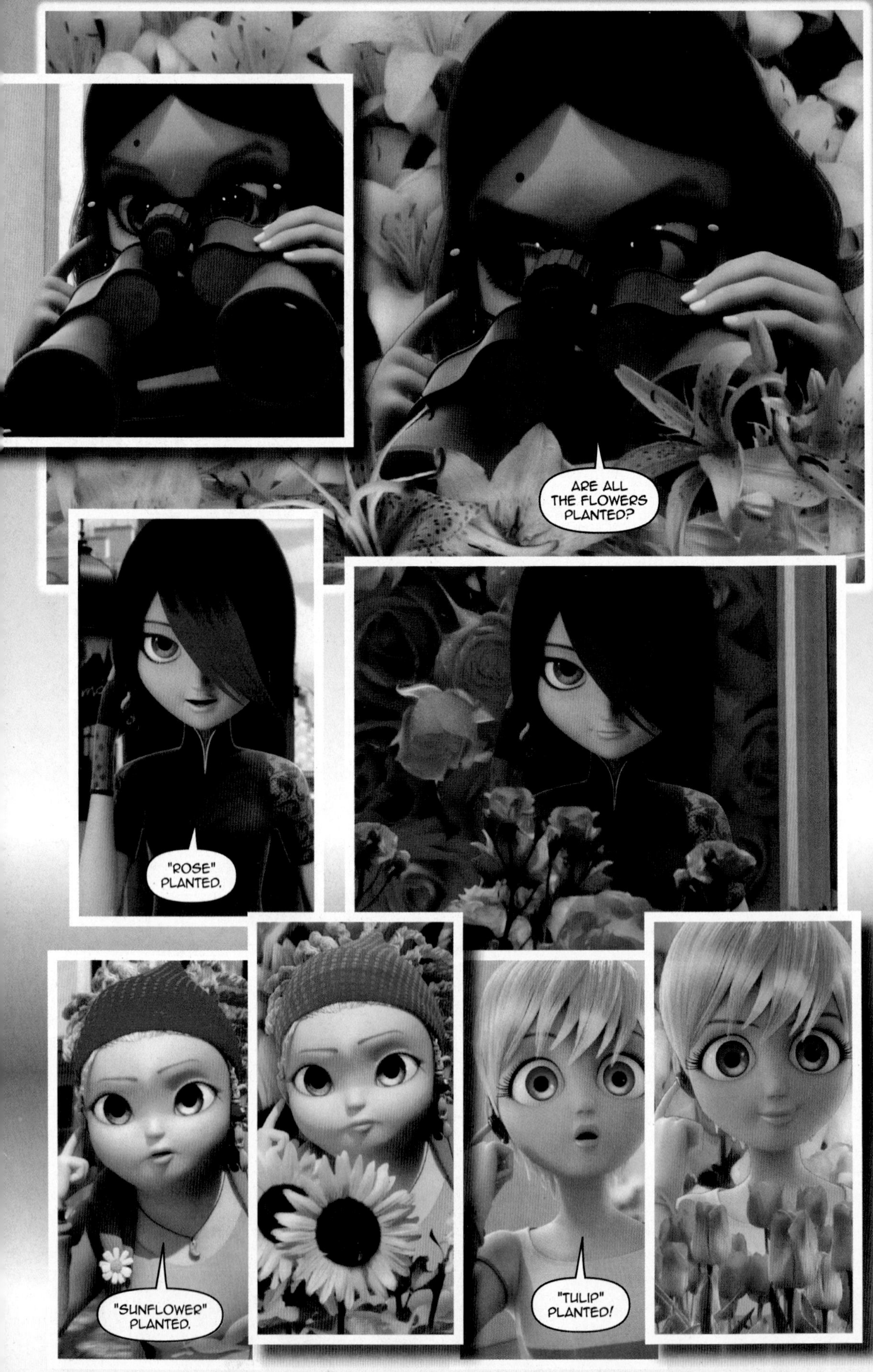
ARE ALL THE FLOWERS PLANTED?
"ROSE" PLANTED.
"SUNFLOWER" PLANTED.
"TULIP" PLANTED!

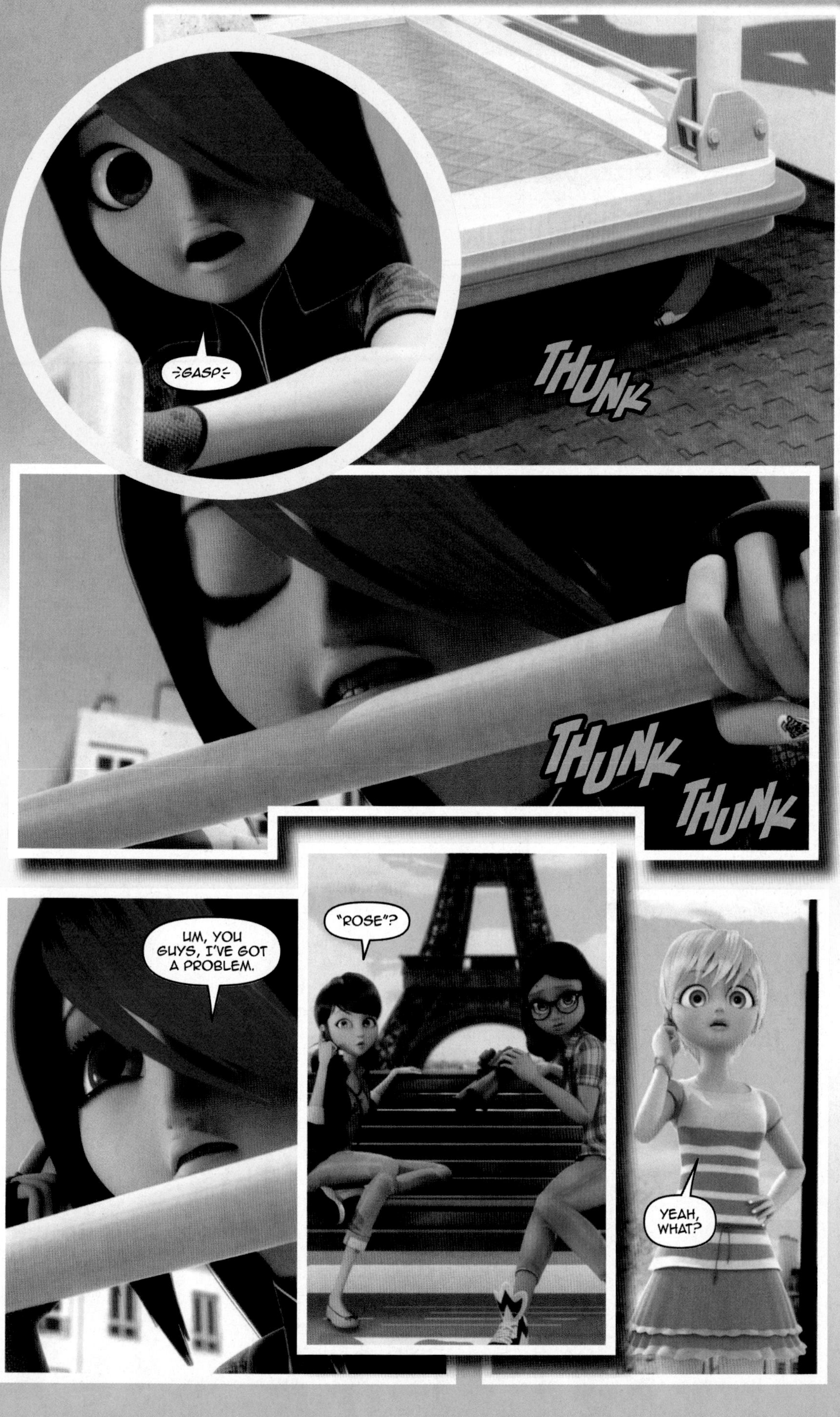
GASP
THUNK
THUNK
THUNK
UM, YOU GUYS, I'VE GOT A PROBLEM.
"ROSE"?
YEAH, WHAT?

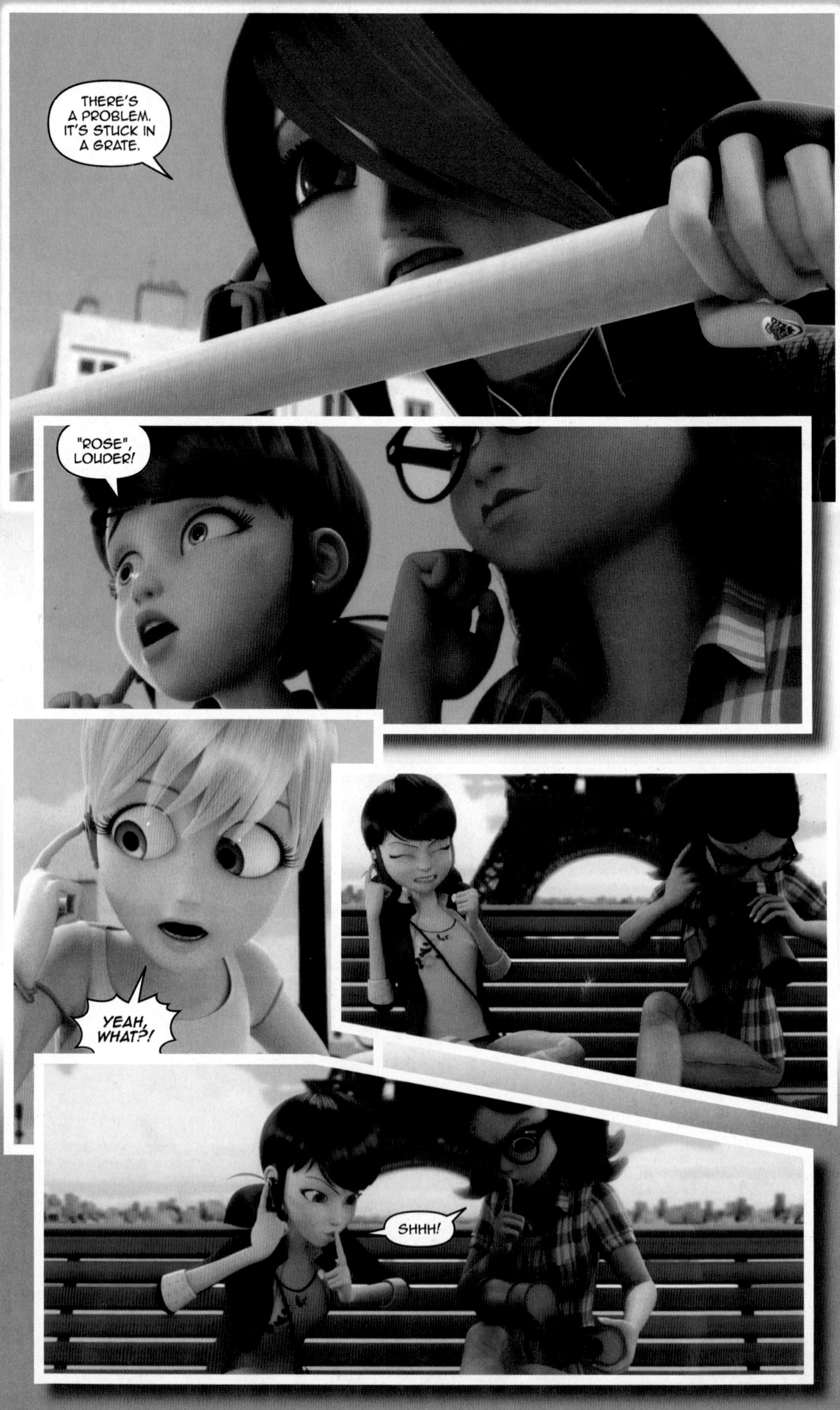
THERE'S A PROBLEM. IT'S STUCK IN A GRATE.
"ROSE", LOUDER!
YEAH, WHAT?!
SHHH!

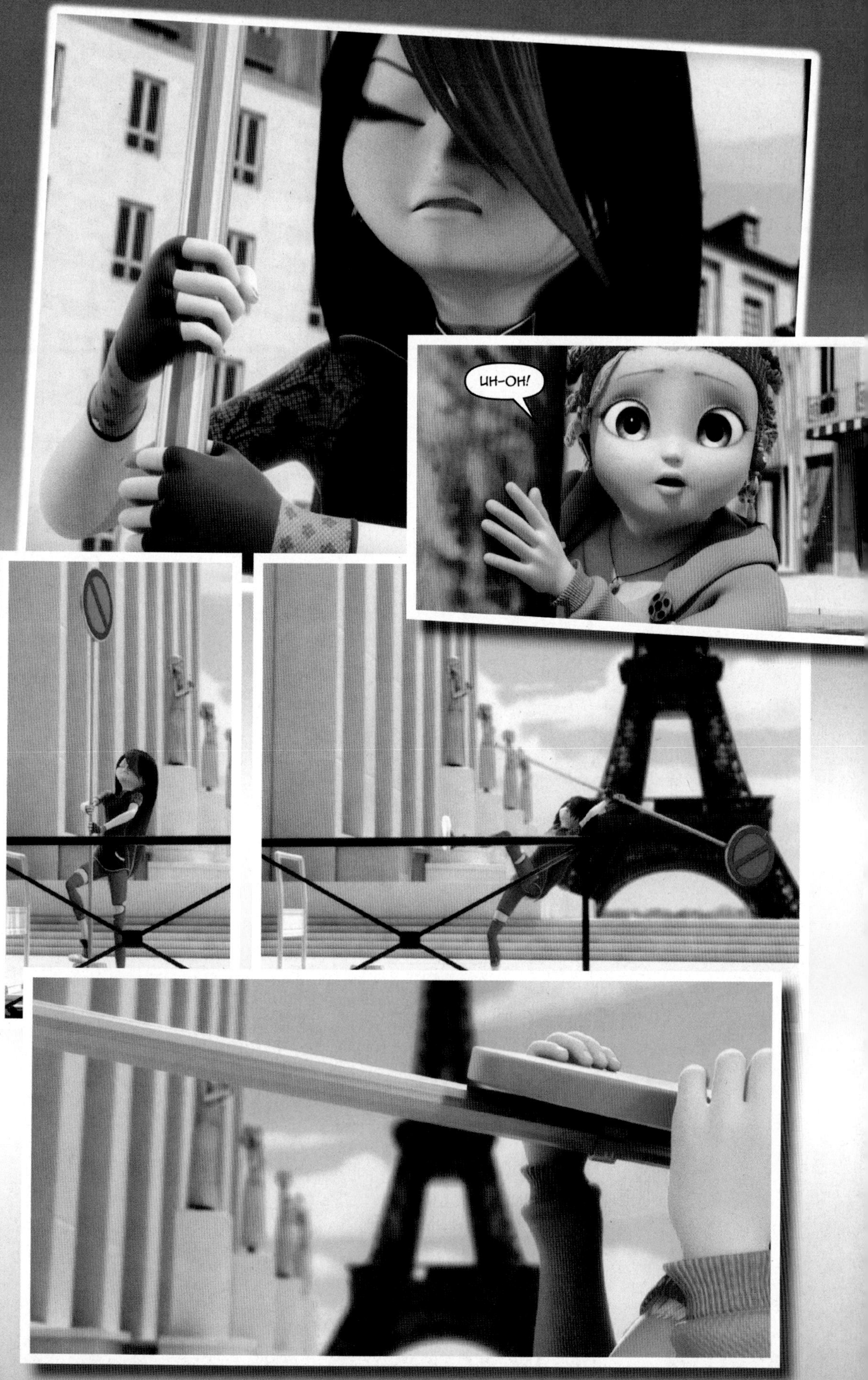
UH-OH!

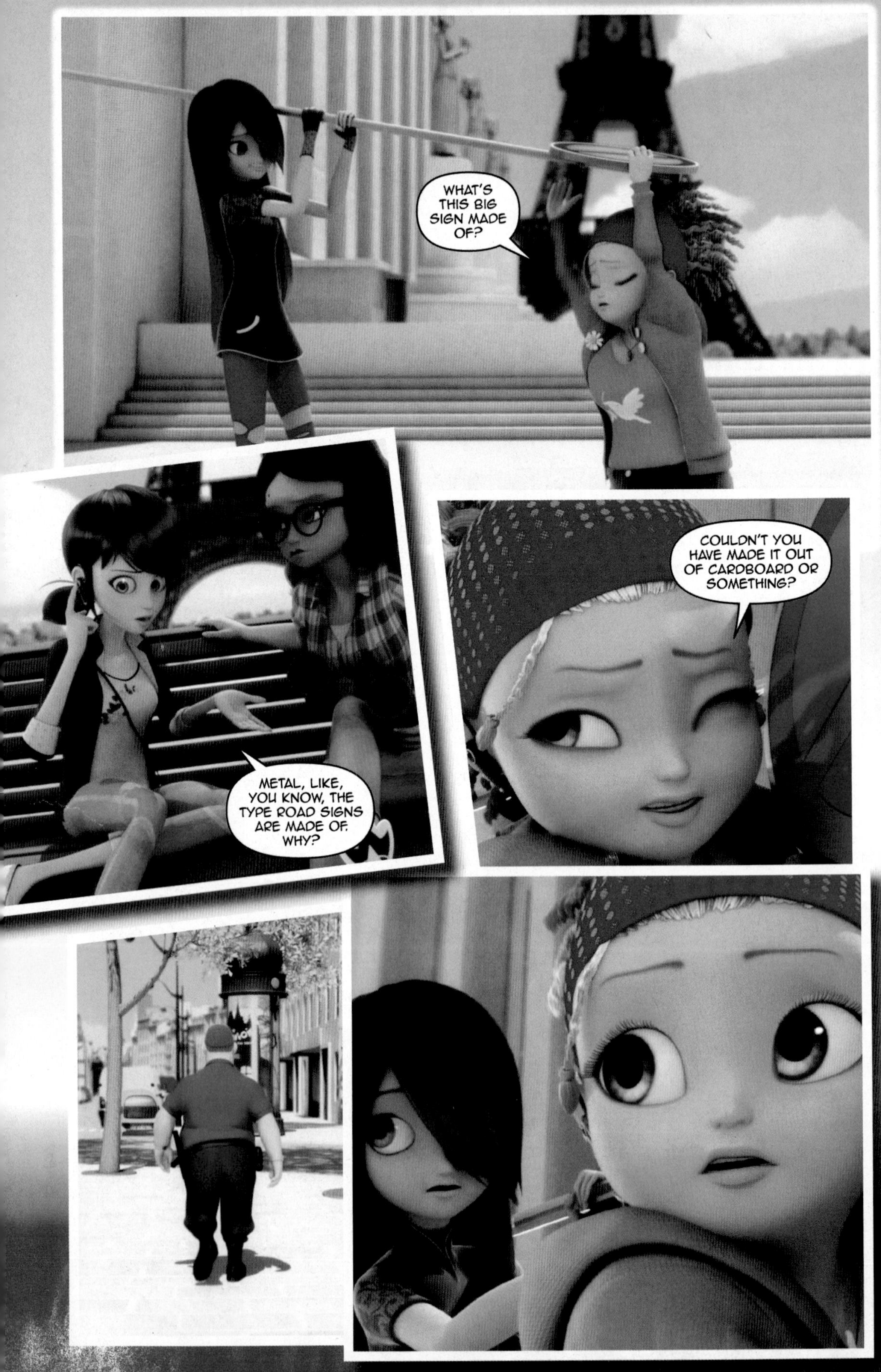
WHAT'S THIS BIG SIGN MADE OF?
METAL, LIKE, YOU KNOW, THE TYPE ROAD SIGNS ARE MADE OF. WHY?
COULDN'T YOU HAVE MADE IT OUT OF CARDBOARD OR SOMETHING?

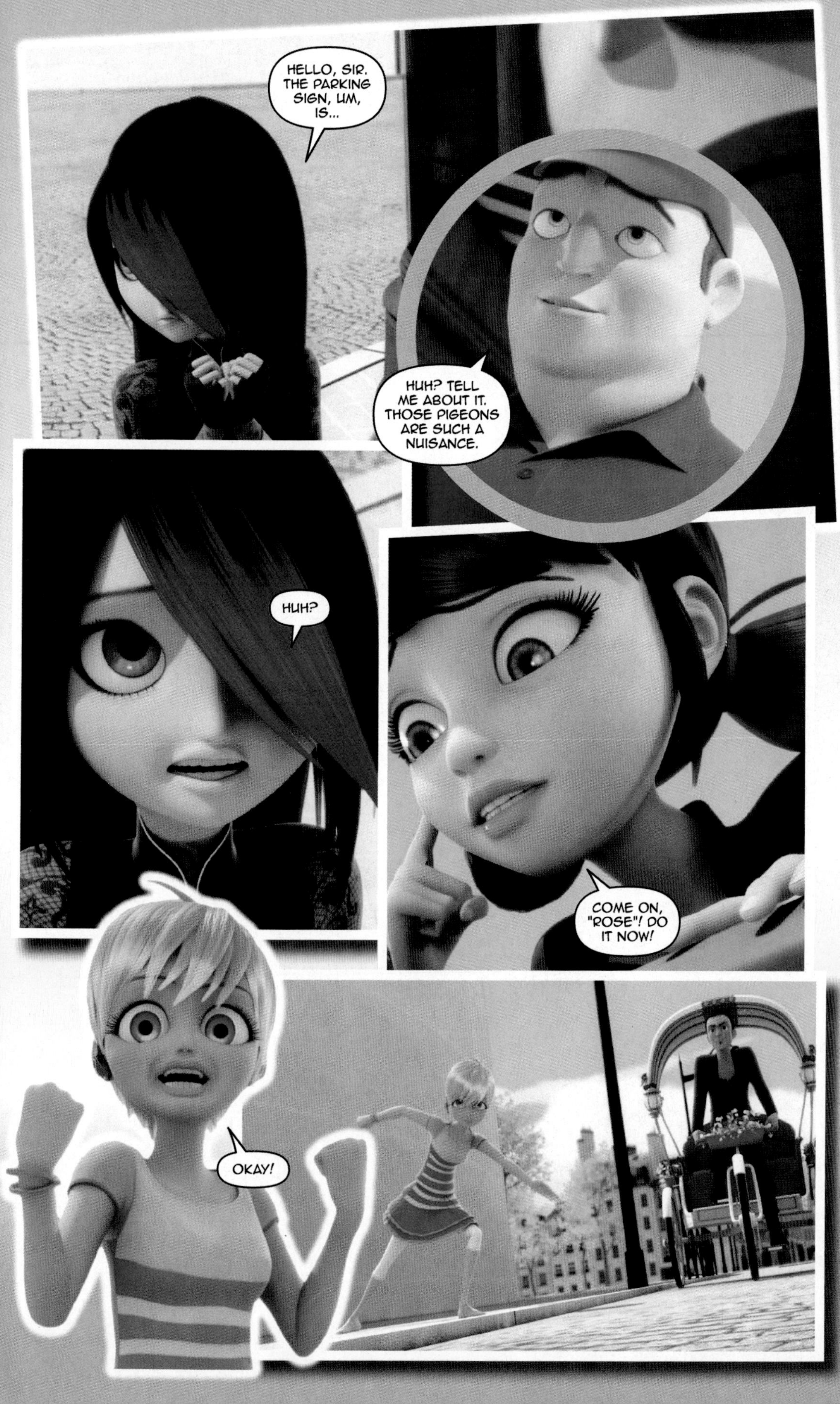
HELLO, SIR. THE PARKING SIGN, UM, IS...
HUH? TELL ME ABOUT IT. THOSE PIGEONS ARE SUCH A NUISANCE.
HUH?
COME ON, "ROSE"! DO IT NOW!
OKAY!

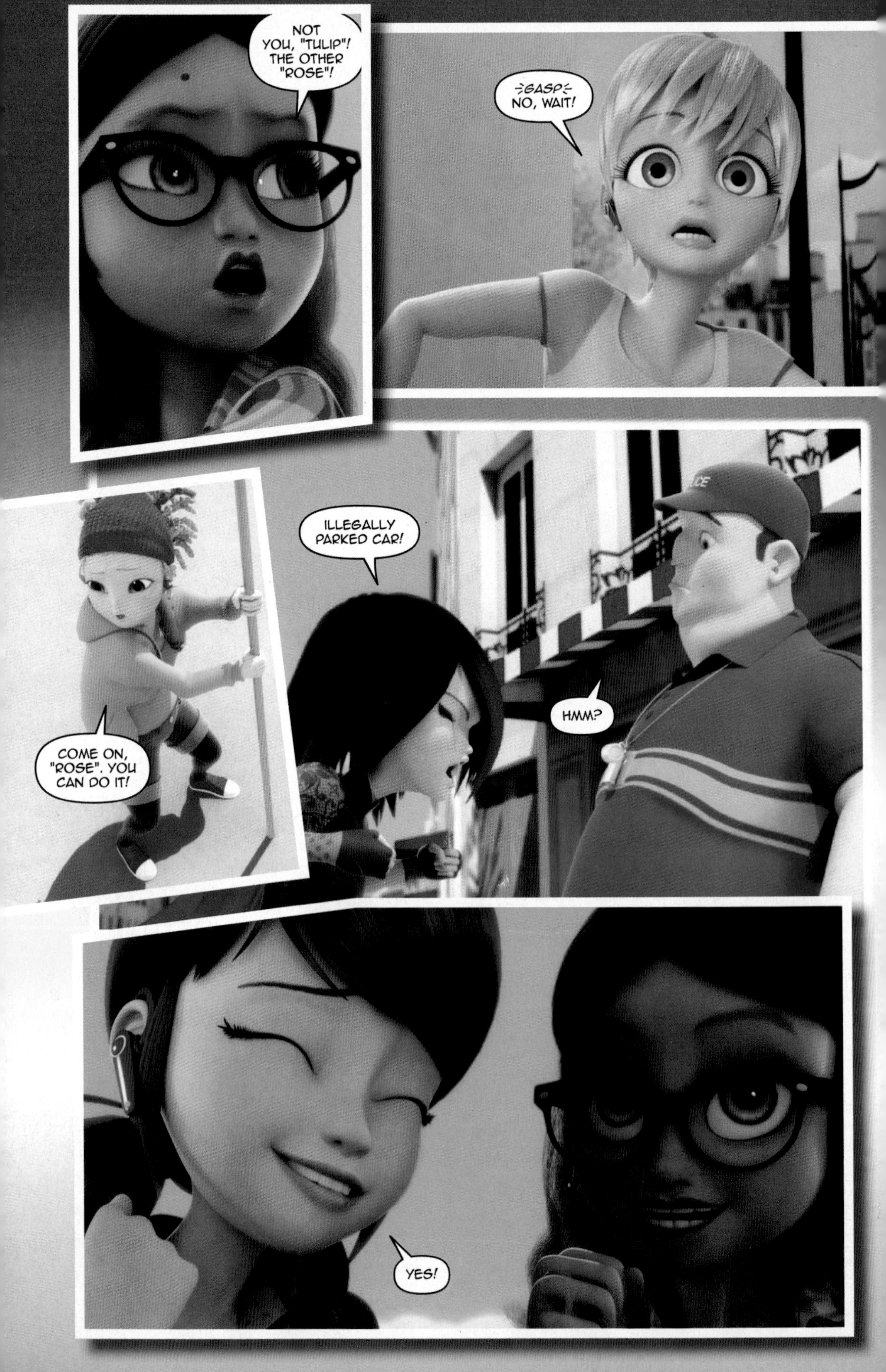
NOT YOU, "TULIP"! THE OTHER "ROSE"!
GASP NO, WAIT!
ILLEGALLY PARKED CAR!
COME ON, "ROSE". YOU CAN DO IT!
HMM?
YES!

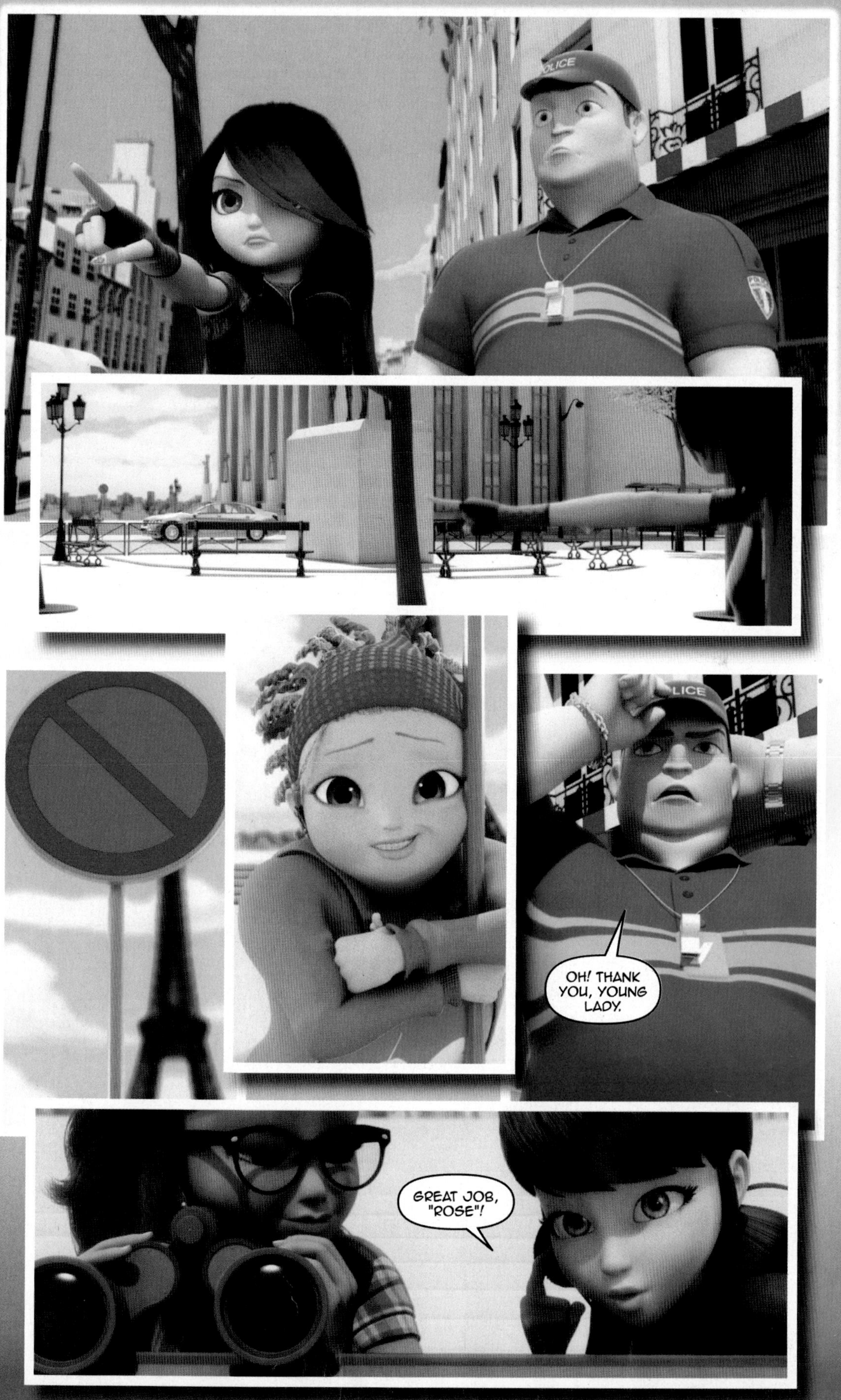
OH! THANK YOU, YOUNG LADY.
GREAT JOB, "ROSE"!

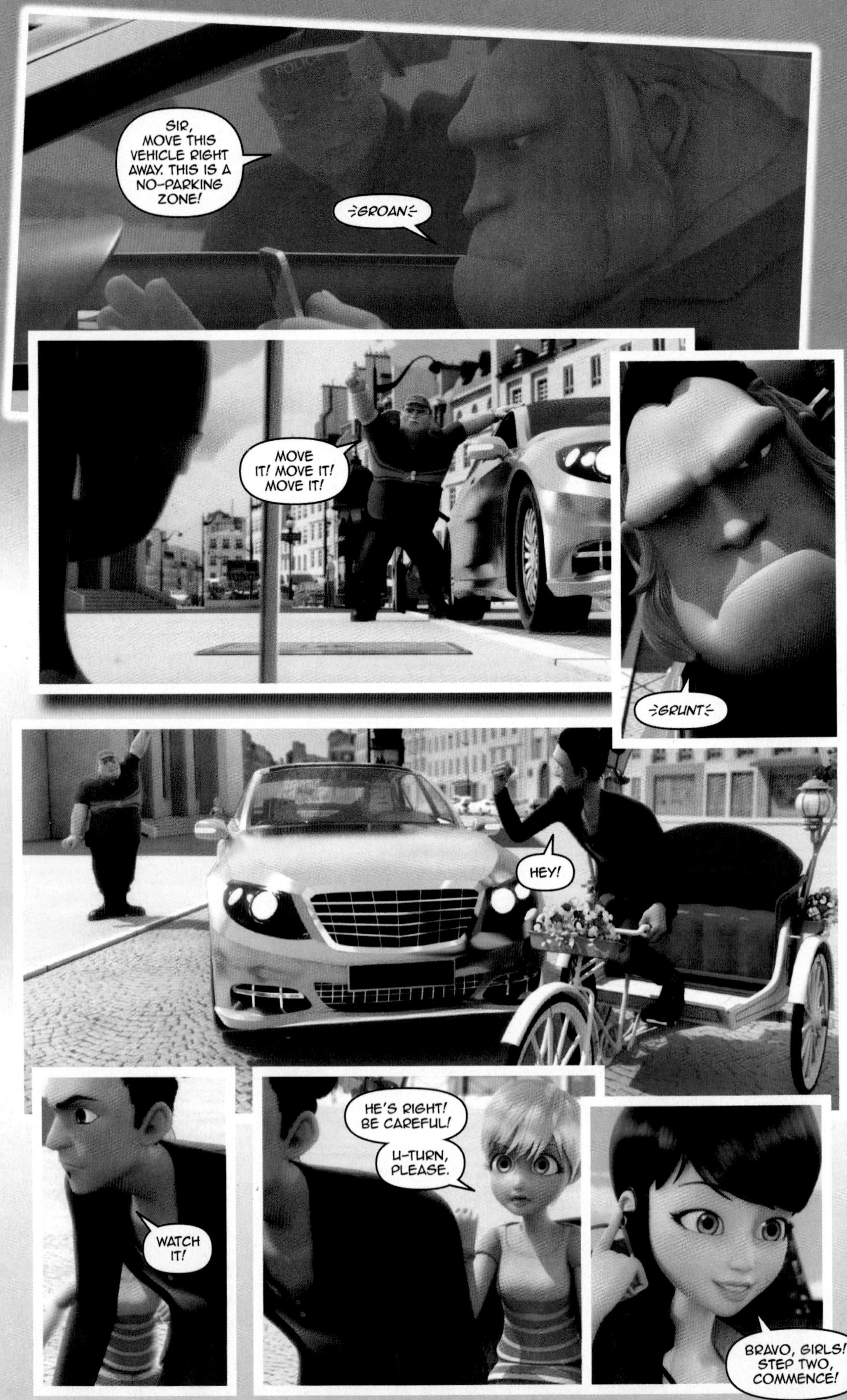
SIR, MOVE THIS VEHICLE RIGHT AWAY. THIS IS A NO-PARKING ZONE!
GROAN
MOVE IT! MOVE IT! MOVE IT!
GRUNT
HEY!
WATCH IT!
HE'S RIGHT! BE CAREFUL!
U-TURN, PLEASE.
BRAVO, GIRLS! STEP TWO, COMMENCE!

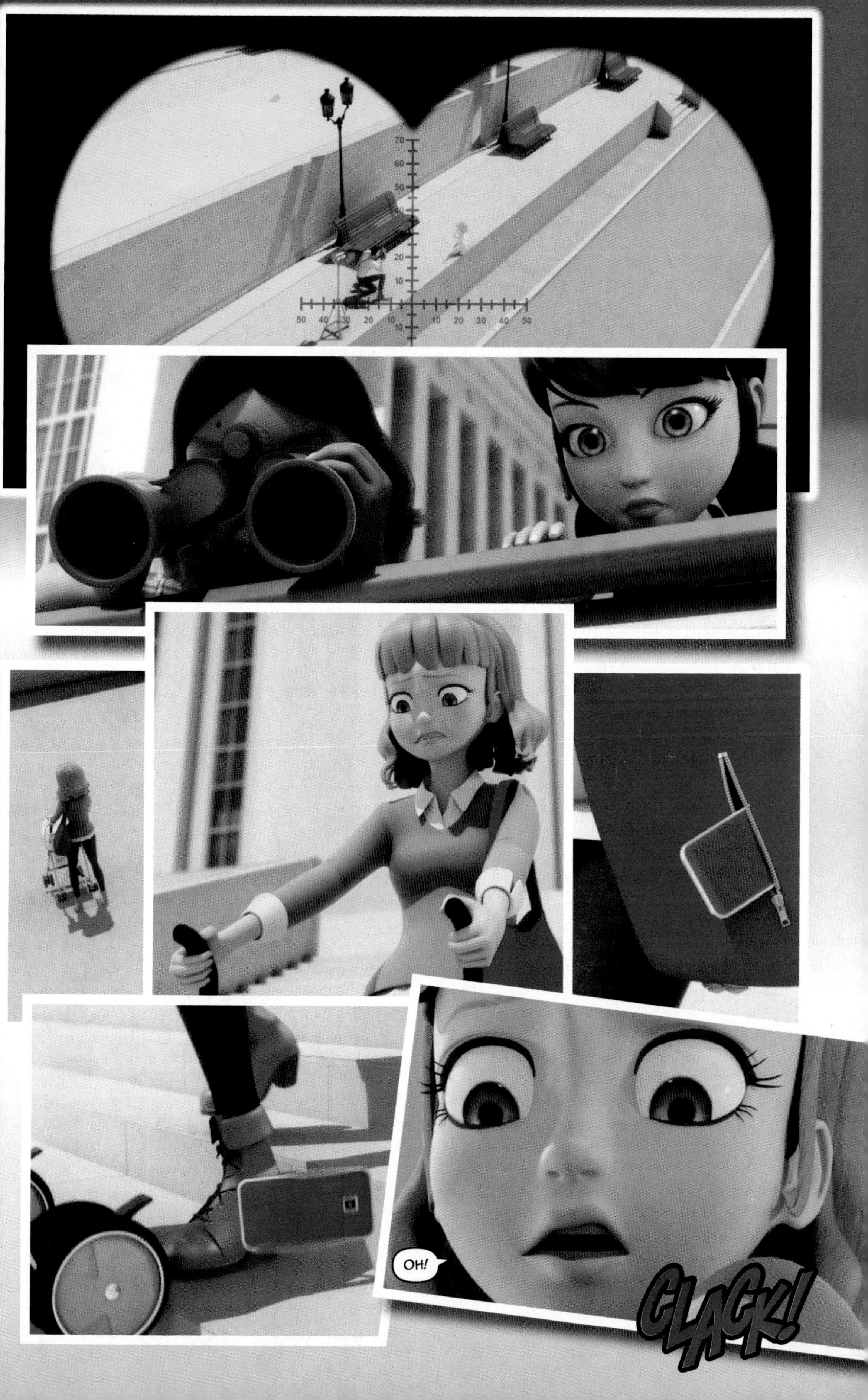
OH!
CLACK!

"LOTUS"—ER, MARINETTE—STAY HERE!

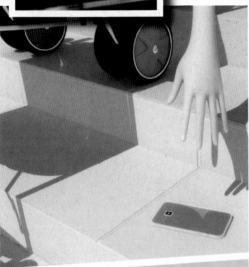

HELLO, MA'AM!

THANK YOU SO MUCH!

HELLO, LITTLE BABY!

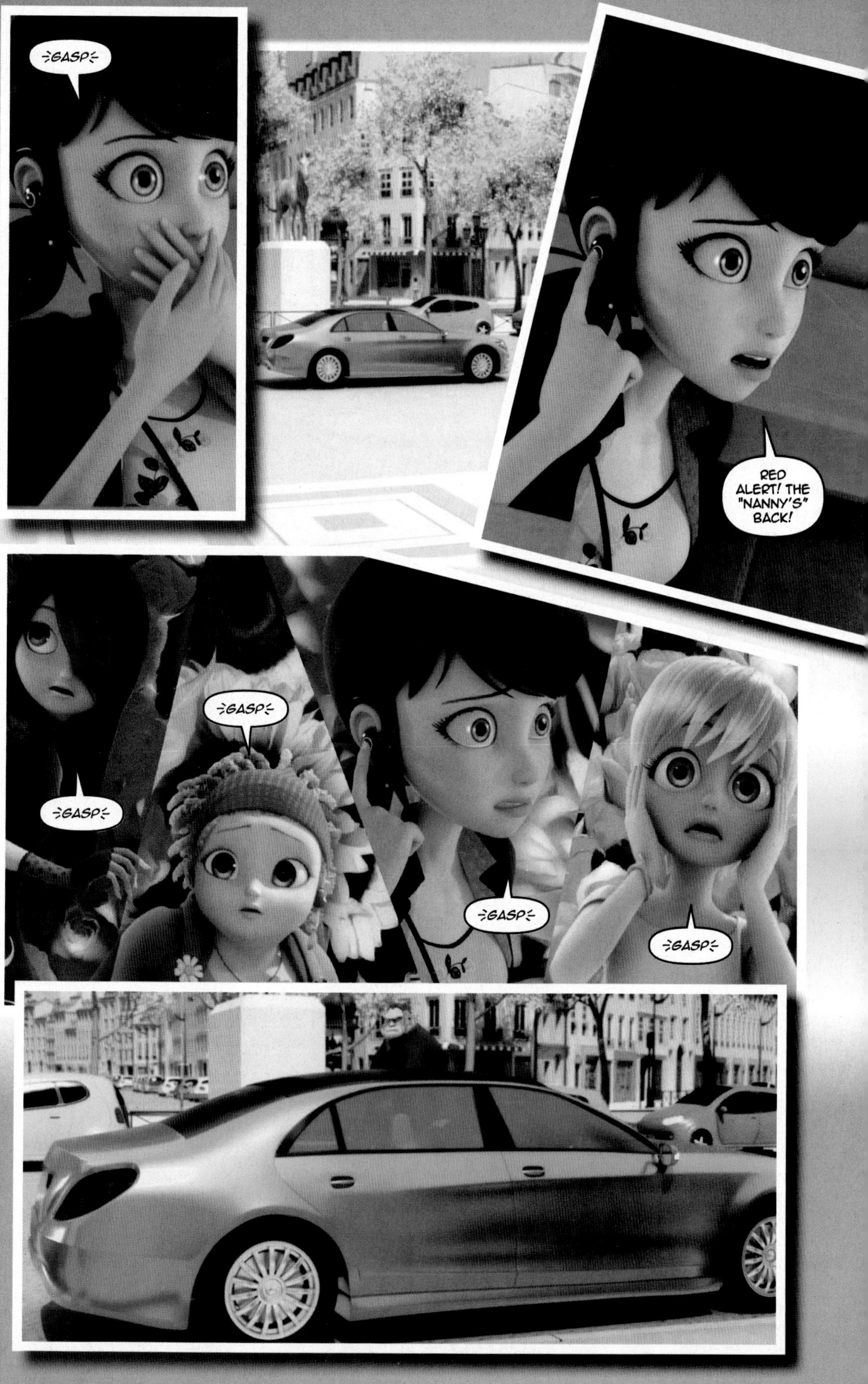

GASP
RED ALERT! THE "NANNY'S" BACK!
GASP
GASP
GASP
GASP

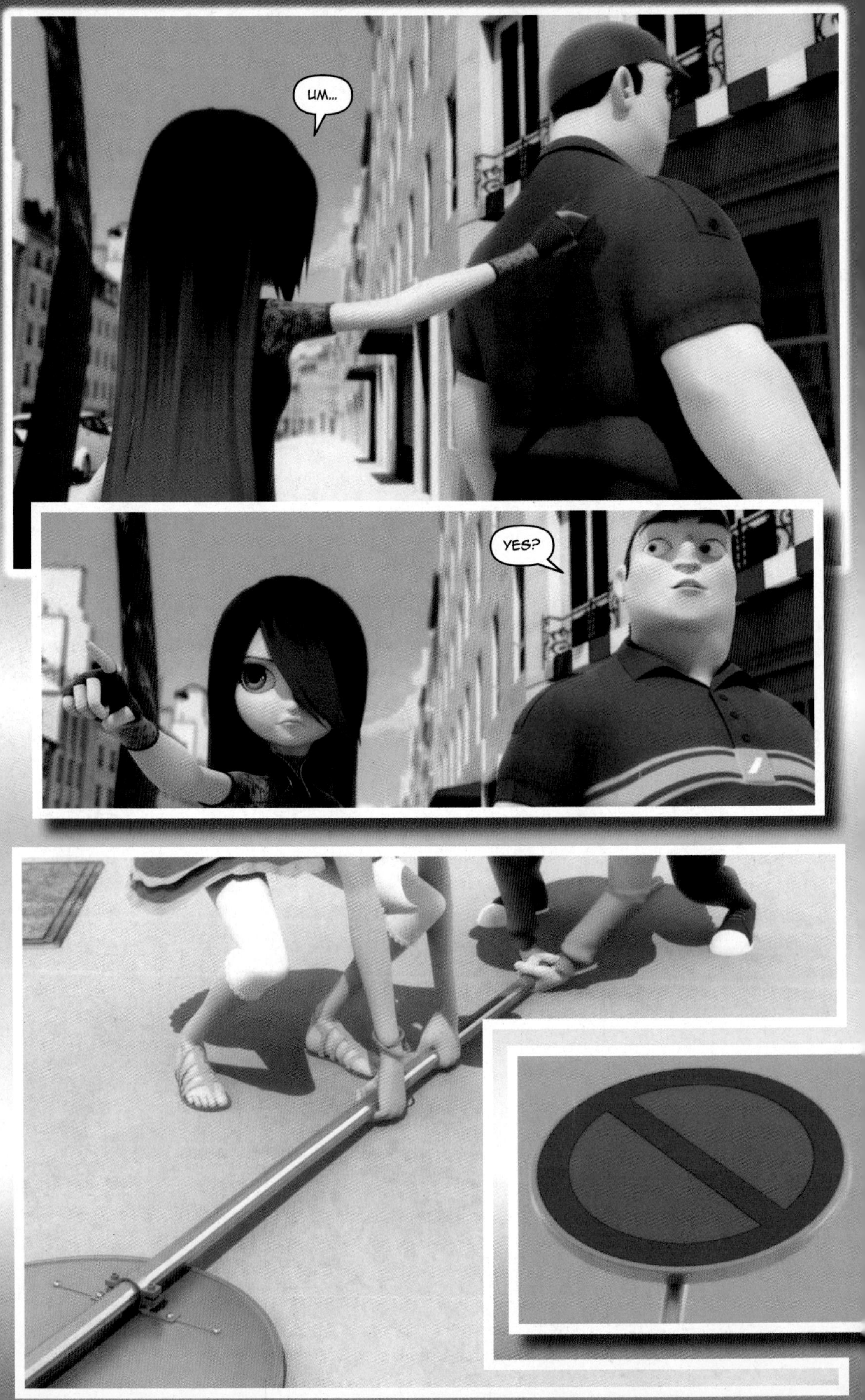
UM...
YES?

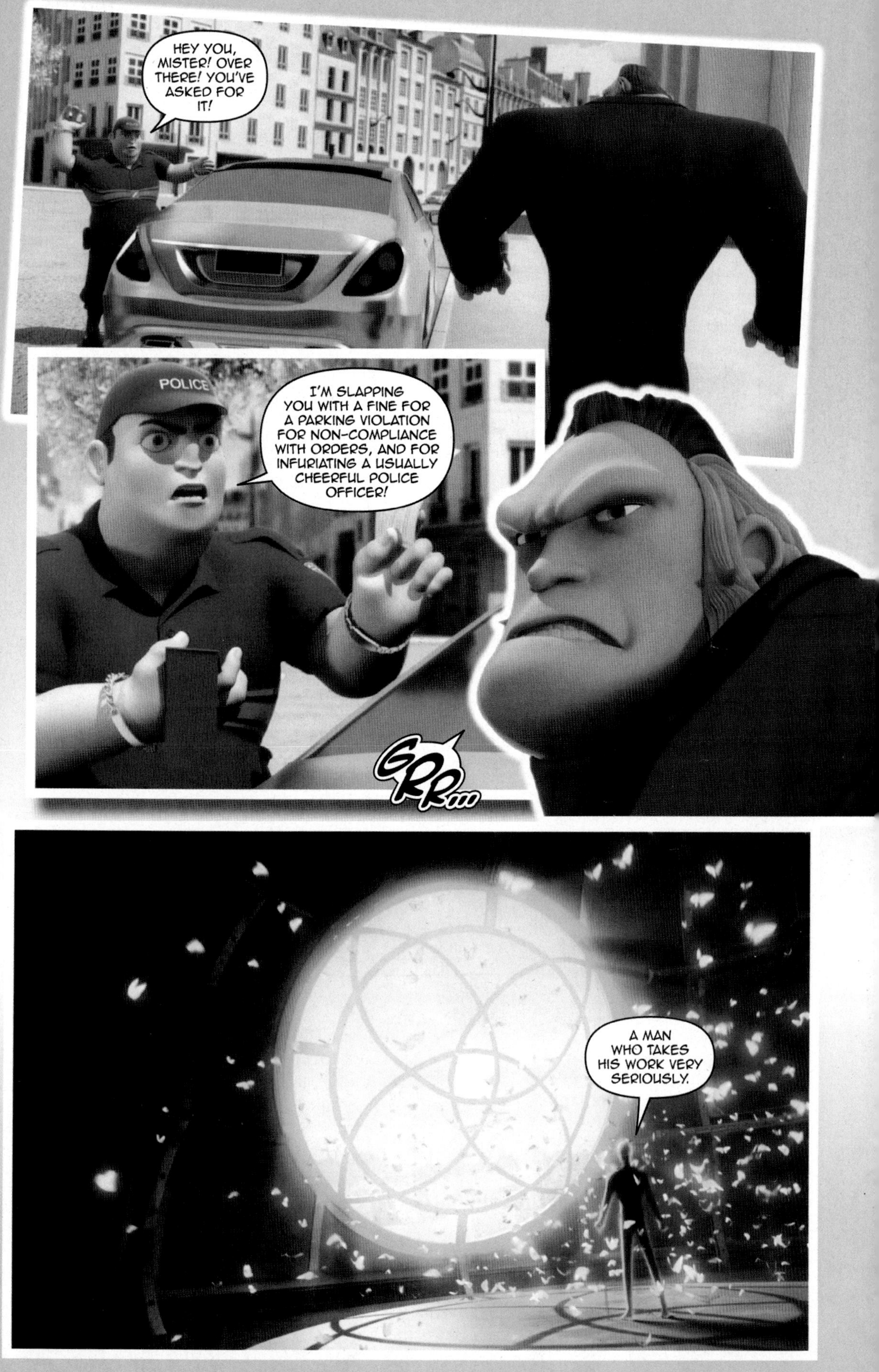
HEY YOU, MISTER! OVER THERE! YOU'VE ASKED FOR IT!
I'M SLAPPING YOU WITH A FINE FOR A PARKING VIOLATION FOR NON-COMPLIANCE WITH ORDERS, AND FOR INFURIATING A USUALLY CHEERFUL POLICE OFFICER!
POLICE
GRR...
A MAN WHO TAKES HIS WORK VERY SERIOUSLY.

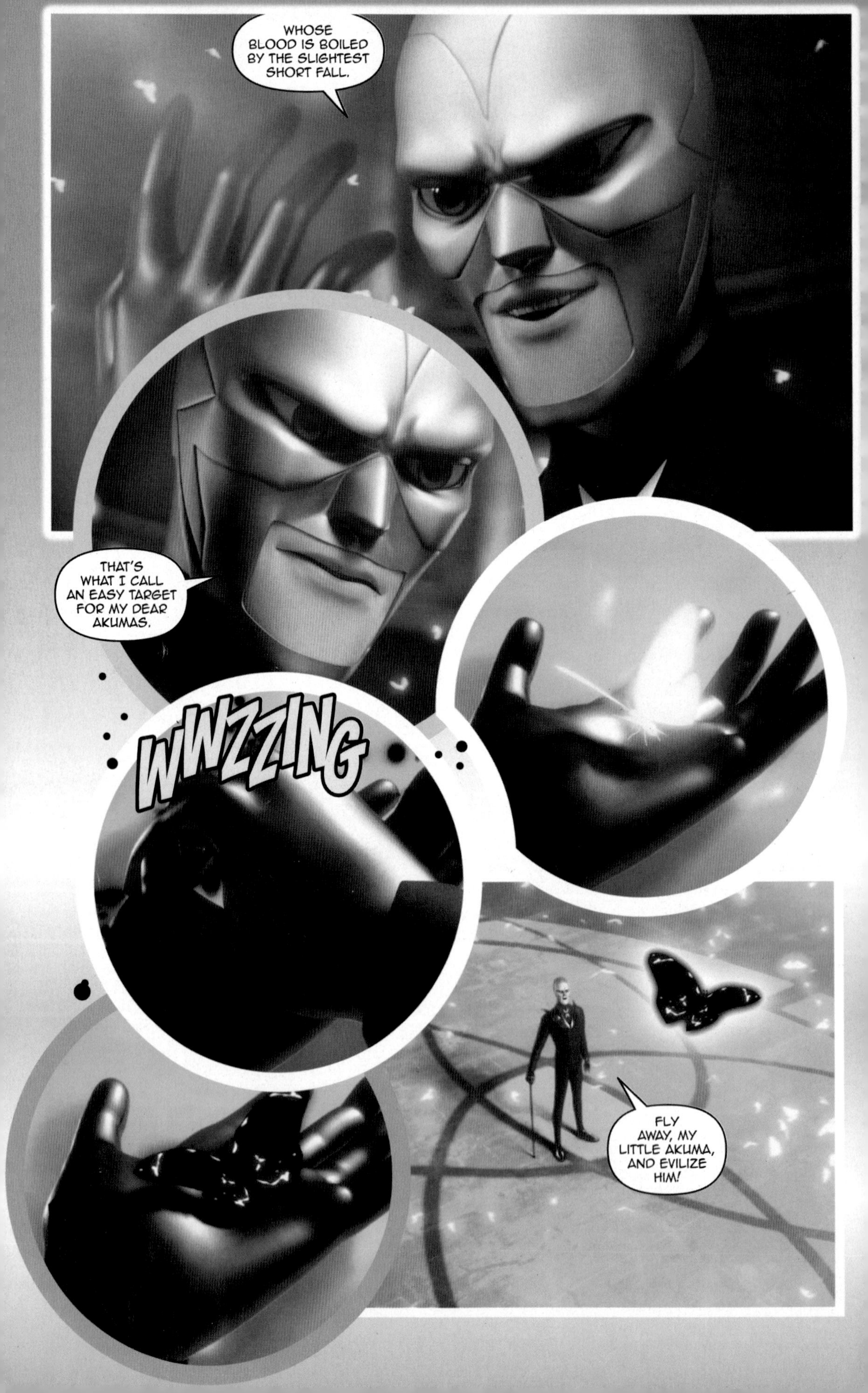
WHOSE BLOOD IS BOILED BY THE SLIGHTEST SHORT FALL.
THAT'S WHAT I CALL AN EASY TARGET FOR MY DEAR AKUMAS.
WWZZING
FLY AWAY, MY LITTLE AKUMA, AND EVILIZE HIM!

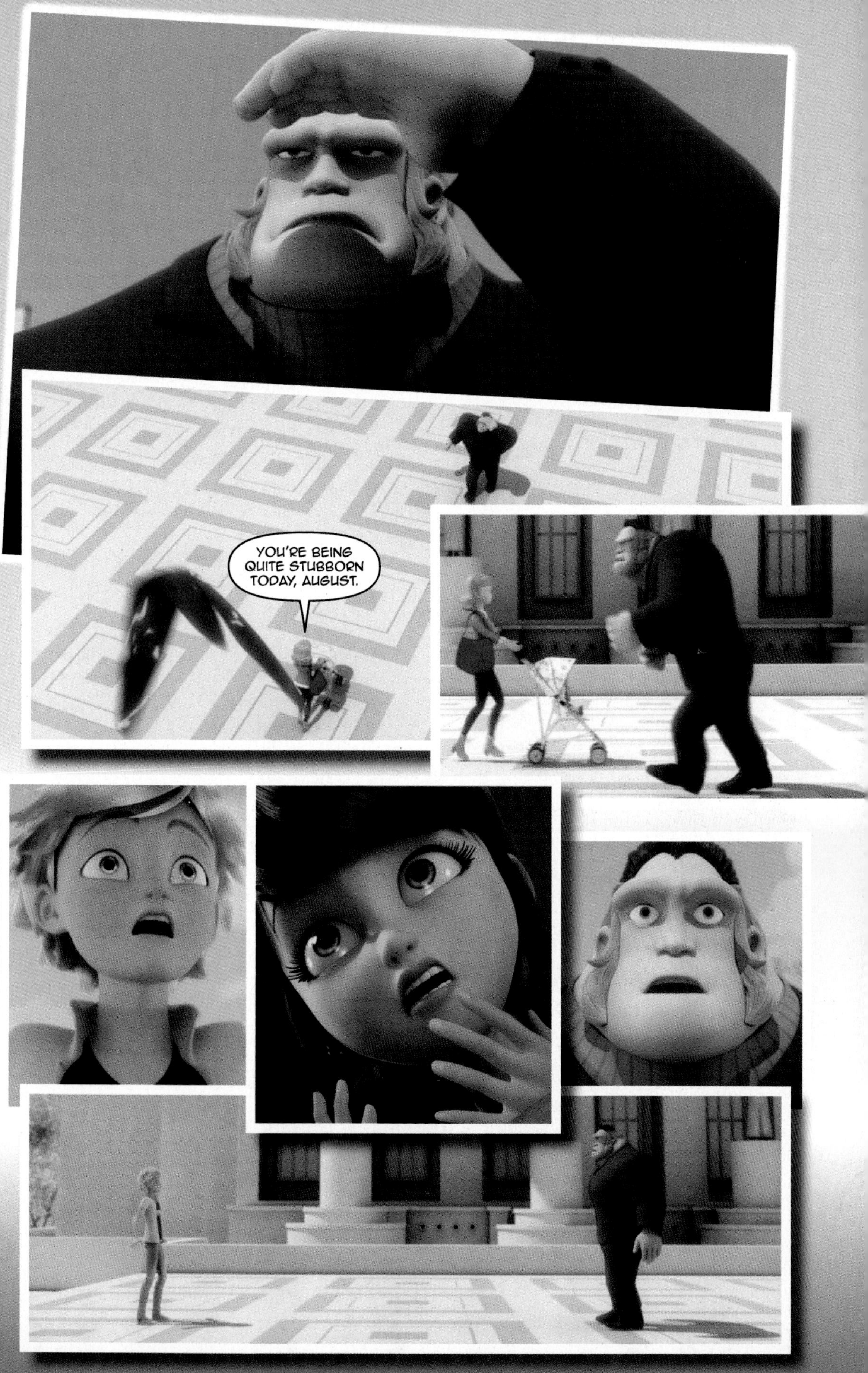
YOU'RE BEING QUITE STUBBORN TODAY, AUGUST.

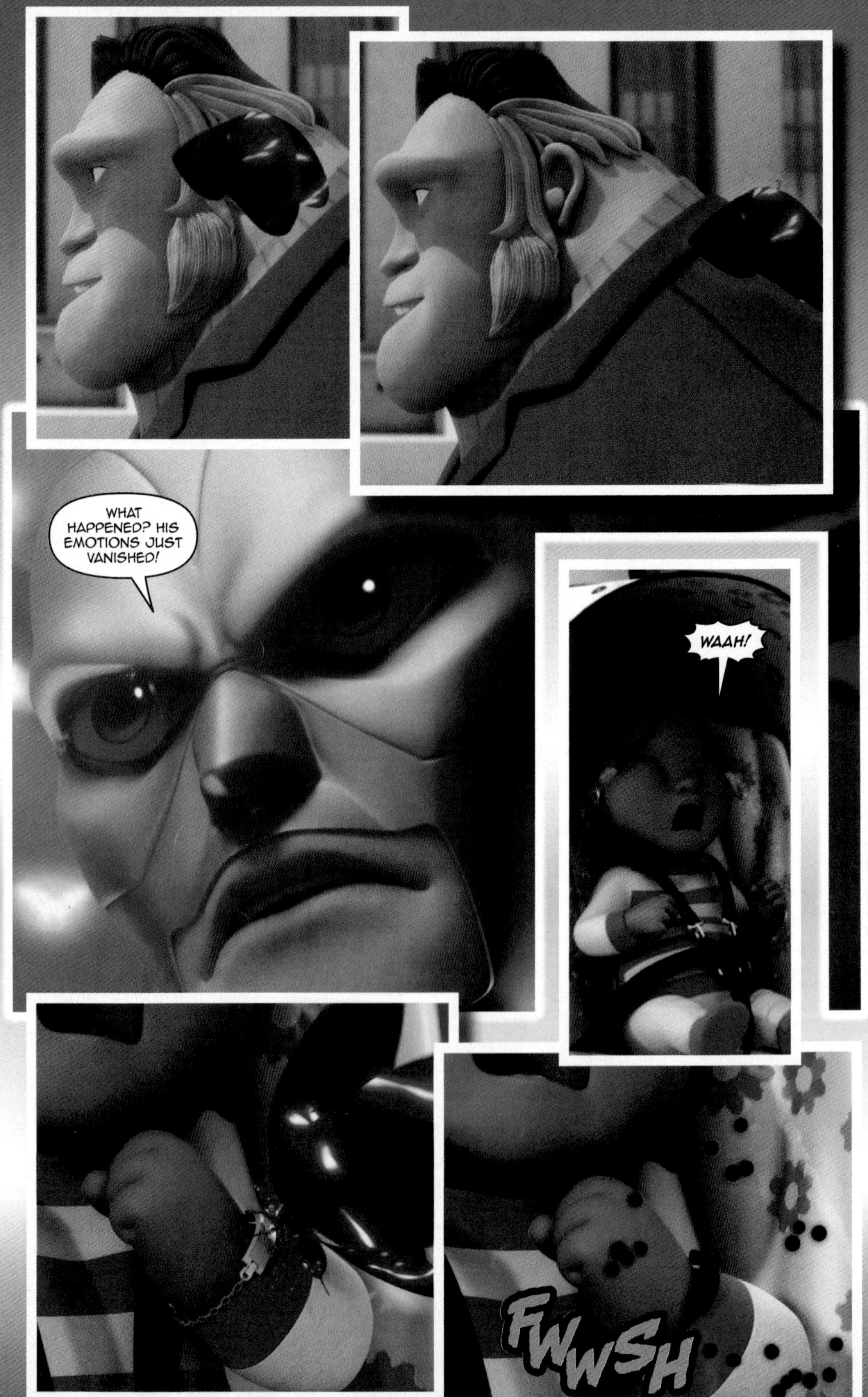
WHAT HAPPENED? HIS EMOTIONS JUST VANISHED!
WAAH!
FWWSH

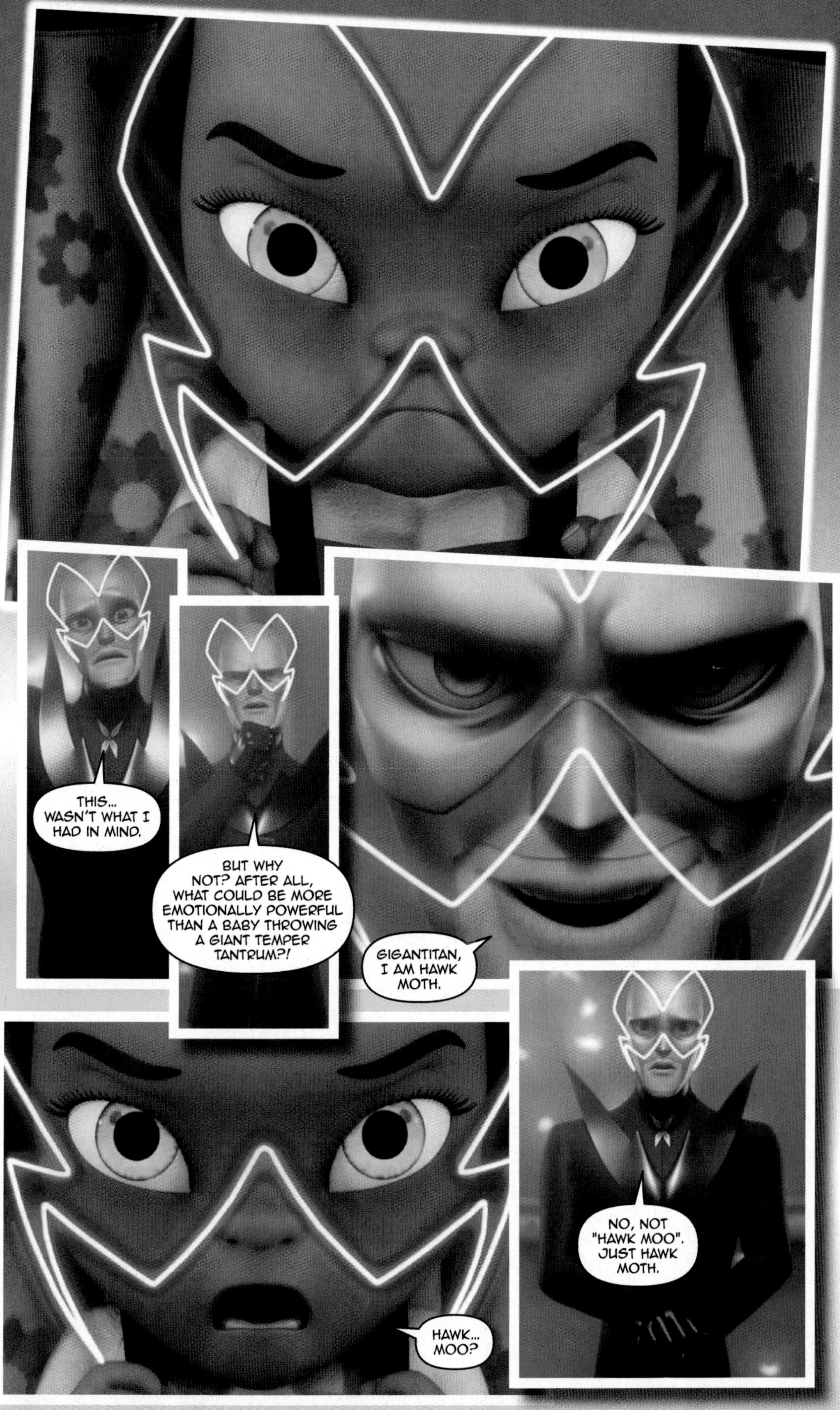
THIS... WASN'T WHAT I HAD IN MIND.
BUT WHY NOT? AFTER ALL, WHAT COULD BE MORE EMOTIONALLY POWERFUL THAN A BABY THROWING A GIANT TEMPER TANTRUM?!
GIGANTITAN, I AM HAWK MOTH.
HAWK... MOO?
NO, NOT "HAWK MOO". JUST HAWK MOTH.

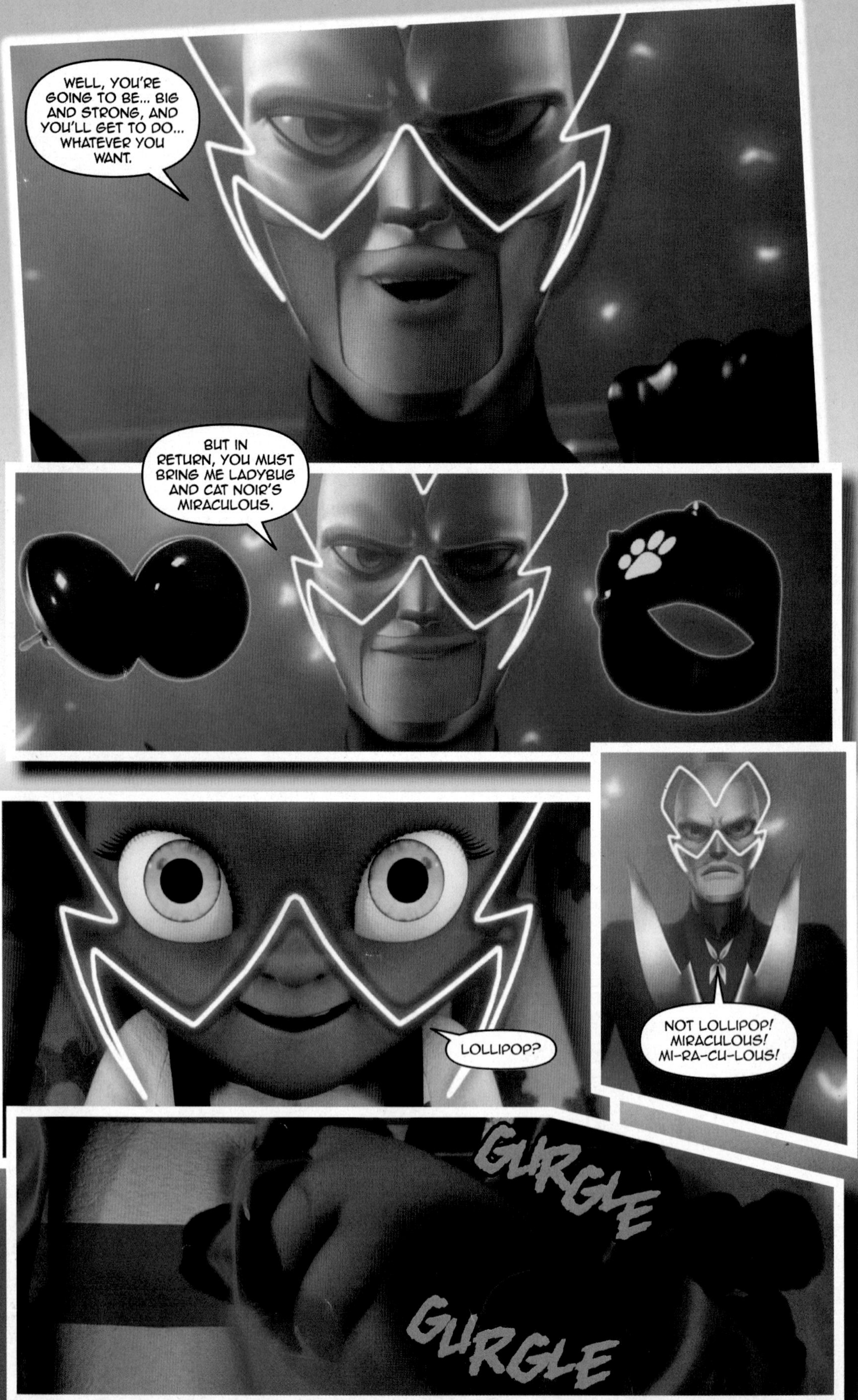
WELL, YOU'RE GOING TO BE... BIG AND STRONG, AND YOU'LL GET TO DO... WHATEVER YOU WANT.
BUT IN RETURN, YOU MUST BRING ME LADYBUG AND CAT NOIR'S MIRACULOUS.
LOLLIPOP?
NOT LOLLIPOP! MIRACULOUS! MI-RA-CU-LOUS!
GURGLE
GURGLE

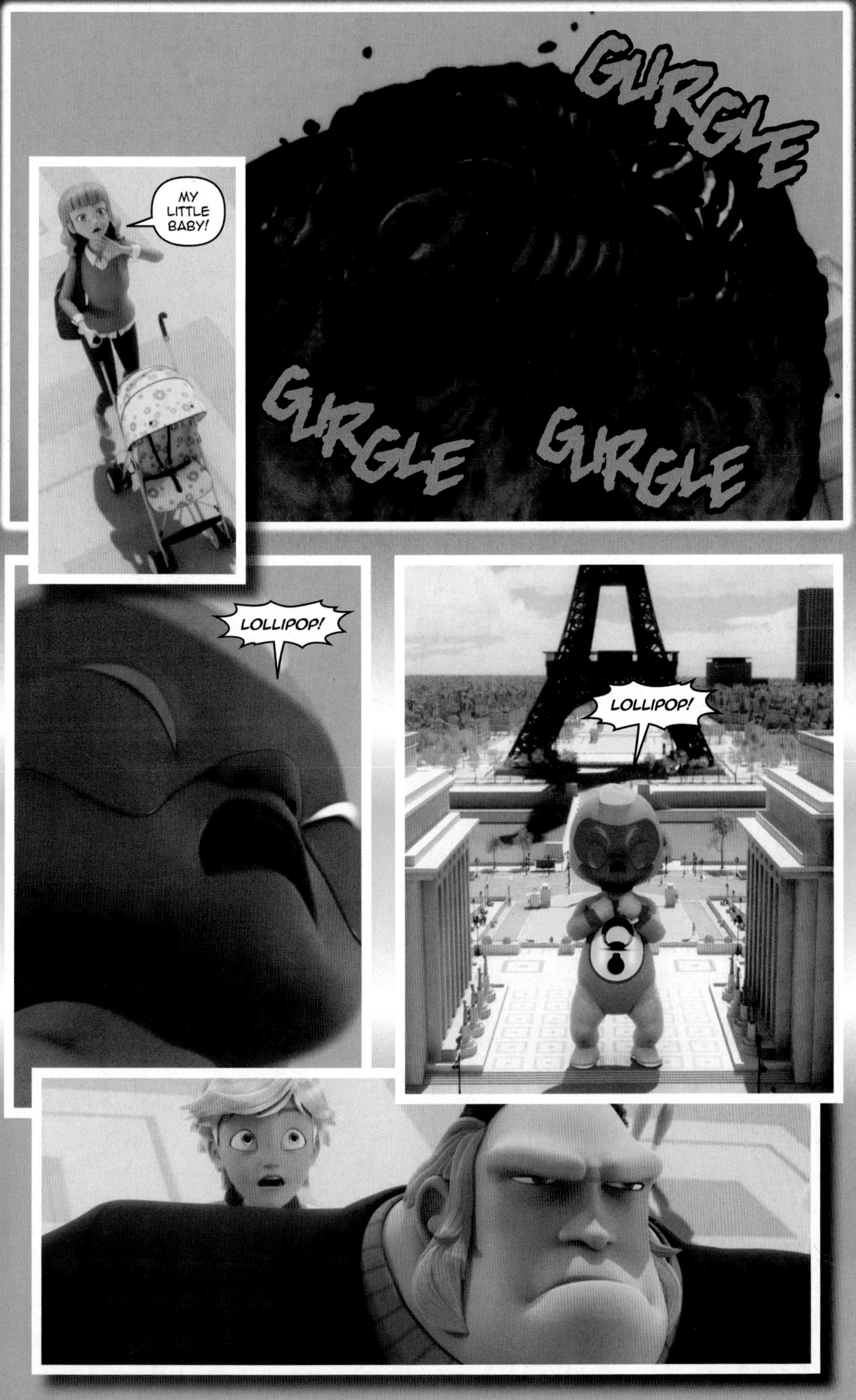
GURGLE
MY LITTLE BABY!
GURGLE
GURGLE
LOLLIPOP!
LOLLIPOP!

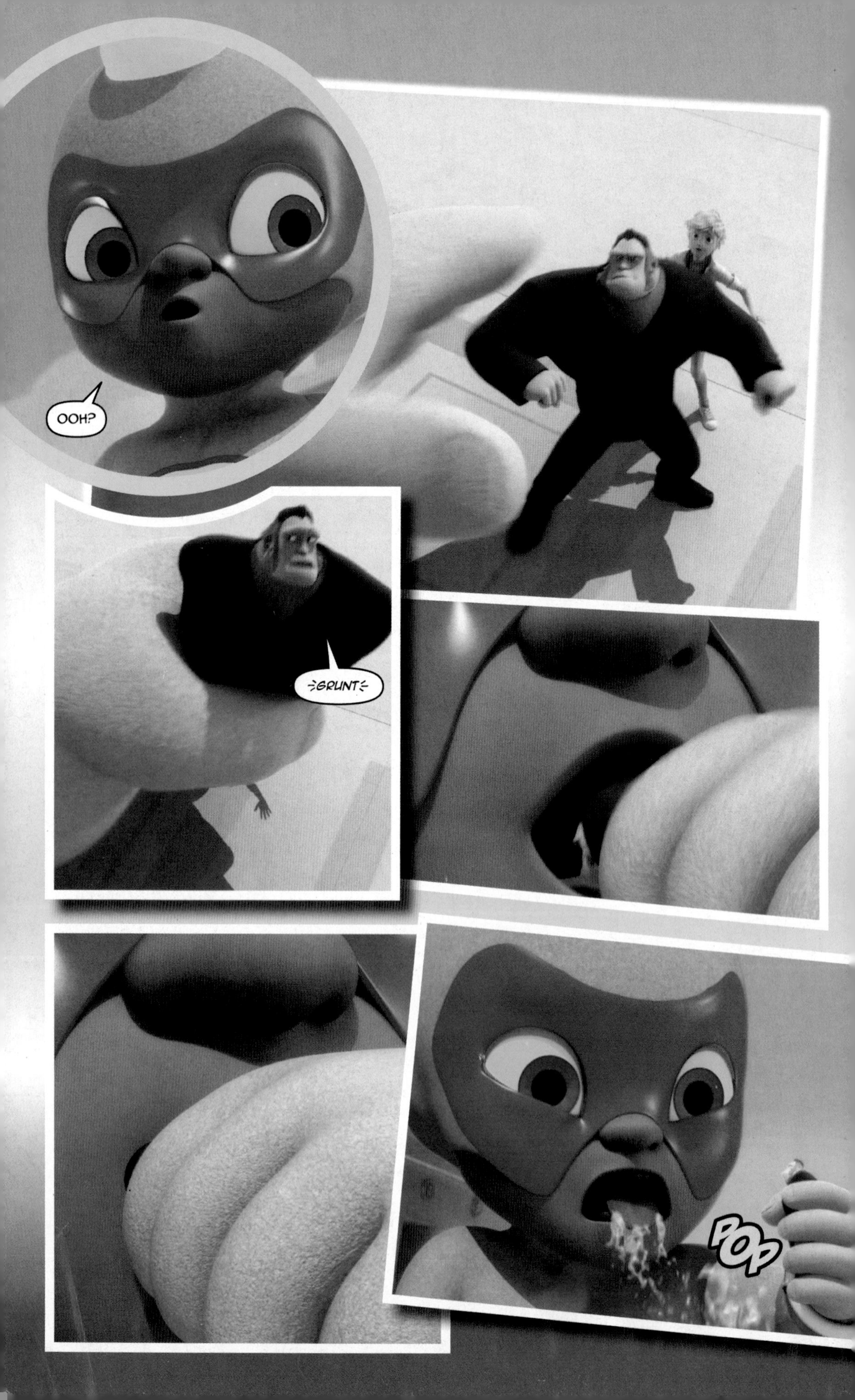
OOH?
GRUNT
POP

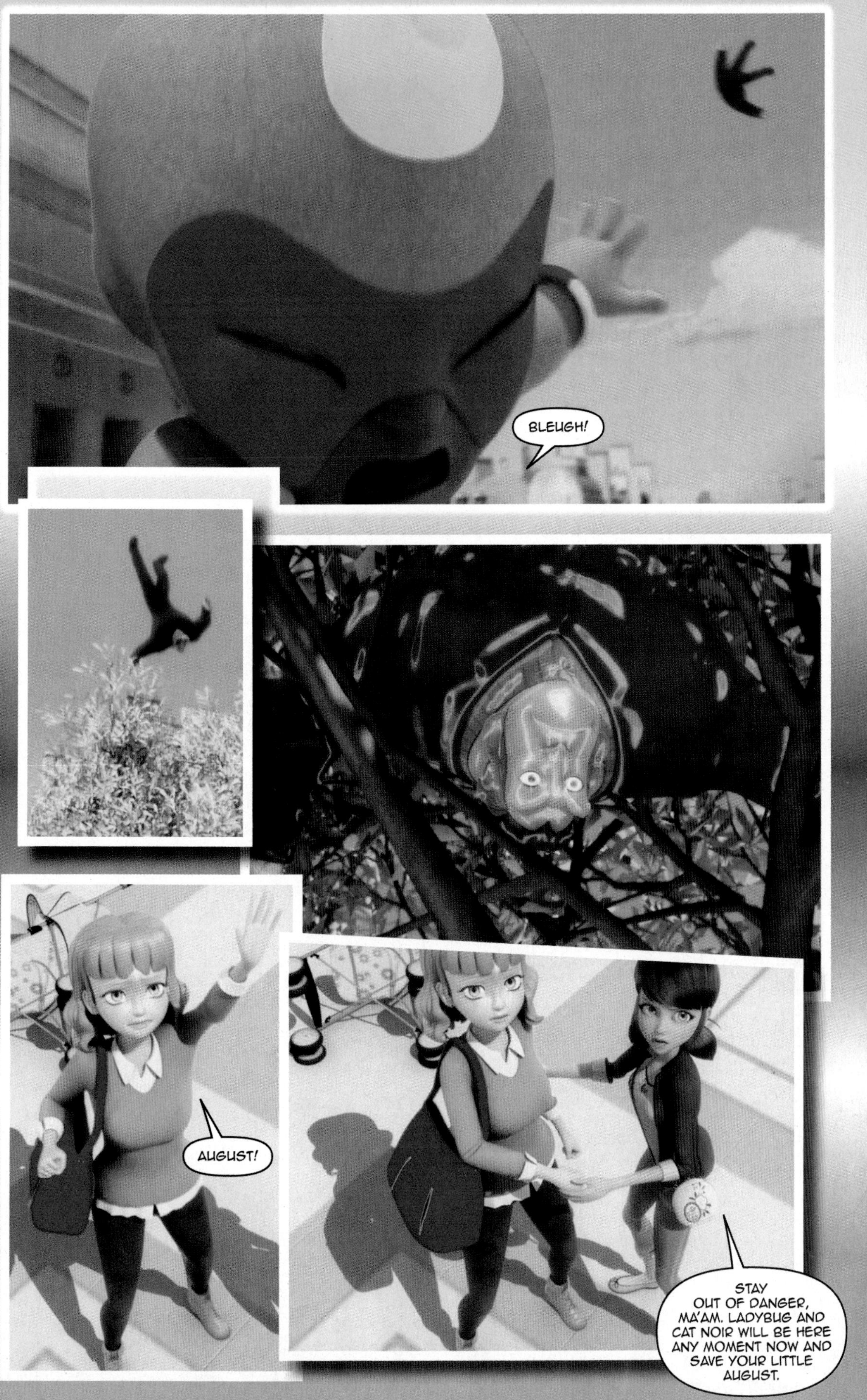
BLEUGH!
AUGUST!
STAY OUT OF DANGER, MA'AM. LADYBUG AND CAT NOIR WILL BE HERE ANY MOMENT NOW AND SAVE YOUR LITTLE AUGUST.

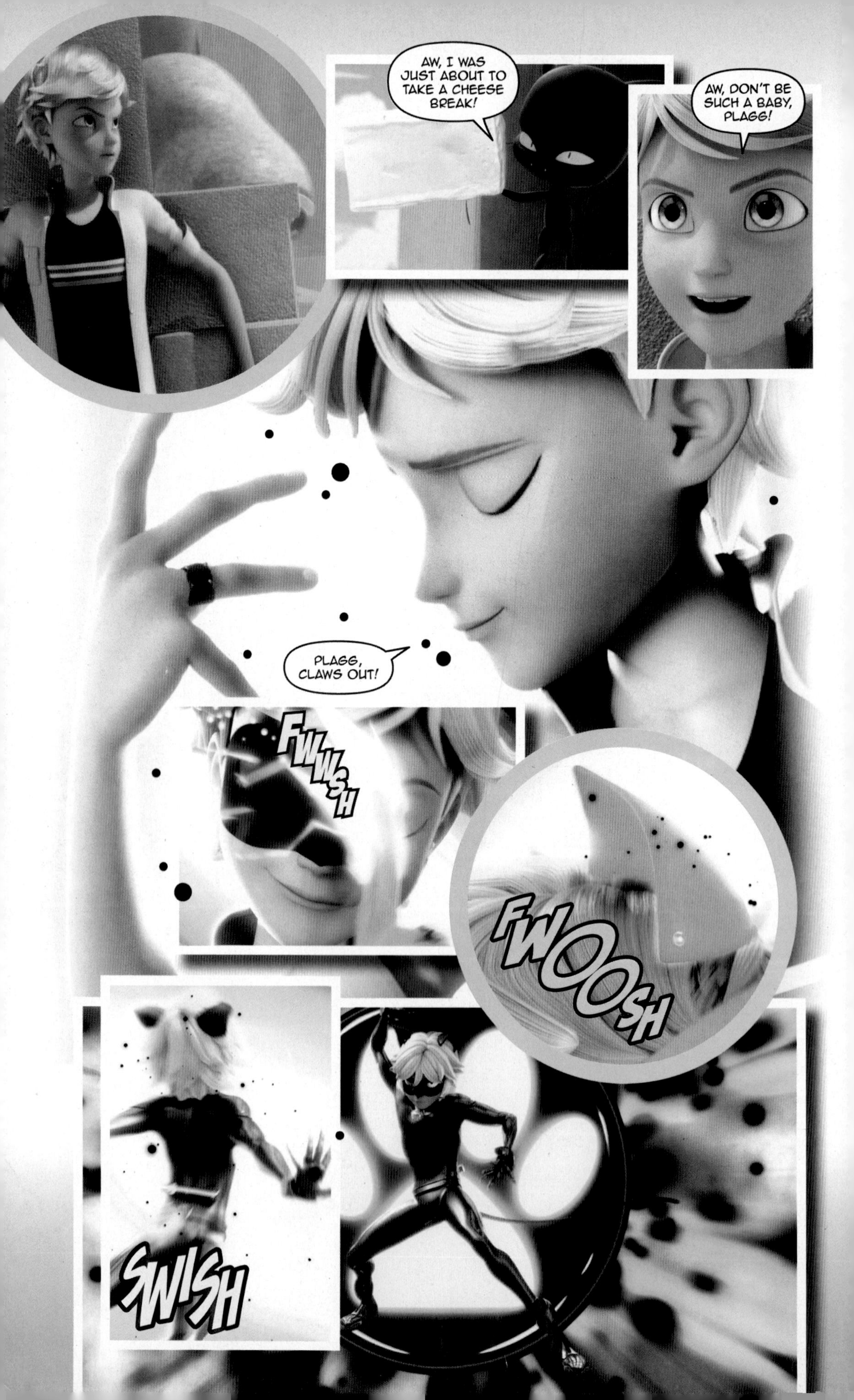
AW, I WAS JUST ABOUT TO TAKE A CHEESE BREAK!
AW, DON'T BE SUCH A BABY, PLAGG!
PLAGG, CLAWS OUT!
FWWSH
FWOOSH
SWISH

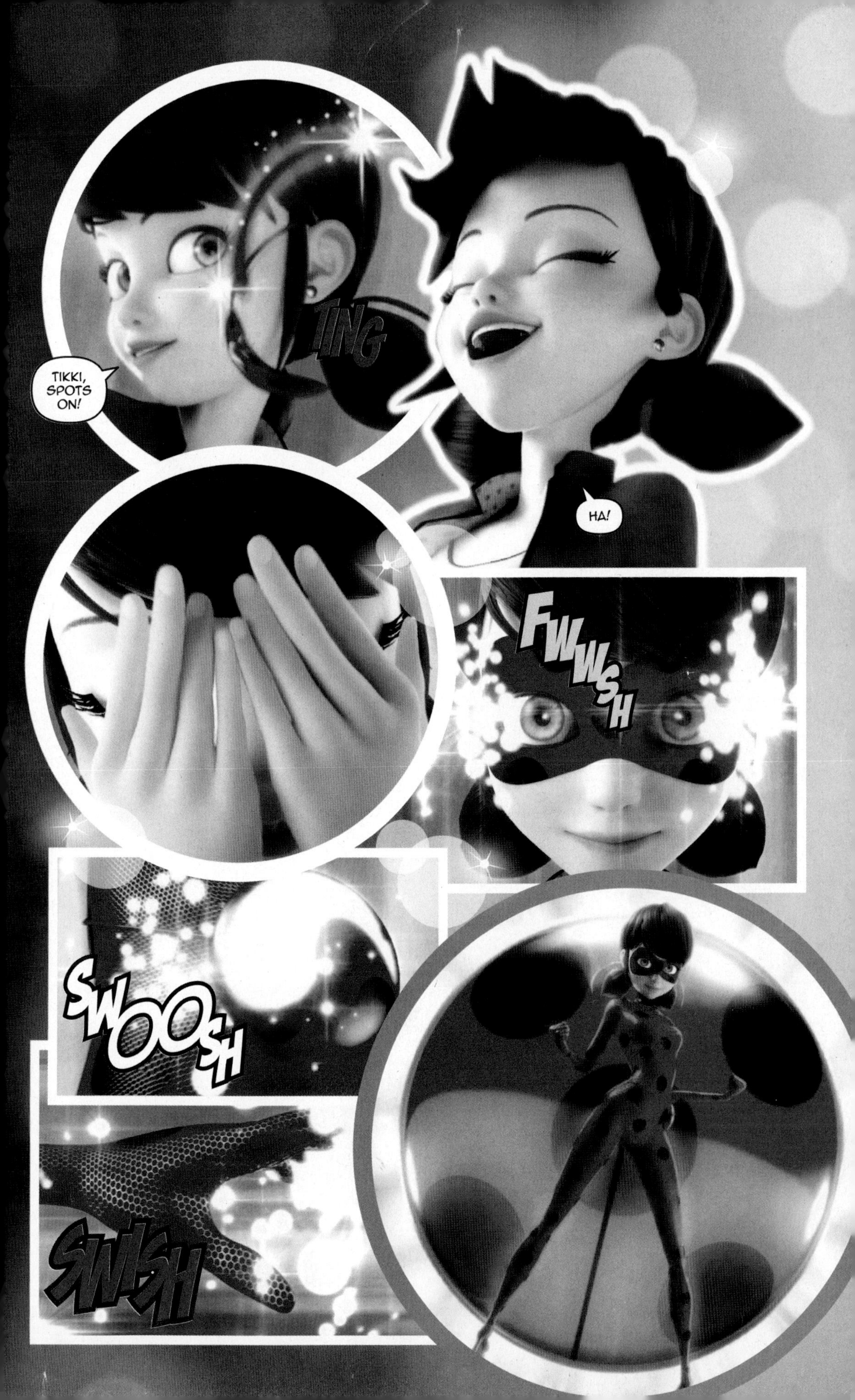
TIKKI, SPOTS ON!
TING
HA!
FWWSH
SWOOSH
SWISH

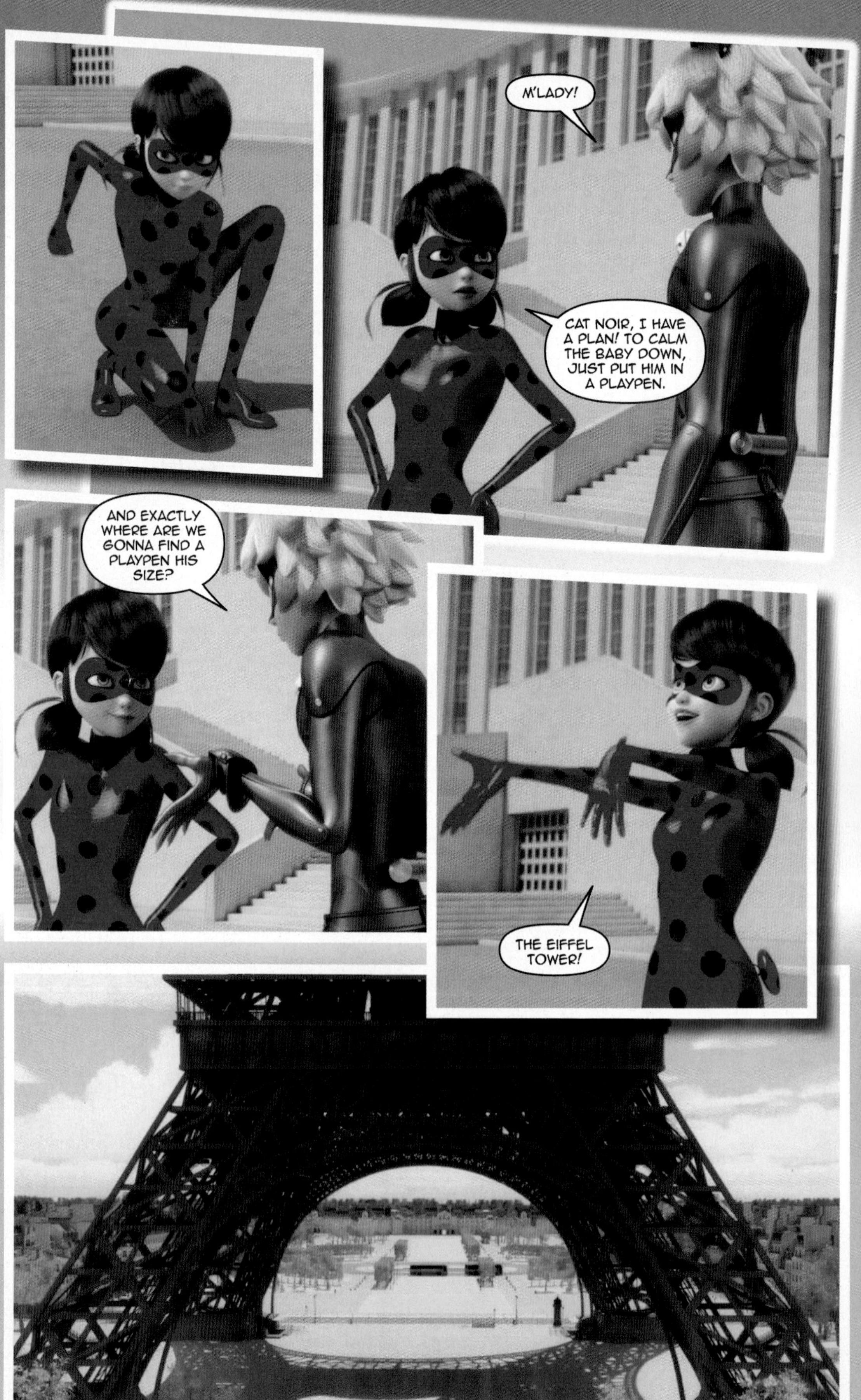
M'LADY!
CAT NOIR, I HAVE A PLAN! TO CALM THE BABY DOWN, JUST PUT HIM IN A PLAYPEN.
AND EXACTLY WHERE ARE WE GONNA FIND A PLAYPEN HIS SIZE?
THE EIFFEL TOWER!

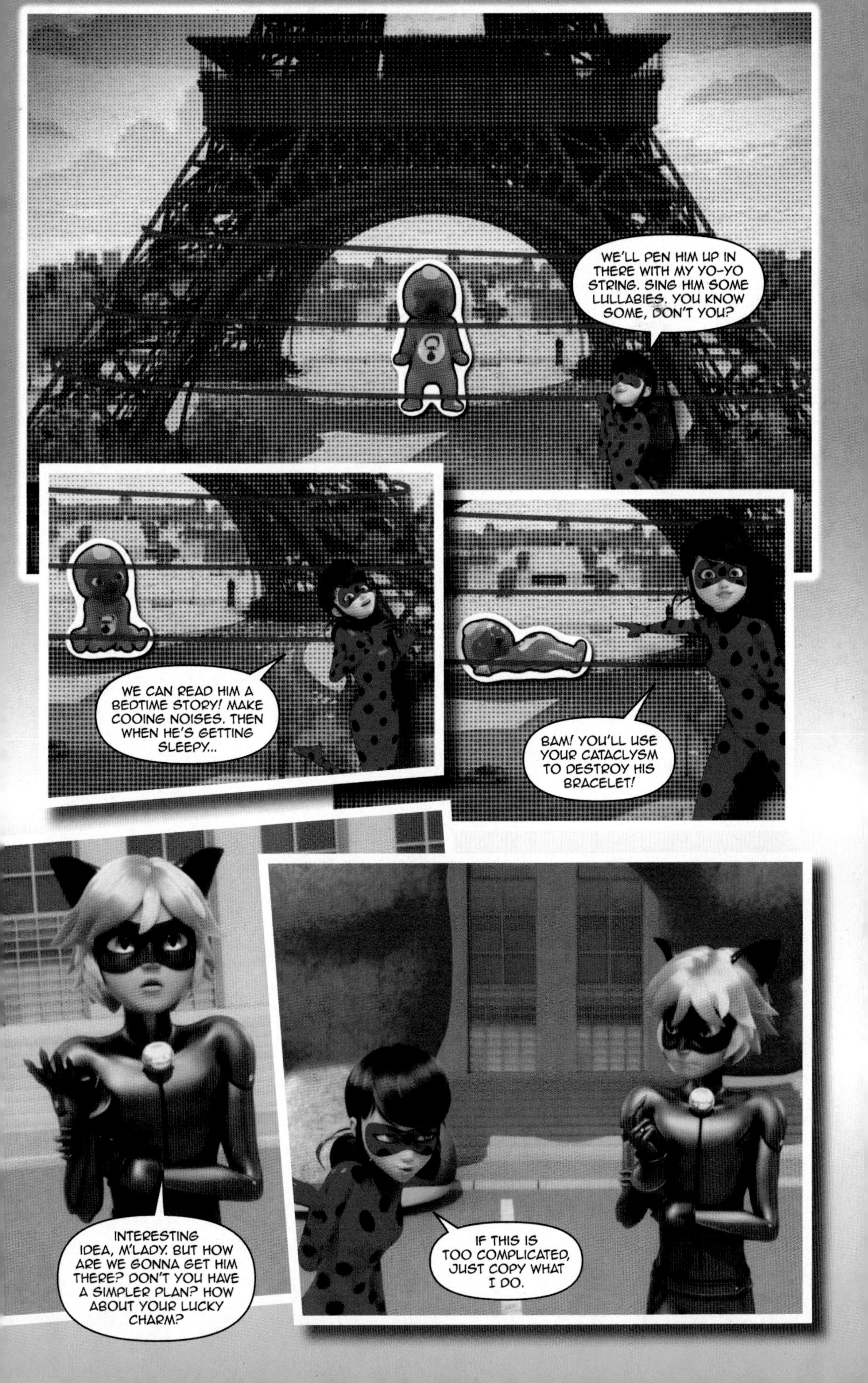
WE'LL PEN HIM UP IN THERE WITH MY YO-YO STRING. SING HIM SOME LULLABIES. YOU KNOW SOME, DON'T YOU?
WE CAN READ HIM A BEDTIME STORY! MAKE COOING NOISES. THEN WHEN HE'S GETTING SLEEPY...
BAM! YOU'LL USE YOUR CATACLYSM TO DESTROY HIS BRACELET!
INTERESTING IDEA, M'LADY. BUT HOW ARE WE GONNA GET HIM THERE? DON'T YOU HAVE A SIMPLER PLAN? HOW ABOUT YOUR LUCKY CHARM?
IF THIS IS TOO COMPLICATED, JUST COPY WHAT I DO.

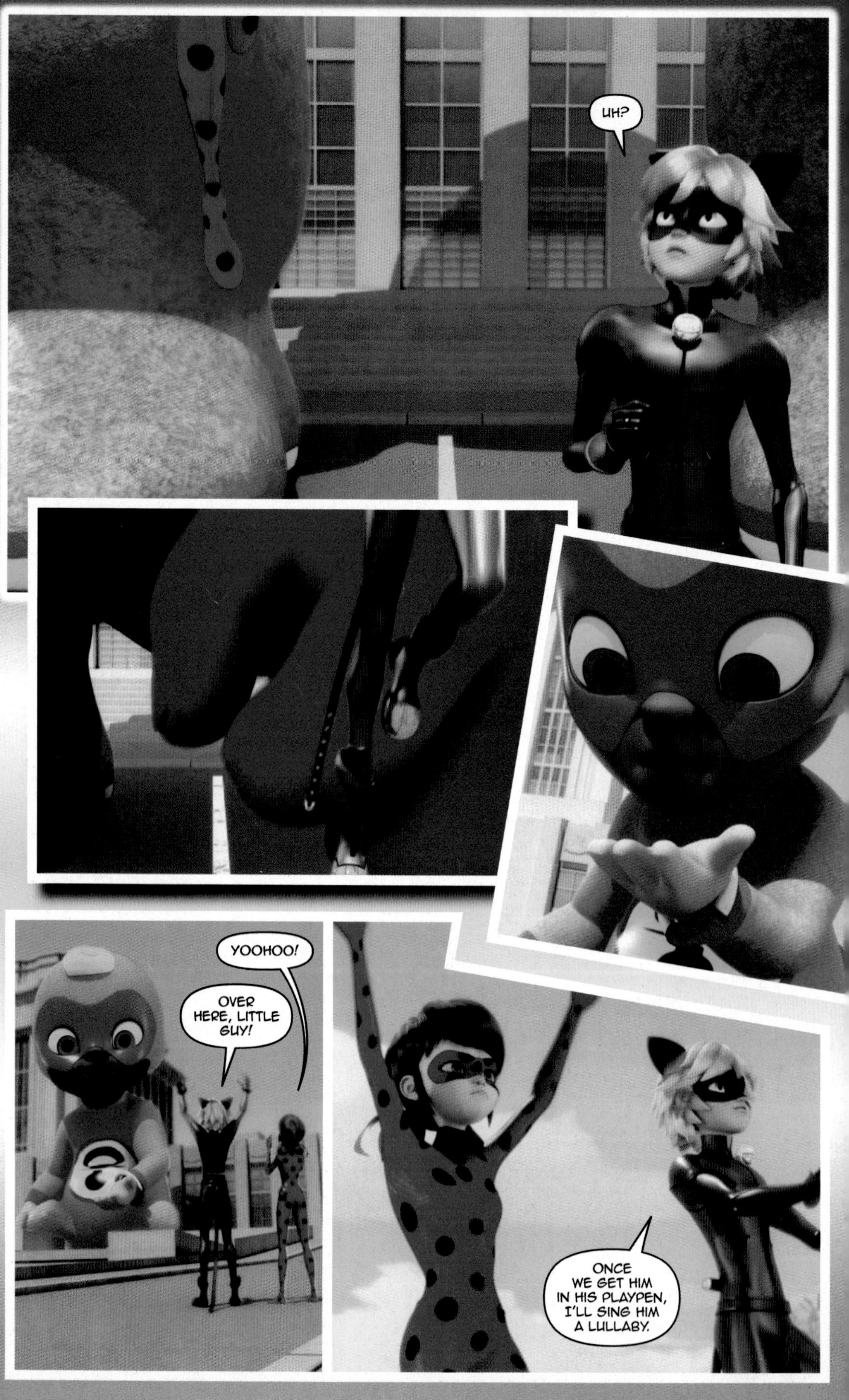
UH?
YOOHOO!
OVER HERE, LITTLE GUY!
ONCE WE GET HIM IN HIS PLAYPEN, I'LL SING HIM A LULLABY.

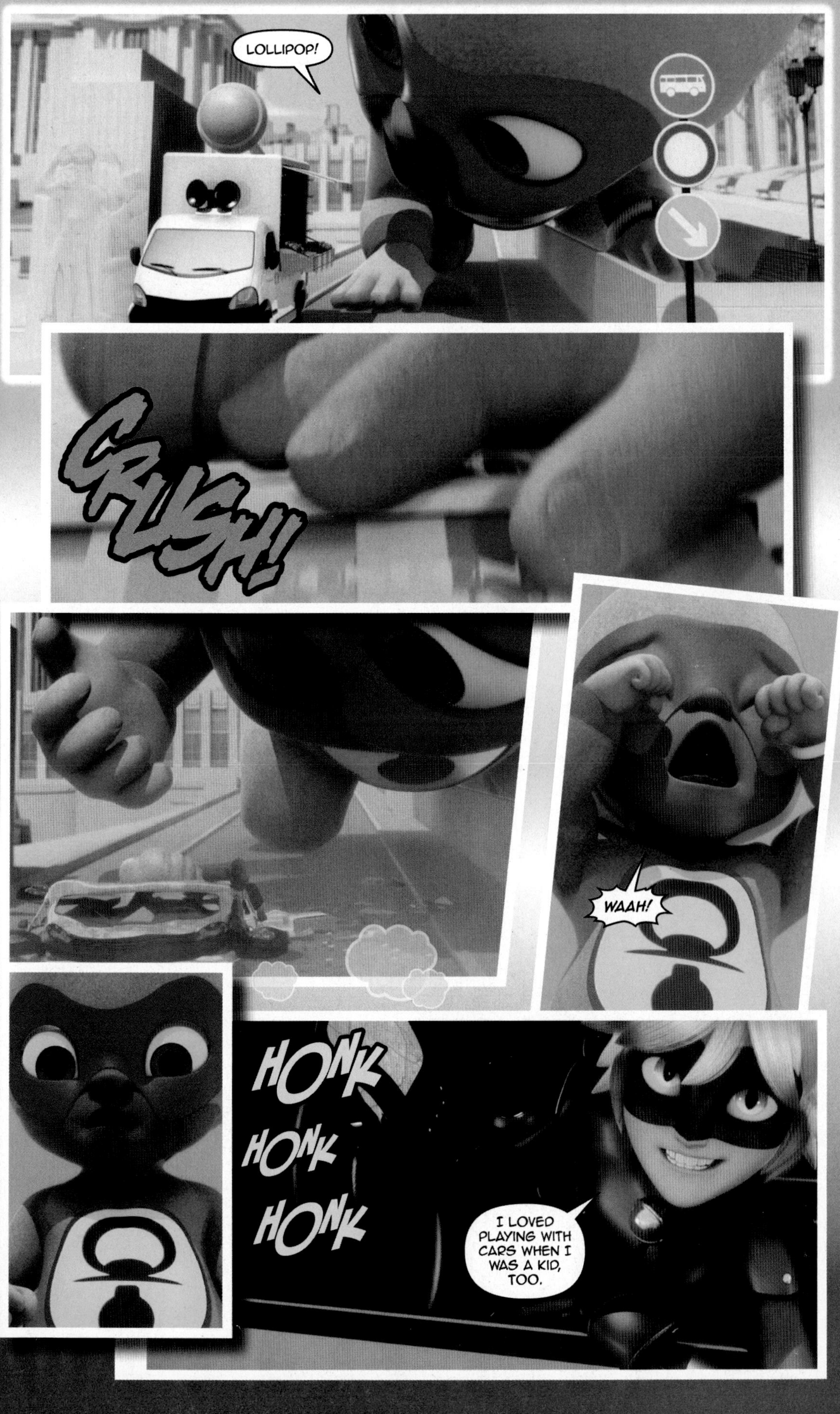
LOLLIPOP!
CRUSH!
WAAH!
HONK
HONK
HONK
I LOVED PLAYING WITH CARS WHEN I WAS A KID, TOO.

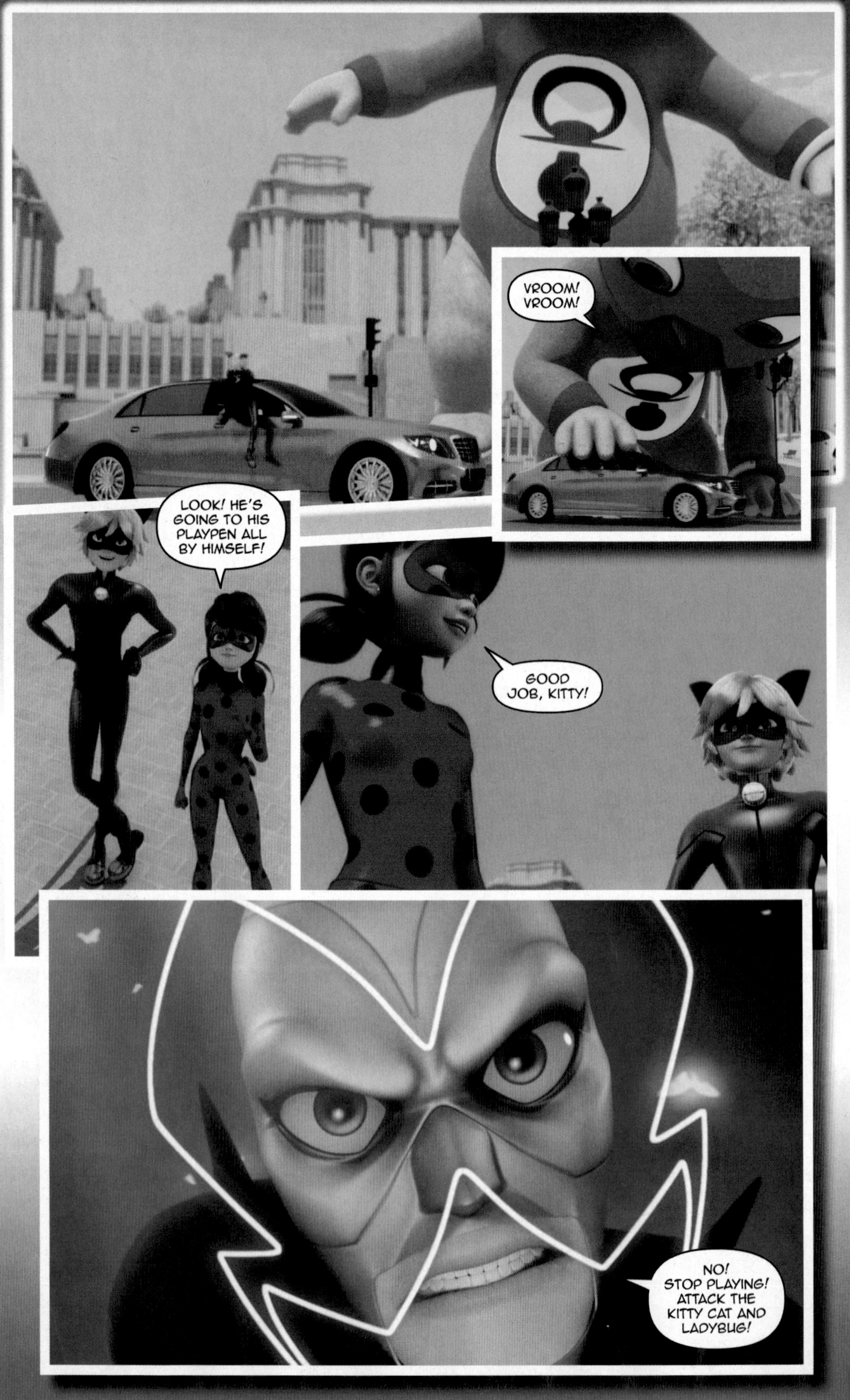
VROOM! VROOM!
LOOK! HE'S GOING TO HIS PLAYPEN ALL BY HIMSELF!
GOOD JOB, KITTY!
NO! STOP PLAYING! ATTACK THE KITTY CAT AND LADYBUG!

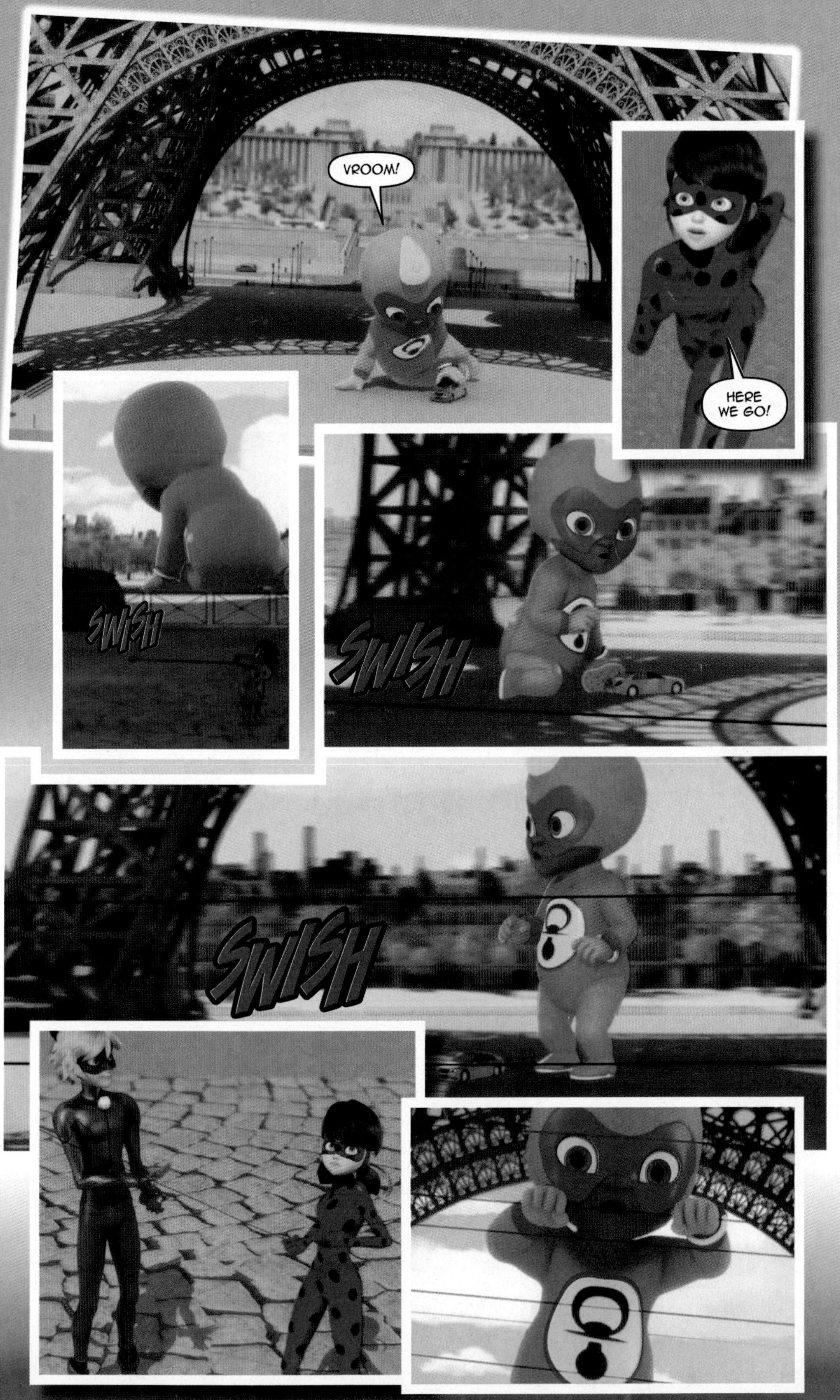
VROOM!
HERE WE GO!
SWISH
SWISH
SWISH

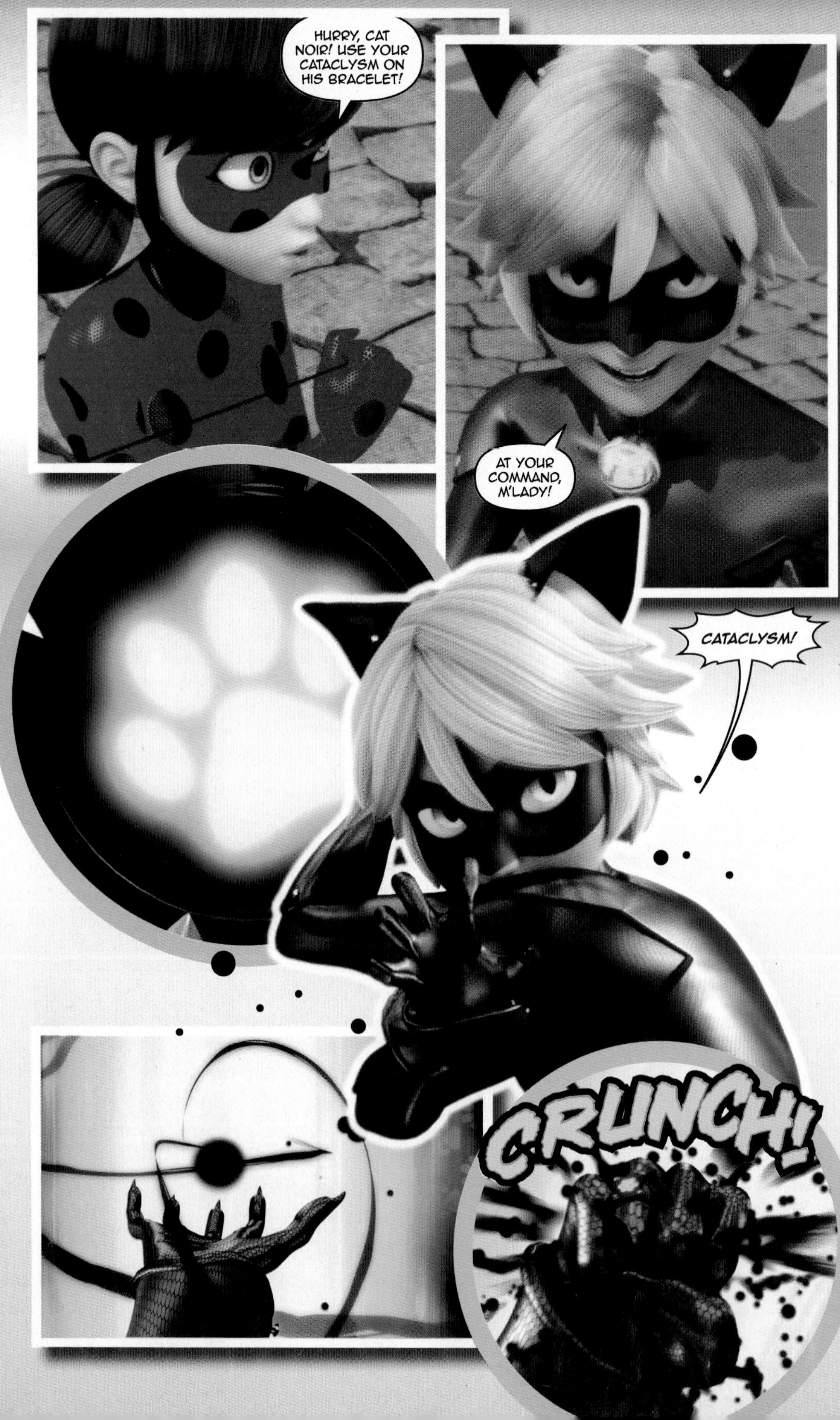
HURRY, CAT NOIR! USE YOUR CATACLYSM ON HIS BRACELET!
AT YOUR COMMAND, M'LADY!
CATACLYSM!
CRUNCH!

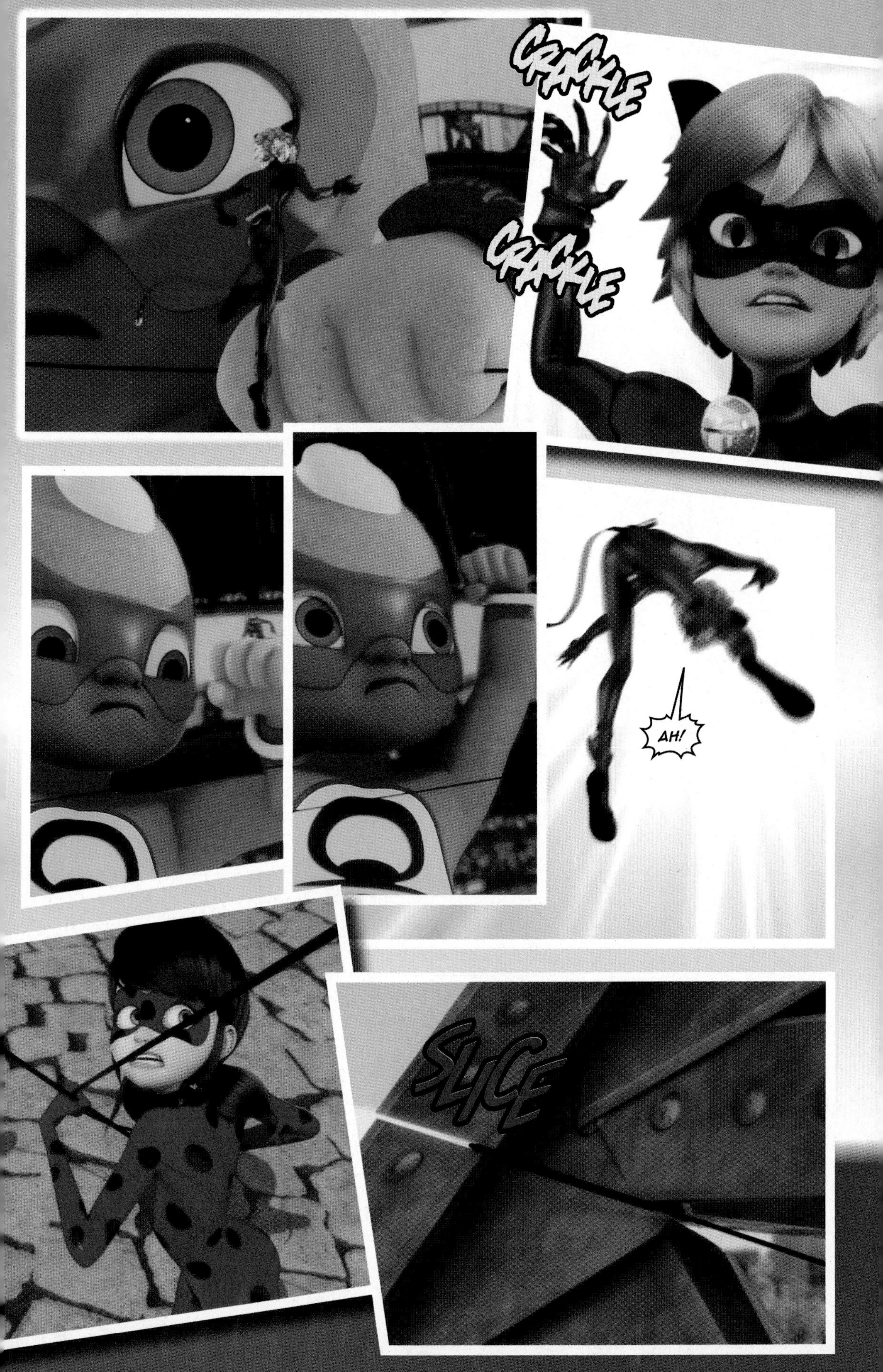
CRACKLE
CRACKLE
AH!
SLICE

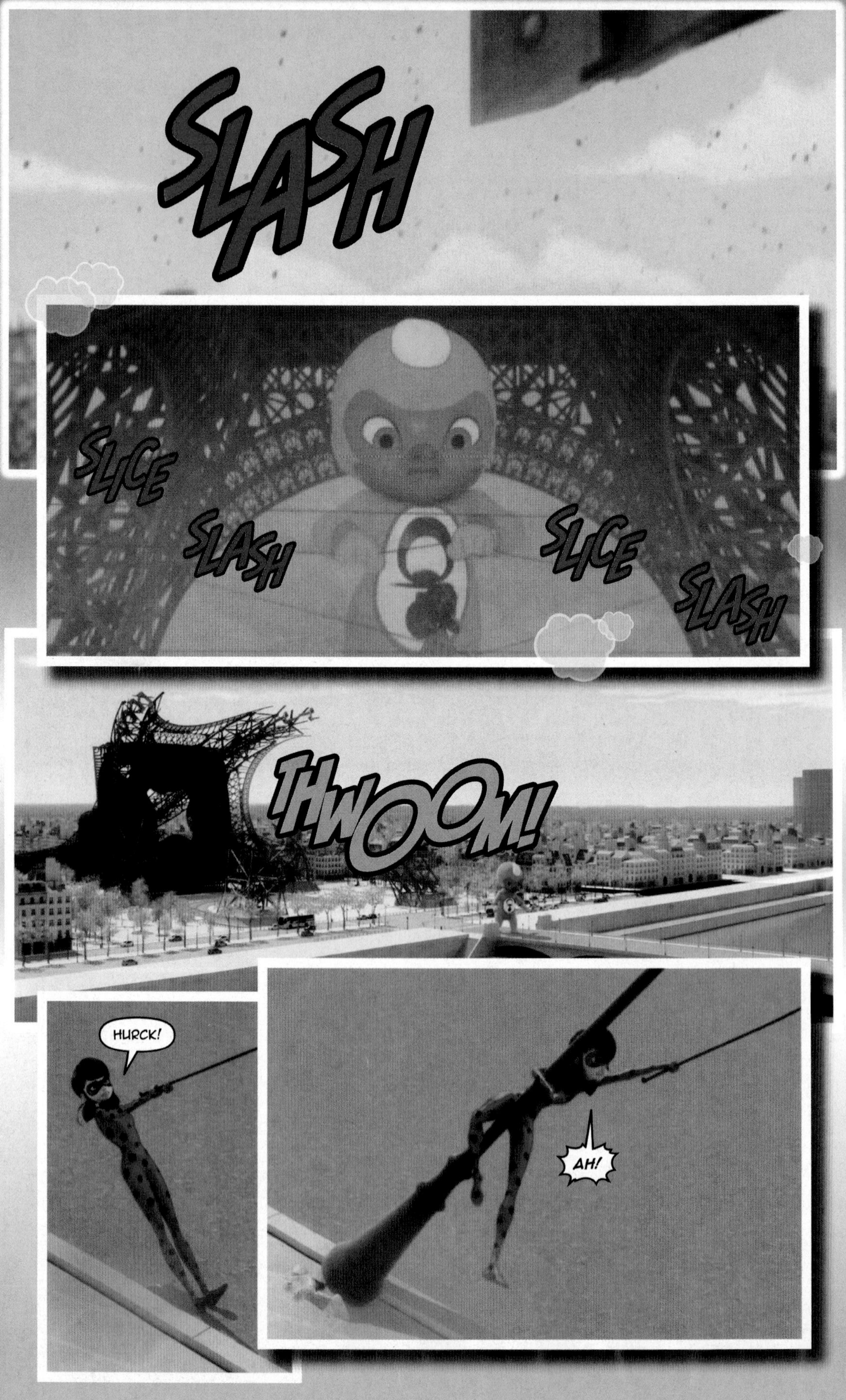
SLASH
SLICE
SLASH
SLICE
SLASH
THWOOM!
HURCK!
AH!

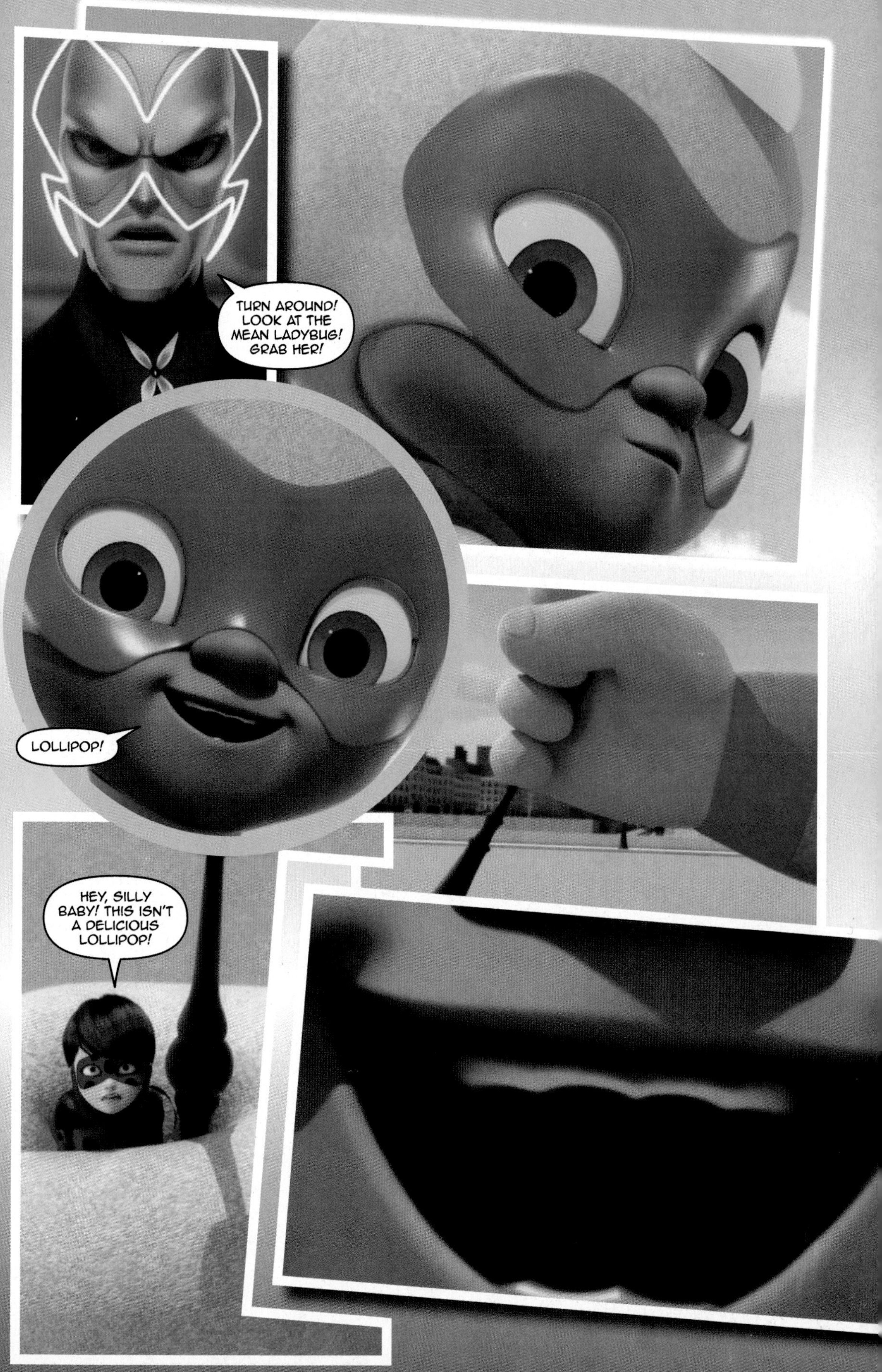
TURN AROUND! LOOK AT THE MEAN LADYBUG! GRAB HER!
LOLLIPOP!
HEY, SILLY BABY! THIS ISN'T A DELICIOUS LOLLIPOP!

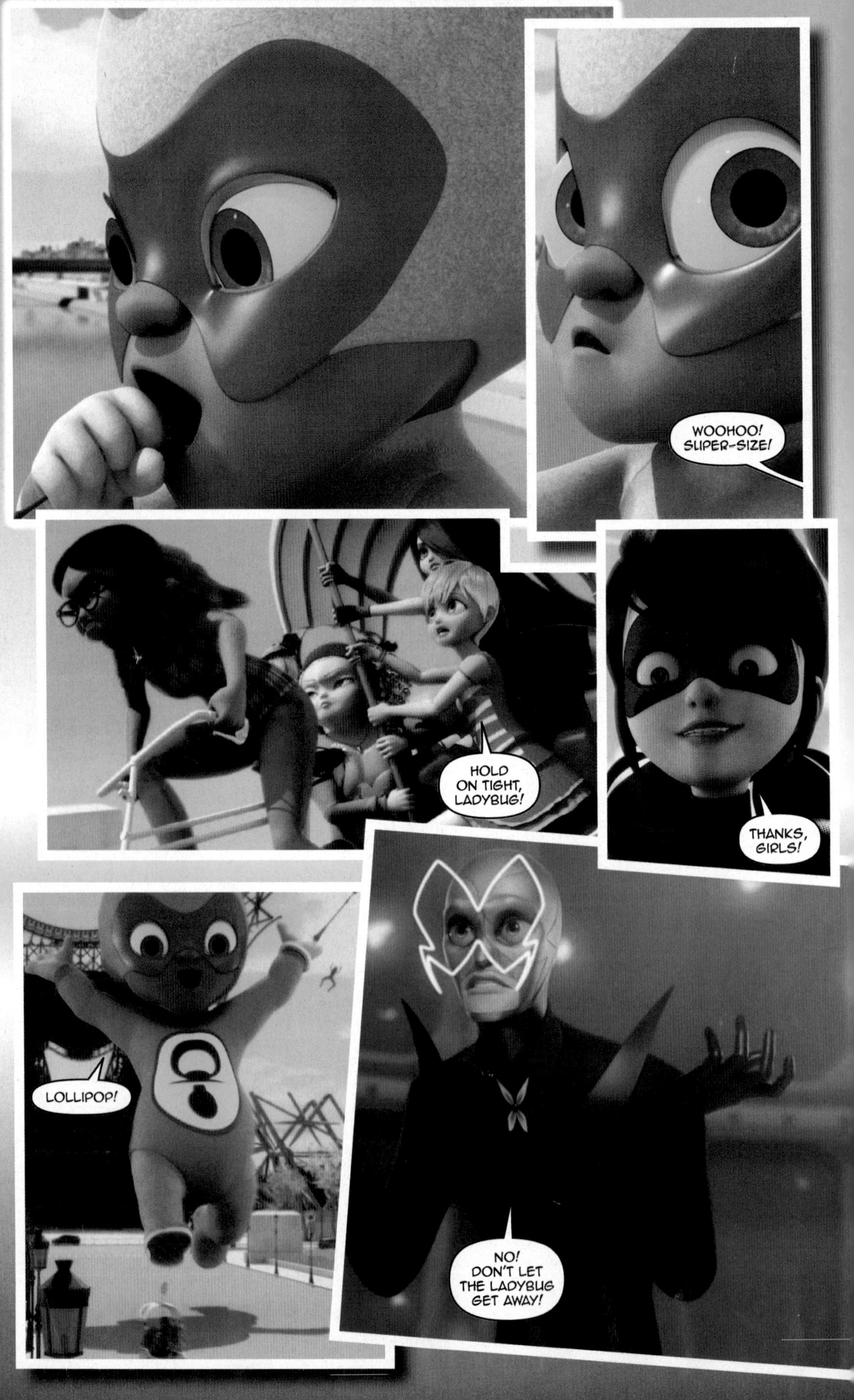
WOOHOO! SUPER-SIZE!
HOLD ON TIGHT, LADYBUG!
THANKS, GIRLS!
LOLLIPOP!
NO! DON'T LET THE LADYBUG GET AWAY!

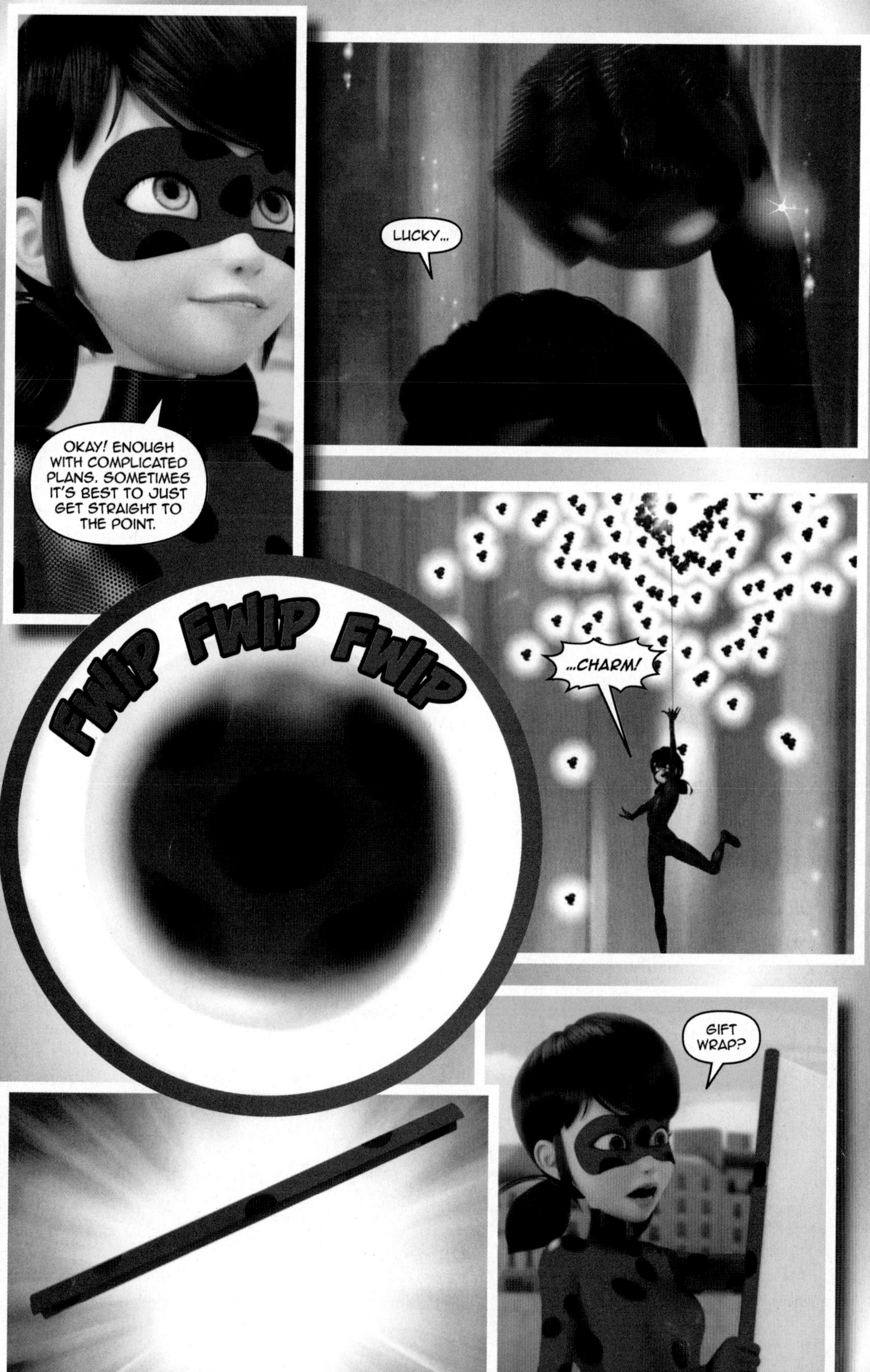

LUCKY...
OKAY! ENOUGH WITH COMPLICATED PLANS. SOMETIMES IT'S BEST TO JUST GET STRAIGHT TO THE POINT.
...CHARM!
FWIP FWIP FWIP
GIFT WRAP?

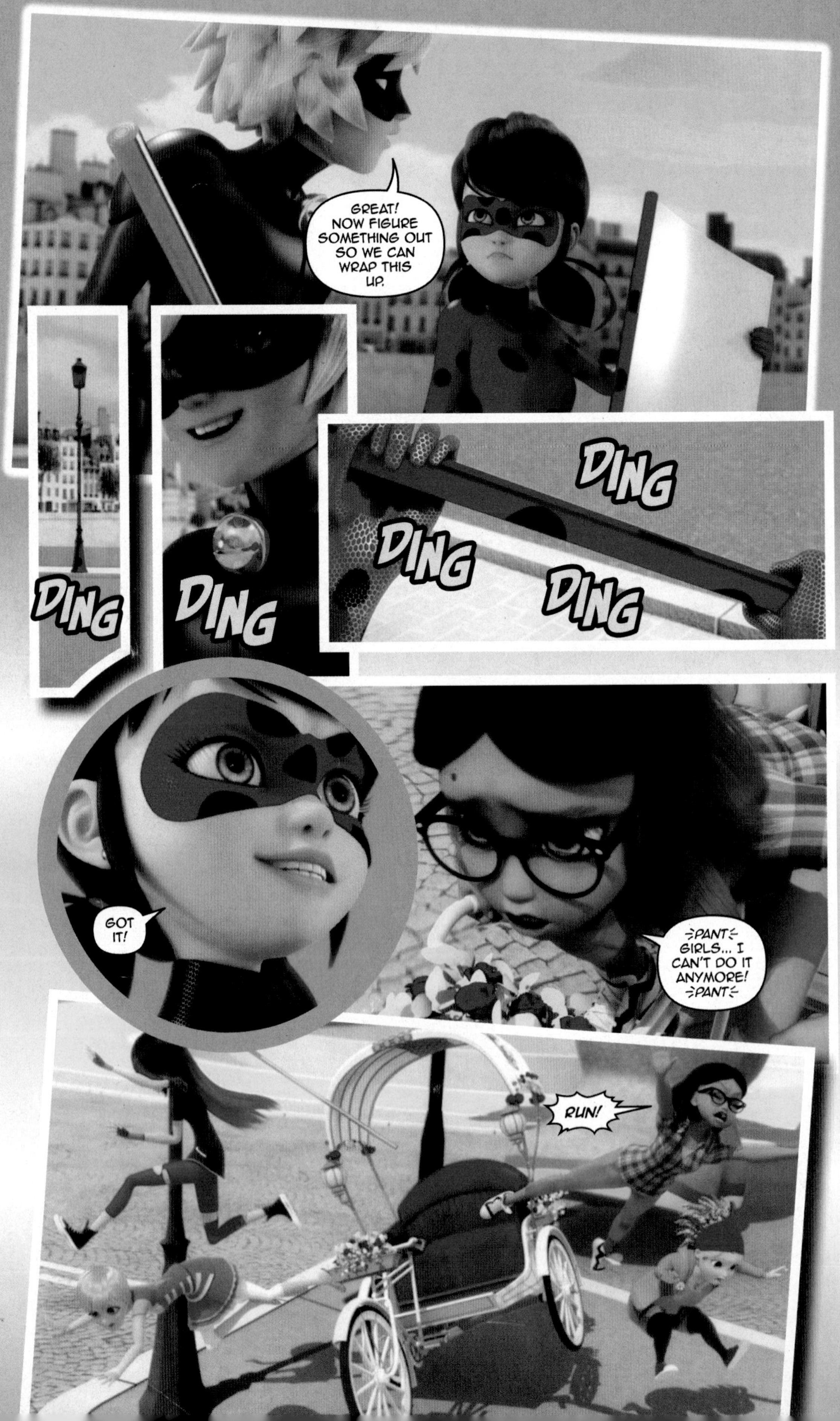

GREAT! NOW FIGURE SOMETHING OUT SO WE CAN WRAP THIS UP.
DING
DING
DING
DING
DING
GOT IT!
PANT GIRLS... I CAN'T DO IT ANYMORE! PANT
RUN!

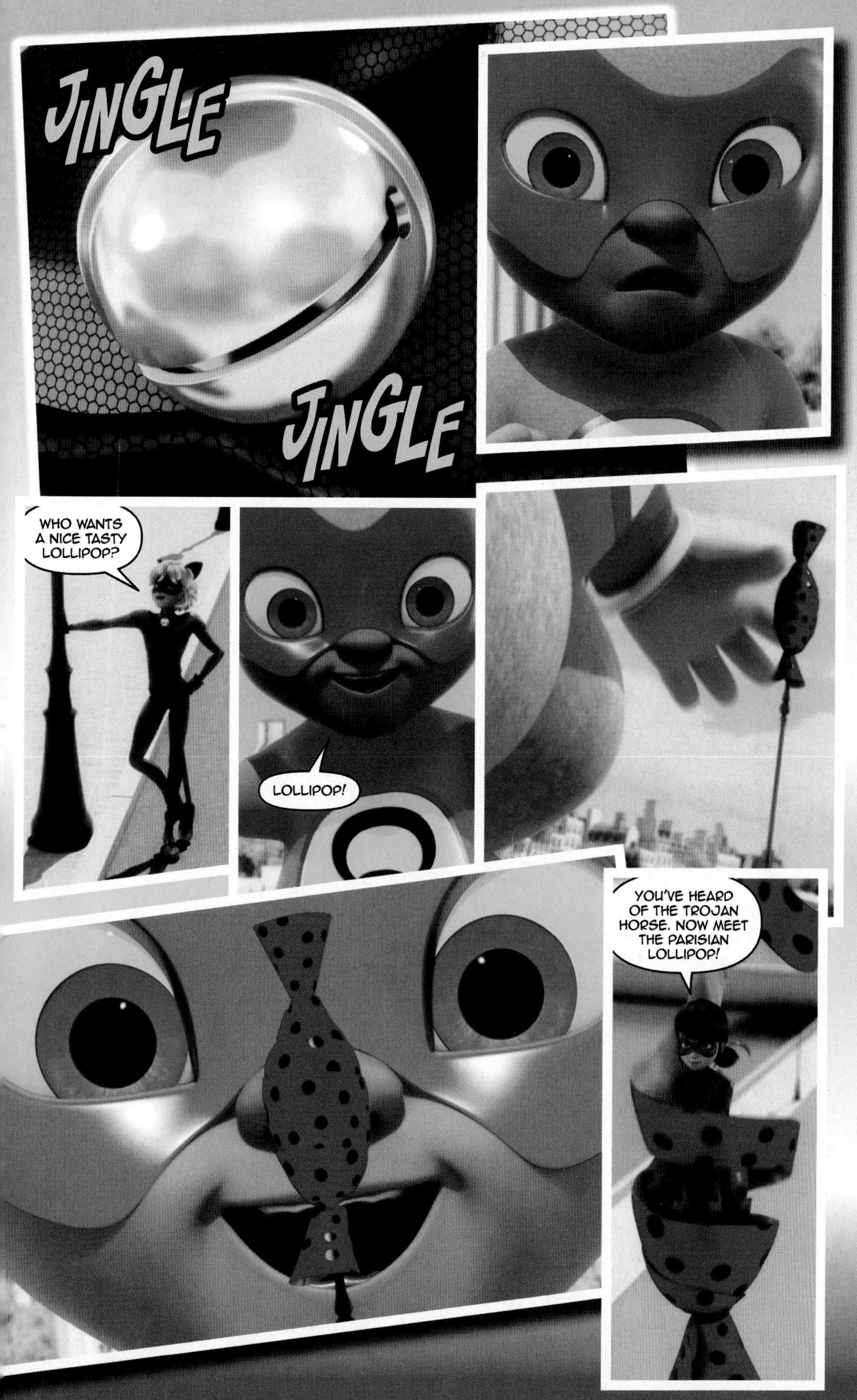
JINGLE
JINGLE
WHO WANTS A NICE TASTY LOLLIPOP?
LOLLIPOP!
YOU'VE HEARD OF THE TROJAN HORSE. NOW MEET THE PARISIAN LOLLIPOP!

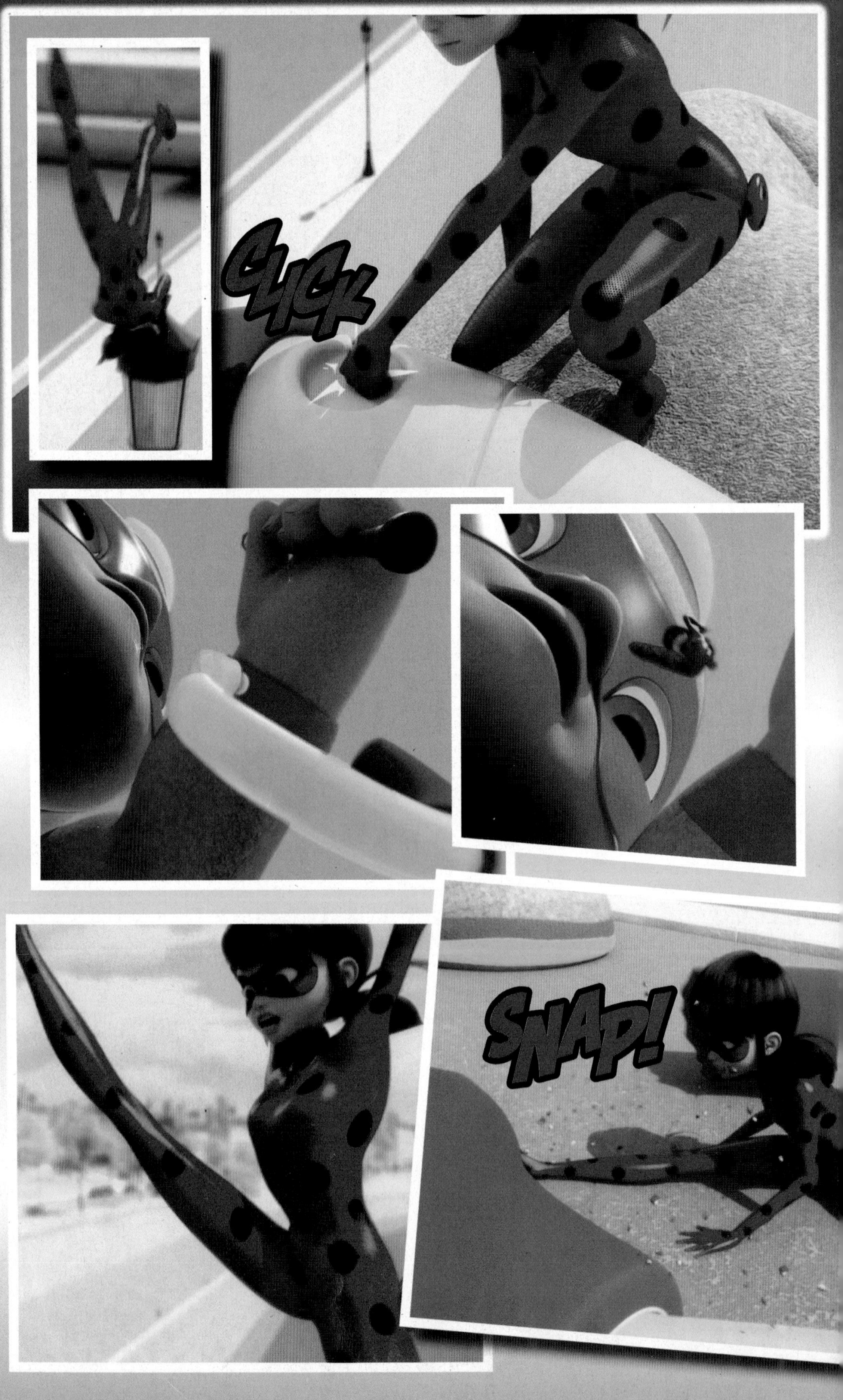
CLICK
SNAP!

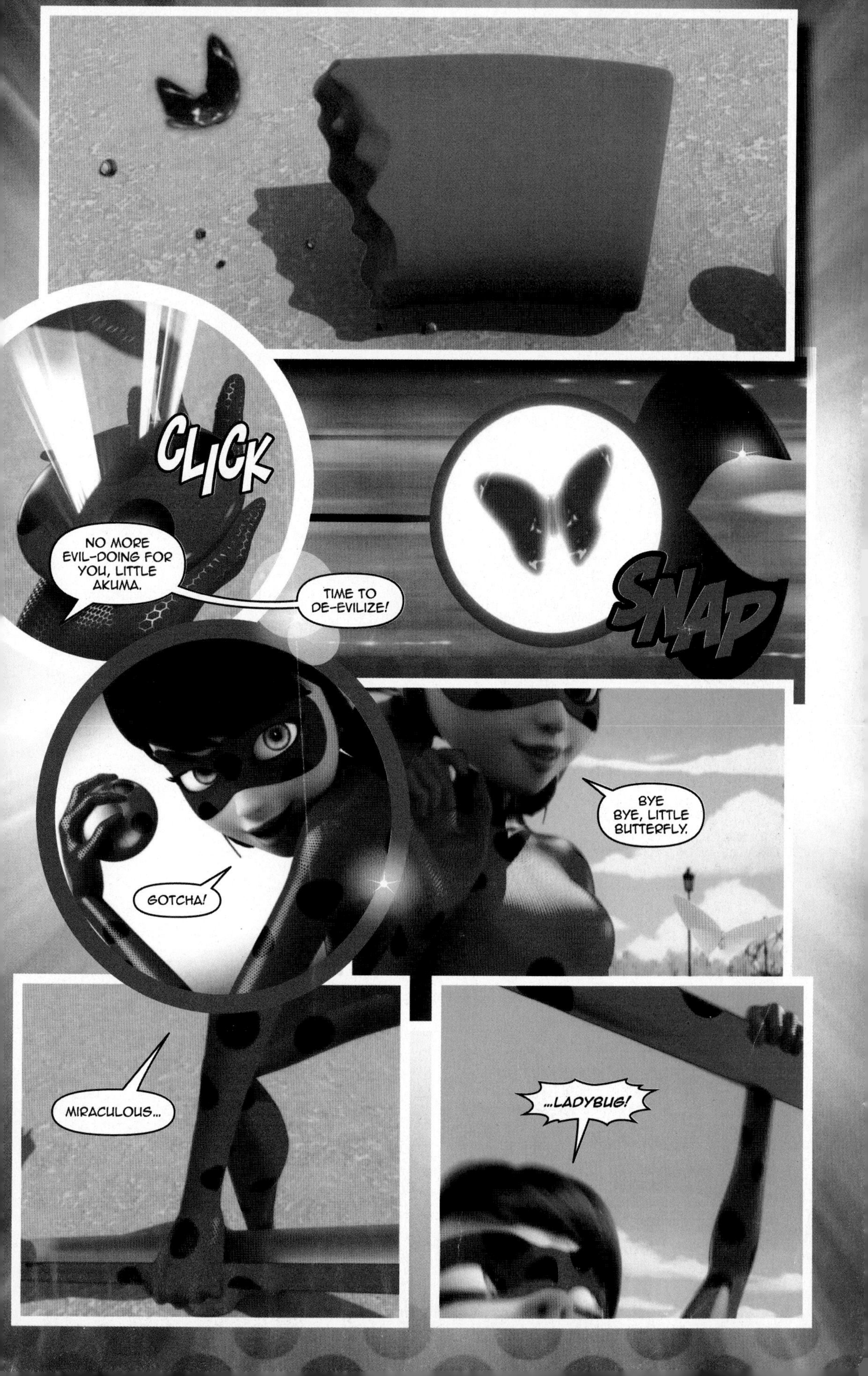
CLICK
NO MORE EVIL-DOING FOR YOU, LITTLE AKUMA.
TIME TO DE-EVILIZE!
SNAP
BYE BYE, LITTLE BUTTERFLY.
GOTCHA!
MIRACULOUS...
...LADYBUG!

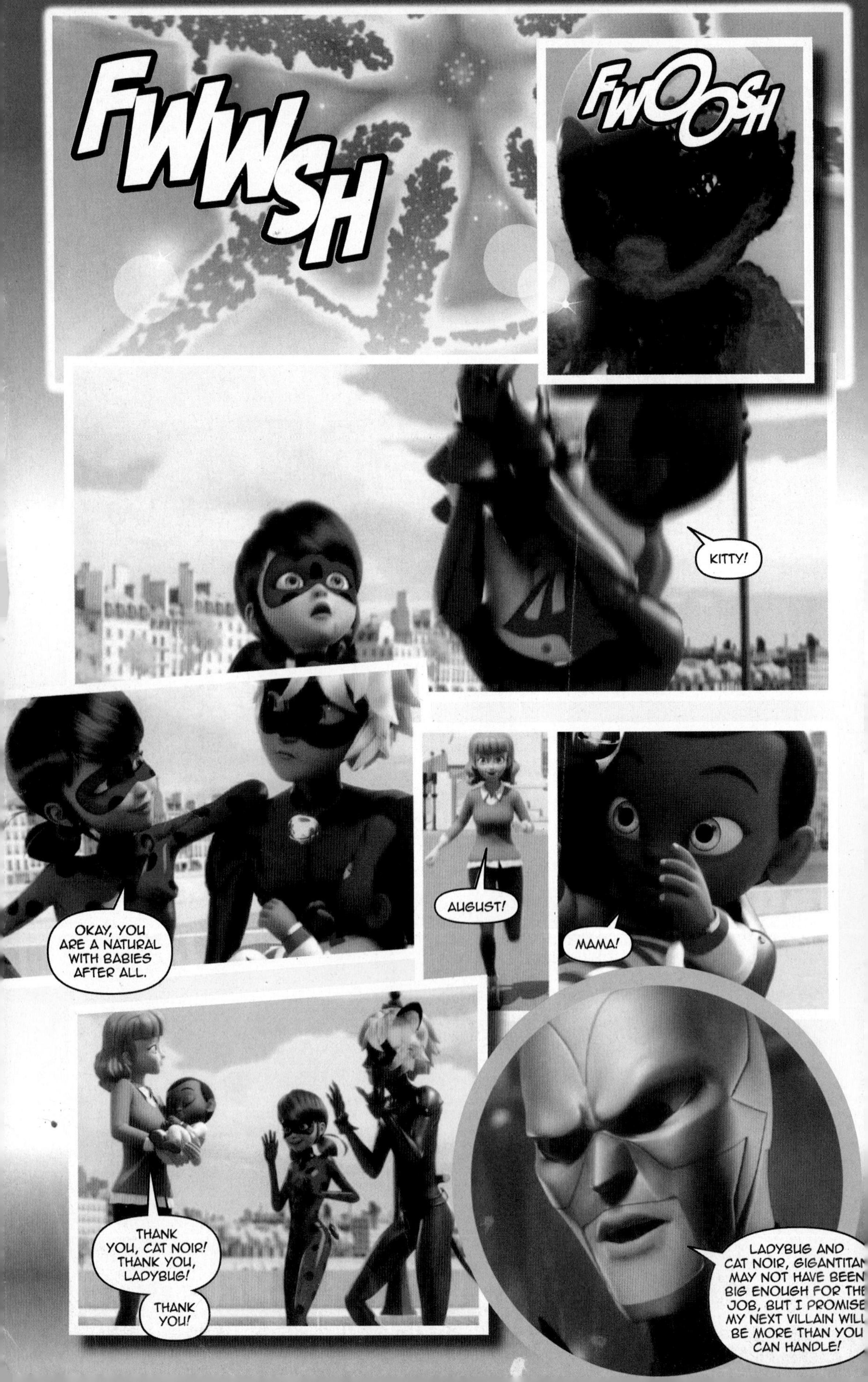
FWWSH
FWOOOSH
KITTY!
OKAY, YOU ARE A NATURAL WITH BABIES AFTER ALL.
AUGUST!
MAMA!
THANK YOU, CAT NOIR! THANK YOU, LADYBUG!
THANK YOU!
LADYBUG AND CAT NOIR, GIGANTITAN MAY NOT HAVE BEEN BIG ENOUGH FOR THE JOB, BUT I PROMISE MY NEXT VILLAIN WILL BE MORE THAN YOU CAN HANDLE!

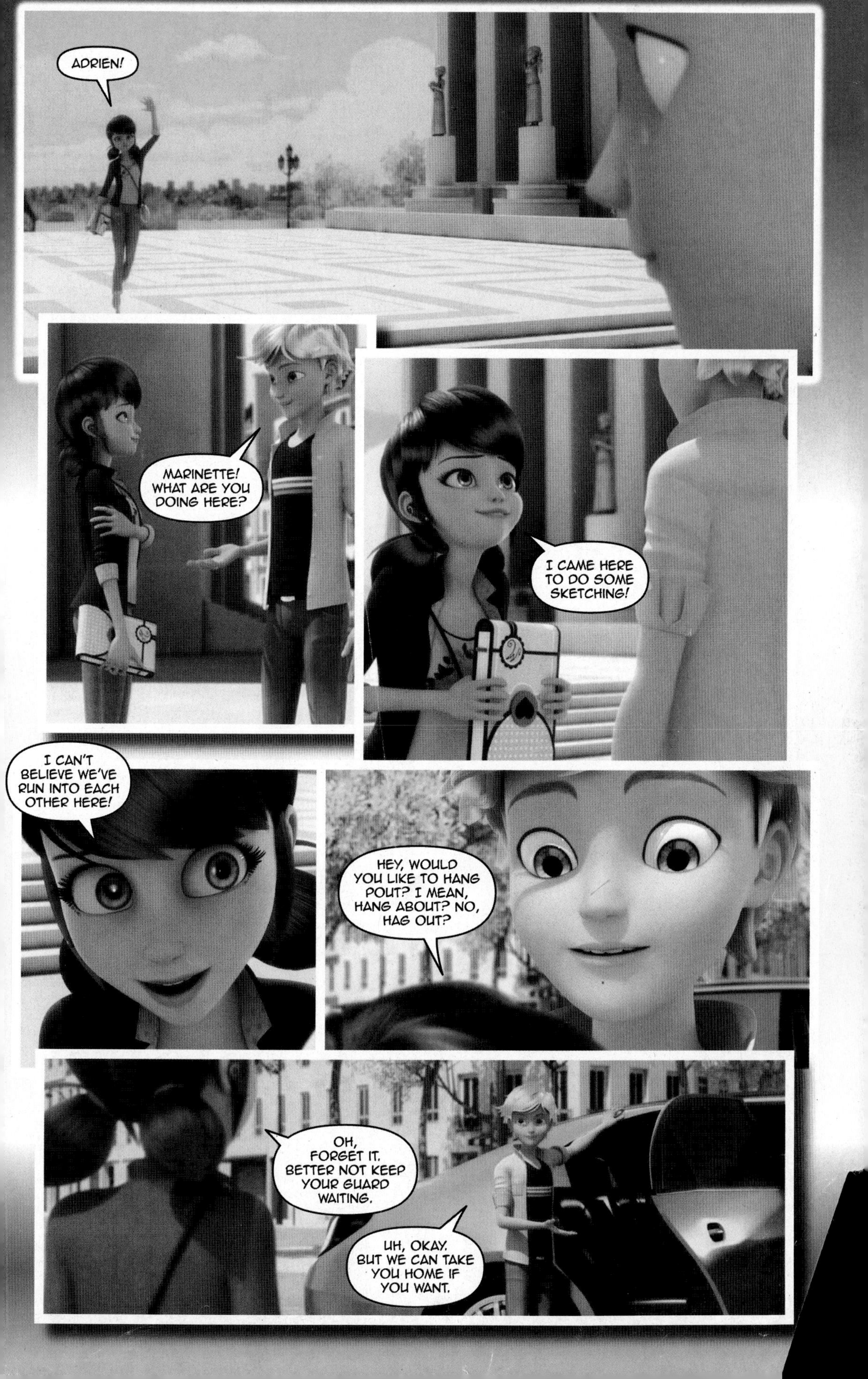
ADRIEN!
MARINETTE! WHAT ARE YOU DOING HERE?
I CAME HERE TO DO SOME SKETCHING!
I CAN'T BELIEVE WE'VE RUN INTO EACH OTHER HERE!
HEY, WOULD YOU LIKE TO HANG POUT? I MEAN, HANG ABOUT? NO, HAG OUT?
OH, FORGET IT. BETTER NOT KEEP YOUR GUARD WAITING.
UH, OKAY. BUT WE CAN TAKE YOU HOME IF YOU WANT.

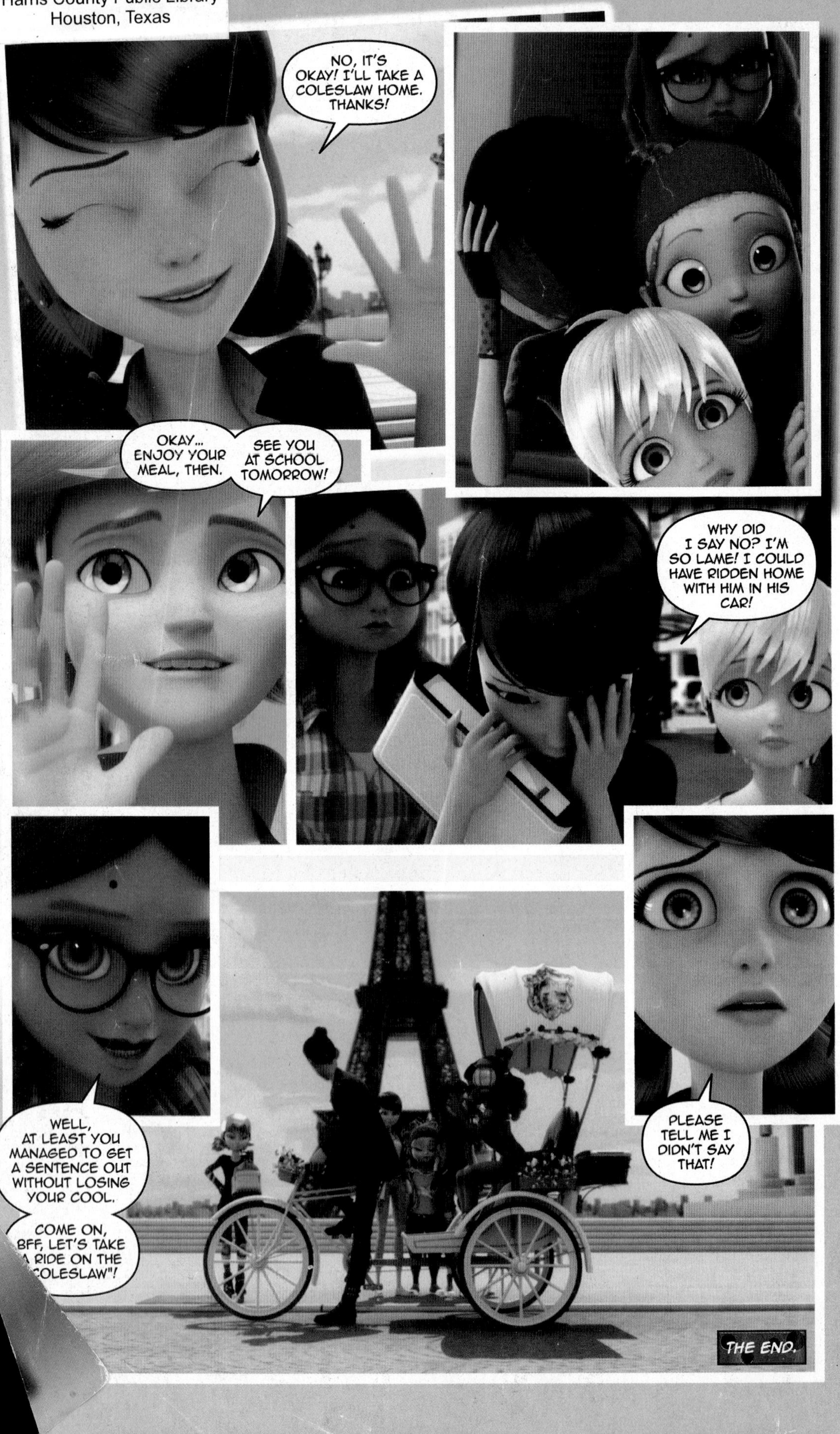
NO, IT'S OKAY! I'LL TAKE A COLESLAW HOME. THANKS!
OKAY... ENJOY YOUR MEAL, THEN.
SEE YOU AT SCHOOL TOMORROW!
WHY DID I SAY NO? I'M SO LAME! I COULD HAVE RIDDEN HOME WITH HIM IN HIS CAR!
WELL, AT LEAST YOU MANAGED TO GET A SENTENCE OUT WITHOUT LOSING YOUR COOL.
COME ON, BFF, LET'S TAKE A RIDE ON THE "COLESLAW"!
PLEASE TELL ME I DIDN'T SAY THAT!
THE END.